# THE DEAD SEE

MARCUS GIBSON

# CONTENTS

**PART ONE**

**PART TWO**

# PART ONE

## 1. '...CAST FORTH AS A BRANCH...'

*Tuesday, September 11, 2012*

Jenny Wilson was ten minutes from the deadliest place on earth, for the fifth time in two hours.

She turned, at the clatter of suitcase wheels over the step...

A tall figure stood a few feet away in the open door of the metro carriage, towing a bulging vinyl case into the aisle.

Jenny's gaze flicked to the other passengers on the train. They'd noticed him as well – glowering suspiciously before returning to newspapers, staring blankly through windows, or looking for her reaction.

It wasn't unusual for passengers to stare at Jenny.

An oversized security ID hung from her sky-blue lapel. On the shoulders of the knitted vest were the embroidered letters 'TSA'. Half the passengers had done a quick double-take when she walked aboard. The newspapers had gone wild about the Transportation Security

Administration decision to put Behaviour Detection Officers on subway trains in the lead-up to September 11. The media hadn't been positive. ...*How exactly do you pick a terrorist from their facial expressions?*

Jenny had worked JFK airport for three years, without much success. And even though these passengers were less anxious, the surprise on their faces when they saw a petite, five-foot-two blonde in a TSA uniform didn't make the job easier. Surprise and self-consciousness were difficult to distinguish from fear: The inner and outer eyebrow muscles and eyelids rose, and the lips parted. A look of fear could just as easily be surprise. Less helpful, every person on the train knew why she was here.

Jenny wished she'd been allowed to work in plain clothes.

The man with the suitcase stared at her intently, eyes grim.

His features were difficult to place. His skin was about *20* on the *von Luschan* Chromatic Scale, making him Native American, African, Arabic, Indian, or Southern Asian... the most common pigmentation in the world. Racial profiling was pointless anyway. In New York, ethnicity bore fewer correlations to other demographic indicators than in any other city on earth.

The man stared back at her as she worked to hide her own fear.

*Keep your hair on, Jen! It's all in your head.*

Suitcase-man glanced at the NYPD officer by the far door. The burly patrolman – hands stuffed in his windbreaker, fleece high around his neck – was distracted by a young woman in tight jeans dangling playfully from an overhead rail.

"*Stand clear of the closing doors, please,*" announced the cheerful recording. The doors clattered shut.

Jenny studied the suitcase-man's face. His *orbicularis oculi* and *pars palpebralis* were tense, raising his upper eyelids, and tightening the lower lids. It wasn't fear *or* surprise. His upper lip was stretched horizontally at the *risorius* and *platysma*. It was *almost* an expression of disgust – nose scrunched, eyebrows downcast, eyes narrowed...

No...

It was contempt.

Jenny felt her gut clench. *Poops McGee, this is a bad shit-uation.* South Ferry was the last subway station before the target.

The Joralemon Tunnel was excavated a hundred years ago, making it the oldest tunnel under New York's East River. If a bomb went off in the soft riverbed bud, it would rip through the old iron casing like shit through a short dog. The East River would flood the whole New York subway. Metro Transit Authority had commissioned classified modelling. *Five* times as many people could die here as were killed in the World Trade Centre attacks, on the same day 11 years ago. The city would be crippled. Worse, Homeland Security had called in the TSA and *told* them to work the train, meaning they knew something...

Jenny approached the tall figure, smiling. "Hiya!"

He scowled darkly. Depressor glabellae, depressor supercili, corrugator muscles...

Jenny glanced out the window. The dim casing of the tunnel rushed by in a blur. She twisted her neck, making eye contact. "Where ya headed?" she forced a smile.

"Jay-Eff-Kay," muttered the man.

There wasn't enough in the curt answer to place an accent.

From the corner of her eye, she saw the patrolman notice the two of them – *finally!*

Seeing what was happening, the young girl in jeans had straightened and backed against the door.

"You know... there are at least *two* better ways to get to J.F.K. from South Ferry?" Jenny suggested, helpfully. "Ya coulda ridden uptown to Broadway-Nassau... taken the blue line out to A-C..." She pointed in the general direction. "Or... up to Chambers Street, and taken the brown line to 'Jamaica'?"

"My mistake," the man's expression flickered with something else...

Maybe this was the source of his contempt: That the City had failed to build a direct link to the airport?

"Just thought I'd help," Jenny smiled, trying unsuccessfully to put him at ease. *'Reverse Psychiatry'* her son would say. "...You goin' on holiday?"

The man shook his head. "...funeral."

*Funeral?* Jenny studied the muscles around his eyes, and wondered if she'd misread them. Maybe he was mourning? "Mind if I take a look in your suitcase?" she asked pointedly, still smiling.

The man's eyes darted to the corner of the train.

Jenny turned to see...

A second figure lurked at the end of the carriage, holding a cell phone.

She barely had time to look back at the suitcase (*Oh God!*) before the bomb ripped through the carriage.

At least... this is what might have happened.

If anyone on the train had lived to tell the story.

Hundreds of New Yorkers witnessed the great geyser of grey water that shot up out of the East River, forty feet off the bow of the Weehawken Ferry – soaking screaming passengers with spray.

Maybe a thousand people felt the earth shake on the bank of the East River.

In Lower Manhattan, passengers on the bustling platforms of ferry terminals from the Battery all the way up to Pier 11 at Wall Street, felt a *thump* under their feet and heard the *whoosh* of water... all turning to see what happened.

On the east of the river a half-mile section of the Brooklyn Queens Expressway heaved. Cars swerved and braked, skidding into each other screeching and banging in sequence.

Underground, a pressurised jet of smoke, flame, shredded metal, and a century of soot blasted down the iron tunnel like a cannon.

Behind the racing fireball, a roaring, brackish torrent gushed through the transverse crack in the ceiling of the Joralemon tunnel.

Borough Hall station in Brooklyn, and the bustling South Ferry station in Lower Manhattan, erupted with volcanic force: A pyroclastic flow of pressurised dust boomed from the stairwells into the streets, shattering store windows. Chairs, masonry, litter, and bodies tumbled into the traffic, colliding with cars and buses.

Then... there was a moment of unnerving silence throughout south Manhattan – a collective gasp – followed by the hellish reverberation of fifteen thousand screams.

In the hours that followed, nobody remembered the woman in the diamond necklace walking down 42nd Street toward the cross-town subway platform at Grand Central. At the time, people turned and wondered what she was doing on the street at ten o'clock on a Tuesday morning.

Madison Mueller was the kind of New Yorker you saw on a billboard, not a sidewalk... She looked like she *should* have been stepping out of a limousine: tall, leggy, tanned, and impossibly photogenic. She came to a stop at the Grand Central ticket window like it was the end of a catwalk; leaning on a long leg, hand on hip, propping open her overcoat to reveal a silver evening dress that clung to her like mercury. Owing to a life-long dedication to spin class and Elastin, Madison also *looked* like she was in her Thirties. She'd kept her age a secret for so long she barely remembered. There *had* been at least three consecutive 35th birthdays. Or maybe four.

Madison didn't notice the stir she caused walking through Grand Central. After fourteen hours straight on three-inch heels, all she was thinking about were her feet. As she sauntered painfully past a Tuxedoed string quartet busking in the concourse, she noted something vaguely ironic about the scene: Evening gown... Concerto...

Male violinist grinning at her over his chin rest. Smiling uncomfortably, Madison opened her clutch purse and flicked fifty bucks into the upturned top-hat near the busker's scuffed shoes.

Walking away, she'd tried to remember if she had any food left in her apartment. She hadn't had time to go shopping, between flying back from Boston the night before and answering a dinner invitation... Well, if the cupboard was bare, she'd have to say 'yes' to another date tonight, but she wasn't in the mood to put on her 'people' face again.

Reaching the narrow cross-town platform for the IRT Flushing Line, she stopped again, posed. A neatly-pressed executive strode over and planted his briefcase a few feet away. After a short pause, he turned and smiled. "Going or coming?"

Madison glanced at her jewelled wristwatch. "Pardon me?" She wished for a bench. There were black fibreglass seats further down the long 11-car platform, but that meant more walking.

"You're headed for Broadway..." clarified the young exec. "You're dressed like you're going to a *show*, but..." He glanced at his fat, lustrous wristwatch. "...It's two hours until the first matinee. So, maybe you're heading home?" The exec had clearly put some thought into the monologue. Madison wondered how long he'd been following her. She swivelled her hips, gave him the well-practiced look that said *not today*. But the pain in her feet whispered *fuck off*. The string quartet was still audible, echoing out of the concourse. *If he'd asked for a dance,* she thought, *THAT might have been funny...*

"Can't a guy be friendly?" He flashed his doctored smile again, off-script, wondering simultaneously if the fish was too big for the line.

"Usually not."

He looked perplexed. "—Buy you a coffee?"

Madison was ready to decline, when she noticed a rat scurrying down the tracks, past the edge of the platform.

The young man saw her expression, and turned... Another rat emerged from the shadows, scampering frantically on the tail of the first. Then a third. "*Jeezus—*"

A rush of dank, fetid air coughed out of the tunnel, stirring Madison's hair. She blinked the dust out of her lashes. *What—?*

Desperate shouting erupted from the foot-tunnel at the top of the stairs, then a burst of static on the public address system:

"All passengers on all platforms are instructed to IMMEDIATELY make their way to the concourse level! All passengers on all platforms...!"

Madison heard the announcement, but she was transfixed by what was happening on the tracks...

A tiny trickle of water had appeared, bubbling over the ballast between the rails at the end of the tunnel.

An NYPD patrolman leapt down the stairs to her right, halting on the bottom step. Gripping the rail, yelling for people to *'run!'*...

There were *hundreds* of rats now, tumbling over each other ahead of the rising water. Madison could hear their strained screeches. She'd seen plenty of rats in New York, but she'd *never* heard a noise like this... She was intrigued by the shrill chorus, barely noticing the young exec abandoning his briefcase, and dashing for the stairs.

It wouldn't be the first time a metro water main had burst and flooded a line. But to evacuate *all* platforms? *In Grand Central?* To *'instruct'* people to evacuate, not *'advise'*...

The water surged, catching up with the rats; all thrashing as they came into contact with the brackish wave... With a hiss of sparks, the tiny bodies burst into flames as the 625-volt 'third rail' that powered the subway electrified the water!

"*LADY!!*" bellowed the patrolman.

Madison heard another shout at the far end of the platform.

A man in a torn suit, covered head-to-toe in dust, came running out of the darkness in the tunnel. His face and clothes were grey with dust... a streak of blood down his cheek.

The water boiled down the tracks in that direction as well, close on the man's heels. He struggled up onto the platform, screaming desperately. "*Turn off the POOOOWERRR! There are still PEOPLE in THERE!*"

"*LADY!!*" bellowed the patrolman.

The sickening stench of death and mire filled the chamber. The water roiled suddenly in a three-foot swell along the IRT Flushing Line. The roaring torrent, the fizz and crackle of sparks, became deafening. *And screams!* There were screams from the tunnel! Madison turned to the policeman. "*Turn off the pow—!*"

But she didn't finish the sentence.

If they turned off the power, the trains would stop.

The tunnel was flooding.

If people tried to flee the stranded cars, they'd be drowned. But if the power was left on, *some* of the trains might escape, and the rest would die like rats – swimming, *burned, boiled...*

They were damned if they did, and damned if they didn't.

The torrent rose to the edge of the platform, leaping in a bow wave ahead of an arriving carriage. Smoke and steam and water spilled across the tiles between Madison and the stairs. The subway car stopped halfway out of the tunnel, billowing smoke. The tip of an umbrella wiggled through the door as an invisible passenger tried to prise his way out.

Madison looked down at the deadly, electrified water as it pooled between her and the stairs. She was trapped.

An overweight man in baggy jeans and a faded college sweater came running toward the Exit stairs from the far side. As soon as his feet hit the water, he *stumbled,* grunting, legs curled, falling hard on the concrete, skidding forward convulsing violently, his face contorted like a Japanese Kabuki-mask. Electrocuted. Madison gasped as the man's body tightened into a foetal curl, twitching, clenched. The electrified water sloshed across the speckled tiles, between her and the Exit-stairs in both directions.

It had only taken a few seconds.

There was no way out.

In the distance, she saw the fibreglass bench she'd thought about walking to. Now, it was the only refuge for a huddle of terrified commuters, clinging to each other atop the chairs, watching as electrified swampwater pooled around them.

Another clutch of passengers – including the neatly-pressed executive who'd been flirting with her minutes ago – stood gathered on the stairs behind the patrolmen, backing away in terror from the rising flood, shouting for her to *"RUN!"*

But it was too late.

There was nowhere to run.

Smoke and soot billowed out of the tunnels, into the terminal.

Madison coughed, and covered her mouth with her collar. She peered up at the curved, off-white ceiling, with its tiny black stalactites from decades of leeching groundwater. A row of fluorescent lights zigzagged between suspended rods and signs in the filthy ceiling... The light fittings were too high to reach.

Looking down at her feet, it would be seconds before the floor was completely submerged.

Water gushed over the platform, sweeping away the briefcase near where she was standing...

650 volts coursed through the slurry, and the skidding briefcase bursts into flames as well, sinking as it drifted off the edge of the platform.

Then the overhead lights flickered, and died... plunging the station into darkness.

Echoing over the sinister *hiss* of sparks and roaring water, reverberating off the ceiling of the blackened chamber, the sounds of desperate screams rose. She could only *hear* now, as water gushed out of the tunnel, down the tracks from both ends. She stood frozen in shock and fear.

At eighty feet below street level, the Number 7 Line platform was the deepest subway platform in Grand Central terminal.

Whatever was happening, the water was *all* flowing here.

This platform would be the first to be completely flooded.

And, unexpectedly, Madison found herself thinking about what happened yesterday...

## 2. '...DIVIDED FROM DARKNESS...'

*Friday, February 26, 1993*

It all started at the lighthouse keepers' cottage.

Mohamat al-Lideen dragging a suitcase full of kitchen flour and industrial bleach onto the South Ferry metro...

Madison walking to the 10:15 IRT Flushing platform...

My whole life...

It *all* starts at the lighthouse.

It's 1993. Annie and I are in college. I'm sitting in the passenger seat of Annie's '85 compact Benz, reclined, like a boy on the sundeck of a boat – happy for the sunshine of her love, but seasick with nerves.

Green to the gills.

The window is open, pummelling my face with a frigid jet-stream. Outside, diagonal lanes of snow-laden spruce strobe hypnotically in the car's headlights, cold black branches bristling like iron filings. I'm pretty sure I'm about to puke, and reach for the radio, to trick my head I'm okay. Everything is normal... *Mmmbop, Ba Duba Dop Ba Do Bop, Ba Duba Dop Ba Do Bop, Ba Duba Dop Ba Do... Oh Yeah!*

We're hurtling over fallen sleet. Annie smacks her bright lips, and sucks in her breath – ready to remark on the addition of more noise.

'*...At seventeen minutes past twelve today in New York, a truck bomb exploded in the garage beneath the North Tower of the World Trade Center...*'

"Turn it off," she pleads softly. "I can't listen to *that* any more."

'*...Experts have speculated the bomb was intended to collapse the North Tower onto the adjacent tower, but instead left a thirty-metre hole through four sublevels, killing several people eating lunch in a basement office, and injuring as many as a thousand–*'

I switch the radio back off.

"Relax. You'll be *fine*," she sooths, and pats my knee.

I swallow. "I don't have enough money for a coffin."

"Shhh... He's not going to kill you."

"I'm serious. What if I die, and I can't afford a coffin?"

"*I'll* pay for your coffin," Annie laughs.

I smile. "Thanks. That's so sweet."

I'd hoped tonight would never come. Three months of rising expectations, and now only a complete catastrophe can save me: A patch of black ice on the next bend... A fox darting onto the spot-lit macadam... Fifteen minutes from now, I come face-to-face with the man I fear more than god.

Annie grins. "Maybe I'll put you in one of those pet cemeteries?"

I don't have an answer, for too many reasons to list... *Am I her pet?*

I've already been introduced to Annie's mother, Tessa, a week ago. Tessa is party to our secret plot, previously committed to a glowing report of Annie's new beau – in spite of all her best instincts. Fastidiously groomed, with a fixed smile and fearsome eyes, Tessa was waiting for us at a table by the garden window at the upmarket restaurant *Aujourd'hui.* Over lunch, mother and daughter whispered conspiratorially, discussing 'our' strategy to meet MISTER Mueller.

However, the rendezvous only made me more nervous than before. *Much* more. Seated in the ritzy venue with a snooty waiter repeatedly refolding my napkin and slipping it over the arm of my chair, I realised for the first time how terrifyingly far out of my depth I'd swum. The whole conversation was uneasy. There were too many unspeakables. I *knew* this was all for show... Tessa's kindness and chit-chat. Favour on favour, heaped grudgingly. She wasn't even *remotely* enamoured with me. I could see it in her eyes as a lump of Savoy cabbage crashed off my chin, toppling from the tenderloin, and splashing red truffle-Madeira juice onto the cut-rose centrepiece.

Annie beams at me from behind the wheel like she's the only person who doesn't get it. Or the only person who *does*. "Hey – I want to show you something!" She swings the car onto Main Street, in the small Cape Ann township.

"What?"

She brakes, tail lights flashing red in the black easement between two old houses, crooked like children's drawings, leaned-over clapboard walls strung with fluorescent lobster-pot buoys and crawfish cages.

She leaps out of the car into the bitter gale.

I watch her trot around the hood, over a split-rail fence, long-legged in ripped jeans. Her flimsy Boston *Patriots* sweatshirt snaps around her waist like a sail. "*C'mon! BOB!*"

Arms folded, I climb out onto the warped pavement, and she unhooks my elbow, taking my hand. "C'mon *Hunny!* Quick."

Her fist warms my pipes.

"We'll be late," I protest. "I don't want to be late."

"Shhh..." She tows me up the pebble path, through the clapboard canyon, onto the wind-blown back of the bluff. Her chin is aimed up at the lighthouse on the bald hill, with its rotting Keeper's cottage, signal building, oil house, and rust-stained minaret lurking in shadow.

The crooked, aged structures reek of fear and obsolescence. I peer up at the wrought-iron balcony at the lighthouse's zenith. "You're kidding me?"

"C'mon!" Annie hauls me along the winding path, and raps on the blue wooden door of the cottage.

I'm too distracted to see the young man in his early twenties with long red hair, and spidery speck-like eyes, hands stuffed into his pockets, lurking behind the crooked fence near the clapboard house. It's too dark to see him as he flexes his fingers against the cold, and rearranges the miniature tape-recorder in one pocket, and thumbs the oily metal of the safety-catch on the revolver, like a rock in the other.

"He's blind," mentions Annie hurriedly.

"Who?"

"The lighthouse keeper..." The hatch cracks open. "Vantcha!" Annie throwing her arms around the grim spectre.

"Anne!" he croaks in an Eastern Bloc accent. His wrinkled face tilts up into the moonlight, revealing a mask of folded skin and empty eye-sockets.

His eyes are *gone*, replaced by puckered scars.

*Jeezus!*

"*Hunny*," Annie grins, unperturbed. "Can I take a *friend* up to the light?"

Hunny?

Vantcha extends his bony claw. "Hello *friend*..."

I shake the withered hand, still struck by the mutilated, vacant eye-sockets – realising too late what the old Lighthouse Keeper is doing, as he runs his fingertips over my knuckles. Shivering, I snatch back my paw.

"What's your name, *friend?*"

"Bob!" I blurt uncomfortably.

Vantcha shoves his way between us, the cuffs of his oversized corduroy slacks whispering on the cement step. He walks to the sheet-metal security door at the base of the lighthouse next door.

There's a warning – emblazoned on the door in red paint:

**AUTHORIZED PERSONNEL ONLY DANGER HIGH VOLTAGE KEEP OUT**

"Don't look into the light," he whispers.

"Follow me." Annie slips in front of me, towing me by the wrist.

Vantcha lurks by the door as we start up the steps. The treads of the wrought-iron stairs are powdered with chewed wood, ant eggs, and bird shit. My footfalls echo like artillery fire. Squealing down from above is the rhythmic squeak of pinched metal, like a playground swing.

"*Cheese-and-rice* Annie," I whisper, echoing. "'*He's blind*'? How about 'brace yourself, his face looks like a twisted sandshoe—'"

"Shaddup." Annie's laugh echoes madly. At the top of the stairs, she takes to the ladder that leads through a small hatch. "QUICK!"

Puffing, I peer over the lip of the light-room floor.

A hot flash erupts to my left, striking my ear like a truncheon. I rise up to stand in the brilliantly-lit turret, glancing at the spinning sun before me... A sparkling ten-foot trio of lenses whirl on a giant screeching ring gear.

"*Christ!*" I cringe from the glare. Snapping one eye shut, peering down at my church shoes, I hook a thumb through the belt-loop in the small of Annie's back. "We're gonna be *late!*"

"*Shhh*! Stop being so *serious.*"

"I'm not '*serious*'. I'm *shitting* myself," I mumble.

Annie glances back, ready to clarify. *No*, it's *not* the lighthouse I'm shitting myself about... "*Jeezus* Bob, come on."

On the rusted balcony, the wind shoves at my back. With every sweep of the lens, the searing white light illuminates the antique iron rail and swings out into the night sky over the black ocean.

"Wait..." Annie tenses.

"For what?"

The balcony trembles, and I reach urgently for the wall.

"See?!" She points over the small town, thrilled! For a moment, everything is lost in a haze of iridescent sea spray.

"What?"

"The hill!"

Another blinding flash sweeps by. And as the lamp spins away, I see sparkling windows on the next bluff.

"That's my house!"

"We should get going."

"Now look at the moon," Annie beams brightly.

The light blasts past me again, and I twist my neck, peering skyward. "What?"

She digs me in the ribs with her elbow. "See? The reflection of the moon... It's like the windows on the hill!"

"Huh?"

"The reflection of the sun!"

And suddenly, it's the smartest thing I've ever heard.

The whole idea of the solar system plummets into perspective... The way the light of the sun, 93 million miles below my feet, reflects against the distant moon... In just the same way, the windows on the adjacent hill reflect the beam of the lighthouse.

I grin at the cold orb in the sky above. It suddenly seems close, shining with the atomic light of a searing photosphere on the far side of the world... I'm reminded, gazing at the moon, it's nothing more – and nothing less – than the reflection of 700 million tons of hydrogen burned per second, rising for a million years to the sun's surface, leaping untrammelled through space past the dust of nine planets and 134 moons, into the cold void past Pluto.

This is the moment, right now, when my last doubt evaporates.

*This* is the girl worth dying for.

If I had a ring, I'd ask her to marry me right here...

The lamp strikes again, casting its beam across the sea. "So... If the lighthouse is the *sun*, and the balcony is the *Earth*, and your window is the *moon*..." I ask wryly. "Who's the blind lighthouse keeper..?"

"Ha! Come here," she whispers, checking over her shoulder.

Out over the Atlantic, a thundering nimbus catches the glancing beam of the lighthouse. What appears to be an oddly uniform string of stars on the horizon, takes the shape of faraway booms, bows and wheelhouses of fishing vessels out on the ocean shelf.

Annie's breast brushes my forearm, and I get a magically instant hard-on.

The distorted form of the keeper warps behind the light chamber window like a carnival monster. "Jeezus!" I jump.

"Shhhh."

"Is he *watching* us?"

Annie shivers. "Um. *No*, he's not. *Idiot*." She grins.

"Are you cold?"

"Whatever happens tonight, I love you," she says plainly.

"Are you *trying* to scare me?"

The light flashes by again.

"You'll be fine."

The balcony shudders as Vantcha rattles into the wind. "How's the view?" he cackles.

I look down over the rail, contemplating the fall.

"How's Matthias?" Vantcha asks Annie, too familiar for my liking.

"I'm taking Bob to meet him now."

Vantcha's shrivelled face puckers like an elbow. "Ah! I *see*."

Annie tugs at my wrist. "I'll come by again, soon, Vantcha. I promise. We have to go." She nudges me past Vantcha, toward the door.

"It was nice to meet you Bob," adds the withered man with an unusual finality, eye sockets aimed over my ear. I know I should feel safe in his blindness: he can't see my bad shoes, worn down heels, thread-worn pants paired up with a second-hand jacket of mismatched Kensington grey. Or my internal pockets damp with sweat, off-white China-cut shirt, five-dollar shear, and hard-working eyes. But nobody ever *seems* to notice, do they? They're too distracted by the prodigious scholarship grades, and the young face so full of promise. Still, something about this guy scares me. He *smells* my nerves: the penniless financial-aid student from Ohio, junior in Applied Mathematics, somehow... *somehow*... dating the rich-beautiful-talented daughter of the Provost of MIT, Vice President of Academic Affairs, Dean of Science... Matthias Mueller.

Nobel laureates tremble to meet him. He's former chairman of the Nuclear Safety Oversight Committee under two previous Presidents, a former college roommate of Charles P. Tunic, ex-Dean of MIT Engineering, now CEO of IBM. And John Germaine, former Dean of Chemistry and MIT President, now Federal Director of Intelligence. When the MIT Board of Trustees vote next month, it's widely acknowledged that Annie's father will become the President of MIT Corporation... Maybe the most influential man in Boston... And the most powerful scientist in the world. *And here I am, sacking his youngest daughter, so far out of my depth the light from my depth takes a thousand years to reach me.*

I go to shake Vantcha's hand, but of course the old man doesn't know.

Stomping down the promontory, I wait until the wind is high enough to cover my voice. "How do you know him?"

Annie wriggles under my arm. "He's a friend of my father."

"Oh?"

"His eyes were cut out in the War," she adds strangely.

Of course they were...

Seeing my confusion, she elaborates. "Catholics terrorists overthrew the Serb-Croat-Slovene government in April 'Forty-One and issued a 'Law concerning the Conversion from one religion to another' – legalising forced conversions. They executed non-Catholics who refused to convert. Vantcha was lucky only to have his eyes cut out."

"Cheese-and-rice!"

Annie nods, definitely. *Cheese-and-rice.*

And as we walk back down the hill to the car, we pass the crooked fence near the clapboard house where the wiry young man with long red hair and spidery eyes, wearing an oversized Army Surplus parka, lurks with a tape recorder and a gun.

# 3. '...THE MEEK INHERIT THE EARTH...'

*Friday, February 26, 1993*

Annie's headlights sweep over the verge as the car rounds the cliff, arriving at Matthias Mueller's sprawling mansion.

The layered granite and concrete structure stands proud like a cliff-top war nest; a Prairie-style masterpiece perched on a rocky precipice. The house bears a striking resemblance to Frank Lloyd Wright's Pennsylvanian mansion *Fallingwater,* but instead of a tranquil cascading stream running through it, the Mueller home hangs out over the crashing sea. Textureless concrete platforms cantilever above the glacier-milled rock. Braced against the granite core of the home, three floors of glowing living spaces are suspended into the snow-whipped squall.

Annie told me the story, as we drove out of Boston: A State Lottery winner from Carson City commissioned the house in Cape Ann granite from the same quarry – just outside New Bridlington – where the Statue of Liberty's plinth was milled. The home took two years to build, and the day the last painter drove away, Matthias

Mueller walked up the hill with his chequebook - Annie watching from the car - and returned ten minutes later with the Deeds.

Annie brakes on the gravel parkway at the brick colonnade, and flicks off the headlights. We sit for a moment, deciding on our final words.

"Don't say it," I plead feebly.

"I *have* to."

"No, you don't."

"Just don't tell him." She takes my hand.

"About what?" I feign ignorance, wanting her to *say* it.

"You know."

I *do* know. However, it's the first time it's been mentioned. Or *not* mentioned. "Why would I tell *him* about my father?"

"He figures things out. Just be careful. I want him to like you."

"Me too."

"I'm sure he will."

"How could he not?" I scowl unfairly.

"Let's go." Annie pops the door.

"I'd prefer *you* liked me," I blurt, too late to be clever. The French have a name for it... *L'Esprit De L'Escalier.* 'Staircase wit.' Thinking of a comeback on the way home.

She frowns at me. *If I didn't like you, you wouldn't be here,* I expect her to say. But instead, she just takes my hand fiercely. "I love you."

I'm done for.

I don't deserve her. I know it. She knows it.

All that's left now, is for her father to issue the decree.

I step out into the annex. There's an eerie shimmer in the sprawling dark to my left. The dappled light materialises into a steaming spray of moonlight on water on glass. "Is that an indoor pool?"

"*Natatorium,*" corrects Annie.

"*Nata*-what?"

The front door swings open. "Annie!" Tessa gasps. "What in god's name are you wearing?!"

Conscious of the fact that I'm again popping out of the same dusty Sunday Best I wore to lunch two weeks ago, I hang back, and let Annie draw the fire.

"I came straight from a lecture." Annie marches into the foyer.

Tessa tries to decide which is more troubling: that her daughter dresses like a vagrant to lectures, or to dinner. "You couldn't change?"

"Of course I *could*. I just didn't."

I push through the invisible force-field on the stoop.

Tessa shines her smile on me. "Robert! Let me take your jacket."

Then a third female voice, cool and aloof, splashes down the hall. "Annie?"

Right away, the voice gives me the all-overs.

Annie's nineteen-year-old sister struts into view.

"I didn't know *you* were here, *Madison*," groans Annie.

"I wouldn't miss this for the world." Madison sips from her beer, swivelling her hips like she's warming up for a workout. "How are you *Robert*?"

Madison's piercing blue eyes fix on me. I try to look away from her chestal region. Her tits look about ready to pop out of her blouse, and as she folds her arms over her chest, I hear a *squeak* like party balloons.

Annie's mother frowns. "You two *know* each other?"

Madison laughs, as if that's impossible. "Know *of* each other, Mommy!"

*She knows 'of' me?* I certainly know *of* Madison... even before I met Annie. Every boy on campus knows of Madison. In the Biblical sense. That's how I met Anne, after my roommate boasted that Madison Mueller's little sister was in his study group. Annie is studying Cognitive Science. And I with my Pure Maths, I figured out the two of us shared a module on Statistical Analysis. I never consciously *decided* that by joining the study group I might get into Madison's undergear, or that Annie might get to know me, and tell her little sister what a swell guy I am, after which Madison might then drop round to the dorm and tear off her clothes... *No.* I knew Madison was *beyond* unattainable. I just wanted to see if Annie looked anything like her, so impossible to miss, so searched-for in every single lecture hall by every last boy... There's even a guy, Tim Holden, who'd moved from Delaware and enroled for three years in the new 'Womens Studies' degree, because he met Madison at a party two years ago, and guessed she might be in that course from something she'd said.

No, I just wanted to *see.* I didn't want to *meet* either of them. Madison Mueller is just as widely feared, as she is yearned for. She established her Pornocracy in the first week of term, goading a promising young computationist named Steve Wells into taking Polaroids of her, rutting doggy-style on the Common Room floor, fully aware that Wells - aside from wearing a length of Ethernet cable for a belt - was one of five guys on campus with a Tandy computer, and access to the Microtek scanner. The pixellated photos were loaded on Wells' Bulletin Board within the hour, and downloaded onto two hundred guys' floppy disks another hour after that.

The next day Wells was gone. *And* his Tandy computer. His Polaroid camera. His footlocker. Every mention of his name. So too, the boy seen sweating over Madison's long torso, and every one of those actually in attendance at the event. Nothing remained of *any* of them but a few crumpled 300dpi sheets of tractor-feed paper with faded dithered renderings, sold in locker rooms for twenty bucks a page... That, and an all-pervasive fear of Madison Mueller *and* her father, the Provost.

Strangely, I can't quite remember the first time I saw her - 'Onion Arse' - with her butt so nice it makes you want to cry. It's like *all* boys are born with Madison Mueller on our minds. But I do remember the first time I saw Annie, vividly.

I stumbled into the library, out of breath, collapsing the circle of students in on itself as an associate professor browbeat the group, and gave me the kind of look you gave a clock. The professor was gnawing at the silence as I scanned the circle for her. There she was. The resemblance was obvious. A year older. Shorter hair. Bright, quizzical gaze, as she blurted brazenly, "Professor! You can't disregard centuries of applied thought!"

It was honest-to-goodness from that instant. My curiosity for Madison withered. Worse, she became repellent. The aggressively fussy gimmicks: tit-slings, hair management, lip shine, eye paint, lash-gadgets, lock steamers, cantilevered boobs, leg mesh, orchestration, and pretence.

Annie is effortless. She presents a complete contrast; satisfied with her dimensions, rational, cognisant, studious... It's instantly apparent how much effort Madison puts into being Madison, when you see Annie.

I was hooked right away on big sister.

Now, it's my second-darkest secret that I ever felt anything but wary indifference for Madison. That I *ever* spent twenty bucks on her photograph, lustrous legs and freckle-necked-freshman akimbo on her back... I can't even speak her name for fear of giving something away. It's the worst thing Annie could ever *possibly* know. The filthy thoughts. Sweet Annie. But now, standing in the foyer of their house, I feel a brief flash of reprieve, knowing Madison's secret. It gives me a toe-hold. *Doesn't it?*

I glance at Madison quickly. She looks unflappable. *'How are you, Robert?'* she has already proclaimed loudly. For the benefit of everyone. To make them wonder? Make *me* wonder? Hoping I know? *Knowing* I know? She doesn't even flinch, when I give her a brief, knowing glance. Because she alone survived the extermination. No, I realise: I'm in even *worse* condition now. Another unspeakable, another reason to disappear. Their father will see right through me. I'm walking right into the nexus of power, like some dumb kid out of *'Fast Times at Ridgemont High'*. It seems like a good idea right now to fake an illness... roll an ankle on the rug... on my worn-up heels. It's too much all at once:

Madison, the evil Man-eating sociopath – boobs with a magnetic effect on my corneas.

Annie... *surely* she *already* has her doubts about me?

Tessa, only wanting Annie to be happy. The moment she sees otherwise, she'll bomb the invader into oblivion.

And Matthias, operating at a superhuman altitude I can barely fathom, his sprawling signature governing hundreds-of-millions in bursaries and dispersals. On this man's professional whim, livelihoods are toggled like light switches. He has erased decades of academic effort for less than defiling his daughter.

And this is the principal issue: Tonight, the Provost Himself will inform Annie whether or not, she may see me again.

Since that first study group, it has always been inevitable. I see now, with painful clarity, that I've been clinging to a ledge. A fissure. Eyes closed, thinking I was near to the ground. It's a dizzying sensory overload – my mind is diverted by the details of the house, glancing at Madison, looking away, feigning indifference, watching Tessa, plying their faces for a read on my status, ear on the conversation, anticipating the moment HE appears... Which door? In this next room? Where is he? My head is out of space, looping in expanding concentric circles, ready to slingshot into the void.

I follow the three women down a step I don't actually see, *trip* into the humid living area, and Annie snatches my hand – catching me.

The room beyond is unlike anything I've ever even heard of. It bears no resemblance to my childhood home, with its single rug, damp papered walls, and mismatched sofa chairs. This looks like a fancy hotel. The size of it. The neatness. Here, every angle is perched with oil paintings, standing lamps, throws, cords and tassels, flower arrangement, and international knick-knacks. The kitchen is crowded with flashy pots and utensils. A shale island bench like a billiard table is strewn with the spoils of a ruptured Horn of Plenty – figs, cheeses, legumes in jars of oil, decanted wines stood to breathe.

In the next room, the dining table overflows with piled and polished silver.

Further on, beyond a densely-furnished lounge, it's all shadow and glass and spotlights on sun-bleached wicker, and a wide deck over the darkened sea.

To the left, down three steps, lays a deep cave warmed by a granite fireplace, overstuffed cowhide couches, side-tables piled with a potpourri of bric-a-brac: Everything is buffed and shining. I'm lost and sick. And – where am *I?*

"Can I... fetch you a drink?" asks Madison, sweetly.

I slap my crown. "I brought wine. It's in the car."

"Don't worry about it," says Annie too quickly.

"It's good," I add. *And those were my last twenty bucks!* "I'll be back in a sec—"

"Nobody *said* it wasn't good." Madison's cleavage swings into view.

Look away!

"Have a beer." Tessa moves to a fridge under the bench.

"You'd *love* a beer, wouldn't you honey?" Annie squeezes my damp fist.

Madison flops lazily against the bench and tugs at the neck of a beer bottle. "Dad ships these down from Canada by the truckload. The names are priceless. *Au Benite.*" Angels' bathwater. "Here, look. *La Fin Du Monde.*" *The End of the World.* "*Nine* percent alcohol."

Tessa hands me the heavy, black-labelled ale. "Matt doesn't like taking dinner this late. Let's start serving."

*Taking* dinner?

Annie pours the wine. "Where is he?"

"In the den. Help me fetch the roast. Madison, get the salads out of the cooler."

And so the mythological Mueller women busy themselves, conversation running to Madison's desire to quit her degree in *Political Science and Writing* at the MIT School of Humanities Arts, and Social Sciences, to switch to a degree in International Studies at the new MIT campus in Frankfurt or Berlin – whichever it turns out to be, if Daddy ever makes up his mind, and sorts out where the new campus will be in Europe. Madison thinks Berlin. Her desperation to travel. The ethical wrongness of the Wall... And I stand there, nodding, drinking the Provost's beer, waiting for HIM to appear.

Even in his absence, he fills every corner.

Suddenly, Matthias emerges... as if the mention of his name summons him from Olympus: Silver-haired, deep-creased face, eyes like neutron stars held in tow by sheer force of will. He's taller than I thought, inspects the women's labours from on-high, as he joins the conversation. All their words became an incomprehensible buzz as I stand motionless, leaking, waiting to be noticed, the voyeur, the stranger, occupying territory I can't hold, hurtling towards the surface of the sun propelled by every universal Law. Sweat beads on my cheeks as I wrestle with my unclean thoughts, hiding my shoes behind the bench, regretting my choice of Curriculum, parentage, and all the secret burdens I've been warned not to speak of.

Matthias turns. "Robert?"

"Yes?"

"Can I get you something?"

I can't tell if it's a jibe. It could be. Is it unusual for a Provost in his *own* house to ask a junior Math major if he can *get* him something? It might be an obtuse reference to the fact that I am already kitted out in HIS kitchen, drinking HIS beer, sleeping with HIS daughter, studying at HIS university... interloping in HIS universe. *Yes*, I'm fine? Or— *No*, I'll have another?

"I'm okay."

Pause.

"*I'm glad* you're okay."

And Matthias returns to the conversation.

Just *okay?*

Annie is busy at the oven. She doesn't seem to have noticed the exchange.

Condensation from the beer trickles down my wrist as I stand, still frozen, heart thumping, sweating, and suddenly unable to think of a single word to say.

I sit at the dining table, decked out with a glass of Grenache-Syrah-Mourvédre, a dry white, another of champagne, and an unfinished *La Fin Du Monde ('End of the World')* by my plate. "This is a *very* good wine, Daddy," observes Madison, smirking. I swirl the red in my glass like I've seen the others do, and accidentally send a red fan across the tablecloth.

Tessa softly mitigates the destruction of her linen.

"I'm sorry!" I exclaim, too loudly.

"It's nothing."

"Happens all the time," Madison quips.

The conversation becomes even more stilted, decaying exponentially, running around the table skipping Matthias. Skipping me. Like a rapidly deteriorating game of Totem Tennis.

Annie takes a swing at the ball. "So Daddy, *Bill* gave you a mention in his speech..."

Last week, President Clinton delivered his first State of the Union address. "Really?" I blurt, surprised.

Matthias grumbles.

"Robert," explains Tessa. "Matt led the Committee for Nuclear Safety under Reagan and Bush."

It's the first time I've heard anyone abbreviate the Provost's name that way – 'Matt'. He doesn't *seem* to mind...

Realising I still haven't caught up, Tessa adds, "the President made a very passing reference to defence, and 'the proliferation of weapons of mass destruction'."

"Three sentences," Matthias barks. "And *one* of them was '*responsibly reducing the defence budget*?"

I nod. Ah! Hmmm. Yes. I agree.

Annie peers at me curiously.

"Bush lit a fire in the Middle East," inserts Madison. "And Clinton turns *off* the fire hose. Look at this thing today with the World Trade Centre! It's just the beginning."

Matt nods, agreeing with Madison. *Yes, good girl.*

"It's *disgusting*," Annie scowls. "Killing *ordinary* people."

"Not *so* ordinary," I add.

Annie blanches.

"What do you mean, Bob?" asks Madison, sweetly.

I can't say it. But I've been thinking all day of the possible arrogance of naming a place the '*World*' Trade Centre.

"Bob has started his thesis," volunteers Annie. "Tell dad about it, Bob. It's very interesting."

"What subjects are you taking, Bob?" asks Matthias.

"Probability and Random Variables. Statistical Inference. Automata, Computability and Complexity. And Modelling and Simulation."

"That's funny," Madison sucks the flesh off an olive. "Ben did modelling as well."

*Ben?*

"Madison," Tessa frowns. "Please."

Annie nurses her wine, arms curled like a boxer.

*Who's Ben?*

Matthias is watching me expectantly.

Annie looks strangely sullen.

*Who is Ben?*

"Bob?" urges Madison.

"Oh, I'm calling it *Impossibility Science*, like Complexity Science."

Matthias looks away at nothing in particular, like I've spontaneously vanished.

But I'm safe here. I know this ground. "The probability that relationships like the Pythagorean triangle will occur is *zero*. All true numbers *should* resemble *pi* in complexity. So, what we observe are just patterns in our own mathematical—"

Madison frowns. "Speaking of *pi*, does anybody want some?"

"The probability of us being here right now," I persist, "since time is infinite and life is finite - is *zero*."

Madison pinches her arm.

"That *is* interesting Bob," smiles Tessa, convincingly.

"I think it's very clever," smiles Annie.

"So... What's your conclusion?" asks Matthias, distracted by something outside a window.

"We've created a language which allows us to *think* we understand the universe, when we only understand the language."

A visible shadow forms across Matthias' brow. He rises from the table suddenly. "That was a lovely meal. Thank you ladies. I'm going to the den. Bob. Come with me."

For a moment, I think my roast lamb is about to have a reversal of fortune. I'm dropping hard gas at the same time. I look to Annie for my status. She throws me a futile glance.

Matthias dumps his napkin, and heads for the hall.

"Thanks for the lovely meal, Missus Mueller," I offer, rising from my seat, selecting my beer. *La Fin Du Monde.*

My moment of judgement.

I circle the table, looking for a way over to where Matthias is headed...

Madison pushes her chair out in front of me.

Before I realise what's happened, she's standing in my way, with her head turned slightly so Annie can't see her face. She's so close I can feel her breath, as her boobs sweep through my field of vision. She turns and flounces toward the kitchen.

"Bob?" Matthias stands at the doorway.

Intoxicated seven different ways, I trip after the Provost down the long, shrinking corridor.

# 4. '...THE ROAD THAT LEADS TO DESTRUCTION...'

*Friday, February 26, 1993*

"Come in." Matthias gestures me into the den.

I peer into the mythological lair: A huge Persian rug fills the floor, under the Napoleonic desk. A second river-stone fireplace reverses onto the riser in the adjacent room. An entire wall is filled with gilt and burnished spines.

Matthias touches a contact switch. A miniature spotlight fades up on the far side of the room, illuminating a shining spectacle. Hanging in a tall glass cabinet at the back of Matthias' study, is a slab of basalt the size of a fridge door, hung on wires, tones of grey graduating up its sheer face. I know the relic from photographs. It is a full-size replica of the Rosetta Stone.

Matthias turns his back, not quite noticing my fascination, as he reaches into the layers of costumes on a stout coat-stand – Harris Tweed and scarf, fluorescent anorak, khaki fishing-vest gaudy with lures – and he unhooks a burgundy velvet smoking jacket.

Matthias draws on the jacket, walks to the desk, opens a mahogany cigar humidor, and selects a pair of *Hoyo de Monterrey* as fat as truck driver's thumbs. "Here."

With fluid movements, Matthias snips off the nose off a cigar with a gold cutter, and hefts a fat marble desk lighter into my limp hand.

The lighter weighs like a bowling ball. My wrist drops, whacking the desk. *Shit!* I urgently accept the cigar, pretending not to have already made a mistake, copying Matthias' movements, sucking and puffing above the long flame, knuckles throbbing.

Matthias seems focussed for now on his own smoke.

This doesn't feel so bad, I smile.

Maybe the situation isn't as bleak as I thought?

"What are your prospects after college, Robert?"

"I'd like to be an Operations Analyst, or a Systems Analyst," I answer smartly. My eyes are drawn back to the basalt slab. Who else has stood here? Who else has been privy to this scene? MIT board members? White House Science Council? Former Presidents?

"I'm not normally given to discussing a thesis with a second-year student," prefaces Matthias. "Especially a *math* major. However, since you are seeing my daughter, I feel it's in her interest..."

"Sir?"

"Your thesis: It is too abstract. We live in a market economy. There are certain practicalities. Have you read Church, and Turing?"

"Yes."

"Of course you have. Do you know why?"

*Why?*

"They showed a practical application for their ideas - fluid dynamics, economics, computing... for a thesis to have *any* interest for anyone, like Shaw's application of Chaos Theory and strange attractors to information flows, it must do the same. Or it's a waste of time. *Nobody* will care about it. It won't see the light of day, outside of your own classroom. By definition, there isn't a commercial market for 'Impossibility Theory'. And in *this* world - the *real* world - the ideas with legs are those with a market." From a pair of crystal decanters, Matthias mixes a highball of scotch with spring water, and hands it to me.

"Thank you... I'm not sure I—"

"Here. Put this on." Matthias hoists down another smoking jacket on the hook of his thumb. "If Anne is like her mother – and she is – she won't tolerate smoke on your clothes."

Swaying like a metronome I grapple with the logistics of holding the lit cigar, and navigating into the black jacket. The silk lining is cool on my wrists, funereal, at the death of my world view. *Did the Provost just trash my thesis?*

"You're interested in Probability?" continues Matthias.

"I guess so."

"You should think about getting into Insurance."

I consider embarking on a rejection...

"This is an egalitarian society," Matthias proceeds self-importantly. "And a comparatively passive government! When small groups are permitted to drive change based on private opinion, they foster oligarchies: like Fascism and Communism. This is *our* way of life in America: The market rules. It is a demand-driven society, not *supply*. The same goes for ideas. If there isn't any *demand* for your ideas, they aren't *useful*, and they'll never see the light of day. As scientists we have to accept that. Here *ideas* are the tail, not the dog. Science is not about *changing* the world, not this century. Science is about service. *That* is the price of liberty."

And just like that, my thesis is dead.

If I submit it, I'm a Fascist.

"You'll learn," Matthias adds. "The majority rules." He watches me closely, rolling the chubby cigar in his curled fingers.

I have never been alone in the company of a man like him. I've never even had a conversation like this, not even with my own father. And this man is the antithesis of my namesake in opinion, education, and vice. Right at this moment, all the thoughts that Matthias would cringe to know, shuffle to the top of my mind. I'm not sure how I'm meant to respond...

"You know what *that* is?" Matthias nods at the glass case across the room, firelight flickering in his eyes.

"It's the Rosetta Stone," I answer, staring at the beautiful tablet. "...A replica."

The achromatic slab is profoundly elegant: Three paragraphs are engraved on the spot-lit face of the stone... Finely detailed pictography, cursive demotic and immaculate parallels of engraved Greek... "It's the most beautiful object in all of human history," I add.

Matthias looks surprised. "Do you know what it says?"

It's a strange question. The Rosetta Stone is well-known for its role in deciphering the first Egyptian hieroglyphics. But hardly anyone could recite its contents. Only those with an avid interest in Egyptology...

"It was written on the first anniversary of the reign of thirteen-year-old Ptolemy Five, Epiphanies," I answer. "It reaffirms his church, and lists duties of the priests in worshipping him." I step closer, and point to a portion of the text: "'...*the priests shall pay homage three times a day...*' and... *'there shall be set upon the shrine the ten gold crowns of the king'* and... a list of days for religious festivals, including Ptolemy's birthday, the thirtieth day of the month *Mesore*, which is October seventh."

Matthias puffs smoke. "I'm surprised Anne thought to tell you about this..."

"Hmm?" I blanch, sensing a problem.

"Memorising the Rosetta Stone? What else did she tell you...?" Matthias' piercing black pupils lock onto mine with withering intensity. "Did she tell you I like crossword puzzles? *Hall and Oates, Live at the Apollo* maybe?"

"No, I didn't—"

"Tell me Robert, how does a Math junior know so much about *this?*"

I realise suddenly I've skated too far. I'm out on the ice. "I—" Maybe I expected more time before he closed in, more preliminaries. Here it comes... "I don't know... I guess I just remember things."

"You didn't agree with Anne's comment about today's terrorist attack... But you have an interest in *religion?*"

I freeze. Here I am, at the precipice, witnessing the rising ire of the man who can sway Annie's will, excommunicate me, banish me to the abyss, send me out of his home to find my scholarship revoked for some small infraction... And with no home to return to, I will serve my days in a part-times job in a hardware store in Akron and grow old, regaling tradesmen with notions of Impossibility and dreams of dreams... And there is more to lose here than Annie. Much more! This man holds something over me. The way Annie speaks at length of the strength of his protection. Here is the man I wish I could become. If I could have chosen my father – and I've often wished I could – *here* he is: master of science and learning, commander of a nation's greatest minds. In this room, at this moment, my fate will be decided. As in all of science – the birth of a sun, the beginning of an ice age – everything swings on an infinitely small pivot. A shift in the wind. A sensitive dependence on initial conditions. Two glancing molecules. What do I say? Now or never. What's the correct answer, out of the million possible incorrect ones? Annie tried to warn me. Stay off the subject of religion.

"I guess I'm interested in religion," I explain meekly. "As a derivative of my interest in numbers."

"How so?" Matthias sets down his drink.

"*Three* sons of Noah, wise men, crosses on the hill, denials of Christ, cries for Bärabas, days in the grave, Holy Trinity... *Seven* Days of creation, years of famine, plagues of Pharaoh, seals of Revelation, hills of Babylon, laps of Jericho by seven priests on the seventh day... *Twelve* vines, apostles, tribes of Israel. The Book of Numbers. The Number of the Beast. The Hebrew alphabet written in numbers. The name of god, a Number... The way we apply simple rules to the universe to comprehend it – like maths – we also apply simply rules to understand god," I pause, wondering...

There is an awful, hanging moment.

33

Have I dug myself deeper? Maybe even dared to sound patronising?

Matthias' gaze drops, downcast. And not for my sake. "It is an unlikely sequence, Robert. It takes more than whimsy to motivate a man to seek knowledge," he replies, softly, sadly. "Augustine, Wallis, Pascal... All enlisted mathematics to prove god - but *not* because they *first* believed in *mathematics*. No... They were missionaries before mathematicians. Which are *you*, Robert?"

The sweat is coming out of my head in marbles. I can't change the subject now. I can't hide. "Respectfully - people are not always so neatly compartmentalised."

Matthias darkens further, cigar propped sideways on his thin lips. "May I speak without prejudice, Robert?"

What have we been doing already? I nod.

"I'll be straight with you. And I'll appreciate, if you are straight with me."

"Yes—"

"Anne's mother has done her utmost to convince me that I should like you. She thinks it will make Anne happy. However, I am a scientist. And her father. As such, I have more practical expectations. I wish to see my daughter protected and provided for. I want my daughters to marry men of character. I want my *grandchildren* to be healthy, and have outstanding role models."

I'm blushing. Am I witnessing the pink parts of Mister Mueller? The delicate emotional organs... The matured anxieties? Peel away the cloth, and behold...

"Anne was born smart, Robert. She doesn't care to be nurtured, and she knows her own mind, and she can make her own way. But she is my daughter, and this is my home. I do not have to be polite if I know better. Don't you agree?"

"Ahuh."

"Then there's one thing I'd like you to be *especially* clear on, Robert."

*Here it comes.* Whistling, like a bomb.

"I don't like people who believe in god, Robert. In any form. God, or gods. I *dislike* them. However, I have a particular loathing for *all* forms of monotheism, with special regard to returning messiahs. It infuriates me... immensely. Do you *understand?*" He leans forward.

I nod.

"It flies in the face of reason. Worse, it has led us as a race to shirk our responsibilities in the real world for centuries. Responsibilities which, according to science, include the protection of *natural life*. And, as if all this is not enough, this god now has us planting bombs in the basements of high-rise buildings! So when I ask you, how a Math junior knows so much about religion, and you tell me how much *more* you know, it bothers me. Do you 'follow'?"

I recall vaguely, months ago, when I first approached Annie... I interrogated myself in that moment. What I mistook for an act of bravery, I now know, was not bravery at all. How did I *ever* think I could survive this? How did I expect the Provost to react? Pity? Disregard?

"*This* is what *offends* me about religion, Robert." Matthias glowers. "That it is considered harmless. That our government will spend billions to crush a poisonous threat like Communism, which falls very narrowly into the sphere of politics... but will *not* crush a *more* poisonous threat like god. No, instead we give them tax concessions - as if stupidity is a human right? I tell you, religion divides countries. Divides families. Precisely because it is irrational, flimsy, imaginary... it allows individuals to devise absurd logics for all forms of bigotry and discrimination - racism, sexism, class... Despots and villains are easily able to pervert it to their own ends *because* its words and ideas are pliable and ambiguous. Religion has killed more people than Fascism or Marxism combined. In fact, neither of these other two abhorrences could have succeeded without the church! Churches *put* them into power. Khrushchev used the Polish Catholics. Mussolini, and the Lateran Treaty, as did Chancellor Hitler, who proclaimed to the Catholic German Nation when he was democratically elected that he regarded Catholicism as '*the foundation of our national morality*. Stalin even used the Orthodox Church to appease his people, in spite of Marx—"

"'Religion is the sigh of the oppressed creature...'" I quote, hoping to stem the tirade.

...The heart of a heartless world, just as it is the spirit of a spiritless situation. It is the opium of the people...

Matthias nods, impatiently. "The *only* way we will *ever* have peace in this world, and accept we are responsible for our own fate... is to destroy god. So - this is my question, Robert. Again— Where does your interest in *religion* come from?"

The heat from the fireplace grows even fiercer.

Sweat streams down my temples. I swipe at my brow, and shrug. "Like you said, '*the market rules.*'"

Matthias's dour glare remains set, as stony as the ancient tablet.

"If there isn't any *demand* for an idea, it isn't *useful*..." I elaborate, quoting him from a few minutes earlier.

Matthias instantly produces a thunderclap of laughter. "Ha ha! Robert! *Well said!* Well said!" He hands me an ashtray for the grey nub of ash at the end of my cigar. My head is spinning. "Very good." The Provost's sudden good humour fills me with relief.

"Sir, may I say something... '*without prejudice*.'"

"Please."

"I guess I'm a bit *circumspect*... about religion. I only recently stopped believing in god... To my father's disappointment."

Matthias jerks slightly, smile evaporating.

"It's been maybe a year— It's hard to pick an exact date. It was less like stepping *off* a cliff, than climbing one."

"How old are you Robert?"

"Twenty-six," I clarify, being closer to Annie's age than Madison's.

"I was your age too."

"Who's winning?" asked Annie, silhouetted in the doorway.

I jolt, startled.

"We're getting to know each other, aren't we Robert?" Matthias claps me lightly on the arm.

"Something like that."

"I came in to see if either of you want an espresso?" Annie looks confused at the sight of Matthias petting me like a pug.

"Robert?" Matthias turns. "Espresso?"

"Yes please."

"Ristretto," replies Matthias. "Two."

Annie comes to my side, and touches my wrist, concerned – like a nurse checking a pulse. For a moment, my arms form a physical link between father and daughter, and I shiver. Annie turns reluctantly to leave the room, glancing back.

"Robert, I have something you'll be interested in." Matthias draws a heavy sheaf of paper from the shelf, and places it carefully in my hands. The card-covered document is bound with a constellation of star-shaped metal split pins. The title reads: *Banking and Financial Services Committee, U.S. House of Representatives, Hearing on Intergovernmental Insurance Regulation.* "If I were a Math major studying Probability and Statistical Simulation, with your range of interests *this* is what I would choose for a thesis."

The cover is emblazoned with the pyramidal logo of the American Academy of Actuaries: three triangles stacked to form something resembling the 'all-seeing eye' from the one-dollar bill.

"Take a look at page one-forty-four."

I wrestle into the reference.

The chapter reads 'New Financial instruments: Catastrophe Futures and Acts of God Bonds'.

"Do you know what this is?" Matthias asks.

Actuarial Science is part of my course, but nobody bothers to study. Jobs in the sector are impossible, unless you're a certified genius. "Insurance risk?" I begin. "Figuring out how many times a year rooves in Galveston will flip into a ditch, and how much it costs to fix them. Then sell Bonds to cover it."

"Good. That's good. There is a big *future*," Matthias elaborates, "excuse the pun, in State and Federal Governments issuing bonds for catastrophes, *Acts of God* futures, to offset the risk of major disaster recovery: Earthquakes, floods, and forest fires. Think of it as insurance on a national scale. They may even cover acts by civil or military authorities. And terrorism, like this World Trace Center bombing today. There's a certain irony in calling a terrorist attack an 'Act of God' – don't you think? Anyway, take a look. You'll find it interesting."

I'm intrigued. The contradiction of Insurance versus Divine Will in the detail of human lives *is* curious... God versus science, exemplified in the notion of mathematical modelling to *forecast* his will. It's interesting, framed this way. And better still, the Provost himself has handed it to me.

"Don't be mistaken, Computer science will take off," adds Matthias. "But guys like you will be a dime a dozen. The only thing this century that will grow faster than computers, is disaster. And there are far fewer men for Washington to come to when things go wrong."

"Thank you, Sir."

"And by the way, Robert..." Matthias stubs out his cigar, mashing the crackling leaves into the spotless dish.

"Yes?"

"If you *eeever* upset Anne..."

The phone on Matthias' desk rings softly. He picks up the handset. He is watching me, as he listens.

A curious expression that I can't quite place flickers across his features. The Provost whispers into the phone:

"Don't call the police. I'll be there in ten minutes."

He sets down the handset, and bows his head. Staring at the blotter on his desk.

"Robert..."

"Yes?"

"You'll have to come with me."

"Hmmmm?"

Matthias' tone is that of an instruction, issued to a subordinate: "Tell Tessa and the girls *we* have to step out for a few minutes. The lighthouse keeper has had an accident. It's nothing serious. However, we'll just make sure he's okay. If not, we'll drive him into Boston. I'll need you to come with me, in case I have to stabilise him while you drive."

"Wh—? I—"

"*Annie* will stay here. Is that clear?"

*The lighthouse keeper?*

I trip out of the cave in my black velvet smoking jacket to the kitchen, head swimming. *'We' have to step out?* What just happened?

*Don't call the police... I'll be there in ten minutes...*

That's what he'd said on the phone.

The skin at the back of my neck is tingling with danger.

The lighthouse keeper has had an accident?

Madison is seated on the kitchen bench, feet swinging – while Tessa clears the table, and Annie operates an espresso machine the size of a church organ. They glance at me, smiling at first...

"Annie?"

"Hmm?"

I repeat Matthias' instructions, verbatim.

Annie pales, steam hissing into a jug of milk. "He said that?"

"'You stay here.'"

She nods solemnly, without question. *His word is not questioned.* "Okay."

I hurry back to the hall, seeing the front door to the house is wide open and Matthias is waiting behind the wheel of a Range Rover on the floodlit porte-cochère, passenger door ajar.

I pull the house closed, and rush across the pebbles.

On the passenger seat sits a white sheet-metal first-aid kit with a green cross.

Seeing my hesitation, Matthias barks. "Come on! Quickly!"

My brain is screaming. What the FUCK is going ON?!?

I pull the first aid case into my lap.

With a spray of gravel, Matthias races down the tree-lined drive under the moonless canopy of trees at break-neck speed. "Where are we going?" I ask redundantly, half pretending not to know.

"In the first-aid kit, you'll find a blister pack with two point-three millilitre plastic ampoules of ammonia inhalant. Get them ready."

I pop the latch on the case, and rummage through bundles of gauze, zip-locks and sachets, locating the ammonia.

I can only guess what they're for... an 'inhalant' might be used to prevent fainting? I wonder, fearfully whether he means to use them on me. I grab at the dashboard to steady myself as Matthias swerves down the hill, punching through the gears, engine roaring.

My heart is pounding like a marching band drum.

I've been shot from a torpedo tube.

Launching into the familiar black easement between two clapboard houses, Matthias pulls on the handbrake, and leaps out of the car.

Running up the hill, where Annie led me hours ago, light streams from the open door of the lighthouse keeper's cabin.

Before, when we came here on the way to the house, the cabin had been darkened – when Vantcha answered the door. Why would he now have a light on, if he's blind?

Matthias runs ahead of me, up the windblown back of the darkened bluff. His voice echoes in the gale. "Hurry up!"

Fear tightens around my neck like a Chinese finger trap. I have no choice but to follow, into whatever waits in the cabin.

I tuck the first-aid kit under my arm, and run after him.

Reaching the door to the cottage... the first thing I notice is the neatness. The single room barely looks lived in. The furniture is limited to a lone chair, and a small radio on a side table. There are no bookcases, no TV, no photo frames. Rubber blinds are drawn on two windows. A small lead-light table lamp sits on the floor, filling the cabin with an amber glow. An unnerving odour of burned fat and plastic fills the air. The burner on a tiny gas stove in a corner juts blue flame, and a copper kettle lays upturned on the floor.

The old lighthouse keeper - in his ill-fitting corduroy slacks - is sprawled on his back on the floor, a bright welt in one empty eye socket. Matthias huddles over him, trying to revive him. "Give me the ampoules!"

I hurry inside, and hand Matthias the plastic tubes. He snaps the ends off both, and holds them under Vantcha's nostrils.

Blearily, the old man rouses, mumbling: *"He found me..."*

Matthias raises Vantcha into his lap, and inspects the back of the old man's shirt, grimacing. Overpowered by curiosity, I move to see at what Matthias is looking at. An oozing blister the size of a dinner plate, ringed with molten polyester, covers Vantcha's shoulder. I gag involuntarily.

The acrid smell is burnt flesh.

"Matthias?" Vantcha reaches up to touch the Provost's cheek with his blind fingers.

"You're in shock. You need to stay calm." Matthias glances around the room. "Robert! Fill that kettle with cold water!"

Vantcha shrieks suddenly! "The boy! —might still be outside... listening!"

"What 'boy'?" ask Matthias.

Vantcha mutters feverishly: "He knew *my* name... *Velajcic! His* name was Lujko... from Nassua— He *said* he was a student... He found my name in the Witness Statement! He said he was writing a paper! He wanted to ask me questions... I told him to leave. But he said his father was in Jasenovic—"

"His father was in the same *camp?*" queries Matthias.

Vantcha nods.

*Camp?*

I struggle to fathom the strange conversation. *Jasenovic?* The old man is barely conscious, slurring his speech, spittle foaming on his lips.

"Bring the light closer!" Matthias waves a hand at me, as I pass him the kettle. "What else did he say?" Matthias pours the water carefully over the burn on Vantcha's back.

41

The old man mutters disjointedly: "His mother... Decree One-One-Six-Eight-Nine... The *Office of Religious Affairs* – He asked about the *Ustashi*" Vantcha's voided eyebrows rise up, stretching the scars in his sunken sockets. "His father was in *Jasenovic*! He met a man..." Vantcha shifted his weight painfully. "The *Ustashi* were looking for the treasure! With the Nazis– That's what he said! The massacre at Oradour-sur-Glane, the secret convoys– *Das Ahnenerbe! Parzival* The *Holy Grail* – not a cup... a stone! *The word of god!*"

"He pushed you against the stove?" asked Matthias. "To make you talk?"

"He had a gun..."

"What did he ask you?"

"The *tablet*!" Vantcha gasps suddenly. "He asked about the *tablet*!"

"What did he *say?!*" whispers Matthias gently. "About the *tablet*?"

"I begged him for mercy," whimpers Vantcha. "Like in *Jasenovic*! On my knees on the cobbles... over a basket full of eyes... Last thing I saw... A basket full of eyes... The same cruelty... The Ustashi..."

Matthias inspects Vantcha's back more closely. "Vantcha?"

"Yes?"

"It's bad, but I can't take you to the hospital. It's not safe. I'll take care of you, alright?"

"Okay."

Annie's father turns to me. "Robert. Take my car home. Ask Annie to take you back to Boston, and Tessa to come and pick me up in two hours."

What changed since we left the house? He said we were taking the old man to the hospital? What changed? And I'm busy studying Vantcha's wrinkled face. Tears stream out of the old man's dead sockets, reliving a distant memory... The agony in his eye, the searing pain in his burned shoulder, the horror of what had happened, all his present pain pales in comparison to something he sees in his mind.

"Robert!" Matthias snaps. "Did you hear me?"

"Yes."

"And don't say a *word* to Annie!"

Annie is rapturous as we race back to Boston. "He *really* liked you. I mean, *really...*"

"I don't know..."

"What were you doing *talking* about in there all that time? And going to see *Vantcha?*"

She knows I'm hiding something.

I just wish I knew what I was hiding. "He asked if you clued me up on the Rosetta Stone!" I offer as a decoy. The sight of the old man's burnt back is like a mental scar. *Jasenovic. Ustashi. Oradour-sur-Glane. Das Ahnenerbe.* None of the words made any sense. *Something about a 'treasure'?!*

"Really?"

"He nearly fell over when I knew what the Rosetta Stone says."

Annie's eyes widened. "You know... what that *rock* says?"

"It's not a '*rock*'!" I blurt. "It's a *tablet.*"

"It was sweet, Bobby... The way you threw yourself to the lions tonight." Annie chuckles. "Daddy *never* liked any guy *either* of us brought home."

Either?

Annie cuts the engine in the dormitory parking lot, and climbs across the console into my lap. "Maddie is *insane* with jealousy. Did you tell him?"

"About what?"

"About your father, silly."

"It didn't come up."

"Phew. You did good, Bobby." Annie deftly unravels my belt.

I can't make eye contact. "Hey, *Hunny,*" I grab at my pants. "Maybe we should just get some sleep?"

Annie scrunches her nose. "Very funny!"

I baulk. "Really."

"Yes, Bobby."

"*Hunny*, I'm tired."

It dawns on her that I'm not fooling. "Are you effing *serious?*"

I rub my eyes with one hand, still holding my pants together. "I'll see you tomorrow?"

Annie flounces back into the driver's seat, banging her knee on the wheel. "You're so fucked up. You know that?"

*I guess I do.*

I lay awake all night replaying the evening in my mind... The conversation at dinner... cigars in the den... The strange scene at Vantcha's cottage.

I'm not sure what happened, anywhere throughout the entire evening. The whole thing was a mad rollercoaster.

By dawn the events have already begun to fade, and the world has returned to the satisfaction of markets, noisy as a nest of sparrows. I toss my Impossibility thesis in the trash, and go to work on '*Catastrophe Futures*' and '*Acts of God Bonds*'.

Three weeks later, Annie takes me back to New Bridlington for lunch at the *House*.

Slumped in an awkwardly-shaped wicker armchair on the wide sun-bleached deck overlooking the day-lit sea, Tessa mentions the 'New Brid' town council is looking for a lighthouse keeper.

Matthias suggests I call him 'Matt.'

Four months after that I stride into his office, full of hope and hubris, and hand-deliver the second-to-final draft of my thesis: '*Predicting Acts of God.*'

Matt accepts the star-pinned bundle.

"How's your friend? The lighthouse keeper," I ask nervously.

"He's fine. It's was just an accident. He gets a little mixed up." Matt jerks a thumb at the TV in the corner of his office. "Like I told you..."

It's on the news... Last night, President Clinton ordered a cruise missile attack on the Iraqi intelligence headquarters in Baghdad, in retaliation for an assassination attempt on former U.S. President Bush.

Overnight, the USS *Peterson* and the USS *Chancellorsville* fired 24 cruise missiles at Baghdad.

"You watch," Matt suggests, as he scans my thesis. "This is just the beginning. If a *Democrat* is bombing Baghdad now, the next Republican President will invade."

But I don't think it was Matt who first said that: 'this is just the beginning'.

I think it was at dinner. It was Madison.

# 5. '...A THIEF IN THE NIGHT...'

*Sunday, September 2, 2012*

Washington's New York Avenue radiates purposefully in a direct line from the White House, out to the rambling Brentwood rail yards, where it snakes east to the Anacostia River.

The straight section of *NY Ave* cuts a direct line from the luminous residence of President Obama, past office buildings, apartments, and shopping malls, to the warehouses and grimy railway easements of the 'Ward 5' district – a seam of glitter and grim in the industrial hem between Washington's city and suburbs.

Past the first bend in the Avenue is a cross-street occupied by cabarets – red brass and velvet foyers, naked neon women, and pin-boards filled with Polaroids. At the bottom of the street, on the intersection of Bladensburg Rd, a man stands staring into the mirror of the men's washroom in the Kazco gas station. Security camera footage shows Lujko 'Lou' Maas, 41, dressed in a faded army uniform: leg cuffs tucked into sand-coloured combat boots, and tan t-shirt visible at the Mandarin collar. Tattooed on his forearm is a sword crossed by three lightning bolts. His eyes have sunk deeper since 1993: the skin around the tiny, spider-like pupils is wilted, but retains the same speck-like quality his blood-shot face gave those eyes as a youth when he visited the lighthouse keeper in New Bridlington. His scalp is bald, eyelashes plucked, eyebrows and – on close inspection – the fine hair on his ears, has all been removed with depilatory cream. His ruddy complexion bears an angry red tinge where the ointment burned the skin.

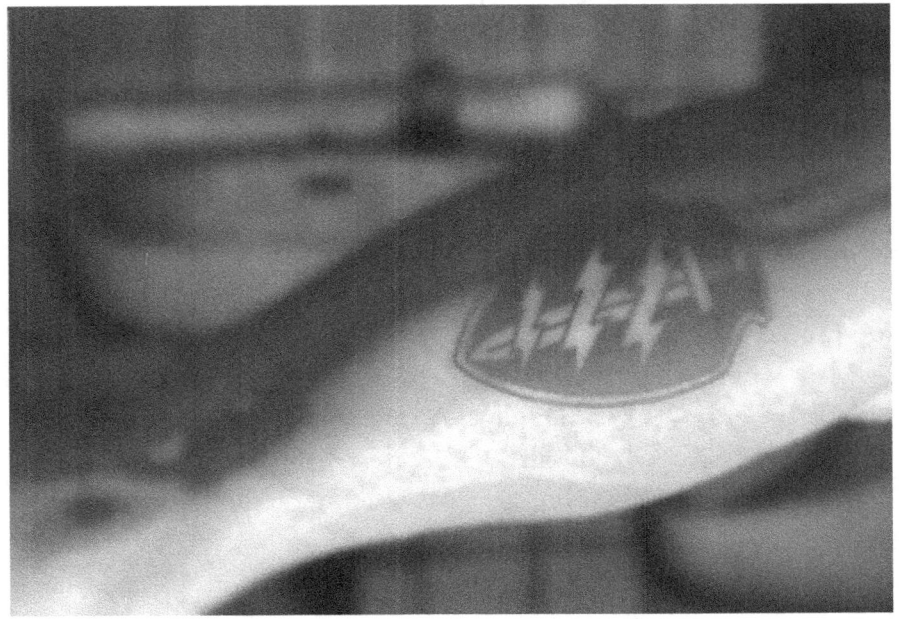

*(Diagram 1- Lou Maas tattoo)*

Lou reaches into a plastic bag on the counter in the dank piss-stained bathroom, and takes out a small nail brush. He scrubs his nails, then the top of his head. Finally, he rinses a pair of RayBan sunglasses under the tap, and slips them on under a thread-worn patrol cap, pulled down hard on his narrow skull.

Not a hair, not a scrap of DNA, will be left behind.

He examines himself in the mirror. There is a hardness in his expression that bears no resemblance to the wiry boy in New Bridlington, nineteen years ago. That boy isn't even a memory.

Stuffing the nailbrush in his pocket, Lou clomps out of the washroom, around the rear of the gas station, and cuts across the abandoned parking beneath a sign advertising *'Kosher Style Home Cooking'*. He marches purposefully down 24th Pine, turning the corner between a derelict warehouse, and the brick back of an adult movie theatre.

Over the past year *Ward 5* has experienced an epidemic of HIV and AIDS. Not for any one reason: needle-sharing, gay and adolescent prostitution... This street has it all. In the alley, deep in the shadows, a drunken resident lays slumped in a doorway. Lou eyes the man coldly long enough that the diseased figure remembers him later, when police question witnesses. Maas takes a moment – realising he'd been seen – to consider pressing his silenced pistol to the side of the junky's dandruffed head, and pulling the trigger. But that would be too much like an act of charity.

Maas approaches a sheet-metal iron door covered in shredded billposters, glued across the hinge. A small faded sign on a bare circle of beige brick reads '2ND HAND.' A tiny display window beside the door advertises the spines of a half a dozen esoteric books. The pane is so grimy and the dust-jackets so faded, it's impossible to make out the titles. On the glass, is painted a crude outline of an open hand with an eye in the palm.

Maas leans on the door, but it stays stuck. Frustrated, he shoves harder. The hinges give way with a *crack*, spilling him inside. He catches his balance quickly, stomping his boot.

A buzzer announces his arrival inside.

Maas bends slightly, and inspects the latch on the door, before stepping on into the derelict store.

Struck by the thick smell of mouldy old paper, squinting into the darkness of the blackened shop, Maas props the door open, allowing the weak nimbus from the alley in past his shoulders.

The rows of bookshelves look desolate.

He listens for movement... As a tiny angular woman with wispy hair limps out of the darkness. She wears a floral housedress, and lime-green cooking apron held together by iron-on binding. Stopping short of Maas, she shields her eyes, as if the weak light is a cosmic supernova. "You got the wrong place, Mister."

Maas shifts so the dim glow lights her face. Her lip is split. One eye is rimmed red, and a cruel blue-yellow welt runs down her neck, disappearing beneath her collar.

It might have concerned Maas that somebody else got to her first. However, she's still alive, so that can't be it. "Do you know who I am?" he whispers.

She moves stiffly behind him, takes the door out of his hand, and closes it. "Maybe!"

Maas' eyes adjust to the dark enough to see the old woman feel her way over to a moth-eaten recliner by the cash register. On a fold-up table of pressed tin, is a pile of books, a rubber stamp, an inkpad, and an empty cut-glass Sherry decanter.

"Do you know how I *found* you?"

"I emailed some people about the *Litthamer* crossword," she supposes. "You traced the emails."

"Do you know Samuel Litthamer?"

She shakes her head.

Maas considers for a moment if she's lying. By the look of her, she doesn't know anybody of importance. But that's not true, or he wouldn't be here. "You have it?" he asks.

The woman thinks for a minute, then reaches into the lap pocket in her apron, fishes around inside, and pulls out a curled newspaper clipping. "Here."

Maas walks to the edge of the fold-up table, takes the clipping, and peers at it – tilting the page in the weak light.

*New York Times Sunday, September 2, 2012...*

Puzzle by Samuel Litthamer — 2/9/12 (No. 5551)

## ACROSS

2. Rapacious
9. Units of electrical resistance
13. US cryptology bureau
16. Missouri river valley Siouan
20. Cold aloofness
25. Sumerian city-state
27. Strenuous objects
29. Polonium
30. Consume too much
32. Dutch scent
33. Gambling houses
34. Rhodium
35. Irish guerrillas
36. Thames' North Sea anchorage
37. Babylonian creation goddess
39. International System of units
40. Outcome
42. Bunks
43. Workman's kits
46. Eastern Melanesia
47. Instinctive
49. Tidal wave
51. Basin for holy water
53. A representative of 354 down
55. Inactive
56. A thousand litres
57. Site of battle in the Fourth Diadoch war
59. Reliant person
60. Concerning
62. Edible mushroom
64. Foreilmb bones
66. Wife of a rajah
68. Two under par
70. Norse god of strife
71. Within the vehicle
72. Grain in whiskey
73. French currency
75. Push
77. Den
79. Assignation
82. Tiger nut
84. Gratified by pain
86. Estimate value
89. Black-winged kite
90. Half the width of an em
91. Sails on frozen lakes
94. Engrave
95. Washes
96. Blaggards
98. Stop up
100. Small Māori conifers
101. Lubricates
103. More uncommon
105. Ligature ash in 150 across
107. Terrapin
109. Afternoon or night
110. Breast feed
113. Gender discrimination
115. More desperate
116. Of teeth
117. A parking lot
120. Transfer a plant
122. 47 down
123. Transmit
124. Court favour
125. Brussels-based military alliance
126. Mathematical shine
127. Circulatory fluid
128. Area
130. Demonstrate truth
132. Ancient casket
133. Rodent genus
138. Of a Christian church in Egypt
142. Imitators
145. Sedative
147. Acts on behalf
148. Fungal spore-bearing cells
150. Roman emperors
151. Solid state of water
153. To familiarize
155. Hindu sun-swallowing demon
156. Single-masted vessel
157. Levantine father god
158. Modern Laodicea
160. Not downs
161. Mohawk river city
162. Tin
163. Holy book
164. Maps
165. A purple-blue orchella weed dye
167. Danish king of England
169. With reference to
170. Thousandth of a second
171. Mongrel hound
173. Alkane, alkene, alkyne
175. Funny lonely heart
176. Novice recruit
178. 54 down
179. Long key
181. Artistic category
182. Nothing
184. Servile
185. Calling oneself thus
187. Formerly Persia
189. Provoke
190. Cobalt
191. Pollen-bearing organ
192. Yiddish commentary
194. Cry for attention
195. Surprise or apology
197. Lower-melting fractions of a fat
199. Portion
200. Biblical Heliopolis
201. Capital of Kazakhstan
202. Not out
203. Dusks
206. Only queen of Lithuania
207. Northern English nightshirts
208. An eighth of a gallon
210. Tellurium
211. Long tooth
214. Horace's poems
215. Bottom
217. Bitter
218. Yiddish dismay
219. Son of Hermes Trismegistus
220. Nuclear authority
221. Old ones
223. Chose
225. Imitates life
226. Luxembourg's domain
227. Blood red
228. Tunisian industrial port
229. Green-eyed
230. Loch monster sobriquet
231. See Also
232. White supremacists
234. Revs
236. Ginsberg
237. Electronic post
238. Ship Security Alert System
239. Roman sun god
240. Product of fire
241. Transportation Security Administration
243. Lemur
245. Analyse
247. Orwell's pig Trotsky
252. ...It May Concern
257. -Fi
258. Lent to Mark Antony at a funeral
260. 1,000 pounds force
262. Article
264. It will
265. Female advisors
268. Egg-shaped
270. For animals
272. Steadfastness
274. Something lent
276. Ludicrous act
277. Two letters but one
280. Twin Turbo
281. Hairy hide
282. Automobile
283. Ulcer-causing bacteria (2, 5)
285. South wind
287. Petite
289. Midday
291. Ski lift (1, 3)
293. Gloomy disposition
294. Cupid's lover
295. Wood-boring beetles
298. Member of Parliament
300. Little violone
302. Inexpensive
303. Nordic god-father
304. Serpentine symbol (1,5)
305. Delete
308. Western hemispheric union of States
309. Connects a head and body
311. Greek god of shepherds
312. Sulfur
314. Unit of pressure
315. Sprightliness
316. Computer network
318. Red
321. Not due north
322. Re-emitted electromagnetic radiation
324. Strategem
325. 190 down
327. Fervent
330. Has the symbol at
332. 20 down
333. Audiovisual
334. Journalists' opinion
336. Obsolete expression of annoyance
337. Measles, mumps, and rubella
338. Trade swap
339. Solo
341. Norwegian word
342. Sidelong glance
344. Chatter
345. Dinner nook
348. Seen
349. Glancing ray of light
351. Stains
352. Sung, Goodnight...
355. Of thread
356. Front of the page
357. Other than implied
359. Less than six fathoms deep at low tide
360. Cut previously for fodder
361. Supreme Hindu god
363. Turkish mountains of Holy Light
364. 25 down

## DOWN

1. Columbarium
2. Five-leaved ivy (8, 8)
3. Breadfruit tree
4. List Unix files
5. Stand up
6. Disorderly retreat
7. New food (8, 7)
8. Unit of energy
9. Aleppo boil (8, 4)
10. -Man
11. Butter substitute
12. Aft
13. Non-specific urethritis
14. Own appreciation (4, 10)
15. Way for cars
17. Beats a king
18. Inclination of a fault (geo)
19. Posit
20. Point of interaction
21. Blue darter (7, 4)
22. Organisation Internationale de Normalisation
23. Erb's palsy (3, 8, 9)
24. Will
25. 25 across
26. Train track
28. Son of Poseidon
31. Spain
35. To be
37. Sumerian sky god
38. Crests
41. Unchangeable (3, 2, 5)
42. 1,055 joules
44. After Helium
45. Tropical American palm trees (5, 6)
47. Expend
48. French sword
50. Ancient sanctum
52. Ride in Japan
54. Pharaoh before Ka
56. Small barrel
58. Puzzle
61. Windpipe
63. First Taoist philosopher (3, 3)
65. Studies old paintings (3, 9)
67. Sober group
69. 5 Across
74. Above SC
76. Sex god
78. An hour in Belgrade
80. Meaning 'bright spear'
81. Ejected
83. Failure or silent h
84. Wrestler
85. King novel
87. Rocky Mountain jay (10, 10, 9)
88. Aiding memory
93. Young urban professional
97. Civil disorder
99. Morsel
100. Circular ratio
102. French pronoun
104. Donkey
108. Spanish wave
110. Hereditary translation
112. Not down
114. Seventh prime
116. Russian affirmative
118. Quake scale
119. Moon of Saturn
121. Exist
122. 25 down
127. East Tunisian port
129. Presidential security advisors
131. NCAA ranking system
132. Monthly flow of blood
133. CC (6, 6)
134. Argentum
135. Spoken
136. All... (2, 3)
137. Those without god
139. Count's territories
140. Yiddish suffering
141. Amorous bite-size butterscotch
143. Blessed Abraham
144. Alveolar click for shame
145. Drugs
146. Anatomical cavity
149. Speed in inches
150. Of enduring quality
152. Praises
154. Hobbies
156. Trimmed
159. Worship of icons
160. 25 down
162. Landed a punch (6, 1, 4)
164. Genus of chameleons
166. Plant disease
168. 25 down
170. Island provinces
172. Heisenberg's rule (11, 9)
174. German Lake Balaton
177. Egyptian sun god
180. Pont Pierre-Laporte
181. Fortune teller
183. East Hellenic tribe
186. Forefeet
187. Powhatan axe
191. Skewered meats
193. Pigment
196. Davidic praises
198. Not far
204. Hawker
205. Public two-way
209. St Petersburg's river
212. Genus of Guillemots
213. Russian Don River city (6, 2, 4)
216. Purification rituals
218. Twelve months
222. Data by phone line
224. Strolling in Spain
225. Over again
228. Above critical temperature
233. Yes
235. Furtive glance
242. Keenness
244. Causes turbulence
246. Essential oil
248. Tower formerly Sears
249. Killing games (5, 6)
250. Having wings
251. Retreated into Washington
252. Equipped for cold
253. Detest
254. Egyptian god of the dead
255. Thus
256. Modify text or film
259. Process of decay
261. Hospital ward for acute illness
263. Non-magnetic metal in steel
266. Most achromatic (3, 9)
267. Slice of ham
269. 25 down
271. Covers 186 across
273. Vascular retinal membrane
275. Feathery Asian palm
277. Complex exercises
279. Before a vowel or silent h
280. Confronting such as fears
284. Ytterbium
286. In capital letters
287. Didymium
288. Indoleacetic acid
290. Science of natural language information
292. Rod
293. Grumble
294. Protactinium
295. Those in a bee
297. Helter-skelter (4,4)
299. Most jaunty
301. Burdened
303. Bachelor of Science
305. Religious costume
307. Greek goddess of crime and punishment
310. Medieval trumpet
313. Expert
319. One who cuts
320. Rudder lever
323. Flows into the Drava
325. Outer garment
326. Small Hawaiian tree
328. Inner membranes enclosing embryos
329. Müller's sacred Asian texts
331. Christmas
335. Odd tread
336. Northernmost Scandinavian
340. At any or all times
343. Icelandic Ð (d)
346. UN investment agency
347. Numerical prefix for three
350. End of the line in Unicode
351. Near-
353. What?
354. 27 westernmost Eurasian states
356. Rhenium
358. Original Russian dot-com

*(Diagram 2 - Second-hand bookshop crossword puzzle)*

The neatly cropped crossword puzzle on the clipping is the most marvellous piece of cryptography Maas has ever seen. He turns it over. There is a string of numbers and letters scrawled over newsprint on the reverse. "You worked it out by yourself?"

The woman returns to the task of taking books from her left pile, stamping fly-leaves, and piling them to her right. She shrugs slightly. "I do a lot of puzzles."

"You know what it says?" he asks, incredulous. How *can* she? How can she *possibly* have figured it out, and not *care*?

"Yep."

"Who hit you?" Maas asks. Not because he's concerned, but because he can't understand how she's still alive... or why she's giving the clipping away so easily.

"Go to hell," she croaks.

Maas sneers at the irony. "Was it your husband?"

"What're *you* gonna do about it?"

Maas is perplexed. "Can I keep this?"

"I guess that's up to you."

"Thanks... I'll be going."

"Then go."

Maas turns, and walks back to the door, closing it behind him as he steps back into the laneway. With a sudden burst of speed, he runs across the alley, turns, pushes off the far wall, and hurls himself back into the sheet-metal door.

Raising his boot before the step, he smashes into the reinforced panel, popping the door inwards with a *ping* as the lock erupts, spitting the metal faceplate across the floor.

Maas sprints through the store toward the moth-eaten recliner, drawing his silenced pistol, seeing the woman sitting quietly, with a cell-phone to her ear.

As she moves to stand up, her knee strikes the tin card table sending its contents crashing to the floor.

Maas waits until he's close enough for a bullseye.

His tiny eyes stare at her coldly, as he fires a round into the woman's right eye socket.

Her head snaps back with the muffled spurt. She folds in half.

Hurriedly, Maas bends and puts a second bullet in her left eye, before picking up the cell-phone. The call is still dialling. He slides the back-plate off the phone, flips out the battery, and drops all three pieces in his pocket before pivoting to the cash register, and thumping the 'SALE' button with the butt of the pistol. The till *clacks* open.

He scoops up the meagre bundle of notes, stuffs them into his pocket, and hooks his fingers under the edge of the drawer, yanking it out of the register. Everything he has touched, he takes with him.

Finally, he turns, and runs back to the alley, spilling coins onto the floor – a shower of change bouncing after him.

The dead woman in the floral housedress lays slumped on the floor of the second-hand bookstore, blood pooling in the books around her.

Of course, it will be the eyes sockets punched through the back of her skull that will connect her to what happens next.

# 6. '...FLESH AS GRASS...'

*Monday, September 3, 2012*

I park the BMW on Massachusetts Avenue, outside Boston's Southern Mortuary, and mount the grey stoop leading into the grim structure.

The foundations for the morgue were laid in 1929, seven years after the discovery of King Tutankhamen's tomb prompted a revival in Egyptian architectural themes in Boston. Stepping into the ornate lobby, I find a pair of sphinxes leering back at me. The two beasts are mounted on pedestals on either side of stairs that lead down into the building's bowels. There, at the bottom of the stairs, a winged hourglass hangs above the door.

I stop for a moment, gripping the ornate handrail, transfixed...

The years since college have gone too quickly, until yesterday. The passing of time has taken a macabre twist in the past twenty-four hours, and now seems to be running in reverse...

Only twelve hours ago I was driving home to New Bridlington.

It's been six years now, since I sold the house in Lexington and bought Matt's house. Matt wanted to move to Back Bay to be near Tessa's doctor, and take a summer cottage on Cape Cod. He wanted to keep the house in the family. Annie loves it. She has a pair of Lipizzaners stabled out the back - the kind of horses that run backwards and do jumping jacks. They're really something - and smart. I strongly suspect they stand around in the stables afterhours on their haunches like ten-foot bowlegged ranch-hands, spitting chewing tobacco, swapping trail stories, and plotting to steal Annie - bolting away with her on their backs... So everyone is happy, most of all Tessa's housekeeper, knocking on sixty and tired of cleaning the bigger venue. That said, the house didn't come cheap. But the money might as well be Matt's anyway. My first gig on Catastrophe Futures with the Chicago Board of Trade was Matt's idea, and that almost paid for the place by itself. Then there was the role after that, at *Standard Sapiential and Life*. Anyway, it's a fair commute every day from New Brid to Boston. An hour each way, if I beat the traffic. But Annie had been 'commuting' up there every weekend since college. So now it's mine and Matt's turn to go the other way.

Mostly, the move to New Brid was good for Joe. He's home from boarding school in Marlborough on weekends, and the property is all boyhood splendour. A piece of beach at the base of the cliff. A walk through the moth-wild woods to *the crick*, space to run in circles. Four seasons. All up, the daily haul out of Boston is okay.

In early Fall, the rocky townships around Cape Ann are like scenes from a devotional calendar. The way the chemical clock touches every fifth tree with flames.

On my way into town, the disused granite quarry has filled with blue rain, and echoes of a hymn in the sky. The township is still four blocks square, folded into the rocky headland, aged like a shipwreck. Its pavements are still warped, grey power poles, and leaned-over clapboard walls decorated with fluorescent lobster pot buoys, and crawfish cages. Nothing has changed in New Bridlington since I first met Matt and went to the lighthouse, except the lighthouse itself. The majestic Fresnel lens in the tower was replaced some years ago by a stationary solar-powered optic in a powder-coated housing. Vantcha is long forgotten, moved into Boston on a Coast Guard pension. These days a maintenance man treks up the hill once a month to service the lamp, and the humming bank of power cells. The keeper's cottage is hollowed out, windows broken, blackened walls marked with rust, wood rot, dry vine, and spray-painted teenage gibberish: *WARP. ZZIIPP. Vooz roolz.* I never saw the old man again. I haven't even *thought* about him, until today.

A handful of fishing vessels huddle by the pier in the cramped black crescent of the bay, tired from the slap-slapping through the rough break, over the rocks, lights beaming like cars, and great spools of net on their gunwales.

It's all familiar now, the way the sky like frosted glass filters out the colour of the sun. The black shale beach beats the crooked night-time settlement in grimness – a great spill of chewed moraine, ground out of a deep gouge in the ancient ice shelf, invisible at night but for a bright speckle along its wet edge. Most days the fishermen clatter and clamber across the shingle beach between the broken wharf and the tavern, the steep slope hammering like spoons under their booted waders, prickling the hair at your collar. Lost in time, they cart just enough of a catch in their scoured orange bins to cover a table at the tin-roofed market at the toe of the cove. The townsfolk all gather on Sunday morning to buy, emulating the slow walk of the fishermen. Black Bass, Bluefish, Dogfish and Fluke stack on the folding tables like ingots.

Down the end of the beach below the lighthouse is the dim foul-smelling tavern, 'The Bee's Wing': Its exposed beams are crowded with curled clippings about big storms and bigger catches. The disappointment is evident in the shoulders of the fishermen as they trudge into the tavern like a school of red-cheeked National Geographic cover-shots. I often wonder if a man would accept their lot if it were handed to them in this condition.

As I turn my his car towards the leaned-over boats with their high booms and the sea, I try to imagine what it's like, out past the horizon – where they bark at each other, squinting into the spray, rocked by the waves. *What draws these men back?* When the winter oceans freeze the brine to the masts and hulls, weighing the boats down so deep they have to chip at it the sea-ice with axes to keep from sinking. Five thousand fishermen have died off Cape Ann in a hundred and thirty years, and still they travel back.

I sail past the boats in my silver sedan, and the fishermen gawk at me like I'm driving a UFO. I doubt I make any more sense to them, than they do to me.

That was twelve hours ago. I pulled into the garage to find Matt and Joe busily untangling a pair of rods by the tool vice. Joe is a foot bigger up down and sideways than the other kids his age. He cops five kinds of heck for it, but at sixteen, he's getting by a good dose better than I ever did. He's a handsome little shaver, thanks to Annie's eyes. And he's gentle with the other juvies and bed-wetters. He brings these kids home that make me wonder how I'd go as their old man, fearful little birds with broken wings, bristling with hang-ups. Joe just takes them out in the yard, lets them bounce off him with all their nerve, pitches a few balls through the tyre swing, then sends them skipping home.

"We're going fishing," announces Joe. "Want to come?"

I check my watch. "It's half-five."

Matt frowns, picking at a knot in his line. His hair is silver now, and thinner than it used to be. "...Joe made a new fly with a buck tail collar on the shank..." he explains, head down. "We're trying it out." He frees the rod and smiles. "There." Matt is transformed in Joe's company. Where I'd once hoped I might be the son he never had, I've since discovered I was just warming the seat for Joe.

"There's no time. We're leaving for dinner in an hour..." I reply. "Annie and Tess will be waiting."

Every Sunday for fifteen years we've driven into Boston's North End for dinner.

"Plenty of time," Matt replies. "Come on. Grab your waders."

If it's okay with Matt, it's okay.

Through the side gate to the horse fence, father, son, and father-in-law whisper our way through the spun grass to the creek. The air is frigid. In another six weeks the tributary will freeze over. This time of the year the water bites like an electric shock.

I watch Joe move hip-deep into the rain-swollen current, exhibiting Matt's hunting vest, riffles hula-hooping the man-sized waders around his pits.

"Fish! Fear me!" growls the boy.

The water eddies in the pockets, dappled with the afternoon light between shadows of moss-green hardwoods. Joe flicks his line at the glassy slick in the deep current in the elbow of the creek, in the spot Annie brings the horses in summer – throwing a rope around their necks, her own hair tied-up, long legs wheeling in the gin-clear water, black mares swimming with their deadly propellers circling beneath hers.

Striped bass and the occasional wild trout hold near the bank of the freestone stream. A ten-minute walk across the pasture, down the cliff into the Northeast Salt, and you can dip a net into the sea shoals, and come up with silversides, sand eels and clamworms, and bring them back to the creek still wriggling. There's a place where a rock splits the current into fast-running lanes that carry the baits down-tide, where I've seen Matt throw in a three-fly dropper rig, and come up with two big-ass Bass hanging off a single line.

Here – behind the house – in the same duds I've handed down to Joe, Matt taught me the back-cast on a Double Haul.

"Joe!" Matt remonstrates. "Start with the tip down! Keep your hands close."

Joe turns to see if he's doing it right.

I flick my line and the thrilling silver string unfurls over the stream. "You want to know the *secret*?" I offer Joe, conscious of the heritage of the rite.

Joe cocks his big round head. "Think like a fish?"

"No," Matt shakes his head, exaggerating his disappointment.

I allow the old man the honour...

"The fish thinks like a fish... What do *fish* do?" he asks.

Joe beams, seeing the answer. "Go after bugs!"

"So... you think like a bug." Matt's movements are calmingly familiar.

Joe starts bobbing his lure, popping his elbows like bug wings. "Oh-aaay get it."

I smile. Matt sidesteps toward me. "Bob."

It's the moderated tone of a mindful man. "Yeah?"

"You know the old church across from the Revere house?"

The building is an aberration. Across the park from the Paul Revere house on Boston's Freedom Trail, the ghastly church is highly conspicuous. An illuminated pentagram hangs suspended over the head of Jesus on the exhaust-stained brick. On the sunniest of days an unfortunate angle darkens the grim facade. The ghoulish facility has only survived so long because it was designed by Bulfinch after he served as the architect for the Capitol Building in Washington, and JFK's mom was buried there. It has withstood two hundred years of better judgment, and not without some strange modifications.

"The Archdiocese is *reconfiguring* the parishes," Matt spluttered, spittle flying into the water. "It's like a damned fast-food franchise. *'Rationalizing their branches.'*"

The comment is out of character. I looked to see whether Joe is paying attention, but he's too busy still thinking like a bug.

"*That* bothers *you*?" I ask, surprised.

"What they're doing... any of the smaller parishes with money in the bank, they're shutting them down and emptying the coffers."

"Ah-huh."

Matt's line drifts across mine. "What about the people who've gone to that church their whole life? *Married* there. Buried their loved ones..."

I just bounce my head, for a lack of anything to say. "Sure. That's rough."

"My father took me there when I was a boy."

"To Sacred Heart?" I gawk.

Matt shrugs – an immature gesture inherited from Joe. "He had a friend in the rectory. When I was ten... we went there on Sunday nights for meatball dinners, and played *bocce* in the courtyard..."

Sunday night: The same night we've gone to North End for dinner every week for fifteen years, across from the old church – Matt *always* ordering meatballs. I'd often suspected the Little Italy ritual had some kind of significance for him. Catholic Mass was held in *Italiano* every Sunday, which drew a Romanesque crowd sympathetic to Matt's own enthusiasm for ristretto and bolognese. His inexplicable affection for the vigorously Catholic neighbourhood at prayer-time had gone unsolved for two decades. Especially back when Hanover Street was a dreary neck of town. However, these have become pleasant evenings. Just like the Jewish property boom on Salem Street in 1900s, the tenements and warehouses in North End had been systematically gutted and converted to studios. The street was now filled with open-air trattorias attracting a bevy of undergrads, off-hours executives, and Freedom Trail deserters. But we were the *only* people I know who could say we'd been eating dinner there every week since the Nineties.

"It wasn't always a Catholic Church," adds Matt.

I pull back on my line. "Really?"

"It was a red-light district. The harbour once came all the way up to North Street. It was called the *Murder District,* full of gamblers and criminals. A reformed sailor, Reverend Taylor started the church in North Square to preach to the lost, from the bottom of a cistern of degeneracy. '*Delight is to him who gives no quarter in the truth, and kills, burns, and destroys all sin though he pluck it out from under the robes of Senators and Judges.*'"

"What's that?" sings Joe.

"*Moby-Dick*," Matt answers. "The church was named Seamen's Bethel. When Taylor died in seventy-one, the Archdiocese bought the building, put in a Mary, and it became the Sacred Heart."

I'm still not completely sure what Matt is getting at. "We should head back."

"I want you to hold my funeral there," adds Matt.

I trip on a loose stone in the riverbed, and stumble to keep my torso out of the water. "Huh?"

"Daaad! The fish!'" Joe yelps.

"I thought you wouldn't be seen dead in a church!" I blurt.

"You'll gonna live for at *leeeast twen'y years* Grandpa," wails Joe, laughing. "By then it might be a mosque!"

Matt frowns. "'...all flesh is as grass, and all the glory of man as the flower of grass. The grass withereth, and the flower thereof falleth away.'"

I squint, looking at Matt through the sun, bewildered. He suddenly looks frailer than I ever remember seeing him before.

"Deceased members of interchurch families can be buried with Catholic rites," he adds. "My father was a Catholic. And the way the Archdiocese is screwing the parish over, they won't mind bending the rules."

"You can't be *serious?*"

The old man's eyes roar brightly. "Of *course* I'm serious!"

I'm confused... the late-afternoon fishing trip... the fit of mortality. This isn't the place to ask, but as soon as Joe is out of earshot I'll have to find out if Matt is having some kind of health issues. These are the hallmarks of a 'Lady Hope' moment - 'Lady Hope' claimed Charles Darwin sought forgiveness from god in his final illness. Or Diego Rivera, the lifelong Atheist who marched into the *Hotel del Prado* aged 70 and painted over the original inscription *'Dios no existe'* - *God doesn't exist* - on his own mural.

I trudge toward the shore, dragging my line.

Matt is staring at the water. He shrugs again - just like Joe.

I beckon to Matt to follow me.

Joe squeals. "*I got a fish!*" He's yanking the line directly with his fist. He sends up great splashes as he runs to meet the catch.

I step back into the water to help, but Matt holds me back with a small gesture.

Joe hauls up the angry, twirling bass.

"Thank you River!" howls Joe, and slings the catch to the shore.

"Yeah, '*thank you river*,'" I laugh.

Joe sees my mockery. "You *have* to thank the River! So she gives you another fish next time!"

The desire to thank nameless fortune springs from our acquisitive nature.

"Bobby," whispers Matt strangely.

I frown, curious. Matt *never* uses Annie's nickname for me. I step closer, where I'm sure Joe can't hear: "Matt, what's going on?"

"Nothing." Matt opens his lids, and stares directly into my eyes.

That's it.

He turns, and walks away.

But it wasn't nothing. It was *something*. I'd forgotten all about it. Until now.

I step past the pair of sphinxes, down onto the mortuary stairs. It is an act of sheer will. The eye-watering stench of something like gasoline holds me at bay. The sense of foreboding is overpowering.

Resolved, I descend through the archway, and approach the counter to the right.

A burly young woman with short black hair, wearing a lab coat, hears my shuffling at the desk and appears in the doorway.

"Robert Travis?"

The stench of formaldehyde opens my tear ducts. "That's me."

The technician hands me a form: *Verification without Viewing.*

"What's this?"

"I need written permission before I can take photos."

"You need my photo?"

"—Of the remains."

I struggle to recall the basic information for the form. *What is my phone number again? I can't remember...* I've had this problem before, jet-lagged at a hotel desk. But this is something different. The technician takes the page, checks it, slings a Polaroid camera over her shoulder, and disappears down the corridor.

A minute later she returns, flapping a picture in her hand and blowing on it.

"So I don't go in?" I ask, having been prepared for a cold-room full of stainless doors with bodies rolled out on drawers.

"Uh-uh. You *don't* want to go back there." She hands me the photo. "Please sign, and write your name and date on the back."

I watch as the muddy yellow film develops...

It's not what I expect.

*(Diagram 3 - Morgue Polaroid)*

The sight of Matt – laying on some kind of stretcher – sends time flashing backward again.

Last night after dinner, Joe thunders upstairs and Annie lights the *faux* fireplace in the living room, and curls up on the couch with Mark Twain's *The Mysterious Stranger*.

I've only just sat down opposite her, knotting my legs into hers, cradling my laptop – when the phone rings.

Annie and I look at each other across the couch hoping the other will move first. I've always questioned the imperative, the way people heed that bell with such a superb eagerness... It's not this way at the office. A blue-haired lady in a windowless room in Kansas fields my calls. And nothing filters the noise out of daily life like making folks express themselves to a surly septuagenarian crone with a pencil.

"Honey?" Annie mumbles, nestled in the deep end of the sofa, cushions arranged on her socked wheels. "It could be important."

"Maybe they changed Joe's football practice again," I answer tiredly. Alternatively, it's Tessa with some torpid dilemma. Some New Brid Civic Committee melodrama. Maybe Joe gave our number out on eBay, or Annie filled in an entry form at the IGA for 'free' carpet-cleaning.

I get up, grumbling. *Snick*. Handset to ear. "Hello?"

"Who is this?"

"Who is *this*?"

"*Bob?*"

"Who is this?"

"It's Madison." Her voice is hoarse with potent potables or smokes or screaming, or all three. We only see Madison maybe twice a year now – Halloween and Christmas. A call is highly unusual. "I'll get *Annie*." I load the name with all my affection.

"Bob, *wait*."

There's agony in her voice.

"What?"

"Dad's dead."

# 7. '...WHAT SHALL BE AFTER HIM...?'

*Sunday, September 2, 2012*

I gawk madly at the hall mirror. The look on my face is hysterical. I look like my father, mean and serious and old.

"You have to tell her," Madison croaks on the other end of the phone.

"What did you say?" I mumble, dazed.

"You have to *tell* her..."

It takes a moment to realise the ache in my chest is linked to her words. "How?"

"It's complicated."

"Complicated?"

"What *happened*— is complicated."

"What happened?"

Madison growls. "Robert! Get Annie!"

I set down the phone before she can say another word, and start toward the living room, unsteady on my feet. I stop.

"*Who is it?*" calls Annie.

I turn back and pick up the receiver. "Tell me what happened."

Maddie is severe. "For *chrissake* Bob. Just *get* her."

I walk back into the living room again.

"Who is it?" Annie smiles over the spine of her book.

I concentrate on seeming okay, not too okay, but maybe not okay enough. "It's Madison." But I can't keep it off my face. My eyes are a showcase.

Annie launches off the couch, across the dining room, past me into the hall. I'm fixed to the spot. *Dad's dead. Details later...*

"What happened?" Annie asks into the phone, catching it right off the bat. "*What?*" Her face is aghast; her hand goes to her mouth, cheeks tightening like drying paint. She looks pinned, crushed, suffocating. "No."

I slump into the rigid chair by the door, watching her. *What is this?* The two sisters linked by phone, popping and guttering... Annie frowns like I'd never seen.

"The *police?*"

I can see her aging before my eyes.

Sensing a tremor in the house, Joe storms down the stairs three at a time on his long flippers, like the kid-brother in Norman Rockwell's *Homecoming*. "What happened?!" Seeing his mother's expression he whispers to me, "What's wrong?"

"Come to the living room," I herd Joe out of the hall.

"Why?"

After a long silence, Annie creeps in, eyes wrung red. She sinks back into the couch between Joe and me, and puts her arms around our son's neck.

"Grandpa had an accident," she lies. She is distraught, tears trickling unblotted to the collar of her *Patriots* t-shirt.

Joe looks at both of us, tears welling in his own eyes instantly. It's quick with him. Next thing I know, the two of them are sobbing. I grit my teeth, suppressing my own contortions. The day my own father died, I couldn't squeeze out a drop. Now I'm struggling. This is a disaster. My two bright lights crying. It's *Annie* who always turns things around in times of strife, saying something so helpful you can't tell how she does it. Now it's my turn, I'm supposed to say something. But I'm useless. I put a hand on her wrist, and her goose-flesh spreads up my arm.

"Joe," Annie says softly. "I need to speak with Dad for a minute. Then I'll come talk to you, okay?"

"Okay." Joe nods and returns upstairs, reluctant.

"What happened?" I ask.

Retelling the story hurts Annie even more than hearing it: A pair of Boston hard-shoes found Matt laying in the laneway behind his townhouse, spread out on the grimy pavement in his slippers and nightgown. With cigarette burns on both eyeballs.

"*What?!*"

"Someone put a cigarette out in... his eyes."

"In his *eyes?*" It's typical of Madison to unload the worst of everything. I picture Matt vividly: Face like crushed paper, feathery grey locks, bitumen wet with blood, chocolate brown robe, and neutron-star eyes, cold and dead as space. "Who *did* it?"

Annie swipes at a stray hair. "They don't know."

"They don't know?" I echo redundantly. Holy fucking shit. What kind of fucked up...crazy..."They don't know?"

"Mum said he went out the back to the fire escape to take out the trash – and didn't come back."

That doesn't make sense. "The *fire escape?*"

Annie nods. The movement shakes a tear loose from her cheek.

The end of the fire escape behind the townhouse is six feet off the ground. I've walked under it a dozen times to take out the trash, through the *side* door. The iron stairway runs four steps down from a concrete landing, and terminates in a telescopic ladder. The back door to the kitchen is *never* used, except to go onto the Juliet balcony in Spring and shake a rug.

Anne is barely breathing, then finally gasps. "He just went out the back, and some lunatic attacked him."

I'm shaking my head. *Why would Matt go out on the fire escape at all?* He wasn't senile. He was in the pink. He never missed a thing. He did the New York Times crossword every week in less than ten minutes. He was as sharp as ever. *So why suddenly go dippy, and walk out on the fire escape in the middle of the night?*

Anne sucks in another wild breath.

I rub her neck. "I don't get it."

It's too strange. How can he be dead?" We only said goodnight a couple of hours ago. The suddenness is stupendous.

"Tessa was asleep when they found him. She'd gone to bed."

But the other word still rankles. *Mugged?* "What are the *chances* of that?"

Annie shifts uncomfortably. Her head comes around, and she lamps me with her lightning-blue eyes.

"What?" I raise my hands in surrender.

"Don't you dare."

"Don't dare *what?*"

"Don't go to *work* on this." She bites the back of her hand. I know what she means. "This isn't one of your *jobs*," she adds, to press the point. She's barely holding it together now.

"You should go down to Boston to be with your mother," I suggest quickly. "I'll call Joe's school. He can stay home for a few days."

Annie magically produces a scrunched Kleenex from that secret compartment in her sleeve. "I'll take him with me."

"You want me to come too?"

"You can't."

I press a kiss to her nose. "I know. I was just being nice." I smile. The effort at humour comes out completely wrong.

Annie tries to smile back, but it doesn't fit her face. "I'll talk to Joe. You better get to bed. It's late." She tries on the smile again. This time it plays. And I owe her for it.

"Okay."

She heaves onto her feet, and marches upstairs.

I plod to the den to stow my laptop.

The room feels different than it did an hour ago. The new Norwalk furniture is still lit by Matt's old emerald desk lamp. The old man's cigar smoke is still deep in the wall panels. The shadows are dark with nights in his company. It's still his study.

I leave his lamp on. The action is irrational, but I can't bring myself to switch it off. I stand beside the desk, looking at the chair.

How can I sit there *now*?

Annie warned me not to go to work on this, but it's impossible not to. This is what I *do*, thanks to Matt's guidance right there on this spot in his den. This is my daily bash-and-graft, working up odds on disaster. *Catastrophe Futures* and *Acts of God Bonds*.

I know there's no such thing as an accident, or insurance wouldn't offer predictable returns. The only way insurers make money is if *X*-many people tip over their cars, *Y*-many planes go down, *Z*-many tornadoes spin out of the clouds, and so much domestic merry hell takes place on a regular basis. It isn't Fate. It *seems* that way, in the eye of everything, when you're reaching out to heaven for help. But the Numbers always add up. We're all walking Mandelbrot Sets, like snowflakes, set by the air we drop through, a conglomeration of cells based on finite factors... Any other opinion is the product of some archaic illusion that invisible magic sets us apart from the physical world.

What are the chances of Matt going out on the fire escape, and some crazy mugger burning his eyes out? *Does that even happen?* Or did a trillion Numbers make it inevitable, just like every other moment, all based on finite elements... The number of footsteps he took this week. The minutes of sleep he got last night. What side he slept on. How many strokes he made with his comb. A memory. Notches in his belt, chinks in his wheels, pips in his juice...

"FUCK!" I grip the edge of the desk. *Cigarette burns on his eyeballs?!* That this catastrophe is the product of infinitesimally-small conditions seems impossible. Not the great Matthias Mueller, former

President of MIT Corporation. And *yet*... in an infinite universe, it had to be inevitable. Right?

Some of us reach for god in a disaster.

Maybe *reaching* is just something I never got over.

Then I remember... Matt's mood that afternoon, standing in the creek, the zing of the fly-line fresh in the air.

I switch off the lamp.

Now, standing in the foyer of the Southern Mortuary... holding the Polaroid... Matt's gruesome death-mask materialises in the yellow film.

His grey, bruised visage is dominated by swollen eyelids.

"His eyes— were burned?" I ask the burly young mortuary technician.

She frowns at me strangely. "Sorry, I don't— I guess so."

"Can I keep this?"

"You wanna *keep* it?"

"Yeah."

She flinches. "Hang on a sec. I'll get another one."

"Wait," I raise my hand.

"Yeah?"

"I want to see."

She grimaces. "Are you sure? It's—"

"I'm sure."

"'Kay... Usually only reporters and Med students want to see." She leads me down the hall, walls scuffed with trolley crashes.

As soon as she opens the door, I see them.

Dozens of them.

The TV image of a sterile room with neatly rowed fridge-drawers suddenly seems naïve. The bodies are inelegantly parked on gurneys down a long hallway, out through the far door into the next room. There are no body bags, only cotton sheets draped ingloriously, or knotted at the chest.

"You sure you wanna do this?" asks the technician again, holding the door open.

But I'm not moving, or thinking.

Through the stench of Formaldehyde ebbs the funk of bleach and rot. I clench my throat internally, trying not to be ill, eyes leaking, and stare through the door. Heads and feet protrude from crooked shrouds. There are corpses of every dimension, laid out on inch-thick brown vinyl mattresses.

One skinny lump is so small it can only be an underfed youth. Another, an obese man, gut bloated so high it raises the bed-sheet off his bare, bruised flank— A stray arm. A patch of hair.

I nod, freeing up my throat briefly: "Yes."

"'Kay. C'mon." She moves down the hall with startling nonchalance, sidestepping the log jam.

I follow. It's impossible to look away. There are rickety, tube-steel trolleys parked at every angle. I squint, eyes following the floor, counting the canted plastic castor wheels... but the horrors still enter my peripheral vision.

A hand brushes my hip... where it hangs off one of the trolleys.

"Sorry about the smell," says the girl. "A couple of them are a bit old. That one there," she casually calls my attention to a swollen bump, "was a week old when we got him." The exposed feet and arms look black, but the head is rigored up at an angle, raised off the gurney – pale white where the blood has drained to his back.

"That's him." The technician rests her hand on the top-rail of Matt's gurney.

I freeze.

Matt is parked midway down the hall, indistinguishable from the others, amid the offensive fetor and failed logistics. The shame and ignominy make me want to say something.

This isn't right.

But this is what happens. In a few days Matt's broken-down body will be boxed up, and dropped in a hole. He's gone. It's just my own flawed mental rig that identifies this inert shape with the man I loved.

The technician peels back the sheet to the neck, and raises her camera.

At first, I think she's made a mistake.

It doesn't look right. The lifeless face. Matt's jaw is slack beneath the skin. His lips are concaved, pronouncing the wrinkles around his mouth. The skin looks sodden; his grey locks are askew. But it *is* him. And the angry red seams, where his eyes are pressed shut.

"Are you okay?"

I realise she's watching me. "Yeah. You got the photo?"

"Here."

I stuff the Polaroid into my pocket, and try not to run for the door.

*Monday, September 3, 2012*

It feels like a long day already. I check my watch as I walk out of the lift. It's 9:00am.

There are five pink Post-it notes on my computer screen. One is from a cop at the Boston Police Department, Detective Cullen. Two more are calls from Gordon at *Standard Sapiential and Life*. Gordon used to be my Line Manager at SSL – for six years. He sponsored my MBA at Sloane before I went out on my own. When I kicked off a consulting outfit at Matt's behest, I went back to work for SSL on twice what I was making before. SSL was big enough to wear it, and Gordon didn't mind. Now, SSL occupies nine floors above my office: ten thousand tons of Numbers, of which Gordon very dependably brings me the lion's share.

I dial my assistant.

"Good morning Mister Travis."

"Hi Ruby. This message from Gordon—"

"He said he's got '*two tickets to the Super Bowl*'," explains Ruby.

I'm not sure exactly what that means. It can't be literal. Not with Gordon. I doubted he's ever watched a Super Bowl in his life. "Thanks."

I check my diary. A decorator is coming in at ten to replace the timber Turing Machine in my reception with a glass sculpture that looks like the middle four letters of the day before Sunday.

Today's newspaper sits folded on my desk.

*(Diagram 4 - Newspaper headline, 'mind readers')*

I notice the 'SIGN HERE ->' sticky note at the margin, and fold the broadsheet open to the obits. This is where the newsworthy people receive journalistic mention, after the paid death notices. If you worked as a Packer's scout, photographed Lenin, taught at Milton Academy, wrote a book on slavery, or led a similarly curious life, you get your entire worldly existence expertly distilled to twenty words:

*Leon Patmor, at 74; star of radio, music executive - by Nicholas K. Short, Globe Correspondent... John LaVenne, at 85; testified at Senate Select Committee hearing - by Julietta F. Beattie, Globe Staff... K. Willett, at 69; with passion, sold houseboats - by Tom Baum, Los Angeles Time.*

And there it is...

*Matthias Mueller, at 66; MIT president and Reagan advisor - Associated Press. Matthias Mueller was a chemist, historian, won the Aldus Medal for contributions to science, died yesterday the government said last night. He was 66. (Associated Press, 9/2/12)*

News of Matt's death made the wires before the paper went to bed.

I speed-dial Anne.

"Hey. How're you doin?"

"Fine. Did you go?" she asks.

"Yes."

"I don't want to know."

What else do I say other than "Okay"? Sharp corners remind me the Polaroid is still in my shirt pocket.

"Did you get Joe's teacher to email him some homework?" asks Annie.

"Yeah. How's Tess?"

"A rock."

"Where's Madison staying?"

Annie hesitates. "Um. The *Harbor* I think. Dunno."

Whoever the current boyfriend was, he'd probably furnished her with a consolatory credit card. Madison was probably already on Newmarket Street, spending twenty grand on shoes to console herself.

"You okay?" asks Annie.

"Me?"

"Yeah, you."

"Sure. I'm okay," I lie. Annie could *never* see the photo of Matt. Not for the rest of her life. *Where do I hide it?*

"You sound funny."

"Funny *ha ha*? Or funny weird?"

I hear her smiling. "The second one."

"Nope."

"Okay. Talk to you tonight."

I try to think of something else to say, to keep the conversation going. "Are you okay?"

"You already asked me that."

"Really?"

Her voice strains. "Yesss."

"Okay. Later."

"Ciao."

And the sound of the handset going into the cradle echoes in the phone.

I'm over-compensating with my awkward pity... Mental note: buy a book on helping loved ones grieve... and locate an earlier mental note to buy Joe something as well. Maybe we should take a trip, as soon as Tessa is okay.

My desk phone rings. "Yes?"

"I have Gordon on hold. He says it's urgent."

"Put him through."

"YAHTZEE!" shouts Gordon, gleefully.

"Gordon?" I almost smile, before the storm cloud in my head rains on my face.

"Five sixes, Bob!" Gordon is short of breath, like he's running laps of his desk. "I've *got* something! BIG! Really BIG!"

"I'm well, thank you. How are you?"

"Clear your desk. I'm coming down."

"No, I'm—" but the line is already dead.

Two minutes later Gordon bursts into my office with his tie swept over his shoulder. He's a short man with a luminous, circular bald patch like the Friar from a Robin Hood movie. "Come for a java!"

"Why?"

"We need some Numbers!"

"The level of abstraction here is hitting an all-new high."

"Listen Bob, I just hit pay dirt. Add together *all* the other times we've ever hit pay dirt, and that's how much pay dirt we've just hit! I mean *paaaay-diiiirt!*"

"Gordo. Look, I—"

"Sweet suffering lord this is *big*!" Gordon punch-dances his way around the desk to slap me on the shoulder. "Four o'clock – *this* morning – I get a call from this guy in D.C. named Dodd. They're doing a study, and they want *us* to do Numbers."

The last D.C. gig I did for SSL was a risk assessment on a scramjet test flight. SSL provides aerospace cover to military subcos: Northrop Grumman. Raytheon. NASA is technically a civilian body. So, two years ago they were testing a fuelless atom-fizzing jet NASA had been tinkering with for fifty years. The thing flew at fourteen times the speed of sound when it got started, so they couldn't land it anywhere, and they couldn't slow it down. It just got faster and faster until it tooled itself, so they were tipping it into the sea. It was a write-off. They were looking for coverage in case the jet swerved into a tanker, maybe a town – to brace their ass against general mayhem. It was some kind of statutory obligation. Check-a-box on a form.

So I flew out to the Jet Propulsion Lab at Caltech and spent an hour pissing into paper cups, signing waivers and sitting for photo badges so the pointy heads could put me in a pair of white sockettes and hairnet, and usher me into the hangar. I'd assumed with all the build-up that this billion-dollar bird was going to resemble the space shuttle. Imagine my surprise when they rolled back the screen on this sleek looking novelty bar-fridge. All of them beaming so very proudly.

Another job in D.C. means another trip to wonderland.

*Most* of the time, general insurers like SSL stroll into my office and tell me they're thinking about a policy against bolts of lightning. It might as well be falling pianos, or flying anvils... *'Independent market research shows lightning bolts are a big fear for folks lately.'* Or existing policies aren't meeting market expectations. Annuity streams are down. So I go up to Joe's room, and dig out the *Book of Knowledge* with the red cover.

*'...Lightning hits the earth six thousand times a minute...'*

I find out how many houses, how many trees, how many people catch a line of blue-hot plasma every year. How many park rangers, green keepers, yard boys, joggers, roofers, loggers, beach fishermen, and line workers. I fill a hundred columns in a spreadsheet with anything I can find. *How tall was the guy? How much silver did he have in his wallet?* Then I apply some weighting criteria, some permutation and mathematical ANOVA, and take the glamorous extrapolation back to the client. I hand it over like it's the pristine milk of the virgin, and these guys go running back to their Executives grinning *'We've got the Numbers!'* And paste it into a policy application: *What is your occupation? How tall are you? How much silver do you have in your wallet? Please sign here...* And they make billions.

Half-a-million Joe-regulars pay a buck-fifty a day so when they *do* get hit by a flying anvil, these guys bankroll their misfortune. But we already know when you're going to cop it. On *average.* Of course we do. Because I sit in the back room with my adding machine, working up the numbers, the same way some godless bunko-man designed your slot machines, or equity markets. When people ask what I do, I just say 'I'm a fancy accountant', but it's untrue. I'm a dues-paying dice man. A card-carrying card-counter. A carnival worker stacking empty milk bottles with novelty rings and crackerjack toys. Just enough to keep you throwing softballs. Not enough so you win the pink bear. It all ticks along so neat and clean. Everyone pays Gordo and his buddies to sit on their bread, waiting for the Number to come in, focused on the mayhem. The fear of disaster. The idea of protection. The fluted colonnade between you and your dough. But these guys can't make enough. 'Bring us more Numbers.' Brake failures. Bath-time electrocutions. Home invasions. Seafood chokage. *What are the chances?*

"What's the study on?" I ask, curious.

Gordon leans back, and sweeps his hands apart like a ringmaster. "*Terrorism!*"

# 8. '...DIVIDING UP HIS GARMENTS...'

*Monday, September 3, 2012*

The *Standard Sapiential and Life* building plaza is a bleak angular exercise yard that might have looked good under lights on a draftsman's table, but in practice turned evil the week it lost its brand-new sheen, and accumulated a patina of bird shit.

"Architects never put crap on the models," observes Gordo. "They always put stylish little figures bustling around." There's no one like that here. Just a wary guy in a suit, his manic client, and a guy in a poncho selling pencils.

Gordon finds a space perched on the edge of the fountain, stirring nothing into his coffee. "Sweet suffering lord this is big. This guy 'Dodd' called from the Anacostia Institute. Four in the morning. *Four.* Doesn't *that* beat a hen rooting uphill backwards?"

"You said that already. That is was 'four in the morning.'"

"You've heard of the Anacostia Institute..?"

"Maybe." I might have read something about it somewhere. *Time* magazine?

"You okay?"

"Sure."

"It's one of these independent 501-C-3 tax-special 'Think Tanks.' All government money coming in from the Feds. It's a group of triple-doctorates and their pals working out of a nerve-centre on the Potomac, consulting to the Executive Branch on foreign policy, energy-aerospace-cleantech-defence, risk assessment, capacity planning, knowledge management, disaster recovery... They host a bunch of working groups including... wait for it... the 'International Center for Terrorism Studies.'"

I'm not in the mood for this. I wonder if I should just tell Gordo about Matt. *Cat's Dead. Details Later.* But I don't want to burst his balloon. I've *never* seen him so excited: He's higher than a giraffe's ass right now. Then there'll be questions... *What happened? Am I okay?* "Ahuh."

"The *Institute*," Gordon slurps, "it's the new seat of power in Washington. The government does whatever these independent third-party policy assessment studies tell them to, so the guys with the *Numbers* hold the power. These guys have a lot of sway. This guy Dodd was an astronaut on Mir. He's working on an annexure to a Special Red Paper by the Congressional Subcommittee on Environment, Technology and Standards, for the House Committee on Science. It's called the *RUNE* report. Short for 'Remote Unlikely Negative Events.' There's a whole section on 'terrorism risk' they want to give us... 'What are the chances of another big attack?' 'How many casualties'... Recovery costs... Oh— Get this! He says, this RUNE report? It's *'affectionately termed'* the PITS study. Guess what that stands for? P.I.T.S..."

I try to think of a clever acronym, but my head's not into it. What do the Spanish say? *'Pensando En La Inmortalidad Del Cangrejo.'* Contemplating the immortality of the crab.

Gordon sees my expression, and looks wounded. He's been hauling his red wagon up The Hill for years trying to get in on White House outsourcing. There are piles of cash just laying around D.C. for this kind of thing: Slush funds. Earmarked surplus. 'Not-For-Profit' just means they're not paying tax. These guys are taking the money home in sacks. There's also the boon of limited liability. The work in D.C. is hypothetical. The Numbers never get checked. My favourite example was the '98 Subcommittee on Space and Aeronautics of the Committee on Science hearing on *'Asteroids: Perils and Opportunities.'* The study showed that the chance of being killed by a falling meteor was fifty times greater than being killed in a fireworks accident. Of course, the only reason the statistic was true is that an asteroid would kill *everyone,* which skewed the odds considerably. And of course, no one would be around to collect their insurance. It was a running gag with Gordo...

"It stands for *'Pie In The Sky,'* Bob. P.I.T.S.! Doesn't that sound great!"

"I'd like to, Gordo. I can't."

"What?"

"I've got a lot on—"

"This is what we've always wanted! It's a walk in the park. A very nice park, with big trees made of money."

"You don't need me, Gordo. You need a battery hen picking Lotto balls from a dish."

Gordon hesitates, quizzing me silently. He knows me well enough to see something is chewing at my liver. Even through the din of his own internal cash register. "C'mon Bob. Uncle Sam has deep pockets in that jazzy striped vest. You do some numbers, ask for an even three-hundred. You get paid. I'm in good with Dodd. We all go home happy?"

"I can't," I reply.

"You're joking," Gordon says brightly, finishing his long black. "Go out to Arlington. Talk to this guy. I'll cover your expenses. Dodd just wants to *meet* you, show you around, ask a few questions. This is the big one Bob." Gordon swabs his lips with a handkerchief. "For *all* of us."

"Matt died last night."

"Huh?"

"You didn't see the papers?" I ask, feeling instantly guilty for the implication Gordon should have already known – or that I've been nursing the secret pain for the past hour.

"Matthias *Mueller*? No shit?"

"I need to be here for Annie."

"Christ." Gordon deflates visibly. He peers at me, hoping to gauge how far he can push his wagon. He knows Matt and I were close. Matt was the one who first got me the gig working for Gordo, fifteen years ago. "That's awful," he says finally. "How's everyone holding up?"

"Not so good."

"What about you?"

"It's still sinking in."

"Christ. What happened?"

"He was mugged or something. They don't know. I have to go see the detective this afternoon."

"Fuck."

"I know."

"Well, you know what they say: 'Old Provosts never die. They just lose their *faculties.*'" Gordon smiles weakly, hoping to break the gloom. "Look Bob. Let me have a chat to Dodd, see if we can push this thing back a few days? Okay? It would *really* mean a lot to me if you could do it. I *need* you on this one."

"I don't know anything about terrorism."

"How much did you know about Ramjets?"

"*Scram*Jets."

"See! Look Bob, these guys just want some Numbers."

"You say this guy called at four A.M.?"

"Yeah. Expect a call. I gave him your cell. I gotta run. Give my best to Anne. I'll phone you in a couple days." Gordon rises off his perch.

"Oh, you'll probably get a call from the F.B.I. as well... They need to ask you some questions for the security clearance."

"My standard waiver covers all that."

Gordon shrugs. "Not this time. Non-standard non-disclosure. This is a different ball game."

"Give my love to Sue."

"Okay."

And there it is. Just as easy as getting hit by lightning.

Gordon two-steps out into the street.

I try to look busy for the rest of the day, before bundling my things into a case, stuffing the pink Post-Its in my shirt pocket with the Polaroid, and driving home to the empty nest.

Parking the car in the garage, I pass the bench where Matt and Joe were yesterday untangling their rods.

I can't remember the last time I was alone at the house. Right now, even a hotel room would be better. In a hotel, there is an implication of company in the neighbouring rooms and adjacent days. Here, I'm alone with my regular self. More accurately, I'm *not* alone. Alone would be better. There are ghosts here now.

I fix a sandwich, sit in Matt's old chair, and fire up the computer at my desk, staring at the fluorescing screen in the dark.

It's 7:00pm. I reach for the phone, mindful of the other two Mueller women down at the Boston townhouse, both more likely to answer than Annie.

The phone rings out.

I empty my shirt pocket, careful not to make eye contact with the Polaroid. Shuffling through the pink Post-Its, I find the phone number for Detective Cullen from the Boston P.D. Tomorrow.

*Flying windows* screensaver winks on the computer screen, and I nudge the mouse.

"DAAAD!!"

Joe?

I walk out to the foyer, and open the front door.

Joe is on the stoop wearing an oversized hunting vest, nursing an armload of tackle, saddle hackles, a fishing pole, stamp albums, a book of New York Times crossword puzzles, and a bundle of aircraft model sprues with a record player perched on top.

"Look! Grandma gave me Grandpa's stuff!" He leans forward precariously.

Annie pops her head up behind the tailgate of her car, parked in the driveway. "Bob, come help with the boxes."

"How come you're back already?"

"Shhh!" scolds Annie.

Joe looks uncertain.

"Give me a hand," Annie strains to lift a box out of the car. "Mom couldn't sleep at home. She asked if she could stay here."

"Where is she?"

Annie glances inside the convertible, through the plastic rear window of the raised roof.

Tessa is sitting in the passenger seat of the car, motionless.

"What's she doing?" I whisper.

Annie gives me the look: *Not in front of Joe.*

"Where's Madison?"

"Gone back to the hotel." Annie heads for the door.

I trundle over, and take a look in Joe's bundle. Inside the box are the fixings for fishing lures; colourful wads of Rainbow Krystal Flash, feather, red Flashabou, a hunk of chartreuse bucktail...

I pluck the book of crossword puzzles out of the box. It feels obscenely mortal; the sweat-browned pages thumbed thin. Opening one of Matt's books is like trying on his *clothes*. And near the bottom of the crate, I spot a white Captain Black tobacco can. "What's this?"

"Enn-Ess-Eff-Pee!"

"What?"

"'*Not Safe For Parents*'" Joe grins. "Just jokes. Handmade flies!" It's in his eyes: he's doing his best to keep the mood cheerful, after a punishing trip from Boston.

I resist the urge to tousle the boy's hair.

"Check out the record player! It's broke but I'm gonna fix it. I've got a soldering iron and everything!"

"Bring in Mum's suitcase." Annie nods at the trunk. "Put the car in when you're done?"

The car door opens. Tessa turns to me, red-eyed. Her face is ashen and plain. She's wearing her nightgown. In all my life, I've never seen her without her makeup on, or the impeccably shaped hair. *Nobody* ever has. She begins to speak, her voice cracking... looking a thousand years old.

"Hi Tessa."

She walks past me into the house.

I eye the suitcase with caution, and haul it out of the trunk.

I'm alone on the driveway now.

The hairs on the back of my neck bristle.

Turning to face the darkened lawn, the wind stirs trees at the edge of the horse paddock.

My inner caveman sees the restless darkened woods, and senses monsters.

Five centuries of Middle-Ages sharecropping translates the biological fear reaction of the previous hundred-and-fifty-thousand-years before that, into evil spirits. Nuclear man thinks 'home invasion'. Prowlers who snip off victim's ears with their own garden shears. Shivering, I turn to head inside.

Annie is waiting for me in the bedroom, seated on the end of the bed. "Close the door."

After fifteen years of marriage, you don't say *'we need to talk.'* It's in the line of her shoulders.

I reach for her hand.

She stiffens, and looks me in the eyes.

There's no familiar framework with which to phrase a comment. I feel like I've slipped past the end of the rope. Everything is unstable.

"Have you talked to the police?"

"No," I shake my head. "Have you?"

"A Detective called... He said he'd been trying to reach you."

"I got busy."

Annie rises silently, and walks to the rainbox. The bathroom door locks with a *click*.

I sit on the edge of the bed, disabled, and listen to her shower.

Then I walk back downstairs, and switch on the light to the den.

Tessa is standing in the dark, ghostly in her white night dress, staring at the space behind the desk where she would have once found Matt in his smoking jacket ...

She passes me silently, moving quickly into the hall.

"Wait—" I start to follow, but the sound of her hurried footsteps tell me she doesn't want to talk. I can't imagine how it feels. Even if I lost Annie... *What could I possibly say to make her feel better?*

*Nothing* today is the same as yesterday.

As much as I'd like it to make sense, to find a reason, to make it meaningful, it was just an accident. *Right?*

I pick up the book of crossword puzzles on the desk... The one from Joe's box of loot.

A folded slip of newspaper tips onto the floor.

I fetch up the clipping, and open it...

It's a crossword puzzle from the New York Times: *Sunday, September 2, 2012.*

Yesterday. The day Matt was murdered.

I study the blank puzzle. There's nothing remarkable about it, other than the date. The clues aren't included – just the empty grid. In the bottom left-hand corner, it reads: '*Puzzle by Samuel Litthamer*'.

I stow the clipping in the drawer, with the Polaroid of Matt's death mask.

I switch off the desk lamp, and plod upstairs – the wind in the trees forgotten.

Lou Maas sits crouched at the edge of the horse paddock, watching the house as the bedroom light winks out.

Further away, on the next bluff, flashes the solar-powered lighthouse. After nineteen years, he's right back where he began, with the lighthouse keeper – Vantcha Velajcic.

It's mind-bending.

Lou curses under his breath, and thumps the tree trunk beside him, hard enough to cut up his knuckles. He knows now, he should have watched the old man all those years ago, made sure. He might have found *this* house that night as well... It's tempting to cross the field into the bedrooms – one-by-one. Right now. But he has to be careful. He isn't prepared. It's dangerous going into a strange house without a good recon first. He doesn't know his way around... Too many things might go wrong. There might be a snub nose in a shoebox under the bed, a panic room, a silent alarm... It's better to lure the occupants outside, here into the forest, the way he lured the old man onto the fire escape... *Matthias Mueller.* His driver's license showed a different address to the townhouse with the fire escape in Back Bay, Boston. It had taken a moment to recognise this other town: *New Bridlington.* It was the same town, nineteen years ago... where he'd found Vantcha Velajcic. The lighthouse keeper. Maas wasn't sure yet how it all pieced together, but it was important.

"*Fuck!*" Maas spits again. He can't see the driveway clearly, but he's heard three car doors *thump* shut. Four people are too many to take down on his own, without a floor plan.

But he can't afford to be too patient now either. Every second, somebody else might be *told.* He decides he'll have to come back – soon, and better prepared.

## 9. '...THE WILL OF THE FATHER...'

*Wednesday, September 5, 2012*

*'Annie's fine.'*
   *'Sure, we'll come round for dinner.'*
   *'Call me tomorrow and I'll check my calendar.'*
   *'Yeah, it doesn't make any sense.'*
   'Bad things, good people.'
All the distinguished guests speak about Matt in the most general terms. *'He was a great man.' 'He lived a productive life.' 'He was well loved.'* The pews are lined with MIT alumni, a smattering of cabinet cronies, and comparatively few relatives. To my relief, the interior of the Sacred Heart chapel is surprisingly neutral: No statues of saints, or stained-glass windows. Whitewashed columns support galleries at either side. The lengthwise curved ceiling bears two spidery black chandeliers. The only religious icons are two modest mahogany Virgins in opposite corners, flanked by American flags. The place looks more like a courthouse than a church.

Listening to the priest's eloquent prayer and benediction, I drift off to sleep, head bobbing like a dashboard novelty, air whinnying in my windpipe. I haven't slept for three nights.

Annie elbows me sharply.

The stoic, finely-dressed people eye the closed casket with something like horror. It's clear none of us have any idea about this thing: This *threshold*. This lichgate. Only the priest seems comfortable. This is routine for him. It's his bread and butter. That's why he needs god, even more than we do. But it seems wrong, pretending to have a clue. Still, that's why they're here – right? It's better than everyone standing around looking lost if *one* person pretends to know what's going on. Some proper invocations. A routine. Maybe that's what it's about: Reminding us this happens every day.

We exit through the heavy masonry doors of the Sacred Heart chapel, under the statue of Jesus with the pentagram over his head all lit up like Broadway.

Madison and Annie flank Tessa. The Mueller women step carefully onto the cobbles of the triangular plaza, two of the three dabbing at their eyes. Madison, in her Martini glass heels wears a fixed scowl. She catches my gaze, and so everyone could hear, reports: "Matt *hated* churches."

The rest of us drive home in silence.

On the road into New Bridlington, Annie flicks on the radio to fill the silence, but the pop and chatter seem inappropriate.

I glance in the rear-view mirror to check Joe is okay, and find a glistening blue-and-white Blazer 4WD riding high behind us. The Chief flashes his headlights. Annie twists in her seat, sees the Blazer and flicks the car a wave. "It's Barne."

The Chief burps his siren.

"The *Po*," observes Joe.

"*Joe*," scolds Annie. "How fast are you going?"

"I'm fine." I pull onto the verge, and the Blazer rolls off the tarmac behind me.

Chief Barne Ruberight is toy-like with his stuck joints and pregnant paunch – like the tubby clockwork cop. He climbs stiffly down out of his cab, hanging off the open door, growling loudly when he lands in slush, and swaggers to my window shaking his boot.

Barne's eyes are perpetually slotted, with a golden moustache, and a Kewpie-doll curl on his sunburnt dome, visible when he tips his oversized hat. He's a good guy. He helps Annie carry our groceries to the car. A year ago we had a problem with a guy from Lanes Cove, who tooled Annie's bumper outside the IGA with his pick-up. Bert Morney was the guy's name. Morney was uninsured. So, in addition to not being able to pay for Annie's bumper, he showed up at the house on a hot afternoon, and demanded cash for his own repairs. When Annie declined, Morney swerved on the wrong side of the coast road, forcing her into a ditch. I wanted him locked up, or dead. But Annie demanded I leave it. So, I went down to see Barne at *The Bee's Wing*, where I found him – resplendent in his khakis – standing around with the slack-jawed moon-eyed bar-flies sip suds to the pulse of *Purple Haze*. When I told him the story, he impounded Morney's pick-up that same afternoon. I never told Annie. Barne kept it quiet. I tried to give him something out of gratitude on three different occasions – scotch, cigars, and a Tibor fly reel – but he just laughed it off every time. "Jus' doing my job."

So, when Barne leans down at the car window now, I'm unconcerned. "Hey Barne. How's tricks?"

"Just fine." He tips his hat. "Missus Travis. Missus Mueller. Joe. How're you?"

"Been better," Annie smiles gently.

Tessa smiles weakly from the back seat.

"I heard about your loss," Barne chews his lip. "Jus' wanted to offer my condolences."

"Thanks."

"I hope this isn't a bad time, Bob. Can we talk?"

I try to read his eyes. "What is it?"

"It's *nothing*. I just need to ask you something. Do you mind?" He steps back from the door, his hand resting on the butt of his pistol.

"Now?"

"If you could. It'll jus' take a second."

"Sure. No problem."

Barne shuffles around to the rear of the car and waits for me.

Annie casts me a wary look. I unlatch my seatbelt, and step out.

I circle the fender. "What's up Chief?"

Barne peeks in through the back window. "Sorry to put you out like this Bob. I was going to ring you tonight, but I just saw you driving by—"

"What's the matter?"

"I had a call..."

"Ahuh?"

"I'm not supposed to tell you. But I figure it can't hurt. If it's just between you and me... Okay?"

"What is it?"

"Some guy from Washington called asking a bunch of questions about you. Wanted to know if you ever made any trouble. Where you socialised? That kinda thing. And if I saw you, I shouldn't tell you I'd spoken to him."

I smile. "Oh, that's nothing. It's just standard procedure for some work I'm doing in D.C. - for my security clearance."

"Yeah?"

"Did he say who he was?"

"Said his name was Phil Munce. From the NSA."

"NSA?" I blurt, surprised. This Anacostia crowd don't fool around. "Thanks for letting me know."

"See, that's not all."

"No?"

'That *was* unusual. Then this other guy calls the station this morning. Guy by the name of Benning. Said he was CIA."

"C.I.A.?"

"That's how I heard *all* about Annie's father... C.I.A. guy told me, see."

"Really?" I'm incredulous now.

"He said the opposite – He needs to talk to you. That I should let you know he's going to come visit you."

I glance at Annie through the rear window. She's talking to Joe, keeping him from pressing his ear to the window. "About what?"

"Matt."

"What did he say?"

Barne shrugs. "Asked if I could make regular patrols past your house for the next couple of days."

It's like a speedball out of left field. "Why?"

"He said he planned to fly up here early next week to talk to you." Barne leans in close, like he's coming in for a smooch. "Said I should drive out your way a couple times a day, and keep an eye out, for anything... out of the ordinary."

"Were you at *The Bee's Wing* last night?" I ask.

Barne's eyes narrow. "Ahuh."

"Who else was there?"

Barne thinks for a second. "The usual crowd. Why?"

"Nobody was missing?"

"Nope."

"Not Bert Morney?"

Barne shakes his head. "He left around nine. Why?"

I consider telling Barne about the strange feeling I had last night that there was someone in my yard... But it will just sound crazy.

Barne watches me for a second, and hitches up his belt. "You think it's about Morney?"

I shrug. That doesn't really make sense.

Barne reaches into his shirt pocket, and pulls out two business cards, and a pencil. He scribbles a cell-phone number on the back of both cards. "You get a *whiff* of anything, call me on my afterhours cell. If you can't reach me, that's Patrolman Keegan's cell too. Give one of 'em to Annie. Okay?"

"Sure. Hey. Thanks for letting me know," I pause. "About those calls."

Barne drums his fingers on the tail of the car. "Kinda strange - C.I.A. *and* N.S.A. - right? Same day. I mean, I've never heard from *either* of 'em before."

"I'm sure it's nothing."

"I'll drive by tonight."

"Thanks."

Barne hauls open the door on the Four-Wheeler with a squeal of dry hinges, and wriggles back into the cab. "Bob! One more thing—" Barne calls out from the window of his four-wheeler.

"Yeah?" I walk back to the Blazer to keep him from shouting.

"There's a Detective Cullen from the Boston P.D. trying to reach you *as well.*"

"Yeah, *Cullen...* I need to give him a call."

"Don't waste your time," Barne frowns. "I spoke to him. They've got nothing. No suspects. No witnesses. Nothing. Not a clue. If it does get important, he'll find you."

"Okay, thanks." I wait for the Chief to pull back onto the road, before getting back into the car.

"What did he want?" asks Annie.

"Nothing. D.C. checking up on me for that security clearance."

"What security clearance?" asks Joe.

"Your Dad is working for the government," Annie smiles.

It's good to finally see her smile. I wonder how much she thinks she's joking.

Meanwhile, I've got fifteen things on my mind. If any more questions come up, my ears are gonna fly off. I better call Gordo.

I check my Blackberry. The D. C. briefing is on Saturday. Three days time.

## 10. '...EVERY IDLE WORD...'

*Saturday, September 8, 2012*

A hundred analysts scatter around the darkened Anacostia Institute auditorium like skin-flick perverts, hacking away blue-faced on laptops, wearing badges: FEMA, NOAA, NWS, USGS, CDC...

Bill Dodd stands behind the floodlit podium, poised, feet apart.

This is the Mir astronaut with the triple Doctorate, who called Gordon at four in the morning. There isn't a wrinkle on him: Kevlar tie, chrome teeth, Teflon hair. He looks like Buck Rogers.

There's no doubt this 'Anacostia Institute' is making money faster than they can stack it sideways. You can tell the successfulness of an outfit from their paraphernalia – pens, badges, catering... On a small project, I might get a free backpack and a Bic. On a big project like this, they give you a complimentary Filofax or a Mont Blanc pen at the kick-off meeting. Here, I walked in the meeting room to be greeted by an effervescent 6-foot tall California-brown model dressed in a snippet of fabric. She's handing out conference kits containing security passes on monogrammed silk lanyards, ring binders, name tents, and a shiny new iPad2 for every delegate. On the tablet shines the message: *'With compliments - The Anacostia Institute for Policy Studies'* and a belting-big Great Seal.

I check my security lanyard. The words 'Terrorism Sub-Project Leader' are printed beneath my name.

Dodd takes enthusiastically to the podium, makes his introduction, and gently informs the room that the Remote Unlikely Negative Event report – 'RUNE' – will steer congressional spending on disaster relief, early-warning systems, and a Federal Bond issue.

The iPad screen flashes, in unison with the three projector screens behind Dodd, showing the agenda for the day: First, 'Pandemics.' Then 'Climate Change' followed by 'Resource Depletion'. After lunch, the socio-economic context – 'Population Expansion', 'Energy Security', and finally 'Terrorism'. Seven unstoppered apocalyptic vials.

Team leaders' names are listed in small type next to each heading.

My name is next to 'Terrorism'.

The iPad beeps wildly, presentation notes appear in my lap, synchronised with the screens. The show is all razzle-dazzle. The only thing missing is Chinese sky candy. Dodd starts into a PowerPoint slideshow alternating slides cleverly between the three screens. This is Risk Assessment extrapolated to its grandest manifestation: whole cities, whole states, struck down by *Book of Revelation* scale disasters.

First, he shows Mount Rainier volcano swollen fatter than Saint Helens, wiping out Seattle-Tacoma and spewing trillions of tons of acid into the atmosphere, doing billions in damage down the West Coast. Mud slides. Air traffic disruption. Water sources contamination. Massive fatalities. He draws comparisons with pre-earthquake thermal anomalies in Killari, the Latur earthquake of '93. The Landers '92 surface rupture. Hydrogeological strain fields at Spitak, and Mount Pinatubo, and fumarole emissions at Erta-Ale and Unzen.

Then the Virginia quake last year, less than an hour's drive from this room, the biggest in a hundred years. What if it flattened Washington?

Third, the Calaveras Fault, threatening to swallow up San Francisco. Any day.

Fukushima. Haiti. Christchurch. Chile. After an hour of this kind of thing from Dodd, I'm pretty sure the whole planet is about to tool itself.

I stay in my seat as the group breaks for morning tea, and pretend to look busy with my notes. I don't feel like jaw-wagging. All I want to do is meet Dodd, tell him Gordo is a great guy, and they should do more business, and leave.

A new speaker takes the stage – former Director of the Center for Disease Control.

My attention drifts out during incomprehensible slides on cancer mutating into a contagion... New, more virulent strains of influenza... Four million people dying every year worldwide from respiratory infections... HIV/AIDS becoming airborne – forty million current sufferers, and rising.

The third speaker shows the Earth heating up hotter than a million years of ice core data... Sea levels rising. Hurricanes and tornadoes increasing fifty percent in twenty years, due to rising ocean temperatures... Lost ice-cover taking with it melt-water that feeds rivers and irrigates crops, cutting the water supply to three billion people... Permanent *El Ninõ* – the 'Christ child' – killing the Amazon... And so on... Until there's nothing left on Earth but Martian rock and a steaming, inhospitable atmosphere.

In a year, 'Acts of God' have caused thirty-six billion dollars in damage in the US. Double what it was ten years ago.

In a single year, twenty-five thousand lives have been lost in America.

God is acting up. If *he* doubles the Numbers again, the global economy will collapse.

'Acts of God.' Bang-up job, old man.

These guys have graphs on every disaster. The economic size of it all. The unspoken, unacknowledged, undeniable fact, that it's a tremendous miracle any of us are even alive.

My brow aches, head full of doom. The detached manner in which Dodd and Co. recount recent events... The subdued clacking of keyboards and the eerily lit, impassive faces... The Numbers.

How have we survived this long?

How did we stay free and clear on this whirling mud-ball for thirty billion years? Protected from deadly solar radiation by nothing but the diaphanous *van Allen* belts, never smashed to bits by hurtling space rock? Snug. Surface temperature within fifty degrees of balmy, flowering in this idyllic seam of air, between the freezing-cold vacuum of space and the pimpled crust of a superheated pressure-vessel of molten rock and poisonous gas, orbiting around a gigantic fusion reactor headed inevitably towards collapse, all adrift in an infinite void?

A progression of infinitesimal escapes has led to intelligent life at such slim odds, here in the Goldilocks zone: Any closer to the sun, the oceans turn to steam. Any further away, they freeze. Saturn whirls outside us, sweeping up comets.

Here we are, with an impossible balance of elements, gas, temperature and geography, surviving for a trillion years of uninterrupted isolation, and now we're finally smart enough to look around, our resources are depleting, ecosystems collapsing, and we've sown our own destruction.

"It almost makes you wish there *was* a god," quips a presenter, and everyone laughs.

It's too good to be true, right? How stupendously *lucky* we've been.

If you think about it for too long, it's terrifying... The inevitability with which we'll eventually be crushed, burned, withered...

I creep out of the auditorium, eager to escape. I need air... I need to stand in a calm rain-swollen river current where the water dapples with the afternoon light in the shadow of moss-green hardwoods.

I duck around the corner of the hall, out of sight, and spot a bench in the manicured garden. The hush of turf under my heels, I sit by the fountain in the sunlight, and watch the water splash in an infinitely complex dance of droplets, randomly colliding and splitting. I wonder, watching the mind-numbing display of chaos in the fountain... if *I'm losing my mind.*

Somehow, somewhere in the past few days, I've slipped out of Reality.

The 6-foot tall California-brown female model in the belt-skirt strides purposefully down the path beside the auditorium, and glances at me. Her smile is gone. She looks suitably bothered that I'm not inside where I should be.

I nod politely, pretend to check my BlackBerry and, grudgingly, walk back inside the auditorium.

Dodd is back at the podium. He looks up from his notes at the spray of light from the rear of the room, and sees me enter. "...and that concludes our final session for the day," he announces, "on the *Terrorism sub-project*," he adds pointedly. "Those of you who have been nominated as sub-project leaders - as indicated on your security passes - we'll be scheduling separate sessions with your campaign leaders to brief you on your opportunity statements. You'll find courtesy cars on the parkway. For those returning to the Willard Hotel, dinner is at *nineteen-hundred.*"

Dodd steps down from the stage.

I turn and walk back through the doors, making a beeline for the cars, when Dodd and a suited goon pop loudly from a fire door in the side of the hall. "Robert Travis!"

I force a smile, slowing my stride.

"Hold up!"

Dodd rushes toward me, extending a jewelled hand. "Robert Travis?" I glance down obviously. His knuckles are a ruby showcase of Varsity rings. I've met these ex-Pentagon types before. They pick up PhDs from a military university drive-thru. I'm fairly sure Dodd probably retired on a full military pension at the age of forty, even before he got on the consulting gravy train. That's how Tri-Command keeps the best and brightest out of the private sector - with the promise of these easy years. My eyes drift over to Dodd's companion. Up close, this goon is the antithesis of Dodd. He has rheumy eyes, and a face made of tufts of faded hair, sideburns and eyebrows that all blend into one. His shirt isn't ironed, and he's got on a smile like the underside of a yard tool.

"Sorry you had to step out there, Bob," Dodd smiles. "I understand you're busy. We'll catch you up. I *do* want to introduce you to the team."

"Great," I smile.

"Bob," interrupts the stranger. "Your father-in-law was Matthias Mueller?"

"Yes."

It's no surprise this guy has heard of Matt.

"He was a brilliant man. It's sad to see him go. He spoke highly of you."

A little bell goes off in my brain. This guy *knew* Matt. Properly. This whole adventure suddenly makes sense – Gordon's 4:00am call... The *Anacostia Institute* didn't contact Gordon out of the blue. Matt was still guiding me from the grave.

"Bob, this is Clark Diffner. He's with the C.I.A." interjects Dodd, rectifying the impropriety. I shake Clark's hairy claw. "Clark spearheaded the Vatican Incorporated investigation."

*Spearheaded..?* I smile unintentionally. The Navy-bred Astronaut, with his hands clasped at his back, routinely deploys expressions like *debrief* and *oh-nine-hundred. Whiskey tango foxtrot.*

Diffner pokes me with a business card.

I take a moment to absorb it, hoping it will shed more light...

And while I'm considering how this man could possibly know Matt, Diffner turns to Dodd. "Looks like Bob doesn't know about Vatican Inc?"

"I guess you out-flanked me there." I pocket the card.

"Blackfriars Bridge?" suggests Dodd.

Matt told me about this. Back in the Eighties an Italian Banker with ties to the Vatican Bank was found hanged under Blackfriars Bridge in London.

*(Diagram 5 - Clark Diffner's business card)*

The CIA busted the Pope laundering a billion dollars worth of counterfeit Bonds for the Mafia. Until then, the CIA had been helping the anti-Communists – which meant Fascist-slash-Mafia-slash-Vatican. But the Bond bust, and ties back to Organised Crime in the US, signalled a divorce. The CIA – surprisingly – went after the Vatican Bank. If this guy Diffner had anything to do with it, he was a big deal. "I'm just a Numbers man," I apologise meekly.

"Sure you are," smiles Diffner.

The two men stand there grinning.

"It was nice to meet you, Bob," Dodd says finally. "I'll talk to you soon about setting up a sub-project meeting, and we'll work up some decision quality criteria."

Something about this Dodd character isn't right. There's a Turkish expression, *'The bear knows about forty stories, but all of them are about pears.'* It's like this guy Dodd has no personality outside of the one topic. "Um, okay."

Diffner peeps strangely at Dodd, like he's thinking the same thing. "I'll call you tomorrow, Bob. And pass on my condolence to Tessa."

Dodd clasps my forearm when he shakes my hand. "We're *mike-oscar.*"

"Huh?"

The pair march off around the pond.

*"Moving Out."*

Okay fly-boy.

I hop into a courtesy car, wondering more than ever about Matt.

The limo loops up onto the freeway over the Potomac to the apex of the 14th street bridges where Washington comes into view: monumental, grand and dormant. The Capitol, Lincoln Memorial, and Mill's 550-foot Egyptian Obelisk are swallowed at ground-level by tracts of woodland. From here, the scene is strangely still, as if Humanity has been extinct for a thousand years, and the trees have taken back the streets.

The car drops me at the Willard, a block from New York Avenue, where it radiates out to the seedy 'Ward 5' district.

As soon as I get to my room, I go to my suitcase to change out of my suit.

As my thumbs move to the Samsonite combination lock, I notice the number on the anodised wheels.

*009*

My combination is 220, after my initials: 2 for 'B', 20 for 'T'. Easy to remember. Easy to guess. So, when I lock my bag I spin two numbers down, and one number up.

Most people give the dials on a combination lock a spin in the one direction. The numbers move by 2 or 3 digits – if your fingers don't slip, and the outside wheel doesn't move one space less. Even a double-spin still leaves no more than 72 combinations to trace back. By spinning the dials the opposite way, it's almost impossible to work out the combination.

So I'm used to seeing a number like '448' on the wheels.

009 is one spin from the correct combination.

Someone has been in my bag.

I contemplate calling hotel Security, when the phone rings.

It takes a moment, listening to the dial tone in the hotel phone handset, and the persistent jingle, before I realise it isn't the house line that's ringing.

I walk a lap of the room looking for the source of the bell, rummage through the conference gear on the desk, and uncover the Anacostia iPad.

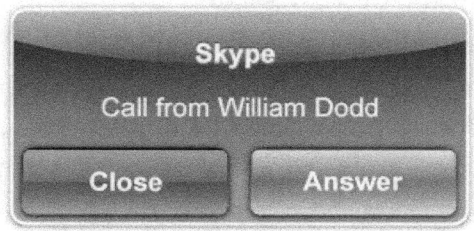

The ringing stops.

I wait a moment...

After some deliberation, I toss the gadget back in the satchel. Tonight, I'm an anonymous guy in a rented room. No innocuous family deaths, or *Acts of God*. I'm... an orthodontist, a salmon breeder, a lumberman.

Restless, I set myself up on the bed with a ten-dollar jar of cashews and the TV remote, and work my way through ten-minutes of sample viewing on every video channel. An hour later, I'm staring at the Menu screen, trying to think of something else to take my mind off the ache in my back teeth. I don't have the will to submit myself to the city. Or the hard-hinged minibar.

Looking for a room-service menu, I pry open the bedside drawer.

The gold-embossed cover of a Gideon's Bible yells:

### Help in a time of need

Scribbled on the cover of the Bible in Super Marker are the words:

## JUST IN CASE YOU'RE A FILTHY SINNER THINKING OF DIALING A HOOKER OR WASHING DOWN A JAR OF PILLS

*(Diagram 6 - Gideon's Bible graffiti, cover)*

The Bible lays open on its spine.

Scrawled into the splayed ends of the pages in more black marker, are the words:

# READ THIS!

Curious, I flip the Bible over in my hands. The spine is fixed open where it's been sitting the same way in the drawer for so long.

The marked page is filled with black lines, omitting sections of text in the same dense pen.

Chapter three: 'The Book of Ecclesiastes.'

*(Diagram 7 - Gideon's Bible graffiti, Ecclesiastes)*

*9 What profit hath a man from all his labour...*

*...in much wisdom is much grief ...*

*...he who increases knowledge increases sorrow...*

*...there is no more remembrance of the wise than the fool*

*...all that now is will be forgotten...*

*...how does the wise man die? As the fool!*

*"Concerning the condition of the sons of men, God tests them that they may see that they themselves are like animals." For what happens to the sons of men also happens to animals*

*...as one dies, so dies the other...*

*...man has no advantage over animals...*

*...All go to one place: all are from the dust, and all return to the dust.*

*...look! The tears of the oppressed...*

*I praised the dead who were already dead, more than the living who are still alive. Yet, better is he who has never existed, who has not seen the evil...*

"Funny," I murmur to myself. 'Help, in a time of need.' Only *if* you don't open the Bible up *here*.

There's a cute symmetry to the vandalism: The Gideon Bible Society was *founded* in a hotel room at the Central House Hotel in Boscobel, Wisconsin, by a pair of salesmen sharing a room during a lumberman's conference. It's fitting a century later an equal and opposite campaign is underway. Maybe a pair of Super Marker salesmen highlighting the godless parts of the book, one room at a time.

I replace the book in the drawer, and lay on the bed, waiting for sleep.

The phone chirps again.

⊠ Madison (Cell)

Sept 8, 2012 10:15:48 PM

Where r u?

*Where r u?*

There's no good reason for Madison to be asking where I am.

I switch off the phone, and lay back, waiting for sleep.

*Sunday, September 9, 2012*

Muhannad al-Baghdadi stands sweating over the stove of the cramped Brooklyn Heights basement studio, wearing a second-hand scuba mask, with a handkerchief tied over his mouth.

Muhannad's only distinguishing feature is his height, his head almost touching the exposed water pipe in the ceiling. The colour of his skin is difficult to place. He might be Native American, African, Arabic, or Indian, or Southern Asian.

Every burner on the stove is lit.

Muhannad empties the colourless contents of a 5 gallon plastic bottle of 'Smart Hair *Ultra*BLOND' into a fourth pot.

He purchased the bleach from three different hairdressers. While getting his hair cut at each store, he had dropped in conversation that he'd just arrived from Iraq, where they used hairdressers' bleach to strip wallpaper. "I have some old wallpaper to get rid of. Can I get some bleach here?"

Boiling the bleach was necessary to increase its concentration, but almost as dangerous as wiring the detonator. The longer the bleach boiled, the more dangerous it became. At higher strengths, spilled on fabric, it could spontaneously ignite. Higher still, the vapour could detonate by itself. It could turn your skin white, and if digested would cause internal bleeding, and blistering in the mouth – called 'Black hairy tongue.' So the handkerchief over the mouth, and the scuba goggles were necessary precautions.

Mixing the concentrated bleach and the paper sacks of 'Atti' flour into the flat plastic tub would be the final step in the manufacture of the Joralemon bomb. It had to be done last, so the mixture didn't decompose.

Next, Muhannad takes a bag of party ice from the freezer, fills the sink around a metal champagne bucket, and mixes a small amount of the boiled bleach with nail varnish remover inside the chilled container. Then, with an eye dropper, he carefully transfers a small amount of acid from a car battery, stirring each drop into the cold bleach-and-nail-polish mix, creating a small amount of tri-acetone triperoxide.

Taking the sturdy cardboard tube from the centre of a roll of wrapping paper, he fits a cork in one end, and tips the mixture inside.

In the other end, he inserts a small torch light bulb with a hole drilled in the glass, and wires it to the speaker of a cell phone.

All told, the bomb takes two hours to assemble and the components cost less than a hundred dollars, with change for a subway ticket.

## 11. '...BY THEIR FRUITS YE SHALL KNOW THEM...'

*Sunday, September 9, 2012*

He's waiting for me: The 60-year-old rheumy eyed goon with the yard tool mouth.

There's no point getting to the airport early just to sit in the lounge sipping complimentary soda and chewing rubberised chorizo for an hour. So I leave my suitcase with the Willard porter, book a car, and walk into the Round Robin Bar.

The Round Robin at the Willard is an elaborate deep-green rotunda with a worn mahogany-lipped bar that plugs the middle of the chamber like a hydroelectric turbine, and the best dressed man in the house is the bartender – tricked out like a coronation prince. Two blocks from the White House, George Washington himself once nursed his Mint Julep here. Mark Twain scotch, sugar syrup, lemon juice, and bitters. And seven score and twelve years ago, Abraham Lincoln brought forth a new whiskey skin, brandy-mash, or glass of pure old rye.

Things feel rosier now, as I sit with my third Old Fashioned swirling in the glass, eager to get back to the farm – to Annie and Joe – when the familiar face walks in, and demands a libation.

I worm around in my wallet looking for his card. *Clark Diffner. Vatican Incorporated.* That guy.

Clark sits on his own in a padded corner, under a field of hand-drawn portraits, sparks up a roaring cigarette in his yard-tool mouth, and a new one in his other hand ready to go, birthing a crazy nebula around his wispy forelock.

*What are the chances?*

So many hotels, so many hours in the day...

Watching him sidelong, I can't help but notice he's smoking with applied effort. Really smoking. It's against the law to smoke in – or near the entrance to – all but six bars in D.C. It catches my attention how hard he's going at it, like he's trying to make himself disappear. It just isn't done anymore, the way smokers huddled like lepers in stoops and side alleys. I've never seen this kind of commitment to the task. Diffner is enjoying himself, one foot cocked over his knee, billboarding the butt-scorched sole of his right shoe, and has already finished his first cigarette before the crown prince can lap the bar, and ask him to stop.

I check my watch. I only have a few more minutes, so I decide I'll go on over, say hi, tell him I have to run, and there's no time to come off the beam.

"Clark?"

Diffner gathers up his briefcase. "Do you have a car?"

"Hmm?"

"You're flying United, Dulles to Boston?"

I pull a face like I just chewed an olive seed. "You too?"

"Yeah. Same."

"No kidding?" We're on a skybus together. That means in-flight conversation, strapped into a cylinder full of folks jetting on grocery-store voucher prizes while a pretty girl explains what to do in the event we're about to die. Normally, if you chat to the guy next to you on a plane he mysteriously has a card for you, wants to pal up and do business. An hour later he's forgotten. But this is different. Diffner is *someone*. He knows Matt *and* Dodd. I'll be hedging all the way to Logan – at the baggage claim, down the concourse – pretending I'm keen on the RUNE report. He'll spot me wheeling past the taxi rank, and offer to share a cab. "That's a real stroke of luck," I lie.

At the check-in counter, he asks to have a seat moved next to mine.

"How did you know Matt?" I ask, as we empty our pockets out into plastic trays at Security.

"You don't know?" Diffner replies.

"He never mentioned it."

"Matt came into the Embassy once looking for help. His hotel room had been sacked."

"Sacked?"

"Ransacked... Sofa cushions cut open. Wallpaper peeled off the walls. It was a real job. Because he was on the White House Security Council, I came down to check it out. We got talking, both being from Boston. We knew the same people. We ended up drinking all night."

I've never heard that story. "Really?"

Diffner peers at me. "Matt had a lot of secrets."

"He did?" I strap myself into my seat.

"So now I'm back to D.C."

"Ahuh."

The Hostess mimes vest inflation. Diffner adds, "I have another project for you."

I'm distracted. It takes a while for the words to register. "Pardon?"

"I've seen your work. *'Acts of God.'*"

An audible seatbelt *click*.

My little epiphany yesterday – Matt sending me on this junket from the grave – isn't the whole picture. The invite to Arlington, RUNE, the meeting outside the auditorium... Dodd ingratiating himself to me, then introduced Diffner...

"I need some Numbers of my own."

There it is.

Maybe Dodd owes this guy *Diffner* a favour. The whole RUNE gig might be a set up, just to help this Agency guy out. Diffner lived in Boston, knew Matt... Am I being pimped out by Dodd, D.C. style?

I give Diffner a second glance. The CIA man is uncomfortable with smiles, but right now he has on a full-blown Jimmy Carter, watching me figure it out.

So why couldn't he hire his own analyst? Is one of them paying off a debt to Matt, flicking the grieving son-in-law work? Maybe Diffner mentioned to Dodd at some high-flier's cocktail party that he needed a Numbers man, and Dodd is eager to get along? Maybe Dodd made an offer he can't fill himself. Or maybe Dodd is the kind of brainiac who locates a resource with family connections, just to impress Diffner. Or maybe Diffner's project is off the books, and I'm not meant to ask questions.

I can't help being a little impressed. The urgency. The big money. The open arms. The tidy manoeuvring. These guys play twenty moves ahead. Like Gordo said, 'this is a different ball game.' And for the first time in a long *long* time, I feel like I'm out of my depth.

"You're not how I pictured you," adds the old jasper.

"Really?"

"The way you were described..." Diffner sucks his teeth.

"How so?"

"This job I have for you, is right up your alley."

"What's my 'alley'?"

"International terrorism attributable to fundamentalist monotheistic dogmas, the most volatile factions: *U.S.S. Cole*, Khobar Towers, W.T.C., Khalid Shaikh, Hamas. Who's doing what. A bit like the RUNE report, but *global.*"

I recognise the spray of references. '*U.S.S. Cole*' and 'Khobar Towers' were Al-Qaeda attacks before September 11, 2001. A boat packed with explosives rammed the *USS Cole* in the port of Aden. Seventeen sailors were killed and thirty-nine injured. Back in '96 – five years before most of us heard of Al-Qaeda – a truck bomb exploded outside the Khobar Towers housing complex in Dhahran, Saudi Arabia, killing nineteen servicemen and wounding 372 others.

Diffner smiles meaningfully. "This is what you do, right? '*Acts of God?*'"

I try to look calm. The way Dodd and Diffner were smirking yesterday...

Diffner laughs earnestly. "I mean, prayer is just people trying to communicate with the weather, right? And you know *all* about weather."

"Sure."

"Good."

There is a monstrous silence.

"The Vatican Incorporated investigation,' I announce. "That must have been something."

Diffner looks at me like I'm a landscape.

"Walking up Vatican Hill to tell the Bishop he's busted?"

"That was a long time ago," Diffner whispers, graciously. "Dodd just doesn't know what I've been doing since. I was a wet-back in seventy-one..."

I nod, because it seems like I'm supposed to know the year. What I'm really thinking, is how much Matt would have loved this guy – busting the Vatican laundering money for the mob. They'd have sat for hours, Matt teasing out every last detail.

"Anyway, new Pope, clean slate," deflects Diffner. "They moved the money into Il Papa's name so it's private wealth. Can't be touched. Can't be seen. And the bishop is living in a white cinderblock house in Arizona, backing onto a country club fairway."

*Ah, the heady days of massive corruption, public assassinations and extortion.*

Diffner shrugs. "The Pope was buying and selling banks like baseball cards. Nothing has changed, they just got wise." It's clear that Diffner is barneying this down for my sake, and he doesn't enjoy taking about it.

I wave off the stewardess. "For two thousand years the Church prohibited the taking of interest," he adds. "Now they *own* banks. Nice flip-flop."

"Yeah."

"*Banco di Santo Spirito, Cassa di Risparmio di Roma, Banca Cattolica, Finabank,* the Extraordinary Section of the Administration of the Patrimony of the Holy See - Vatican central," Diffner muses. "It's a different world now. They're corporatised. The Vatican owns shares in textiles, telecommunications, utilities, steel, finance, pharmaceuticals, hotels, high-rises, automobiles, oil, software, airlines... The money is invested in public companies. Gold from the Indians of the New World. Money from the Nazi's. Eighty-one million from Mussolini in Article One of the Lateran Treaty, about eight-hundred million in today's money... It's all tucked away. The Holy See is the second biggest 'cut-out' country for money laundering in the world. Every administrative unit of every religious Order, and each diocese is an independent corporation with its own assets... We're talking *trillions.* Helluva thing, Bob. *Helluva* thing. It's a crime they keep taking donations - and don't pay tax."

I nod and agreed. It *must* be a hell of a thing. It's a *helluva thing* that I'm sitting here talking to this guy, and he sounds so much like Matt.

"But that's ancient history," concludes Diffner, tiredly. "So, you'll do my Numbers?"

"Yes." Of course.

Whatever this guy is into, whatever the reason the two of us are sitting on a plane, it has something to do with something else.

I peer out the window.

Flying into Boston at night plays with my head. It's the lights, millions of them, spread out over nine hundred square miles - as far as you can see. Homes in rows, a million street lights, headlights moving purposefully... Like every spark is a person, swarming the Earth. Peering down from the sky, arranged on a plane, it's unsettling... The ant farm.

"I doesn't strike you as odd," I reply. "Out of *all* Dodd's 'subprojects' – Pandemics, Climate Change, Resource Depletion, Population Expansion, Energy Security, and Terrorism – most of them are things we've done to ourselves?"

Diffner smiles.

"Do you know a C.I.A. guy named 'Benning'?" I ask, warily.

Diffner nods, distracted. "I had him make some calls before we spoke."

*Of course you did.*

As we swoop toward the tarmac, I consider the possibility of what Diffner is saying.

If an insurer can use Numbers to predict how often *'Acts of God'* will take place, maybe you could also predict acts of terrorism.

Diverting west via the Ted Williams Tunnel, I head for the Boylston Street *Barnes and Noble,* passing the squat, four-storey Lego-like Police Department HQ on Tremont. The windows in the police station are all lit. I remember now I still haven't spoken to Detective Cullen. Tomorrow. I drive up to the Boylston Street and double-park.

I trawl the book shelves for the black spines on terrorism; volumes with ready-made lists of the kinds of things Diffner described.

Hijacking and hostage-taking.

Car bombs, truck bombs, suicide bombs, gunmen, embassy attacks, airliner sieges and kidnappings.

Bell-ringers like W. Deen Mohammed, Louis Farrakhan, Gordon B. Hinckley, and Dimitrios Arhondonis.

Hajj, Fatwa, and Jihad.

I scoop up one of everything, the whole row.

God. Jesus. Allah. IRA. Waco. Holy Grail. Mosques. Priests. The Freakopaedias, and tote the bags out to the checkout, then hump the bundle back to the car.

The house is empty. There's a note on my desk reminding me she's driving Joe back to boarding school.

I drop the stack of books on the desk, takes out a highlighter, and start jotting down anything with the words Catholic, Protestant, Hebrew, Islam or any other fundie group. When I get stuck on a name, I flick through the books and check out who they are, what they want.

I start filling a spreadsheet going back to 2000, adding a bold 'R' for 'monotheism', 'P' for 'political' and 'U' for 'unknown':

|   | A | B | C | D | E | F | G | H |
|---|---|---|---|---|---|---|---|---|
| 1 | Date | Location | Method | Dead | Injured | Target | Responsible | Type |
| 2 | 02-11-00 | Jerusalem | Car bomb | 2 | 10 | Israeli | PIJ (Muslim) | R |
| 3 | 03-11-00 | India | Bomb | 6 | 0 | Muslim | SSP | R |
| 4 | 06-11-00 | Pakistan | Bomb | 3 | 4 | Unknown | Unknown | U |
| 5 | 08-11-00 | Gaza Strip | Shooting | 1 | 1 | Israeli | Fatah Tahzim | R |
| 6 | 13-11-00 | Gaza Strip | Shooting | 4 | 10 | Israeli | Fatah Tahzim | R |
| 7 | 13-11-00 | Athens | Bomb | 0 | 0 | Unknown | Unknown | U |
| 8 | 19-11-00 | Jordan | Drive-by | 0 | 1 | Israeli | Muslim | R |
| 9 | 20-11-00 | Gaza Strip | Bomb | 2 | 12 | Israeli | Fatah Tahzim | R |
| 10 | 22-11-00 | Israel | Car bomb | 2 | 55 | Israeli | Hamas | R |
| 11 | 06-12-00 | Jordan | Drive-by | 0 | 1 | Israeli | Muslim | R |
| 12 | 08-12-00 | Sudan | Shooting | 20 | 40 | Muslim | Unknown | R |
| 13 | 21-12-00 | Israel | Shooting | 1 | 0 | Israeli | Fatah Tahzim | R |
| 14 | 22-12-00 | Israel | Suicide bomb | 1 | 3 | Israeli | Hamas | R |
| 15 | 25-12-00 | Indonesia | Bomb | 14 | 100 | Christians | Unknown | R |
| 16 | 28-12-00 | Israel | Bomb | 0 | 14 | Israeli | Fatah Tahzim | R |
| 17 | 31-12-00 | West Bank | Shooting | 2 | 5 | Israeli | Fatah Tahzim | R |
| 18 | 01-01-01 | Israel | Suicide bomb | 0 | 20 | Israeli | Hamas | R |
| 19 | 12-01-01 | N. Ireland | Bomb | 0 | 0 | Catholic | Protestant | R |
| 20 | 17-01-01 | India | Shooting | 10 | 8 | Unknown | Muslim | R |
| 21 | 23-01-01 | Yemen | Hijacking | 0 | 0 | Unknown | Muslim | R |
| 22 | 28-01-01 | Pakistan | Shooting | 5 | 3 | Muslims | Unknown | R |
| 23 | 29-01-01 | Uganda | Bomb | 0 | 6 | Civilians | Unknown | U |
| 24 | 04-02-01 | N. Ireland | Bomb | 0 | 2 | Catholics | Protestants | R |
| 25 | 08-02-01 | Israel | Car bomb | 0 | 2 | Israelis | Hamas | R |
| 26 | 14-02-01 | Israel | Hit and run | 8 | 20 | Israelis | Hamas | R |
| 27 | 04-03-01 | Israel | Suicide bomb | 3 | 50 | Israelis | Hamas | R |
| 28 | 04-03-01 | London | Car bomb | 0 | 1 | British | IRA | U |
| 29 | 09-03-01 | Spain | Car bomb | 1 | 1 | Spanish | Basques | P |
| 30 | 15-03-01 | Istanbul | Hijacking | 3 | 1 | Russia | Chechen | R |
| 31 | 17-03-01 | Spain | Car bomb | 1 | 3 | Spanish | Basques | P |
| 32 | 24-03-01 | Chechnya | Suicide bomb | 20 | 142 | Unknown | Muslim | R |
| 33 | 27-03-01 | Jerusalem | Suicide bomb | 1 | 27 | Israelis | Hamas | R |
| 34 | 28-03-01 | Jerusalem | Suicide bomb | 3 | 4 | Israelis | Hamas | R |
| 35 | 10-04-01 | Rome | Bomb | 0 | 0 | U.S. | Unknown | P |
| 36 | 11-04-01 | Lebanon | Letter bomb | 0 | 3 | Druze | Unknown | R |

*(Diagram 8 - Acts of terrorism, 2000-2001AD)*

Typing the Numbers, each one turns my stomach another 5 degrees.

I've barely covered six months – just a random 6 months – and *way before* September 11, 2001. Look... There's a bomb ripping through a crowd every few days.

There are literally thousands of pages of this stuff.

The books stand knee-high to my desk. I never saw a quarter of this stuff on CNN! Or maybe I did, and it all sounded the same? *How does this look, from heaven?* All the tiny *pops* and *flashes* going off around the world like a disco ball. I've been skipping through life and everything had been handholding, and daisy chains. Meanwhile, these Hamas with all the suicide work... Don't they ever run out of guys kooky enough to strap on the suicide gear? These Gonzos haven't missed a beat in *ten years*. Every month. And *Fatah Tahzim*. Thriving like roaches.

This is nothing like doing Numbers on weather.

Every one of the 'R's in the spreadsheet is a story. A five-year-old girl killed. An eight-year-old boy loses his arms and legs, brothers and sisters looking on. Mother of five shot. Some guy hijacks a bus and ploughs it into a crowd of pedestrians on their way to work. Nine out of ten of these Numbers are an innocent bystander; a first-grader, a young girl out buying flat bread and milk. Every one of them is a person with their own smell, their own memories... a twinkle in someone's eye.

August 7th 1998, two embassies are car bombed in one day. Nairobi, Kenya and Dar Es Salaam, Tanzania. *224* people are killed, 4500 injured. All regular town folk, just going about their business, riding their bikes, sitting outside drinking tea, and *WHAM!* Mums and Dads, kids, ripped to pieces, wrapped around poles... A seven storey office building next door collapses, killing hundreds more...

All these pages, in all these books, all this polemic about how The West needs an enemy, and how Fundie Muslims want to kill non-Muslims because they can't comprehend religious integration and oil, and blah... It's noise.

Imagine watching some screwball take out your kid?

I can't comprehend it. But I'm dirty about it now. It's *insane*. Four-out-of-five acts of mayhem in the world have an 'R' for 'Religion' next to it. Eighty percent of the bloody, organised terror in the world...

Suddenly all our detachment – Dodd, Diffner, Gordo – feels wrong. All our efforts, too small.

I've seen the headlines before, 'Al Qaeda and Taliban join forces, Attacks on Baghdad', and thought 'Boy that's tough. What a crazy place it must be, wherever that is. Imagine if that was the bus I catch to work, ripped to smoking hell.' And then – just like everybody – an hour later, it's off my mind.

I close the book, get up, and pour myself a scotch.

Lightning bolts and car accidents are one thing. That's physics and chemistry. *This* is different. These aren't 'Acts of God.' These are acts of man in god's name.

Standing by the gin mill with an eel juice in my paw, I wonder what this guy Diffner is onto. If he started out busting crooked Bishops in Rome, and he's back in DC looking at Terrorism, what is he planning? He might be sending the head-kickers in to mop up the smelly little Muslim bomb-maker's workshops, and the sicko bunkhouses? Sweep out all the dark corners of the world. I want to know. What if I ring Diffner right now, and ask a few questions?

I slug down my drink, and settle back at the desk. My mind is wandering again. There's a sizeable flaw here in the general make-up of the world. *Look at it.* Stack it all together, and there's one common denominator, one thread... Tens of thousands of folks being maimed and killed, for *what?*

The front door of the house thumps shut.

Anne clicks halfway down the hall, kicks off her heels, and stops by the door to the den.

I flick off my PC monitor. "Hey! You're home!" I jump up.

"You working?"

"Yeah." I move away from the desk, herding Annie out of spying range, and give her a kiss. "How you doing?"

"You okay?" she asks.

"Why?"

"What are you doing?"

"Nothing. I'm just picking up some Numbers."

"What is it?"

She still wonders, in those tender moments where everything sticks and promises are made... "Just some Federal policy information."

"How's it going?"

"Fine. Thanks. Listen to you! How are *you* doing?"

Annie sheds one of those big bright smiles like a newborn, for no apparent reason. "I'm okay. I'll tell you about it later. I'm gonna go have a shower and fix some supper."

"I'll come help." I can't cook to save my life, but I figure being there when it happens counts for something.

"With supper, or the shower?"

"Ha!"

"Okay." Annie heads upstairs.

I feel flushed. I catch my face in the hall mirror. "How's Joe?" I call out.

"Good... Hey, Maddie said she was trying to reach you..."

"Why?"

"She's in town, staying with *some guy you know*–" Her voice trails off as she disappears into the bedroom.

I trundle back to my desk, remembering how snitty I felt five minutes ago. I need to get out of the room. Get some air. Hang round the kitchen.

I flick on my monitor.

The spreadsheet is still there.

The Numbers are still there.

This Diffner business is bright-and-shiny down the DC end of the trough, but up the other end it's a nasty mess of corpses and bloodthirsty rim-eyed Kamikaze artists. I've seen enough of the Numbers for one night. Nairobi. Dar Es Salaam. *U.S.S. Cole.* Khobar Towers. *I won't sleep tonight.* The ticking street-freaks. Millions of them. All those little scrapers right now, growing up to be just like their dead fathers. I've barely touched the surface. Groznyy. Sarajevo. Bosnia. Tajikistan. Somalia. Tunisia. Northern Ireland. Morocco. Turkey. Kashmir. Gujarat. *Everywhere*, it's Allah, Yahweh, Jehovah, or Jesus. Every time. The whole world over. It's bigger than all the 'Remote or Unlikely Negative Events.' All the Spitaks, and El Niños. All of Nature. This human chaos. Hundreds of thousands of people *dying*.

The more I think about it, the more it has me stumped.

It seems like the most important question of all... The question nobody is asking. The bottom line. The ray of light.

*Why?*

This human necessity to murder and die for the same Muslim-Judeo-Christian god. It's been going on for four-thousand years. The differences between these groups are less than the similarities. So, what is it? Centuries ago it was Catholics versus Protestants, theocratic wars and massacres, conveniently forgotten. Before that, it was Moors versus Christians. Christians versus Jews. It never stops... But it all *started* somewhere. Before Mormons and Muslims, Baptists and Catholics, Moses and Abraham.

It started somewhere.

Some goatherd in a cave.

We take it for granted now – this is just the way things are. *When is it time for it to stop? Burn the tambourines.* If it's alright for a million whack-jobs to get bloody just because someone doesn't take their imaginary friend seriously, who's getting riled at *this* lot? Who's taking them down? Where are the fixers, the people of good will? Where are the angry agnostics?

Where are the heroes in *this* war.

Make me a badge. Sign me up.

The kitchen light snaps off. Annie thumps down the hall.

I glance at the clock on my screen.

It's 12:30. *Christ.* I've been sitting here staring at the spreadsheet for an hour.

"Supper's in the oven," Annie crows, half-snitty.

"I'll be out in a sec!"

There's movement at the door.

"Bob?"

I look up. "Hmm?"

Annie is wearing sweats and the old *Patriots SUPERBOWL XXXI* singlet. "It's twelve-thirty."

"I'll be out in a min—"

She squints her tired eyes, and scratches her hip. "You want coffee?"

"No thanks."

She pads away.

And I'm reminded of that night, nineteen years ago, when I stood here with Matt... Before the phone rang.

*"Ristretto,"* replied Matt. *"Two."*

Then the phone rang. The old lighthouse keeper had an accident.

I look up at the empty space on the wall where Matthias' replica Rosetta Stone once hung on wire, under a miniature spotlight.

And then it hits me like a flying anvil.

It's like if I'm the second person in the world to see the atom, the son-in-law of Bernoulli, or Copernicus... overhearing a snatch of conversation about the Earth orbiting the Sun. But this is bigger. *Much* bigger.

I look back at the Numbers.

The more I consider it – all the notes in all the books, every angle, wondering if I haven't missed something – the more I flip through the book stacks, and double-check my facts... The more certain I am:

I've just made the most important discovery of all.

I reach for the phone to call Diffner, and glance at my screen. It's 2:30. Do I pull Diffner out of bed anyway? No. He'll be awake in a few hours. I'll go to his house.

I tip-toe upstairs and crawl into bed.

This changes everything. *Everything.*

I lay awake until dawn.

## 12. '...A STRONG DELUSION...'

*Monday, September 10, 2012*

I call Diffner as sunrise hits the drapes.

"Bob?"

"I've got some Numbers to show you."

"Now?" Diffner croaks. There's a voice in the background. "It's Bob," whispers Clark, muffled.

I miss what just happened, blurting excitedly, "These numbers are gonna blow your mind." The light of day hasn't diminished the brightness of my discovery. When Diffner sees what I've got, he's gonna backflip out of his chair.

"Okay." He gives me an address on Beacon Street, Beacon Hill, which is like finding Mayfair on a Monopoly board.

I guzzle some eggs, hit the road with a bubble fizzing in my gut like a twisted inner tube. Clenched up against butt-wrongs, I drive into Boston, too distracted to notice the silver-grey Lincoln with Massachusetts registration plates following me out of New Brid.

The whole way, I'm thinking what to say – how to sell this to Diffner. I park the Beemer on Beacon Street, next to Boston Common, barely noticing the Lincoln parking behind me.

As I step out of the car, my attention goes to the five-storey mansion.

There's no way a public servant buys such an extravagant pad. Not even with twenty-five years of exemplary service. This house belongs to a Founding Father tea magnate, a descendant from the *Mayflower*. Not this guy. Unless he's old money, or bent, or well married – and the latter seems doubtful.

I double-check the scribbled note, and mount the path to the stoop.

Recessed in a deep, panelled alcove, the front door boasts a bronze bumble bee door-knocker with the weight and thunder of a cannonball.

A figure ghosts in the glass of the crystal fanlight above the door, and the etched panes on either side, crossing the hall.

The latch turns, swinging away, and in Diffner's place stands Madison.

"Bob."

"Madi–?"

She's standing there grinning, barefoot, with wet hair. One leg is cocked sideways, towel over her shoulder, white elastic shorty-shorts and space-age sports-bra to stop her tits from bouncing when he pounds the stair-master, tits like tow-balls. "Come in."

I lean back to double-check the address against the scrawled note. "Wait– What... are you doing *here?*"

"Jeez Bob, you look like shit," she smirks. "Come in."

"Bad face day– What are you *doing* here?"

"Clark didn't tell you?" She laughs, the muscles in her abdomen bunching. "Clark!" she shouts, twisting her head. "You didn't tell him?"

Jeezus. The guy must ne fifty-five years old!

Madison tilts her head. "Clark's in the *drawing room.*"

"Hang on a sec," I balk. "How do you know Clark?"

"Clark was a friend of Dad's for years," answers Madison matter-of-factly, as if it explains everything. Seeing my surprise, she adds: "Who do you think got you the job?"

Madison turns and bounces down the hall on the balls of her feet, flicking an arm in the direction I should go.

I didn't see this coming. Maddie is making the beast-with-two-backs with her old man's friends? I feel strangely seasick as I step inside, rolled spreadsheet tucked under my wing, and turn to look in the direction she pointed...

I'm past being any more surprised, when I witness the interior of the aristocratic 1920's Beacon Street mansion. I guess I expected sweeping staircases, serpentine-rounded walls, curved mahogany doors, and maybe – beneath the mounds and mildew – it's here. But left and right, all I can see are twisted ziggurats of old books, honeycombed maps, shaggy boles of bundled periodicals sprouting leaflets. Archive boxes occupy every available space. The house is a strew. A horde. The stairs are lined with threadbare tomes; cracked leather spines ranging from aged first editions, to Readers Digest five-in-one condensed biosolids. International periodicals – *Humanité, Le Monde, Alto Adige, Repubblica, Nueu Zurcher Zeitung* – lay in drifts. Amidst the dusty sextants and barometers, faded cartons, and the brooding, sinewed bronze anatomie, I can't see a stick of usable furniture. Not a table, not a chair, that isn't stacked high with paper.

I step through a pillared arch into a double parlour-room, where the book shambles impedes on the floor-to-ceiling view of Boston Common.

The room reeks like a second-hand bookstore, the funk of paper-mould and decayed tobacco are lifted only slightly by the acrid hum of pinecones fizzing in the fireplace. A dusty chandelier hangs – webbed – in the vaulted ceiling. The only light emanates from a pitted chrome floor lamp, reflected in a fenestration of gilt-framed certificates on the panelled wall.

Amidst the chaos in the parlour stands a burnished Chesterfield couch, a chequered sofa chair, a liquor cabinet, and Diffner – seated on the couch. He's hunched over the coffee table, hacking at a tired-looking *DELL* notebook.

I'm reminded again how startling he is to look at, built like a kitted-up Quarterback spliced under a debauched-out Caligula butternut. It's the kind of face you wouldn't trust to take your pooch for a walk.

"Bob. Good to see you," Diffner coughs. "Come in."

I step into the parlour.

"Pardon the mess. I mostly use this house for storage. What can I get you to drink?" The old spook clears a stack of paper from the armchair.

I spot the highball charged by the couch, with a crumpled pack of Ritz crackers spread on newspaper. I check my watch. It's nine o'clock in the morning. Diffner is already taking a whiff from the barrel.

"You *know* Madison?!" I squeak. *In the Biblical sense.*

"She *recommended* you," Diffner offers earnestly. "Sit. Sit."

I sink into the linty wingback, and my knees shoot up under my chin, nearly cracking me in the jaw.

"Did you say scotch?" Diffner moves to the well-trafficked liquor cabinet.

"No. Thanks. I'm pacing myself." My head is spinning enough as it is. *Madison recommended me?*

"*Caol Ila?*" Diffner suggests as he tops up his own glass, as if the incantation will change my mind. It's the same salty, single cask-strength Islay Malt that Matt used to drink.

"No sale."

"I have to say," Diffner takes a sip. "I wasn't expecting your call. You're really attacking this project with surprising vigour."

"I haven't begun anything firm," I reply, wondering already how I'm going to explain this to Annie, when Madison opens her yap. "I just jotted down a few facts last night to narrow the target. Standard process."

Diffner turns to peer at me quizzically. He pauses, silent, thinking. "Wait here." And he disappears into the hallway.

I sit for several minutes wondering where he's gone – where Madison is – before my legs go numb, and I grunt my way out of the chair.

The first picture frame on the glory wall contains a Letter of Recognition for ten years of service as President of the International Society of Atheists. In the upper left-hand side of the adjacent certificate, are the words 'Archbishopric of Boston, Massachusetts. Chancellery-Secretaryship' and a printed seal.

The frame holds a letter from the Archbishop, to the President of an Atheist's Society. To the man who cracked Vatican Incorporated?

I slide back a pair of volumes:

*His Most Reverend Excellency the Auxiliary Bishop and Vicar-General of this Archbishopric is pleased to authorize Mr. Clark Joseph Diffner, a priest that dwells in this Archdiocese, to go into foreign countries in the cause of his ministry.*

*Boston. October 27 1969. Chancellery-Secretary.*

Another surprise.

'Our Man in Rome' was – forty-three years ago – a priest.

I scan the wall for similar insights. Between the elliptical geometry of book piles, I find a Doctorate of Divinity at Boston College, and a series of framed photos of Diffner as a young man dressed in a habit, standing with Cardinal-types in front of Saint Peter's Basilica in Rome.

*A priest?*

Kicked out, dropped out – maybe with a penchant for tall, leggy blondes who look twenty years his junior – he joins the CIA, and runs intelligence on the Holy See...

I can only speculate... An idealistic young man's confusion and dismay, reconciling a vow of celibacy with a repressed 1960's sexuality... The dilemma... Clark, in his youth, flees the church? Tries the old jingly-jangly. And bi-curious George de-programmes himself, and is recruited by the CIA to open up the Vatican? What crucial knowledge must he have as a young Jesuit, tutored in Rome...? To march into the Vatican and eyeball his former brothers as an agent of Federal intelligence...

I hear a squabble erupt in the hall, too polite to be distinguishable, but pitched enough to get the idea.

*What the fuck is Madison doing here?*

"Show me what you've got," says Diffner, standing behind me.

I spin around, thinking Diffner is referring to the two books I've picked up. I hold up the pair of volumes. "Oh." *The spreadsheet.*

I reach under my wing, and offer Diffner the rolled A3 with my usual deference. "The Numbers."

Diffner sits, swills his drink, put on his glasses, and adjusts the cushions. He lights a cigar, shifts in the seat, coughs, wipes his nose, refolds his handkerchief, and unrolls the spreadsheet.

"What the hell is this?"

The hairs on the back of my neck bristle. "Hmm?"

"This."

"Well...I was thinking about how the same religious differences that manifest as terrorism, also manifest in other forms..."

Diffner peers over his glasses. "What?"

"I went broad. To capture the wider issue."

"The *wider issue?* What are you talking about?"

"Look," I whisper. "I had an idea... I actually wanted to talk about something else..."

"That's a relief." Diffner tosses the sheet onto the table.

Madison romps into the room, and props herself on the arm of the fat burnished Chesterfield like she's on the cover a motoring magazine. She slings her arm around Diffner's neck, smitten kitten.

"Bob was just telling me," narrates Diffner. "He didn't come here to talk about the *project?*"

I grab the sheet, unroll it, and point to the top corner of the page. "Here... The Order of the Solar Temple... An infant, aged three months, was killed in October, Ninety-Four in Quebec, a wooden stake through his heart. Because the baby was believed to be The Antichrist...In Eighty-Two, Bradley Lonadier – age three – and the next year John Yarbough age twelve, were also killed during ritual beatings by Solar Temple cult leaders—"

Clark smiles politely. "What on *earth* are you talking about?" He takes out a soapstone pipe, and begins packing the bowl.

Madison smirks strangely, like she is enjoying the show.

I press the page. "Fifteen inner-circle members committed suicide by use of poison. Forty-eight more were shot, smothered, or burned by their friends. November sixteenth, Nineteen-Ninety-Five: Thirteen adults and three children of the group disappeared, and were found dead in a forest. The Coroner determined they didn't die willingly: Two members *drugged* the others, poured gasoline over the bodies, set them on fire, then shot themselves and fell into the flames. March thirtieth, Ninety-Seven, five more burned down a house with themselves in it—"

Diffner sets his highball down hard. "What has this got to do with anything?"

"Hear me out," I press. "April nineteenth, Nineteen-Ninety-Three, Federal agents attempted to execute warrants on Branch Davidians at Waco, and were engaged in a gun-battle with the cult. Four agents and several Davidians died in gunfire. Sixteen more A.T.F. agents were wounded. A fifty-one-day siege followed. Pyrotechnic gas canisters were fired into the compound and eighty-one cult members died, some from gunshot wounds, others burned alive. The bodies were so badly damaged Coroners never established an exact number. I put it down as eighty-one..."

"Where are you going with this?"

"November eighteenth, Nineteen-Seventy-Eight. Armed members of The People's Temple Full Gospel Church opened fire on a Congressman at Port Kiatuma airfield in Guyana. The Congressman, three members of the press, and a cult member were killed. Eleven were wounded. Six-hundred-and-thirty-eight adults, and two-hundred-

and-seventy-six children committed suicide by drinking grape *Kool-Aid* laced with cyanide, liquid Valium, Penegram, and chloral hydrate. Others died by injection, or were shot."

"Bob—"

"Friday, March seventeenth, Two-*thousand*-six-hundred followers of the *Movement for the Restoration of the Ten Commandments of God* in Uganda were boarded up inside a church, and incinerated alive. Bodies were discovered beneath houses owned by the cult. Poisoned, garrotted, mutilated..." I point to the rows on the chart.

Madison leans forward.

"155 bodies in Rugazi, Bushenyi on March 27.

"153 bodies in Rutooma, Rukungiri district on March 25.

"81 bodies in Rushojwa, Rukungiri on March 30.

"55 bodies in Buziga, Kampala on April 27.

"The leader of the church was a Catholic priest named Dominic Kataribabo, who attended Loyola Marymount Dominican College in *California*, on a church scholarship. Police found bodies, including five children under a newly poured cement floor in Kataribabo's house. Another seventy-four mutilated and strangled bodies – including twenty-eight *children* – were found in his backyard. Estimates placed the total *number* killed by the cult at *four thousand*... more than the victims of the World Trade Centre attacks. All were led to believe that the Virgin Mary was coming to save them from the destruction of the world."

Diffner rises off the couch. "I'm really too busy to—"

"Hang on! Al-Qaeda... Vatican Inc... This is about *more* than terrorism. It's happening *everywhere*. It *always* has been!" I pick up the spreadsheet, and wave it at Diffner. "Three billion people believe in this god! Every day, with the prayers and singing. Mums and Dads giving it to their kids while they're going in for Santa and the Tooth Fairy. It's *not* just Islam – Fatah Tahzim, Hamas, Al-Qaeda – with the homicidal whack-jobs. It's *all* of them. Christian! Roman Catholic! The further you go back, the more of it there is, *all* the way back!"

Diffner is staring at me, slack-jawed.

Madison's smile has vanished.

"Look! The Torah, Qur'an, fifty different Bibles, Apocrypha, Book of Mormon, Dead Sea Scrolls, Nag Hammadi, they *all* agree it started with Abraham. After that, they diverged, become inaccessible, obscure. They begin fighting with each other. Each dogma became so convoluted, laden with ritual – one Bible says we live by Faith, the other says Works. One says Baptism, the other says Confession. Predestination or Free-will. They all start adding their own ideas. One group says Israel belongs to the Jews, the other says Arabs. One praises Mary. The other says American Indians descended from Israelites. The *Devil* is in the detail. The ambiguity. Apocryphal books. Different prophets. The rules become vague – inconsistent, compiled centuries after the events they describe. Passages are added and removed. Verses are retracted. Mohammed claims Satan deceived him into writing lies, and recants his prophecies. Gospels are removed a Nicea. Supporting documents are stitched in: the Talmud, the book of Jewish Laws, the oral histories, additional books of laws, the Islamic *ahadith*, the hundreds of versions of the Christian Bible..." I count them off on my hand. "K.J.V., New K.J.V., Revised N.K.J.V., American Standard, New American Standard, Revised New American Standard, New International, Revised N.I.V., the Catholic Bible, Seven Day Adventist, Gideons... All based on different translations, by different experts, from different scraps of papyrus, and incomplete Greek texts. *Vaticanus, Sinaiticus, Alexandrinus, Zacynthius, Ephraemi–*"

Diffner raises a hand. "Okay! Bob, I don't need the lecture–"

But I'm on a roll, chattering like a wind-up robot, shooting sparks from my mouth.

Madison is grinning her piano-key smile again!

"All the ambiguity, human error, inaccessibility, and confusion... The crusades, holy wars, massacres, witch hunts, inquisitions–"

"Bob!" Diffner shakes his head, making blue smoke genies with his pipe.

"You see? It's sticking out like a boner in sweatpants! Four thousand years ago. *Abraham*, back there in Genesis, one-on-one, pals with the Maker. It all started there, *with ONE MAN!*"

Diffner leans out of the couch, and knocks the pipe ash into the fireplace.

"Don't you see? It *all* starts with Abraham!"

Diffner is unimpressed.

"...Then Moses, then Jesus comes two-thousand years later. Three-hundred years after that Emperor Constantine turns Christianity into Catholicism. Another three-hundred years after that Mohammed lifts Judeo-Christian stories from Bahera, mixes in local Qurayš rituals, and starts Islam. A thousand years later, Martin Luther nails his Thesis to the Wittenberg door and starts Protestantism. Now we've got half the world – a billion Catholics, a billion Muslims, a billion other Christians – all knocking each other off and claiming divine precedent, competing for the same real estate! Two-thirds of the mayhem in the world, started with one man!"

Diffner glares at me expectantly. "Are you done?"

"Don't you see what this means?"

"Bob, thanks for the impassioned— Wait, let me guess: By revealing this discovery to the world – that every major religion started with one man – you think everyone will beat the swords into ploughshares, go home, and pack up the hate?"

I shake my head. "No."

Diffner sighs wearily. "So what *is* your point?"

I choose the words carefully. "What if there's a *Rosetta Stone* for religion?"

Diffner opens his mouth, like he's about to laugh, but no sound emerges.

"There have been significant finds of clay tablets dating back centuries before Abraham, at Kish and Uruk in north Babylonia. The first known *writing* was found on a small limestone tablet from Kish in Iraq, thirty-five-hundred B.C. At Uruk, several hundred clay tablets have been found, dated *before* three-thousand B.C. All are too primitive to be read, but some demonstrate cuneiform like the Dead Sea scrolls. So... what if – before the Ten Commandments – there was an original *tablet?* An original message from god. Before the Bible, Torah or Qur'an?"

Diffner breaks into a fit of coughing, trying to speak...

"You'd have a billion Muslims, a billion Catholics, and a billion other Christian sects, *all* sharing the same message. The same god. Before Mohammed. Before Jesus!"

"You're out of your mind—"

"Why?"

Diffner groans. "Boy. You really don't get it."

"It all ends! All the massacres and mayhem. No more terrorism. No more of the people like the guy that went nuts in Norway... Wouldn't that be something? No more! Wouldn't that force the question right round the world, that it's *all the same god?*"

Diffner is just awkward enough, off balance, startled and restless, to give me my big kick. "It would change the *world!*"

Diffner chews his lip for a moment. "Bob, it's a noble concept, but it's not that simple. There are other factors: Sovereignty. Culture. Ethnicity—"

But I'm on a downhill run now. "Bullshit!"

"I beg your pardon?"

"Bullshit! Muslim extremists from Afghanistan don't mind palling up with extremists in Indonesia. Same goes for Jews, Christians, and Catholics... Brothers and sisters under god. Religious unity *transcends* other differences. The only thing missing is a common link!"

"You're being *entirely* unrealistic."

"I'm only asking '*what if?*'"

"'What if' what?"

"What if these three billion people, were *all* on the same side?"

"But there *is* no tablet."

"I know."

"Then what's your point?"

"We make it up."

Diffner is visibly rattled. "What?"

"We set it up! A parchment. *I, Abraham, from Ur of the Chaldeans...* We uncover it in Jerusalem on the temple site. We set up a dig, plant the scroll in a jar, let someone find it. Arrange some credible experts. *Bang!* The scroll does the rest. There are enough people out there just dying for this kind of thing. An end to the violence. It's simple. It's seamless. We can't fall off."

Diffner rises from his chair, and glances at Madison, baffled. "Bob, you're being completely naïve! Even if Abraham himself came back on a magic cloud and told everyone they'd got it wrong, with his own mouth – you know what they'd say as they strapped him into the electric chair? '*Our prophets warned us about guys like you.*' Even in the face of incontrovertible proof—"

Madison speaks for the first time, leaning back on her wrists. "*You* changed."

Clark is visibly startled. "What? That's different."

I'm so busy sandbagging, I miss the way Madison leapt to my aid. "What about the way you guys set up coups to overthrow Arbenz in Guatemala? Mossadegh in Iran... Aidid in Somalia? You can't tell me religious fundamentalism is *less* of a threat than the President of some third-world country?"

"'*Us*' guys?" Clark balks.

"It's the same thing, but you'd be overthrowing the worst dictators of all! People are sick of it. The whole thing. Jews versus Muslims versus Christians. It has to stop. It's the *same damn god.* All that's missing is proof!" I huff. "You don't think it's worth a try?"

"Robert..." Diffner answers coolly, drawing away from Madison. "You should leave." Diffner jerks his smouldering pipe at the front door. "Please."

"Hang on—" This isn't how I'd pictured this playing out.

"I've heard enough. Here." He hands back the spreadsheet.

My head is throbbing like a Jack-o'-lantern. The heat is coming off my brow in waves. "*Jeezus Diffner!* Someone has to stop these Rushdie-bombing, child-beating whack-jobs murdering people for *no fucking reason!*" I raise my voice. "How can you *not* want to do something?"

Diffner remains expressionless.

"Fine." Dissatisfied with the proportions of the fuck-up I've already made, I make a little hand-washing pantomime. "This is the reason nothing has changed for four thousand years," and I start for the door. "'Bye Madison."

As I turn the latch, I can't be sure what's more frustrating: Diffner not sharing my sentiment, the unformed knowledge I've just made a tragic, career-ending error of judgment... or the suspicion that Diffner is right.

As I stamp out of the dim grotto, I hear Diffner mutter to Madison: "Matt would have ripped him to pieces if he'd heard that..."

I'm riled. Mostly at myself. I've made a mistake here. A Himalayan blunder. I stayed up all night reading about the worst horror and mayhem in the world, and had a crazy idea. In a fit of impulse, an ideological fervour, I just took the show on the road and insulted a man who can end my career with one phone call... and I did it in front of Annie's sister.

Diffner is right.

I've slipped off the ladder.

Lou Maas sits patiently in a silver-grey Lincoln on Beacon Street, outside Diffner's house, watching the front door – close enough to pick up a radio signal.

Tucked in his ear is a tiny ear-bud.

'*...This is the reason nothing has changed for four thousand years...*'

He watches me storm out of the townhouse in a huff, fists clenched like I'm pushing a wheelbarrow.

Boston Common is too conspicuous for him to make a move, but it doesn't matter. He knows now what I know.

Maas starts the Lincoln, and pulls out behind my BMW, yanking out the ear-bud, and dialling his car phone.

*"Yes?"*

He says something like, "Travis just showed up at Diffner's house bright and early, and spilled everything..."

*"What about Diffner?"*

"Neither of them know shit."

*"Be careful,"* answers the voice on the other end of the line. *"Diffner is dangerous."*

"Maybe he was once..." replies Maas. "But he's sweeping his house for bugs with a gramophone needle."

*"Just be careful. He's been in the game a long time."*

And maybe Maas is cautious enough to add that it won't be long before one of us figures out what is really going on.

## 13. '...PEACE... THEN SUDDEN DESTRUCTION...'

*Tuesday, September 11, 2012*

It's the eleventh anniversary of the second World Trade Centre attack.

I wake at the Amish crack of dawn. The house phone is ringing.

*"Hi Bob. I'm calling from the office of Bill Dodd at the Anacostia Institute. The Director would like you to come to D.C. today... He needs to talk to you. He's sending a car from Arlington to wait for you at the airport."*

I can't say 'no.'

I creep into the bathroom, and look myself in the mirror.

I'm not sure what I'm looking at. I've seen the way that Annie checks herself over, and decides she needed to change her hair, work out, eat better... I just look at my reflection, and don't know exactly *where* to start. It's not something fixed that easily.

I look wailed-on. There are dark circles under my eyes. I do my best to tidy myself up. Tailored suit, Windsor knot, white cuffs and collar, knife-edge creases... I drive down to Logan, park, and wait nervously to board my flight to Washington.

I find a seat at the bar in the club lounge, and sip a drink, watching a jumbo refuel on the far side of the glass.

Diffner must have called Dodd as soon as I left his house. *Can I level with these guys?* Tell them about my troubles? It had been a terrible mistake. *'Right up my alley,'* Diffner had said. Gordon wouldn't take this well. How do I explain this? If I lose the Anacostia contract *and* SSL's business, I'm folded. *Bustaroo.*

The sky outside is blue. Not a cloud. It's a flying day: A breezy, Orville and Wilbur, kite-flying day.

The TV in the corner of the room is flashing images of the World Trade Centre Attacks, 11 years ago – to the day.

Recap: Friday, February 26, 1993 – A car bomb detonates in the parking garage under Tower One of the World Trade Center.

A flash-back news reader erroneously attributes the 2001 tragedy to a radar error, a technical glitch, guiding flights out of JFK into a faulty antenna on top of the tower. Then, it's a crazed airline pilot. Finally, the word *hijack.* And then someone says *both* flights are from right here, in Boston. Right where I'm sitting. Three hours before the attack, the sick evil fundies were right in this building, checking in their bags with their smiles and their leaky pits. Forty minutes from my house.

Suddenly someone *wails* across the terminal, making me jump. *"Jeezus."*

At first, I think it's the playback...

The crowd in front of the monitor grows. Just like the first time... folks stand and listen, as the amateur footage played of a jumbo jet vanishing into the steel-and-glass façade, to an anthem of screams... News of the last-minute phone calls... a third plane in D.C. Another one, near Pittsburgh...

I rest my head on my arms.

I sense a buzz, a fear-Doppler, gossiping through the crowd behind me, like a primal spine-alert...

People are whispering to each other, overhearing, whispering to the next person. *What is it?*

Something is off.

The woman at the bar next to me turns and said, "Oh my god!"

I look up.

I see the first snoops at the television, and horror rises up around me.

I stand off my stool, and walk over.

The images on the screen are wrong...

There's the same speculation, rumour and panic at the news desk, but they're talking about a *subway*?! The collapse of the towers took out a section of subway track, but it was never *this* big a deal...

There's a boarding call for my flight, but the voice on the PA sounds uncertain.

The vision on the television changes...

This time, the amateur video is shot from the window of a car on the Brooklyn Queens Expressway... The camera swings from swerving traffic... across to the New York skyline... To a geyser of grey water shooting out of the East River.

The title at the bottom of the screen reads:

### TERRORIST ATTACK ON NEW YORK SUBWAY

There are screams, not on the television, around me. Everywhere. Up close in my ears. Telepathic screams.

On the monitor, people are scrambling out of the New York metro stairwells covered in dust and blood. Journalists yell into cameras, hysterical.

I look down, and find the scotch still in my hand, ice melted, condensation dripping off my elbow. I watch the glass as it slips from my hand, shattering on the tiles.

"What happened?" I ask, distractedly. "*What happened?*"

The airport stands frozen. The air has disappeared in a collective gasp. The faces are blank, suffocating. People are circling strangely, looking for something... waiting for god or Jesus or the police...

"We can now confirm," announces a female reporter - people emerging from a dust-cloud behind her on a New York street - "there has been an explosion on the New York subway, under the East River. According to witnesses, there is water flowing into subway tunnels downtown... A number of fires have all broken out... At this time it isn't clear—"

The broadcast cuts to a newsreader. "Reports are coming in of a coordinated attack on subway tunnels in major cities... We can confirm one of them includes San Francisco's Transbay Tube..."

*Fuck!* I grab for my cell-phone. "Shit." I checked my briefcase with general baggage, so I wouldn't have to carry it round... And my phone is inside. I look for a payphone, and see a queue the length of the concourse. I don't want to go back to my car. I have to know more. *What happened?* I join the crowd at the TV screens.

*"...explosions have been reported in Pittsburgh's Allegheny River tunnel... the Chicago River subway, near State Street... and Washington's Green Line tunnel under the Anacostia River, causing flooding at the Pentagon subway stations... and here in Boston—"*

The crazies from the chart.

The sick Rushdie-bombing suicide freaks. Hamas, Fatah Tahzim, the same guys from the Embassy attacks, *U.S.S. Cole.* Khobar Towers. The World Trade Centre. It's the 'R's. The big red 'R's from the spreadsheet. The numbers multiply and blur. *How many people are there on the New York subway? Ten-thousand?* It's rush hour. Maybe twenty-thousand? It's past counting. The weight of it. Worse than all the suicide bombers, and the drive-bys. All the gunfire and rocket launching. The cults and the buried believers. Worse than anywhere. It feels like the end, all over again. If the TV flickers into a test pattern, this is it. It's over. I can't watch. I can't look. More footage... A young girl covered in slime dragged through a manhole... A policeman tripping up a stairwell carrying the slate-grey body... I can't fathom or bear it. My heart is sprained. I rush outside to the pick-up area, clutching my chest, across the street where the cars are stopped still.

I weave home, with the radio off. Then on. Where is god *now?* Where the *fuck* is he? What has *he* done? I know now in my gut, for certain. There is no other explanation. The way everything has gone. For the first time, I *know* it. He's not there. But who else is there to help? And there's no such thing as an accident. Everything is finite. Cause and Effect. Our sick human need led to this. All of it started *somewhere*. It can't be tolerated, the intolerance. No more permission for this... This lack of courage to face reality. The childish fear and stupidity. The false borders, the pointless divisions. The friction and walls. The constant murder. It has to stop.

This supersedes analysis. There's no need for spreadsheets or rhetoric, Uncle Sam. Diffner will be thinking the same thing. They have to tear down the sacred institutions. Right now.

I drive through New Brid at top speed, round the toe of the beach toward the house, blinking tears from my eyes. Stalled people stand in the street, loping into the open for human contact, reassurance, empathy, checking the World is still here.

I run through the front door.

The TV is on. I stand for a moment at the top of the steps.

Annie twists, and comes hurtling at me, flinging her arms around my middle, squeezing me until my legs tingled. "*Thank god you're okay!* I couldn't reach you. I didn't know if there were *planes!*"

*How lucky I am.* How grateful. I'm small and weak and dumb. How would she have heard about, if it *had* been me? What would have happened to her and Joe? "God. Sweetheart..."

Annie looks up at me, overwrought. "Where were you? *Where were you?*"

"I should have called. I should have pulled over." *What if?* Disappeared, in dust and flames. The TV mourns in the background.

"What's *happening?*" Annie asks, forlorn. "What's *happening, Bob?*"

"I don't know."

"I hope Maddie's okay."

"Maddie?"

"She flew back to New York last night!"

It's like a bolt right out of the blue. "*What?!*"

"She had a fight with her boyfriend, and took the red-eye back to New York—"

"You spoke to her?"

"Last night!"

I hem-and-haw. I only saw Madison as Diffner's yesterday! Annie didn't know? "Have you tried to call her?"

"Cell phones in New York are all jammed up." Annie looks terrified.

"She wouldn't take the subway."

"Yeah..."

I can't help it. "She had a fight with her *boyfriend?*" I wade in.

"A friend of Dad... she met at the funeral."

"Really?" I can't pass comment – or pretend not to know. I've already been too economical with the truth...

"I'm sure she's *fine!*" Annie snorts.

I walk to the den, and sink three straight highballs of Hendricks, before slumping at the desk. *Madison didn't tell Annie what happened at Diffner's house? She had a fight with him? About what happened yesterday? Fuck!* She met Diffner at the funeral. There's *nothing* more like Maddie than screwing one of Matt's friends to say 'goodbye.'

Now she's somewhere *in there,* in all the hell and chaos.

Seated in front of the pile of books, it's worse, the frustration. If Diffner won't listen now, others will. I'm certain. Men who topple governments. The kind of men who overthrow tyrants. If these men can bring down Presidents, they can bring down churches. The man-made borders. The walls and fences. There will be a mandate, now, after this. The same agents who took on the Vatican, who destabilised nations, these men will see the need to *depose god.*

The red 'R's on the computer screen bleed together, blurred by my tears.

The desk phone rings.

I pick it up before Annie can get to the line.

"Bob. It's Clark." Diffner sounds drained, distracted. "Come see me. Not at the house. Across the street in the Common. Tomorrow morning. Six a.m."

"Tomorrow morning, Six a.m."

"Bob?"

"Yeah?"

"Let me know straight away if you hear from Madison?"

I try to think what to say...

"You better keep the line free."

Diffner hangs up.

Eyes strained with fatigue, I reach up onto the bookshelf, and take down a Bible.

I used to know this book inside-out, once. I'm not so sharp on it now, the chapter and verse. However, a lot of it lurks in my brain. I trawl through faded recollections, piecing together my plan...

I try to remember how I ever used to pray. *God... If you're there...* Who are you, old man? *What do you want? Are you listening? How do I know?* By reading some thousand-year-old told around the fire by men in sandals? Ignorant, bigoted, fearful, smelly, superstitious men?

No.

You are not there. You are not listening. Not today.

An end to terror.

Diffner will help me now.

On a dry day, the bilges in the Manhattan subway system pump 13 million gallons of water into the sewer.

All over New York, underground motors switch on, straining to force the flood of water down pipes and tunnels. Overflows spew gouts of muck into the Hudson, but not fast enough. The East River is roaring into the Joralemon tunnel. Failing pumps back-up the fetid muck into the transport network, and the roiling water gushes down underground pedestrian walkways connecting the number 4 and 5 lines. The black tide surges down the connecting tunnel to Whitehall station – and the 1, 2, and 3 lines.

Startled commuters flee ahead of foam and sludge, crowding into turnstiles. The surge becomes a waterfall down stairways and escalators. Rapids form in platforms. The panicked screams of passengers echo down tunnels, over the roar and gurgle.

On the number 4 lines – heading north past South Ferry to Wall Street – a speeding Express train slams into the approaching water at break-neck speed, *whipping* to a halt, flinging passengers forward.

The water churns relentlessly north, around the wheels, lurching toward the interconnected tunnels of the Fulton Street Transit Centre Complex and the Dey Street Concourse – with it's spraycrete walls and rows of bare steel piles. There, the water-head crosses to the A, C, J, M and C lines at Broadway-Nassau, boiling westward along the unfinished concourse into the basement of the World Trade Centre transit hub.

The murky flood sloshes along all four of the main arteries through Manhattan Island, coursing into ventilation shafts, pump rooms, maintenance tunnels, sewer overflows, stall tracks, and loops... dusty, incomplete platforms at Houston St, Essex St, and South 4 St... long-abandoned stations at City Hall, Worth Street, and 18th Street... Wherever the water travels – trickling through drains, pooling in culverts, rushing down corridors, flooding into basements – it flushes out a century of filth and litter, setting off plumes of electrical sparks. Fires erupt in cupboards and ducts as shredded, rat-holed newspaper bursts into flame, belching smoke, pumping gouts of toxic ash and coal dust through vents into the boulevards and alleyways. From the Hudson to the East River, the putrid stench clouds the streets, to a million cries of terror.

Fifteen minutes after the first explosion, the narrow cross-town platform of the IRT Flushing Line – deep below New York's Grand

Central Terminal – stands like a concrete island, swallowed by the churning black subterranean river.

Water sweeps away the burning briefcase near where Madison was standing... flames guttering as it sinks off the edge of the platform.

The lights go out.

In the weak glow from the stairs, Madison spots a black, moulded plastic garbage bin in the middle of the platform, and runs to it, hitching up her dress, and climbs on top. With her tail-bone and heels tucked on the rim, knees under her chin, she watches the black water gush over the platform ...

Echoing over the sinister *hiss* of sparks and roaring water, reverberating off the ceiling of the darkened chamber, is the sound of desperate screams.

Madison wriggles forward onto her heels, crouching on top of the garbage can, as the rising water sloshes beneath her, in darkness...

At eighty feet below street level, the IRT Flushing line platform is the deepest in Grand Central. Water gushes down the tracks from both ends, as Madison huddles on the garbage can, listening – frozen in shock and fear.

## 14. '...THE MYSTERY WHICH WAS KEPT SECRET...'

*Wednesday, September 12, 2012*

Diffner leans forward on a park bench under the grand old tree on the high side of Boston Common.

He looks crushed, but a flush of rage is rising through his neck.

I feel the same.

The afternoon breeze rustles through the leaves. Dead leaves cartwheel across the green carpet.

I sit stiff-backed, despite a week-and-a-half without sleep. There's a foul taste in my mouth. I'm beyond exhaustion. I'm sick in my bones with the horror of the past week.

It's strange. The Common is deserted... There are no basking students, lunching office workers, dog walkers, kids tossing Frisbees... Not even the sound of traffic. Nothing. Just the wind, and the leaves. The old park, the historic hub of Boston village, the oldest urban public park in the world, is again virgin pasture.

And two impotently angry men sit together on a bench trying to fathom it.

I've lost every shred of joy or optimism. Everybody has...

For me, everything has been unwinding ever since Matt died. But now, there's nothing. The aftershock of the subway attacks has risen into sickening cocktail of sorrow and toe-curling rage. The sense of loss is overpowering. Not just the lives... The decent hard-working folks... The lost freedom. Everyone is inside, doors locked, huddled, confused, gaping at their televisions, watching the news... In San Francisco, passengers were killed by flooding in the Transbay Tube. In New York, Chicago, Pittsburgh, Washington and Boston, whole subway networks are now flooded. A hundred trains are trapped. Thousands of commuters faced grizzly deaths in submerged chambers. Cities are paralysed. At every station rescue crews are trying to free survivors, and recover bodies of victims. The city streets have turned into field morgues. Drowned, burned, suffocated, electrocuted, crushed bodies lay in rows...

Amateur video and eyewitness accounts of incomprehensible tragedy bombard the news desks: Stark, digitised images of helpless, bloody, weeping, mud-caked commuters hauled out of stairwells... Lost in darkened tunnels... New York is hardest hit. Manhattan Island is crippled. The financial capital of the world lies dying before our eyes, streets clogged with dead. A parade of experts speculate on the consequences of the disaster, the spread of disease, the cost... And every time the camera cuts to the streetscape, I wonder whether one of the wrapped bundles is Madison.

"We have to stop these *fuckers*," I growl, half-pleading.

Diffner just nods, slowly.

There is a long silence, with me checking my phone every few minutes for signs of life... No missed calls... It's 24 hours since the attack. Nobody has been able to reach anyone in New York. The phone lines are overloaded. Bridges and tunnels are cordoned off... All we have is what we can see on CNN.

Diffner tips his chin toward the eastern corner of the Common, at Park Street Station and Boylston Station. "See that over there... They were the first two subway stations in America. They used a horse-drawn carriage underground..."

"Yeah," I snap out of my reverie.

"I made some calls," he whispers. "Through closed channels. I had a guy check Madison's apartment..." His words trail away to nothing.

I turn my cell phone over in my hand where the helpless screen can't taunt me for a while. "You two had a fight?" Diffner and Madison. I still don't get it.

"Yeah... I really dicked the dog." Diffner rubs his knees, agitated.

"What did you fight about?"

"She went in to bat for you. She liked your idea, about the tablet."

When I'd brought him my deranged plan, at his house – across Beacon Street from the Common. *You changed*, Madison had said, speaking about Diffner. "Really?"

"I told her I was gonna have you pulled off the Anacostia project, and she left me." He swallows painfully. "*Fuck* I hope she's okay." He pulls the soapstone pipe from his pocket, and begins packing the bowl with trembling hands. "She said you were badly cut up about Matt dying, and I should give you another chance."

"It's not just about Matt," I suggest. But I have been badly *cut up*.

"Especially not now," sighs Diffner.

"Do you think it could work? The fake tablet?"

"I don't know."

"It seems pretty straightforward. We make up an ancient manuscript from Abraham that lays out some basic commandments... 'Thou shalt not kill'. It automatically overrides the Bible, the Torah, the Qur'an... Surely that changes everything, right?"

Diffner shakes his head. "It can't be clay."

"But all the archaeological finds from that period are clay..."

"But it's impossible to forge. Silicate mud has organic material that's too easily dated. It can't be papyrus either. Or vellum. They didn't exist... and they'd long since have turned to dust. Even the Copper Scroll in the Dead Sea scrolls was so badly corroded it was barely saved and it was only *half* the age we need."

"But you think it *might* work?"

"Maybe it's a stone, like you said. Like the Rosetta Stone."

Like the replica that hung, stately and imposing, in Matt's den. *That* night felt like a thousand years ago...

A tree sparrow pecks busily around in the grass near my feet, foraging for crumbs.

"Even if it stopped *half* these sick fuckers killing people... It would really be something." Diffner sighs. "It wouldn't be so bad if they kept going after each other... The fundies. It's the *innocent people* that get caught in the way!" he snarls. 'Innocent people' being Madison. It's in Diffner's eyes, he wants to kill someone. *Really* make them squeal.

"*If...* we *forge* the stone," I muse, "...it would have to be in some kind of secret dig in Jerusalem..."

Diffner shakes his head, chewing on the end of his pipe, threads of smoke whipping into the breeze. "They don't let *anyone* go digging in Jerusalem, for this exact reason. The Israeli Antiquities Authority has the place all tied up. The Temple site isn't even part of Israel or Jordan. And the Camp David Accord couldn't get *UNESCO* in there under World Heritage protection..."

"I read the Palestinians have been excavating around the Temple site, and dumping the fill in the river. What if something turned up *there?*"

"No. Three thousand years of treasure-hunters have turned every rock for miles around the city looking for relics... If it's not *in* the city on *unturned* soil, it won't fly. And Jerusalem has been razed and rebuilt more times than you can count. It's a layer-cake of ruins. You'd have to get to just the right place, right down the bottom. Nobody *ever* has. The last guy to get close was Charles Warren, two-hundred years ago. And I think he ended up getting tossed out of the country."

"So what do we do?" I ask rhetorically.

*Nothing. It won't work.*

Diffner is silent.

The tree sparrow pecks energetically in the grass. It strikes me, how the bird goes on with its business while all of human society grinds to a standstill.

"Madison had a better idea..." Diffner numbly teases a page of notes out of his jacket pocket, and rubs his tired eyes.

"Madison?"

"She suggested somebody *else* has already found it," Diffner nods.

"'*Found*' it?" The idea dawns on me gradually.

"That's how Oded Golan did it."

"Who is *Oded Golan?*"

"An Israeli antiquities dealer back in oh-one. He claimed to be representing an anonymous collector, selling a tablet from the temple of King Solomon. The tablet's authenticity was questioned, but never conclusively. Most say he found a correctly aged stone already cut to size in the wall of a crusader fortress up the coast from Tel Aviv, carved the inscription in it, and added a fake patina. With a little care, it could be done convincingly enough that it would never be faulted..."

"Wow. Really?" I feel a flutter in my bowels that might be fear, excitement, or a bad corn dog. "What happened to *that* guy?"

"He's still on trial in Jerusalem."

"Wow."

"If you think about Madison's idea, it's plausible... Titus Vespasianus, Emperor of Rome, captured Jerusalem in seventy-one AD. In book six of *War of the Jews*, Josephus wrote... when Titus' *soldiers set fire to the temple, he ordered them to stop, but it was too late. He entered the burning Holy of Holies to see the Ark of the Covenant...*"

The Ark of the Covenant was the Hebrew relic lost two-thousand years ago that supposedly held Moses' original Ten Commandments.

"*...What he found there was said to be beyond all rumor or expectation,*" finishes Diffner. "If the tablet was inside the Ark that would explain how it was kept secret for so long..."

"That was all Madison's idea?"

"Yeah."

"Wow."

"She thought if Titus took the treasure back to Rome, Emperor Constantine would have inherited it. Then the Vatican... That's the pattern. The Ark could easily contain tablets from *before* Moses, that only he knew about..."

I shake my head. "Would people believe it?"

"It works. Uncover the Ark, open it, find a *different* tablet instead of the Ten Commandments... Bait-and-switch... Tie in the Egyptian Pharaoh, Akhenaten who also converted to one god..."

"...Akhenaten of Amarna..."

"Right. He outlawed all previous religions in Egypt, *erased* them, every temple, and the plural word for 'gods' and *replaced* them – with the god, Aten. The same way Constantine did sixteen-hundred years later in Rome. It's a common thread... *both* these rulers were *in possession of the Ark* at the time they switched gods."

I stare at Diffner in disbelief. *No Shit?*

Madison was more her father's daughter than I knew.

"It explains why the Ark went missing."

You have to admire the thinking.

"The king of Babylon, Nebuchadnezzar, also like Akhenaten *and* Constantine, sacked the temple of Jerusalem in six-hundred B.C... He took the Ark as well, before the Hebrews took it back. He *also* converted the Babylonian empire to one god while he had the tablet."

"...It fits."

"In the first room of the Egyptian Museum in the Vatican, Pope Gregory Sixteenth displayed a scroll by Akhenaten. *Why* would a Pope of the Roman Catholic Church, celebrate a scroll from a Pharaoh who never appeared in the Bible? A pharaoh who followed a *sun*-god?"

"Why?"

"Those who've seen inside the Ark, know it's all the same god. Three kings from the *most powerful empires* in history. Rome, Egypt and Babylon... *all* three acquired the Ark, each about six-hundred years apart... And all *three* replaced the religions of their time with the god of Abraham. It works. Constantine's *Roman* church adapted the same rituals as Aten, *Sun*day, the Christmas festival, the Mother and Child symbolism... Ptolemy – Second, King of Egypt, grandfather of the Ptolemy from the *Rosetta Stone* – commissioned the original source for the Jewish Torah *and* the Christian Old Testament. It all works. Right through history the central cord, through at *least* three-thousand-three-hundred years of religion... every one of these people who kept these religions going, had possession of Moses' tablet, and all converted to variations on the same god."

It sounds like a cake-walk... "Imagine... *'proof'* Christians, Jews and Muslims are really all the same."

"The Muslim links are all there too. *Nabonidus* took over Babylon, married Nebuchadnezzar's daughter, and made the god *Sin*, god of the moon, with the crescent-moon emblem, and the lunar calendar, fasting on the lunar cycle... all followed by Muslims today. *He* had the tablet. *There's* the link to Islam... even before Mohammed."

"So Islam comes from the same tablet in the Ark?"

"The men who held this treasure – right down through history – *created* the religions followed by three billion people today. Get the words right, and it's *one god* for all."

"You think we could do this?"

"You still haven't heard the best part."

"What's that?"

"How did the tablet get into the Ark in the first place? From Abraham, to Akhenaten – *before* Nebuchadnezzar, there's a seven-hundred year gap." Diffner smiles crookedly.

"I don't know." I check my phone.

"It's the best story in the Bible... The *one* prophet shared by Jews, Christians, *and* Muslims, aside from Abraham... He's the highest prophet in Judaism *and* the most frequently quoted prophet in the Qur'an..."

"Moses?"

"Bingo. The Pharaohs enslave the Jews... Take Abraham's treasure... Ahmenhotep the Fourth becomes Pharaoh, reads the tablet, *changes his name* to Akhenaten, and converts Egypt to *Abraham's* god... He moves the capital to Thebes. After his death, the vizier rules for four years, then Horemhab, then Ramesses the First, and the whole time the Jews are in slavery. The tablet is gathering dust in a Thebian basement—" Diffner raises his hands, as if the rest is self-explanatory.

It's the Sunday School story everybody knows.

"Ramesses-Second orders all new-born Jewish male children drowned in the Nile. Baby Moses is found in a reed basket by the Pharaoh's daughter. He's raised as a prince of Egypt, educated in the palace, discovers his own Hebrew heritage..."

It fits... Almost too perfectly. "*Moses* learns Aten was really the Hebrew god of his genetic parents, and leads the Israelites out of slavery to Mount Sinai, where he claims to be visited by another version of the same god and given the tablet *by* God."

"And calls it the Ten Commandments?"

"Exactly. And calls it the Ten Commandments."

"So we'd be doing the same thing as Moses," I grin.

"And Akhenaten, Constantine, and Nebuchadnezzar...Uniting a fractured population under the god of the tablet."

"But the Ten Commandments were on *two* tablets? And Moses *broke* them?" I make a small throwing gesture.

"The Hebrew word '*luhot*' was translated to mean two tablets, but it also refers to *two* sides of *one* tablet. There are a bunch of other places where it's translated the other way – two sides of one. In the same chapters, the tablet containing the Commandments is also described as *one* stone. Chapter twenty-four verse twelve, and chapter thirty-one verse eighteen."

"Really?"

"Just like the 'Code of Hammurabi' – the tablet containing the laws of the Babylonians *before* Akhenaten was a *two*-sided tablet. In the *Islamic* faith... in the same story of Moses and the tablet, there's *one* tablet, and it is never broken."

Watching Diffner fit the pieces together, I see a terrifying light growing in his eyes. "The tablet Moses brought down from Mount Sinai came from Abraham?"

"Moses brought it with him from Egypt. It *wasn't* a new tablet. And *everything* we thought we knew unravels," whispers Diffner.

"Or it all makes sense."

"How *else* do you go up a mountain, and come back down with a carved stone tablet?" Diffner asks redundantly. "Moses *hid* in those mountains when he first fled Egypt, before returning. It's the Principle of Parsimony."

"'Choose the simplest explanation...'"

"Where did he get the tablet?"

"It was already there."

"He took the tablet, hid it on the mountain, claimed he had instructions from *god* that nobody should follow him. That, no other man be *anywhere* on the mountain. And returned with a ready-made tablet."

"The tablet he brought down went into the Ark..."

"...He told everyone if they even *touched* the Ark, they'd die," summarises Diffner.

*Abraham...*

*Akhenaten...*

*Moses...*

*The Ark of the Covenant...*

*Nebuchadnezzar...*

*Emperor Titus...*

*Emperor Constantine...*

"So, the Ark is captured by Nebuchadnezzar, then Titus, and passed to Constantine... *All* of them convert their kingdoms to Abraham's god as the tablet passes through their hands... And we've been worshipping different versions of this *same god*, ever since..."

"Yep. That's Madison's idea." Diffner flaps the slip of paper in the breeze, where he's written it down. He winces at the thought of her.

"It *really* would be a kick in the plums for the fundamentalists, wouldn't it," I grin happily at the thought.

"Speaking of *Islam*," adds Diffner bitterly. His voice sounds strangled. "It's in the Qur'an that the words revealed to Mohammed come from a 'well-guarded tablet.'"

"...Really?"

"Mormons too... Their holy texts were written in ancient times on a tablet, sealed up, and *'hid up unto the Lord, to come forth in due time.'* The Bible talks about *'The great mystery that has been kept hidden...'* Even in the legend of *Parzival* – the original myth of the Holy Grail – the *Grail* wasn't a *cup*. It was a stone."

"I didn't know that either."

"*All* these religions have a story about a tablet..." concludes Diffner. "Even Jesus said, on a *stone* he built his church."

"We're just making this up, right?" I add, off-handedly. It all fits so neatly.

"Yeah."

I mumble aloud. "Hidden... for four-thousand-years... by priests, prophets, emperors. All keeping it a secret. It poses an obvious question..."

"What's that?"

"*Why? Why* are they all keeping it a secret?"

Diffner looks across the Common to the Boston skyline, slipping into a daydream. He shakes his head slightly. "That's the only gap. *Why* keep it a secret?"

"There has to be a good reason," I whisper. "Why would you take this to your grave? For four-thousand years, no one sees this tablet, or writes about it? Why has *nobody* wanted *anyone* else to know?"

Diffner shifts on the bench. "If we explain that, it's watertight."

"You think?"

Something shifts in Diffner's face. "I don't know."

"Huh?"

"The Vatican would crush this before it ever got traction. And if anyone had such a tablet now, it would be them."

"The Catholic Church isn't as powerful as they used to be," I disagree.

"Don't kid yourself. They've had *centuries* of practice at this... Scientists, who've sat for decades just waiting for this to come along... setting themselves up on the faculties of academic institutions... Setting up *the faculties.* The same way they propped up the 'Shroud of Turin.' Every major college in the world was started by the Catholic church... Imagine a hundred-thousand scholars in a hundred countries, coming down on this at once..." Diffner glances from the horizon back at me, like I've just arrived next to him.

"We shouldn't even be discussing it," he sighs. "Not at a time like this."

"What? I thought... What else do we do?"

Diffner looks down at his feet.

"There's a new one of these baglickers every *year.* Khomeini. Hussein. Bin Laden. They're like *roaches.* We bomb the hell out of their caves, and when the dust clears *ten more of them* come skittering back out of a crack in the ground!"

"Something like this, *would* ruin them," concedes Diffner. "Their funding, their recruitment, State protection... Without the coverage of a moderate populous *all* the Fundamentalists in all of these faiths would be isolated. It's a smokeless bomb..." He looks pained.

"*What* an idea..." I whisper.

"But you have your family to think of."

I huff. "Yeah... Hey, maybe *someone* at the Anacostia Institute would get a kick out of *workshopping* this?"

Diffner glowers at me suddenly. "Don't even joke about that. If you broadcast this, you're *asking* for trouble. Remember Mark Hoffman? The Mormon counterfeiter? He's doing *life imprisonment* in the Utah State Prison in Draper for faking a letter from the founder of *Mormonism* – and he got half his leg blown off for it. They won't just prove you wrong, Bob. Some nut will drive a U-Haul full of Plutonium into your living room, smiling all the way. You *know* how many murderous *fanatics* there are out there, *gagging* for a visible enemy. This would bring out *all* of them... It isn't worth it."

"Really? It's not *worth* it?"

"What would Anne say if she knew?"

Zap.

Just like that, he's pressed my big red hot button... and he knows it.

Annie would flip if she knew what I was suggesting.

"You don't know how powerful these organizations are," Diffner straightens. "I've seen them at work, up close. I've seen the bodies, Bob... Hanging from a bridge in London in broad daylight. They have *no* fear. This isn't a *theoretical exercise* to them. As difficult as it is to fathom – you slander these churches, *this* god, they will kill you. They'll stop at nothing. This is *real* to them."

"But we'd be *uniting* them—"

Diffner growls grimly. "The psychology of religion attracts the mentally unstable, just as handsomely as it attracts the do-gooders. Not just the Vatican. Or the trillionaire Muslim governments pumping money into paramilitary groups... Look at Oklahoma City... A-hundred-and-sixty-eight people dead, and a thousand injured, by *one man*. One mad coward weasel, in a Ryder truck packed with two-and-a-half-tons of fertilizer and diesel... Or the Utøya massacre last year... One guy shoots sixty-nine people at a summer camp to send a message to his government on Muslim immigration. And yesterday... Six guys with suitcases! We'll be counting the dead for years to come. It's one thing to *read* about this stuff, Bob. You *never* want to be involved..."

"But I *am* involved... My sister-in-law—" I change tack, seeing Diffner's discomfort. "We're *all* involved. Anyone with a stake in the future of this fucked up mess is involved."

"No, you're not even close Bob. Let it go. Stick to the RUNE report..."

I'm so schmangled by the sudden change in direction, I miss the implication; the choice 'A' or 'B'. *Leave it alone, or lose your job.*

Diffner looks at me kindly. "For Maddie, as a favour, I want to make sure you *let this go*... Fly straight. Whatever's eating you up, wherever this is coming from - Matt, whatever else - the world doesn't change overnight. The same way clay figurines of dead grandparents and sun-god worship disappeared, so will Christianity and Islam. In a thousand years people will look back and laugh - as Jesus joins Hercules. Or some goat-herder will throw a rock into a cave in Hebron, and find another Nag Hammadi, or a Dead Sea Scroll, that contradicts everything. Or we'll discover extraterrestrial life, and the aliens will tell us to stop being stupid... But not in our lifetimes. It's a thousand years away," Diffner slaps me on the back. "Don't hold your breath."

I slump.

He's right.

But I'm so fucking riled. Sitting around doing nothing seems impossible.

"It's best you don't repeat a word of this to anyone," Diffner adds, with a hint of condescension. "You know what an opportunity RUNE is... It would be foolish to jeopardise your career. Go back to what you do, Bob. Take a holiday. Before you know it, you'll forget all about this idea."

There it is. Nice and simple. "A carrot, and a big stick." I smile painfully. Play the beach dog, and roll over.

Diffner groans as he rises to his feet. "I have to go." He touches me lightly on the shoulder, as if bestowing a blessing. "I'll call you in a week, about those Numbers, okay?"

"Okay."

He trudges off, across the grass.

I sit, staring at my shoes.

It's impossible to explain, but the idea still feels *important*. It's more plausible than a six-day creation of the universe, Eve being pulled from Adam's rib, Noah's zoo boat, folks rising from the dead, parting the Red Sea, turning water to wine, talking donkeys...

Someone has to do something.

Stop the bandwagon, I want off.

I open my hand and look at my cell phone again.

No news.

Annie will be waiting for me at home.

Then stand and walk up the hill, toward my car. The street is empty.

I glance over my shoulder, thinking for a moment I'm being followed.

All over the country, people are fetching their mail with barbeque tongs they're so scared. A week ago, this kind of paranoia would have been inconceivable. But yesterday was the end of the world.

Maybe that's why it hurts so much. A handful of lone assoholics robbed us of our complacency for the cost of a subway ride.

The real pisser is, there are the same toolheads, these Osamas, who packed a tug with blasting powder and rammed the boys at sea in Yemen twelve years ago. The embassy car bombs in Kenya and Tanzania. Same guys. The World Trade Centre, eleven years ago. And eight years before that. And we all thought things had gone back to 'normal'.

This isn't the end.

I've seen the Numbers.

It only gets worse.

There is no end.

We'll get back on our feet from what happened yesterday... and the same thing will happen again... and one day one of these assoholics will get *really* lucky, and end the whole world for good.

But even at this new pinnacle of depravity, right when it seemed we were all doing so well, I have to think about Annie and Joe. No more carefree, happy-go-lucky Bob.

But no Martin Luther nailing a thesis to a church door either.

I climb into my car, where I parked on Beacon Street, turn on the radio, and hear an audio clip of screams from the New York subway.

And I wonder again, if one of the voices is Madison.

I'm still thinking about what Diffner said when I get home... about one day we'll forget today's religions, the same way we've forgotten so many others.

It takes an hour to find source info, and another ten minutes to run a projection...

Diffner is right.

Based on growth rates over the past hundred years, by the year 7,000 'Anno Domini' there's nothing left but agnostics and atheists.

And if you project the Numbers even further... by the year 4,361,000 A.D., the Atheists win.

Satisfied, I switch off the computer and head for bed.

I'd say you were dippy if you told me now, that tomorrow Diffner and I would both be running for our lives.

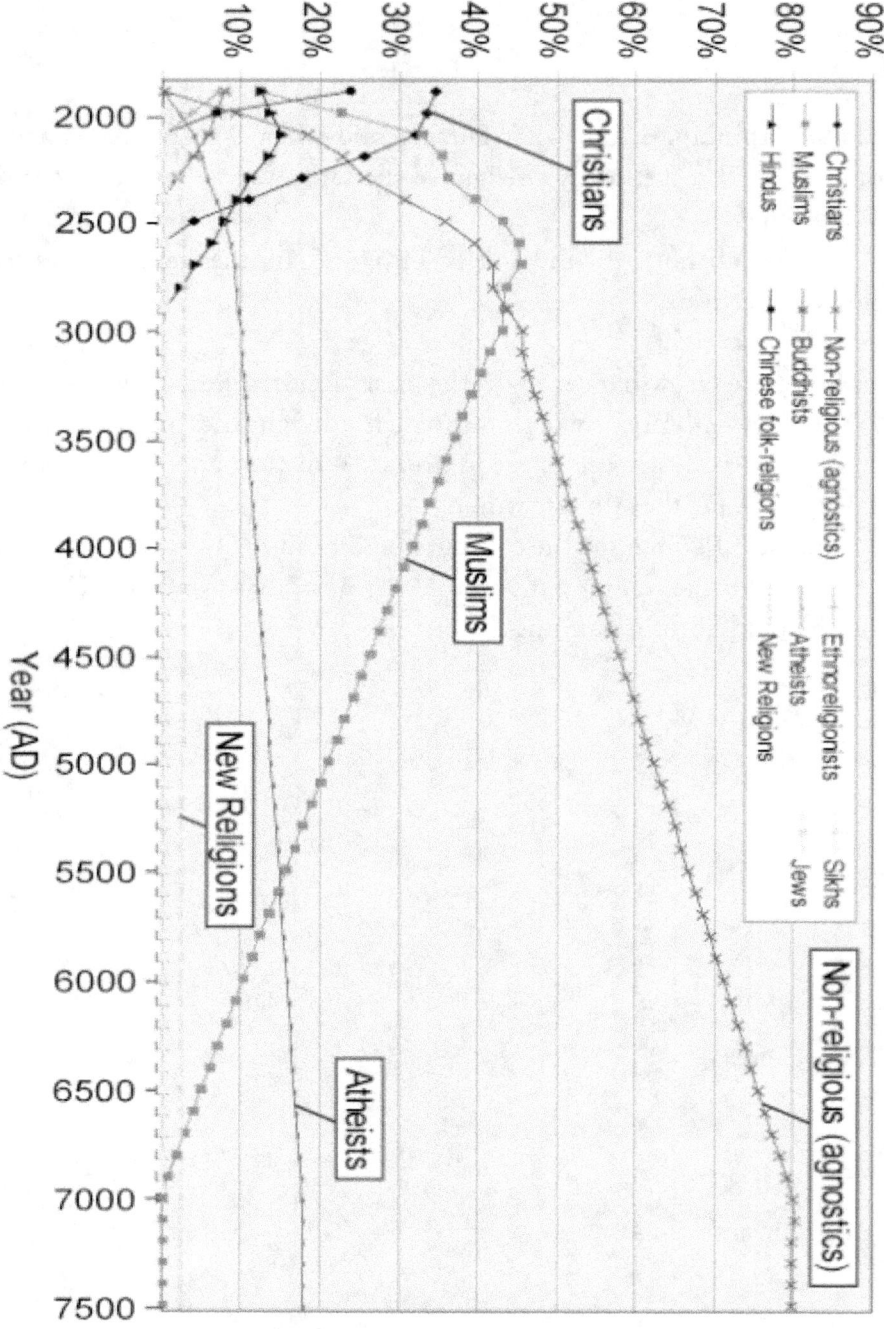

*(Diagram 9 - Religious trend, 1900-7500AD)*

## 15. '...A MAN OF SORROWS...'

*Thursday, September 13, 2012*

The doorbell *never* rings at the house.

It's after midnight when the chimes ring in the walls.

I wake, not quite sure why, and listen like a submariner... The house is still. Annie's in Boston with Tessa waiting by the phone for news of Madison... Joe is at boarding school.

Sure it must have been a dream, I roll over for more log-sawing.

The doorbell rings again.

I stir, napulous, and check the bedside clock. My circadian rhythms are skewiff. I haven't slept this well in weeks. *What if it's news about Madison?*

I leap downstairs, run to the entry in my socks, flick on the external light, and open the door.

Standing on the stoop in a rumpled navy-blue suit, is a new face, with the bald, bony look of a prize fighter – like a sprig of cauliflower wrapped in a wilted collar. There's violence in his eyes.

I glance past him.

Chief Barne Ruberight is standing on the driveway, looking on with a freezinasscold kind of reluctance.

"Barne?" The muscles tighten in my chest.

"Robert Travis?" inquires the lumpy stranger, breath steaming in the cold night air. He looks like a repo man, but talks like a Judge.

"Is Madison okay?" I blurt, slurring the words a little.

The repo man turns to look at the Barne, confused. "My name is Peter *Benning*." He watches my expression closely, allowing the introduction to sink in. "I'm with the Central Intelligence Agency, in Langley."

Barne shifts nervously from foot to foot, watching my sheet-creased face, mouthing the words '*I told you so!*' I try my best to look like I haven't just soiled my bedshorts. "What can I do for you?" I ask, perplexed.

"I need to know when you last saw Clark Diffner?"

"What? Why?"

"I'd like to have a word to you in private," the repo man adds obtusely.

Hang on... What?

"It's important."

I stick out my hand, palm up. "Have you got I.D.?" Like this is a snack. Like I've had five guys around on the porch today, selling national secrets.

Barne climbs the step, nervy. "I checked that."

I examine the plastic sleeve. It looks like a library card. "When did I last see *Clark Diffner...*?"

"Yes."

I return the wallet. "I *was* sleeping. Can we do this tomorrow?"

He lowers his voice. "Mister Travis. I apologise, but – as I say – it's very important that we talk."

I don't want to let this suited goon into my house.

Benning reaches into his jacket, and produces a rolled up issue of the *New York Times*. "Have you seen this?"

I shiver. "Sure. It's a pretty popular newspaper."

"Take a look," urges Benning, presenting the puzzle section, paper flapping in the breeze.

"You dragged me out of bed, to help you finish the crossword?" I smirk.

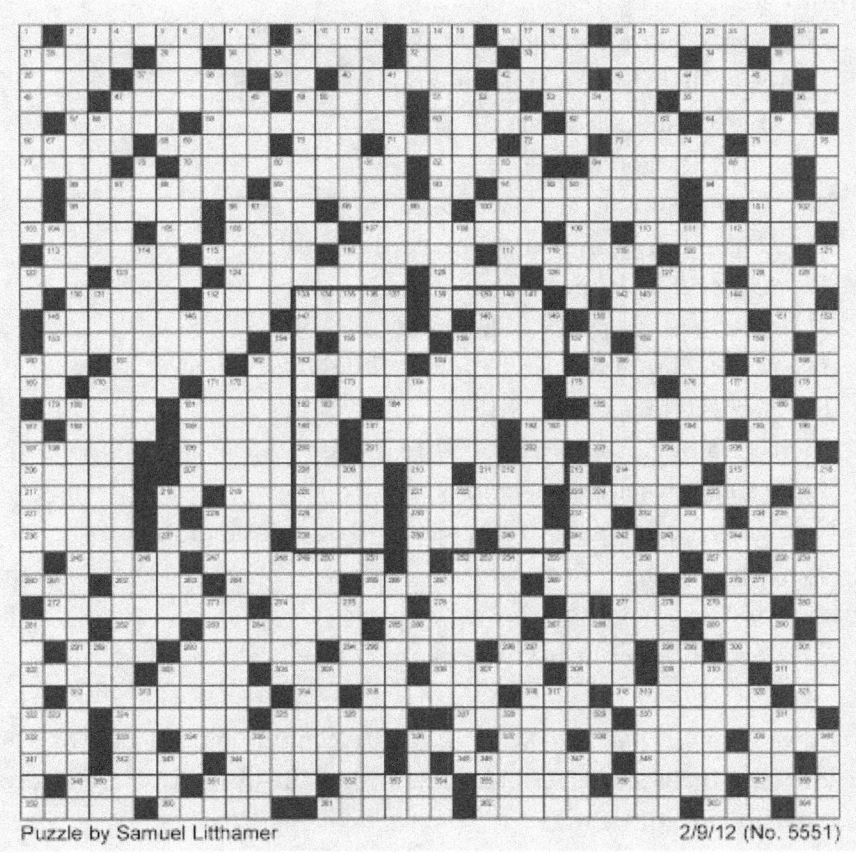

*(Diagram 10 - Empty crossword)*

Benning points back to the masthead. "Do you recognise the date?"

Sunday, September 2, 2012.

That's the day Matt died. It's the same crossword puzzle I found in Joe's box of loot – sitting in my desk in the den, with the Polaroid. "What about it?"

"Look."

"What at?"

"The puzzle."

I squint, perplexed. "It's empty."

"Just tell me what you see," Benning's voice rises.

I scan the puzzle. Aside from an unusual number of references to various gods, I can't see much else...

*28 Down:* Son of Poseidon... AON.

*37 Across:* Babylonian creation goddess... ARURU.

*37 Down:* Sumerian sky god... ANU.

*76 Down:* Sex god...EROS.

*239 Across:* Roman sun god... SOL.

*254 Down:* Egyptian god of the dead... USIRIS.

*303 Across:* Nordic god-father... BURI.

*311 Across:* Greek god of Shepherds... PAN.

*361 Across:* Supreme Hindu god... VISHNU.

*103 Across:* Holy Book... BIBLE.

There's no obvious pattern. "What is this?"

Barne steps closer to take a look.

Now we're both trying to figure out what we're looking at.

"What about the name, *Samuel Litthamer?*" Benning indicates the puzzle's author. "You never heard of him?"

"Dunno. You ever heard of Leonard Dawe?"

"Who?"

Dawe was a World War Two *Telegraph* puzzle-maker who accidentally included secret D-Day landing code-words in a crossword, and was accused of being a spy.

"So you've never heard of *Samuel Litthamer?*"

"If this is some kind of a joke..? I don't get the—"

Benning swoops forward, leaning in close. "'*Samuel Litthamer*' is an anagram of 'Matthias Mueller.'"

I flinch visibly.

Benning scrutinises my expression, stuffing the newspaper back inside his suit.

"Whatever this is—"

"I'd *need* to have a word to you in private."

I look to Barne. There are pit-stains in his shirt. He's sweating in spite of the cold. "Are we going down to the station?"

The agent turns his head, revealing a scar down his neck the size of a mail slot.

"Pete's bar," suggests Barne.

"Left your fishing gear on the desk?" I smirk, hoping to relax Barne some.

"You can ride with me in my car," suggests Benning, pointing.

Benning's silver-grey Lincoln wears Massachusetts plates. The first two letters of the registration are *EO*, short for Executive Office. I've seen these around Washington. The vehicle is registered to the Executive Office of the President, the National Security Council, or some other Federal branch. The '*Mass.*' plate indicates Benning must have flown into Boston on a red-eye, visited the local field office, and picked up a car. The CIA has offices in Boston, due to the number of foreign consulates, and recruiting programs with schools like MIT. I know at least one of these offices is on the third floor of 545 Main Street – a grey, nine-storey concrete building in an industrial district behind campus, across the tracks from the starch factory. The boilerplate on the door reads '*R K Starling and Associates.*' The MIT Department of Political Science occupies three floors downstairs. Although Matt never spoke of it, in his time as Chairman he definitely dealt with these guys – even outside of his friendship with Diffner. So, Benning has flown out of Washington, picked up a government car, and driven up to New Brid at midnight. "What's this about?" I ask.

"I'll explain *everything*, if you could just come with me."

"Something happened to Clark?" I press.

"The sooner we go somewhere private, the sooner I can answer your questions."

"We're talking now." I squeak, annoyed.

Benning's voice changes, taking on a new bruskness. "I'd *prefer* you came without any *trouble.*" The guy is a walking-talking pituitary gland.

Barne looks dumbfounded, wide-eyed, and busting for a leak.

"Fine." I shrug. "I'll take my car... Gimme a minute." I walk inside, and take my time fetching my track-pants and runners, check the fireplace is off, and lock the house.

Benning is waiting in his Lincoln, engine running.

Barne leans on the cowcatcher of his four-wheeler, silhouetted in the glare of the headlights, twisting his heel nervously in the loose stones. "You wanna ride in my truck?"

I shake my head. "It's not a truck. It's a *car*."

Barne looks genuinely disappointed as he sidles into the cabin, easing himself onto the wood-beaded seat, joints popping. "Bob?"

I walk closer, checking if Agent Benning is watching. I can see the CIA man's face, tinged orange in the dash lights.

Benning *pips* the car horn.

I ignore him, irritated. "Yeah?"

Barne jimmies the Blazer's gear lever around. "This is the guy that called a couple weeks ago."

"...I know."

"You know him?"

"Nope?"

"Who's *Clark Diffner*?" asks Barne, concerned.

"...Someone from work." I glance at the dash of his Blazer, and notice a small figurine, standing in a puddle of melted glue. It's a plastic image of the Virgin Mary, with splayed eyeballs. I smile, reluctantly.

"What's so funny?"

"Your Mary is *wall*-eyed."

"She's not."

"She *is*."

"She's authentic hand-painted," Barne contends.

"Wall—"

"She's a holy relic. Show some respect."

"The Virgin *Mary* Feldman," I snort.

"That's a bless-ed object you're making fun of."

"Relax Barne," I force a smile. "This is *nothing*. Everything is just fine. You'll be home in bed in an hour." I turn and walk back to the garage, singing the Jethro Tull song: *"...She's a poor man's rich girl, and she'll do it for a song... Ba bup-ba... CROSS-EYED MARY finds it hard to get along..."*

But this isn't nothing. This is no security check.

This thing with the crossword...

And why is Barne Ruberight along for the ride?

The only thing Barne is good for is firepower. Or a witness... CIA agents are prohibited from investigating US citizens on home soil. So he's also good for an arrest.

I run through the options in my head, like Prince Charming trying Cinderella's shoe on dowager feet. Rolling down the driveway, the spotlights of Barne's Blazer light up my car. The only sound is the thump of my pulse, and a whistle of air in my nostrils. I don't think I'm overreacting... but this feels like the first rumblings of a serious shit storm.

Our small convoy approaches the darkened neon letters B-A-R at '*The Bee's Wing*' under a faded thirty-inch Bud bottle-cap on the timber awning. Pete Hiptmeyer already has tinsel up in the windows, three months out from Christmas.

Barne's Blazer pulls alongside me in the empty lot. Barne shimmies down out of his cab, fastens his windbreaker, and hooks his thumbs over his utility belt, working hard to look at ease.

The old street light chirps like a cricket. The moon and all the stars swim over the fish-skin body of Benning's Lincoln, as he parks on the far side of my car.

The mean-looking Agency man unhooks his jacket from the headrest of the passenger seat, and emerges frowning at the venue – the whole top of his bald head creasing.

It occurs to me as Barne pushes open the padded door, the Chief suggested Pete's bar so folks would believe him, when he told the story later. *The night the CIA came to New Brid...*

The pool tables are bare, and the hanging lights darkened. The only illumination comes from the brightly-lit serving area, glistening like a jewellery case, colourful liquids like precious stones in decanters.

The TV at the far end of the bar plays a *Fox News* report on '9/11-II'. Survivors are still being pulled from nooks and crannies underground. The New York Stock Exchange is still closed. It's impossible for anyone to get into Manhattan. Analysts are forecasting a freefall in stock prices when the market re-opens. Fatalities nationwide are being estimated at twenty thousand. The financial cost, at half a *trillion* dollars.

Pete Hiptmeyer emerges from the back room surrounded by a faint mist, flapping a dishcloth, wearing his usual sleeveless plaid shirt – and a Santa Claus hat.

I smirk.

Pete raises his hand to shoo us away – "We're closed!" – when he recognises the Chief. "Barne? Wazzup?" He licks his sun-swollen lips nervously.

Barne turns to Benning, and suggests "I'll have a word." He jacks up his belt, and swaggers over to Pete.

Wiping his hand on the towel, Hiptmeyer cocks his ear. Barne perches his boot on the rim of the butt-filled bar gutter, leans in, and whispers. The old barman pales, and snatches off his Santa hat. "Hey, can I get choo fellas anything?"

"Black coffee," I reply.

"Make that two." Benning surveys the room.

Barne swaggers over to a padded booth, rotating the 2-way, snub-nose, and nightstick on his belt as he slides into the bench.

Benning drags over a chair, sets it down backwards, and sits with his arms crossed on the seat-back: "On Monday, Special Agent Diffner brought this clipping into the cryptography lab in Langley and asked the Enigmatologists to run it through a high level decipher... The crossword was submitted under a false name to the Puzzles Editor a month ago."

"'Enigmatologists'?"

"Look at the *dots*."

It takes a moment to follow.

"You know how a punch-card works?" Benning asks.

"I was at *M.I.T.* when they ran the *world's first Applied Computing degree,"* I answer shortly, counting the edges. 36 squares. 26 letters in the alphabet plus 10 mathematical numerals equals 36. There are exactly enough 'punch holes' down each side of the grid, for every number and letter in the alphanumeric system. *Just* like an old computer punch-card. "Do you have a pen?"

Benning clicks out a Parker, and slides it across the table.

I scan the grid for a common Hollerith-style 36, 40, or 80 column punch card pattern... But each row in the crossword contains 6 solid black squares. That *can't* be a coincidence, since the probability of that pattern occurring by accident is less than *one in a thousand...*

There's also *one* black in every 6 boxes, all the way down the grid. Statistically, the probability of *both* those patterns together is 36 squared – or 1296... out of... 3.72e+41. About *half* of the possible patterns would be practical crossword puzzles, making the odds even smaller. Something like *one in three trillion trillion.*

So it's more complicated. I scan the puzzle. Vertically, there's no corresponding system. So, the cipher has to be encoded in the *black squares* along the horizontal rows.

I snatch a *Bud Lite* coaster, and scrawl the code on a 6-by-6 grid on the back. I test the first pair of 6 boxes – marking the columns 2 and 6.

*(Diagram 11 - Crossword code, sample grid)*

The position of each black square in the crossword, in each rectangle of twelve squares, corresponds to a character...

"By formula," I explain, "'X' plus six times 'Y'-minus-one equals 'Z'. Where, 'X' is two, and 'Y' is six, 'Z' equals thirty-two. The thirty-second character in the string is 'V'."

The grid on the back of the beer coaster, returns the letter 'V'.

*(Diagram 12 - Beer coaster matrix)*

Barne Ruberight slumps, frowning. "You lost me."

Hiptmeyer emerges from the kitchen with an armload of chipped mugs, and a percolator jug full of burnt crappuccino. He unloads his arm. I reach for my wallet, but he waves it down.

I plot the coded message, scribbling down the string of letters.

Benning's face lights up like a Christmas tree. "What does it say?"

VMVAVIII2VZZJIVJLVHYVOEDVMIOCVDAOTCV
SVNZDVZVJESSGNVWSIKQNHVQBCZLVHOTW32
7VPBUHMI244VKTVLDCVFMBSVAHARVIP2RCXPJ

*(Diagram 13 - Decoded message)*

I lean back, and set down the pen. "The 'V's are probably spacers."
The letter V, the first letter, also appears every few characters.

I rewrite the string, breaking it up:

M, A, III2, ZZJI, JL, HY, OED, MIOC, DAOTC, S,
NZD, Z, JESSGN, WSIKQNH, QBCZL, HOTW327,
PBUHMI244, KT, LDC, FMBS, AHAR, IP2RCXPJ

"What's *that?*" asks Benning, frustrated.

I shrug. "I'm only guessing, but some of the letters correlate to
religious references..." I point at the second letter. "'A' could be for
Abraham, and 'I-One' and 'I-Two' for his sons, Ishmael and Isaac...
Jacob, Isaac's son, was renamed by god to Israel 'J-I'... 'Z.Z.' could be
'Zamzam'... 'P.B.U.H.' could be short for 'Peace Be Upon Him' – used
by Muslim scholars whenever they mention the prophet
Mohammed... 'H.O.T.W.' might be 'History of the Wars' by
Procopius – a Byzantine scholar, in the sixth-century – and a page
reference... I don't know. I'm guessing."

The grid's brilliance is astonishing, even hypnotising in its
cleverness. Whoever devised it, had to find words, and clues, to fill all
the spaces *after* they laid out the pattern of black squares.

"Three-hundred newspapers syndicated this crossword," cites
Benning, "with a circulation of around twenty million copies.
Twenty-five percent of readers attempt the crossword, which means
about five million people *did* this crossword."

Empty, *without* answering a clue, the puzzle contains a message. Five million people studied the grid, and saw nothing. "You say Diffner brought this in on *Monday?*"

"Yeah... Why?"

That was the day I first showed up at his house. "And it was never deciphered?"

"No."

"*This* is why you drove up here?" asks Barne, stumped. "'Cos of this?"

Benning pockets the message. "You didn't tell me when you saw Clark last."

"This morning."

"What time?"

"About eight a.m."

"They just found copies of this crossword pinned to the wall at the apartments of Mohamat al-Lideen, and Muhannad al-Baghdadi."

"Who are they?"

"The New York and Pittsburgh subway bombers."

"*Fuck me dead!*" blurts Barne.

"Last week, you weren't calling me about the RUNE project?" I realise.

"At least three people have been murdered, who had something to do with this puzzle... Do you know where Diffner is *now?*" asks Benning.

"No. I don't. I swear."

Benning stares at me cruelly. "Okay... I need to phone this in." He unpockets his cell phone.

"Wait," barks Barne. "What's going on?"

Benning heads for the door.

I stare at the table. The idea Diffner – and Matt! – had *anything* to do with these terrorist attacks is horrifying.

"Christ," snorts Barne, staring at me, stunned. "*Muhannad al-Baghdadi?*"

Through the porthole-window near the padded door, I see Benning open his car door, cell phone pressed to his ear.

I take a deep breath, trying to handle the swooping sensation in my gut.

Barne shifts uncomfortably, squeaking the vinyl. His usual pluckiness, his lawman's confidence, is shot to hell. He jabs a thumb in Benning's direction. "What's going on?"

I can't speak. My brain is grid-locked. Diffner never mentioned any of this... What *else* has he *not* told me?

Outside, through the round window, Benning's voice is raised just loud enough to tell he's steamed at someone. My bewilderment is multiplying by the second. Did Matt write the crossword? Who for? Was it *for* Diffner?

"Is this normal?" asks Barne.

"Huh?"

"I mean, you know," Barne waves his hand around vaguely, unsure. "Is this normal? For *you* guys?"

I glance at the TV. They're playing CCTV footage of a bomber entering the subway. "Pete!" I shout. "Can you turn that up?"

Pete grabs a remote from under the bar, and aims it at the television.

"...al-Baghdadi was an Iraqi immigrant, who police now believe trained with U.S. security forces after the occupation nine years ago. Osama Bin Laden has released a video claiming credit for the attack, announcing that the world can say 'goodbye to America'..."

Outside, Benning is yelling into his phone. He's smoked. There is steam *literally* coming off his shoulders.

I glance at the door, wondering if I should leave. I have a right to be huffy, being dragged out here, to sit and wait for this gink to get off the phone... I need more than coffee.

Barne slurps at his mug, putting ideas together in his hat. "I mean, you don't *have* to tell me," he pants, at the sheer mental exertion.

"Huh—?"

"You know... Past few years it's all N.S.A., A.T.F., D.E.A., F.B.I., D.H.S... You know. Eyes looking inward. All of a sudden, *wa-la... You* guys are back out of the woodwork..."

"I'm not with the C.I.A.," I mutter, watching Agent Benning as he leans inside his car to fetch something.

"I mean, you guys trained Bin Laden right? There must be some tails in slings over that... now, more than ever."

"I don't know anything about that."

"Ahuh," whispers Barne.

"I need to go part my hair."

Barne slides out of the booth, to let me out.

I spot the *Gents* and angle unsteadily for the door, pin-balling through the S-bend entrance. The place smells like a sump. I run the tap and splash water on my grill. Rising to the pitted mirror, I check my reflection.

There is a strange *whistling* noise inside my head ...

As I walk back out into the bar. Barne is still sitting in the booth. Benning isn't. I hear a loud *crack* – like a door slam – echoing off the building outside.

A second noise – maybe a hammer driving a nail, or a piece lumber dropped on the road – rattles the window. Agent Benning has disappeared from view.

Barne struggles like a kid in a sack-race, to get out of the booth. Popping free, he rushes for the door, holster clapping on his thigh.

"What was that?" I ask, spotting the crossword and *Bud Lite* coaster on the table. I tear off the puzzle page, grab the coaster, stuff both in my pocket, and bounce through the double doors behind Barne.

Outside, on the far side of the Lincoln, the driver's door stands ajar.

A faint bubbling noise comes up from the ground.

I circle the nose of the car, hand slipping on the hood.

"Holy *shit*!" shrieks Barne.

Agent Benning is in the dirt, clawing at the gravel with gory fingers, breath condensed, face pressed to the stones, eyes wide like new marbles.

Barne stumbles to his knees, hands stuttering nervously over the spook's punctured suit jacket. Benning is oozing tinted black blood through the navy fabric.

I stand paralysed, in a dental kind of pain. My eyes go to the street. It's empty.

Barne unholsters his snub-nose. "*Get an ambulance!*" He aims the pistol at the sky, and twists the two-way off his belt. "Keegan! *Come in!*"

Pete Hiptmeyer sticks his head gingerly out of the door to the bar, with his Santa hat back on.

"Call an ambulance!" I bark.

"Keegan! This is Barne. Where are you? *Code red*, ten-thirty-three. State Street and Main. Repeat, *code red*. Come in!"

I shiver. What the hell is a ten-thirty-three? Barne stows his radio. "...CHRIST!"

Benning's contorted face searches out my eyes... Reality creeps through my back like ghost fingers. Barne rolls Benning onto his side. The gabardine jacket is blown wide open, flesh popping out like a can of beans. Lumps of gizzard and slosh spill through a right-angled vent in the cloth. Grunting, Benning tries to raise his head. Barne sputters, "You're gonna be fine! Lay down. You're going to be fine." And whispers sideways at me, "*Dumdum round... went through like a fucking flying hubcap.*"

An ambulance will take at least half an hour to arrive from Gloucester.

There's literally nothing we can do, but watch him die.

My guts twist like an eel in a net. Benning's eyes meet mine. He's looking right *through* me... Glazed... Ashen. His body is assuming room temperature. But he silently, desperately searches out my attention, as the world fades...

I glance at Barne. "He's— trying to say something."

Barne is oblivious, scanning the street.

"What happened?" I crouch, leaning close to Benning.

Barne's radio crackles. '*I'm on my way.*'

"Get your ass here *now! Keegan!*" barks Barne.

"*Shhhh!*" I lean closer, raising a hand at Barne.

He glares down at me. "For chrissake, Bob! He's blowing fuckin *bubbles!*"

"Shut *up!*"

And then— the bright jingle of a glass bottle kicked into the curb rings down from the end of the street.

I arc around the fender of the car like a cartoon cat, sprawling in the dirt.

Peering under the corner of the bumper, I see Barne, lying spread-eagled under a sputter of Benning's black-red deoxygenated blood, searching the darkened corner at the end of the block with desperate eyes...

The blur of movement down the street is fleeting. I can't be sure what it is. "*Hey,*" I croak.

Barne peers at me, like I'm a stranger...

There's a sound like a pelted rock striking the car.

THUNK!

It takes a moment to click. It's a bullet... hitting the far side of the Lincoln. The vibration travels through the air.

*Someone is shooting at us.* It's the weirdest moment of my life, realising someone wants me dead...

Barne pushes up, and scrambles for safety.

There's another laxative *crack*. Barne grunts, is lifted up off the ground, slumps into the car fender, and falls to the gravel.

His eyes stare blankly past me.

## 16. '...A TIME TO GATHER STONES...'

*Thursday, September 13, 2012*

*"Barne!"* I roar, shaking uncontrollably.

The back of the Chief's navy shirt darkens visibly, where he's sprawled beside the Lincoln, legs splayed.

"Barne—?!" My bowels lose their elastic. I try to move, but my legs are boneless.

It's suicide, but I have no choice. If I stay here, I'm dead.

I caterpillar out into the open, under the stadium-bright streetlights.

Even before I reach Barne, I see his face... It's clear there's no life left in him... His eyes are wide, unfocused, aimed at the sky. For a moment, I just lay there and blink... It's stupid. I'm locked up, frozen like a mannequin. *What do I do?*

Another loud *crack* erupts inches over my back, as a third bullet *thumps* into the door of the Lincoln.

I scoop up Barne's snub-nose revolver, and run for the nearest shelter, beyond the corner of Hiptmeyer's bar, landing against the shingle wall.

Twisting to look back, I see Barne's corpse, steaming.

*Fuck!*

My organs are shutting down, one at a time. I peer into the parking lot, vision crazed with the light. *What the hell is this? Where do I go?*

Behind Pete's bar – in the sporadic light of the sparse lamps – lurks a ghetto of crooked crab shacks, lobster cages stacked to the roofs, ropes piled like hair. In the narrow neck between stained shingles, is a mess of buoys, upturned skiffs, plastic drums, and leaned-over poles. The cluttered, shadowy, shanty village is almost as foreboding as the bloodbath at my back... But – if I don't flee, they'll be laying me out next to Benning and Barne, on a gurney in the hallway of the Boston Southern Mortuary, bed-sheet knotted at my chest.

I run south, away from the sound and movement, searching the dark for an exit, holding Barne's revolver at arm's length – not sure how it got there – pressing at the dark with my elbows. I reach the first side-alley on wobbly legs, and leap into the dim, vacant void. A figure ahead of me is making a mad dash around a corner.

I back-flip the way I've come, shoulders pressed to the cladding. My gut turns to jelly.

A second set of syncopated footfalls squelch in the gravel behind me.

I peek around the wall at waist height, in time to see the other Runner ahead of me make a right-hand, past a darkened wall of wire-mesh shellfish traps.

My first instinct is to follow... If a guy in front of you is running, a hundred-thousand-years of Evolution tell me to run in the same direction. *Now!*

I take the corner, make for the last shack, and stick my head into the next lane - in time to see the Runner pass under a rusted lamppost.

The man's head flashes by in a spray of white hair.

He's old, the other Runner - with nothing but escape on his mind. He poses no threat. He's running for his life as well. The old man was probably out in his fishing hut, innocently turned a corner, found the Police Chief's shot, and bolted. I'd have run, too. I *am* running...

I take the corner. The Old Runner disappears into the shadows.

With a flash of light, and a noise like a branch coming off a tree, something thumps me in the face. Hard. I reel, dropping to my knees, the revolver slipping from my hand.

Self-preservation drives me to shelter, wounded, skittering across the frigid stones, squinting, blinded, seeking cover. Squeezing futilely into the wet recess behind a splintered pole, hiding half a shoulder, I pull myself into a ball and freeze, hands pressed to my cheeks, trying to blink my vision clear. My eyeballs feel burned, sliced, split. In the weak, tearful light, my hand comes away flecked with grit.

Ears *squealing*, I peek at the wall behind me where - inches from my head - a new gouge scars the splintered shingles. My muscles are rubber. My gut is unravelling on the floor of my stomach, heart flapping like a bird. I gag, but can't puke. My throat is knotted, acid squirting into my gullet. I check my hand again. No blood. The bullet missed my eye by an inch. The odds are crazy! The way it shattered the woodwork... A twitch closer, a slight gust of wind, and my skull would have been opened up like an egg, spraying yolk down the wall.

Through the *ringing,* I hear footsteps, crunching in gravel... I'm cowering, muscles fibrillating...

The shooter can see me now, huddled there. My back is hanging out of the nook like a billboard.

*Here it comes...*

A mule-kick in the back: The lug, tearing through my chest, just the way it busted open Benning's back, my guts boiling out into my lap.

Struggling to quiet my breathing, cheeks burning, kidneys knotted, I wonder for a second, if I'm already dead...

I should never have left Pete's bar. I keep thinking over and over, *I don't believe this...* and the deafening *ringing* in my ears is maddening. I should have stayed in *bed!* Maybe I should have stayed in Akron when I was eighteen!

Seconds last tens of seconds...

*He thinks he's hit me. Or— he's crouching at the corner, with a Betsy aimed at my spine, waiting for me to twitch.*

...I can't move. I've forgotten how. This isn't me, this violence. Jesus... Where did the shot come from? I needed to follow Barne outside... I had to know. Should I try my legs? Can I run? Or should I wait for someone to find me..? Nobody knows I'm here, huddled a block from Main Street between the lobster shacks, paralysed.

Muscles trembling, I turn my head. Growing it, so slowly, sideways. Enough to peer into the dark. My eyes burn, hazing the street light. I squeeze my lids shut – and blink. The grit in my pupils scratches under the lids.

If I ever get out of this – I'm going to live in the basement. Joe can bring me down hash browns and juice...

A dog barks somewhere.

Another minute passes... nothing.

*Come on folks, does anyone live in these goddamn garrets? Come out in your hair-rollers and bathrobes. Get out here! Come find me, curled up on the footpath, pissing my pants, sucking my thumb! Come out!*

A door slams. Or, is it another gunshot? It isn't close by. I lean out of my niche, half-crouched, and feel around for Barne's revolver where I dropped it, shining, inches away. I snatch it up, and aim the snub-nose up the neck of the lane, looking back to the corner behind me. Then north, past the crooked lamppost. The fear won't let go of my balls. They're nailed to the ground. *Jesus.* But I'm moving now, and I'm still alive. The Old-Runner-Shooter must be long gone by now?

Wobbling against the shingle wall, I roll onto my heels. A distant siren. It's Patrolman Keegan. The gunman will *have* to flee now. And the anonymous Runner-Shooter... They'd be laughing, at how easy it was to shoot up sleepy little New Brid. How feeble the civic resistance! The foot-chase ended with me diving into a wall.

I feel like I *should* have given back some action with Barne's *Smith and Wesson*. When the old silver-haired Runner-Shooter took a pop at me, I should have given back some action right there! But, it isn't my thing. I've never seen anything like this...

I stand slowly, and creep past the lamppost, listening for footsteps, car engines, voices, but the approaching siren impedes my ears. I turn the next corner, weepy-eyed.

The old-man Runner is standing four feet away.

In the dead-end lane, piled up with fishing junk and wire.

His back is turned to me. Close enough to touch. Closer than Jesus. I can hear him *breathing*. I can smell his sweat. I could shoot him in the back right now, if I dared to move.

Holding my breath, turning blue, impulsive, jingle-headed, shitless, witless, I jerk Barne's gun out into space. It's like catching a ball. My arm flies up of its own accord, aimed at the old-man Runner's shoulder. Any instant, he'll turn around and see me up close. I know it. The little man inside me who owns the balls is saying *it's time to jump and run*, but I don't like the idea... Bolting away down a crooked alley, waiting for a pill in the back...

But I can't pull the trigger either. It's not me. Not shooting a guy in the *back*.

Raising the revolver a foot in the air, I squeeze, and with a god-awful *crack*, the recoil snaps my wrist back and up. Orange sparks craze the air. I open my eyes to the clip-clop of running feet, as the old man takes a flying leap at the fence, twenty yards away, and tumbles into the darkness behind Hiptmeyer's bar.

At my own back, a woman screams. I spin around, pistol raised, and a night-robed banshee flees in the opposite direction, dropping a trail of bouncing hair rollers. A sharp pain flies up my wrist. *Christ.*

*The intoxication!* The hysterical guilt. The kick that came out of that little lamb-chop! *Wow.* And the old-man is gone, covering the distance to the fence at full tilt.

I grin widely, chemically high. I was *sure* I was dead about five times just then. It's a jackpot, coming through in one piece! The powder-fumes jazz my nostrils like paint. Another door squeals open in a nearby shack.

"Who's there?" A TV-jockey in his long-johns wields a fire iron.

"*It's okay!*" I yell, hoarsely. "Go inside till the *police* get here!' I emphasise the word '*police*' for *everyone* in earshot. "They'll be here *any second!*" I stumble down the alley, surveying the intersection. Golf clap. Round of applause. *Well-done Bobby. You've got good instincts.* The noise of chatter at my back alerts me to the arrival of more onlookers. Night-robed fishermen, grizzly haired. One with a baseball bat. Another, with a wrench. *A Constitutional Militia.*

"Please folks. Go back inside."

The knot of spectators sees the gun in my hand, and threatens to break.

"Bob Travis?" squeaks Long John with the poker.

I swagger down to the paling fence. "Go back inside," I answer half-heartedly, not really wanting them to. I give the fence a wild kick. The top-rail where the old man disappeared is higher than it looked from the other end of the street. "Hey!" I call out through the palings. "Hey, Asshole!"

...Nothing.

I look left-and-right for a way through the palings, but in the dark it doesn't seem possible. The only way around is over.

Keegan's siren is almost on top of us.

I gave the fence another push.

I don't want the old Runner to get away. I want to see where he's gone... I want him grilled, under a down-light. Who is he? Why is he shooting up New Brid? Has *he* seen the crossword puzzle?

I seize the top rail, and pull my chin up, peering into the adjacent alley at the back of Pete's. The soles of my shoes scuff, as I strain unglamorously to hold the position. I swing a leg up, and manage to hook my heel over the top. My track-pants pocket snatches a nail.

With a shriek of tearing towelling and a squeal of exertion, I haul myself onto the narrow perch, dipping my foot in the dark, lurching, off-balance, and tumble into the wires of a clothesline.

Garrotted, I pin-wheel to the cement. Landing with a guttural wheeze, I curl on the concrete, nursing my elbow, winded. Lightly testing my ribs, I'm sure I've broken something... He didn't know where, but something is broken. Cheek, wrist, elbow, ass. I'm hurting all over. And I've dropped Barne's gun again. I can't see an inch in front of my face!

Suddenly the confidence, the gun-rush of moments ago, has evaporated.

Fuck. What am I doing?

I pat down the pavement for the revolver, touching the warm barrel, and stow it in the good pocket in my track-pants.

I've lost my sense of which way I was facing. My eyes ache with the strain. The night air on my sweat-slick skin gives me a good jiggle as I place my feet. Arms outstretched. Heart pounding. I know, I should have waited for Keegan. My blood chemistry is heading south again. Strangling fear. I *have* to get back over that fence, out of the alley. I have to get home, wrap myself in Annie's arms. Here, in the dark, the mental images are more vivid: Benning turning into a ghost. Barne flipping in the air. Bullets thumping the car. The crossword. Matt. This *new* mystery. The short-lived gloryism has evaporated, replaced by an LSD-style doom.

Feeling my way by smell, I approach a row of dumpsters, wrestling down my panic, and look to scale back over the fence... My phone rings. Fumbling, I fish out the handset. The backlit screen lights up the surrounding bins.

"...Hello?"

I'm too late. The line is dead. Standing in the dark, I dial my message service.

*'Hello Mister Travis.'*

"I just missed a call. Is there a message?"

*'You have one new message from Missus Travis.'*

"Annie? What did she say?"

*'She's wondering where you are.'*

"That's it?"

*'Yes.'*

"...Thanks."

It's 2:30 a.m. I need to get home. To beg forgiveness. I aim the weak light of the phone at the garbage pile.

It takes a second to make out the darkened figure, crouching between two piles of damp newspaper and old vegetables, and the gun, aimed at my face.

"Don't... *move*," whispers the figure.

I can't form a reasonable thought. I peer from the gun to a face that could make a freight train take a dirt road; that grizzly mug, with its distinctive mess of eyebrows and sideburns. "*Clark?*"

"Get *out* of here!" snarls Diffner, like a bulldog chewing a wasp.

"What are you doing—?!"

"Get out of here!"

"You almost killed me!"

Diffner's breathing is irregular. He looks like a duck in a thunderstorm, huddled in the trash. He jerks the gun wildly. "Go! Before I change my mind."

"You're a goddamn lunatic! You almost blew my *head* off!" I smell a strange stench, other than the odour of the rotten waste. It's like bagged fireworks. "What's going on? Who... who shot Benning?"

"How *dare* you," Diffner seethes. "After what you've done!"

"What I've— *What?*"

"Don't *lie* to me!" he bawls, his moonlit face creased with the shadows of popping tendons. "*Don't...* lie to me!"

"How dare *me?* How dare *you!*" I spit. "This business with the fucking *crossword?* In two hours, this town is going to be crawling with Feds! And they're going to question me! So *you* better start talking!"

Diffner struggles to his feet. "Are you threatening me?"

"Yes," I reply too loudly.

"I know!"

"Huh?"

"I *know* you lied."

"*I* lied?"

Diffner steps around the bins, coming towards me, gun aimed at my nose. "Who do you think *you* are?"

I hesitate, struck by the unexpected aggression. The all-running, all-jumping track-and-field marksman. *Our Man in Rome.* I don't have the metal for this, but I'm not going into a corner either. "Look!" I huff. "I'm the only person who can place you here, and you're dancing like a string man to keep out of the fire. So I want to know! What's going on?!"

"You arrogant shit!" Diffner reaches out to grab me.

I see the movement, and recoil. I don't know what this is, but I'm in no mood for it. "I'm talking to the cops," I scowl, and step hurriedly back the way I came. My hand goes to the fence, ready to climb.

Diffner croaks like he's having an aneurysm, and seizes my shoulder in his claw.

Before I can twist free, I'm being spun around, one hand clamped over my mouth, pinned against a dumpster like an empty shirt, lifted up off my feet. My wrist presses against my throat. Before I can yell, I'm twisted like a pretzel, joints screaming, full-Nelsoned in mid-air, one arm bent behind my back, thumb-webbing wrenched sideways. My elbow *pops*. "Nggh!" I wheeze helplessly. My shoulder is just a small push away from snapping out of its socket. "*OOOW!*" I cry, muffled. *What is this Kung Fu bullshit?!*

Diffner, like a hideous Kabuki-masked Karate lord, presses his lips close to my ear and whispers... His voice is uneven, trembling. "*Who did you tell?*"

"What?" I woof, trying to think. I clap my heel against the dumpster, but it makes no sound.

"Who did you *tell?*" Diffner repeats quietly, right in my ear, his breathing damp.

There is such urgency in Diffner's tone. I try feebly to shake my head, sucking air through a crack in Diffner's nicotine-stained fingers.

"*WHO?!*" He shakes me like a doll.

"I don't know what you mean..."

"Tell me!"

"I don't know what *you mean!*"

"The goddamned *tablet!*"

It's a murderous *ache* in my chest. My gut rides up into my neck. ...*Tablet?*

Diffner removes some of his weight, peering up close, eyes inches from mine. "Tell me. Or, I swear. I'll take you somewhere quiet, and I'll pull your teeth out with a claw hammer... Then I'll stick a cigarette in *your* eyes, just like *he* did to Matthias."

I steal another breath, straining, humiliated by his physical weakness. "*What?* Who?" I'm verging on hysterical now. "I don't understand!"

Diffner's hold loosens slightly, and he sighs like a puncture, dropping me and stepping back.

I slump into the fence.

"Get out of here."

I shake my head. "Wait—"

"Get out of here *now*, before it's too late."

"Too late for what?"

"Go!"

"Not till you tell me what's going on."

"The only reason you're even still alive, is because you *haven't* known what's going on!"

A voice calls out through the fence. "Bob Travis!"

It's Carl Keegan, junior lawman. His face is so pinkish-pale, if you stuck a Maglite in his back his crew-cut noggin would glow like a night light.

Diffner seizes me by the collar. "Tell *nobody* you've seen me. *No one.* Or I won't be able to protect you!"

*Protect me?*

"Listen to me! If they find out... you're finished. Just go! Now!" Diffner jerks his gun in the direction of the fence. "*NOW!*"

I shake my head. "Wait—"

"Bob Travis?" Keegan raps on the fence, ten feet away.

"If anyone knows you've seen me, they'll twist your fucking neck," whispers Diffner. "They'll work you over. Anne will find you in the barn, with your head in a tool vice. You have to get *out* of here!"

"But—"

"Hey!" Keegan's footsteps are loud and fast in the shale outside. "Bob!"

"Just pretend you never saw me. Go home. We never talked. I was never here. Trust me. *Never* tell anybody. *Ever!*" Diffner jabs a finger at me in the gloom. "Or they'll kill you. And anyone else you talk to."

I still can't move. "Who shot Barne Ruberight... and Agent Benning?"

Keegan raps on the fence with a nightstick. "Bob? Is that you?"

"The *Twin Lights Inn.* On the road to Rockport." Diffner muffles a cough with his sleeve. "Room Sixteen. Be there before sunrise. Don't tell anybody. Now get out of here." He turns, and slips into the dark.

The real-life horror sinks in. Nothing but a half-inch of timber, and a bad smell, stands between me and jail bracelets. Am I a witness, or accomplice? I'm not sure. *What just happened?*

Keegan calls out again. "Bob! I'm coming over."

"No!" I boost myself onto the dumpster, and lean over the fence, dropping back down into the lane, jarring my ankle.

Keegan is skipping from side to side, revolver aimed at the sky. "Fuck! Bob, what happened?!"

Up the alley, the flock of night-robed residents hold their distance. All eyes are on me.

"The Chief's *dead!*" squeals Keegan. "What happened?"

I gasp, trembling, trying desperately to think.

"Where were you? What were you doing?"

"I– lost him."

"Lost who?"

"I saw him... running," I add. "Here..." I fumble Barne's gun out of my pocket and hand it over.

Keegan stares at the revolver in my hand. "It that Barne's gun?"

"I tried to see where he went, and... he shot me. I mean, shot *at* me."

Keegan looks past me at the fence. "He went this way?"

"'No, he's gone."

"Did you see his face?"

"He was too fast. We– We should get back to Barne."

"Yeah... Yeah... Awright." Keegan notices me nursing my side, pants ripped at the pocket. "You okay?"

"I'm fine," I nod. "I fell."

"Did you get a look at this guy *at all?*"

"No." I'm not lying convincingly. My mind is running out of control. But I can't tell the truth either. I need time to think.

"Nothin'?" Keegan persists, suspiciously. "Short? Tall?"

"He had a thick build. He turned to look back at me. He had like... sandy-blonde hair. I don't really know. I lost him."

"Sandy blonde hair," notes Keegan.

*Christ...* "I guess. He shot at me," I repeat, justifying my confusion. "He almost blew my head off."

Keegan raises his arm, like he's about to throw his gun on the ground. "Christ! Essex County are gonna be *aaall* over this."

"Huh?"

Keegan holsters his revolver. He's more worried about his own ass, than mine. "Come on. We never left the Chief, okay? We were with him the whole time."

I consider bringing Keegan's attention to the half-dozen locals looking on. "Come on," I offer, my jiggled brain finally starting to fly straight.

"*All of you!* Come on!" Keegan waves people off the street. "Back inside."

Around the front, Pete Hiptmeyer is creeping around the nose of the Lincoln to look at the bloodied shapes of Benning and Barne.

"*Pete!*" barks Keegan. Hiptmeyer retreats.

Back at the scene of the original chaos, my main concern is that the *other* shooter is still here – if Diffner wasn't the shooter? Someone is out there in the street, in the shadows. I don't know... Diffner *could* be the shooter, if he got ahead of me somehow, and someone else was behind me? The shot that missed me came from Diffner. But who shot Benning and Barne? *Jesus.* I'm pumping a cocktail of semi-euphoria and terror again, but my head is running okay.

"What the fuck?!" squeaks Keegan, gawking.

The first thing I notice as I approach the cars, are the gallons of blood draining over to the curb, down the street towards the beach. As I round the front of the Lincoln, I see the two prone figures.

What I find, strikes me like a white-hot bolt of fizzing plasma.

Agent Benning, and Chief Barne Ruberight, both have a gory black hole where an eye should be. *Both* of them have had an eyeball cut out – Barne's left, and Benning's right. The opposite eye, intact in both sets of features, stares gruesomely at the moon.

I look at Pete. "He came back?!"

"I went to call the ambulance—"

"He came back!" I point at the two bodies, looking to Keegan. "Huh?"

Keegan spits bile onto the kerb.

I'm unable to look away. The image of Matt's body in the mortuary, eyes burned out with a lit cigarette...

Keegan hovers protectively beside the Lincoln, murmuring something, wiping his mouth with his sleeve.

I'm not listening. The sweat is beading on my forehead faster than I can wipe it down.

The bodies give off a mysterious vapour, like a pair of dumped fridges. Keegan peels off his jacket and lays it over Barne's contorted face. Then he pulls Barne's matching jacket - where the Chief laid over Benning - up over the CIA man's head.

"You sure you should touch them?" I suggest.

"Fuck it."

I don't have a clue what I'm going to say when I'm asked to retrace my steps.

"What the hell do we *do*?" Keegan paces, looking at me like he seriously expects me to know the answer.

It's too improbable. I glance at my car. I have to leave, go to the *Twin Lights Inn*, and find Diffner, before dawn. If he's even *there*? If it isn't just something he said to get rid of me. Diffner knows there's no way I can get away. "Shit," I blurt.

Keegan walks closer. "What?"

I nod downwards. A bullet-hole, the size of an Oreo puckers the passenger-door of my BMW.

Keegan scratches his head.

I've seen enough cop shows to know this makes the car evidence. Technicians will search the chassis for a slug, and use the puncture to figure the line of fire. If they find a bullet, and it traces back to Diffner, they'll put two and two together - I worked with Diffner. The connection will raise questions. Maybe they'll find DNA in the alley, placing us both there, and *wham*. I'll be an accomplice. '*Why else was Diffner running?*' they'll ask. *What was he doing in New Brid?* And if he was staying at the *Twin Lights*, hiding out in a cheap hotel, '*Why?*' Maybe Clark had a reason to take out Benning? Imagine the Feds, when the only witness turns out to be pals with a suspect? The New York bomber connection... They'll lock me up and ask questions later.

Keegan wipes his forehead. "You'll have to leave it here."

"What?"

"Your car."

"I can't. I need it."

Keegan eyes me cautiously. "That's the way it's gotta be. Call someone to come pick you up."

'"My wife is in Boston," I lie. Annie's phone message indicates she's back, but Keegan isn't to know. "We can mark the place where it's parked. Just for tonight. I'll bring it back tomorrow—"

Keegan sours. "Give me the keys. I'll have a Patrolman drive you home." He holds out his paw.

For the first time, he eyes me with real suspicion...

I sigh, and hand over the keys.

"I'll get someone to take you home, and I'll call you in the morning. You'll have to come into the station." Suddenly Keegan is all business, now he's found something to do. I felt my chest tightening. It's hard to breathe. I don't have to worry, right? I've done nothing. I'll be fine. I just have to focus on the *order of events.*

I check my watch. It's 2:42 a.m. My whole world has gone pear-shaped, in under an hour.

I take a long, deep breath, and look down for one last time at the bloodied, prone form of Barne Ruberight...

Tears jump unexpectedly into my eyes, as it hits home. *Old Barne...* He's been police Chief for as long as I can remember. Pete Hiptmeyer tells the story Barne came into the bar twenty years ago with a moustache, wearing a plaid jacket, Pete sold him an orange whip, and all the bar flies rolled around splitting their sides because Barne hadn't seen John Candy at the Palace Hotel Ballroom. Or the time he picked up Bert Morney's kid for breaking a shop window, then sat in the cell with him all night playing draughts to make sure he wasn't scared.

Matt. Barne. Benning. The subway...

Diffner's words by the dumpster, echo in my ears:

*The only reason you're still alive, is because you don't know what's going on.*

Keegan digs around eagerly in his shirt-pocket for something, and comes out with a curled stick of gum. Chewing feverishly, he waves his arm around in the general direction of the bodies, shooing me away.

I move off, one hand cupped over my eyes, faking a yawn, hiding my tears.

## 17. '...KNOWLEDGE INCREASETH SORROW...'

*Thursday, September 13, 2012*

The patrol car trundles up the tree-lined gravel drive. A row of trees form a moonless canopy overhead, bordering the brightly-lit turning-circle in front of the stoop.

The Patrolman leans over the wheel of the cruiser, peering up at the haloed balconies, flood lamps abuzz over the driveway, and whistles. "Some house."

Annie's SL Benz convertible is parked at the door.

"Thought she wasn't 'sposed to be home?" asks the Patrolman, reaching for his radio.

"She isn't." I climb wearily out of the cruiser.

The blue-and-white rushes away.

Annie stamps out into the entrance in her robe, eyes following the cruiser.

From her expression, I know how bad I look. My track-pants are ripped and twisted, my shirt tousled and flecked with grease, dirt, and blood. My face is scratched raw.

"What happened?!" she gasps.

"When did you get home?" I answer, weakly. Out of nowhere, I feel like my knees have been cut out from under me. I want nothing more than to sit down on the ground, right here. I lope past Annie, into the house.

"Where's your car?"

"Someone shot Barne Ruberight."

"You're kidding... Is he all right?" Annie takes my wrist and leads me to the kitchen.

"No."

"God! What happened?"

I follow her to the kitchen bench, lit by the narrow beam of the stained-glass lamp. "He showed up here at the house with a C.I.A. agent, and asked me to come into town."

"Why?"

It's only now that I realise, I'll have to put a fence around how much I tell her, for a bunch of reasons – her father *and* the subway bombers are involved. There's also what Diffner said... *You can never tell anybody that you saw me, Ever... Or they will kill you...and anyone else you talk to.* But– How much to tell her? "To... talk about something. We were at Pete's. The Fed, both of them were shot. Outside Pete's."

"What... what did they want to talk about?"

"I don't know," I lie, again. Nobody can ever know. I can still feel the *Bud Lite* coaster, and the page from the newspaper scrunched in my ripped pocket.

Annie sees me check my hip. "Ouch!" I exaggerate the pain.

She goes to work on the espresso machine, as I pick clumsily through pieces of the story, turning the memories over, trying to join them back together. I tell her as much as I can without mentioning Matt... or Muhannad al-Baghdadi... or finding Diffner between the dumpsters. I can't tell her that either. I know she'd tell me to call the Essex County Sheriff. I can't tell her, not if I want to get to the *Twin Lights Inn* in time to find Diffner...

"Do you want another coffee?" she asks softly, when I fall silent. She knows there's more. But I've told her all I can.

I shake my head. "I was almost shot," I add. I'll refine the story later. Right now, I have to find a way to go.

"So - you've got no idea what they wanted to talk about?" Anne asks again.

"Huh?"

"You said, this man, and Chief Ruberight, wanted to talk to you about something?"

"Oh, I don't know." I hold my head in my hands. "It all happened before we could talk."

"Who did you think it was?"

"Huh? I don't know..."

"Could it be terrorists?"

"*No.* Of course not."

"How do you know? Nothing would surprise me today." She *was* right about that. Nothing would surprise *me*, either. "Have you heard from Madison?" I ask.

Annie shakes her head. "I got a call through to her landline, but there was no answer. I still can't get through to her cell."

"Hmm..." I take my mug to the sink. "I just hope the bullet didn't go through anything in the car."

Anne frowns. "Forget about your car," and squeezes my shoulders. "You've got nothing to worry about, right?"

"Huh? Sure."

"Let's go to bed. You need some rest."

"You go," I whisper. "I'll be up in a minute."

After a short pause, Annie tightens the belt on her nightgown. "Okay."

I've *never* set out to lie to her before. Not purposely. "I'm sorry Honey," I add, with a lump in my throat, and wait for her to look at me.

"Why?"

"My head is all over the place." A part of me wishes she could just read *all* of my thoughts. Or... maybe she *can*.

"Do you want something to help you sleep?" she asks.

"No, thanks. I'll be fine in a minute."

Annie walks away. I lower my head.

Nothing much Diffner said in the alley, made any sense...

I shuffle to the kitchen table, and wait for silence upstairs.

I've *never* seen such violence before. The bloodiest thing I ever saw was a mare giving birth. Now... I need to get to the Twin Lights. Diffner won't stick around. If he hasn't left already. It's three o'clock. I'm zapped. I'm seeing spots. In a few hours the whole town will be crawling with County Deputies, State Police, and Feds...

I take out the scrunched crossword puzzle, and smooth it on the table. *Who else knew about this?* Matt is dead. Benning and Barne are dead. The New York subway bomber is dead... Who is killing people to keep this a secret? I can't imagine a single reasonable excuse to leave the house now. And I'm unable to move, for fear of making a decision.

Finally, I stand and walk to the den. I open the desk drawer, take out the copy of Matt's crossword puzzle book – the one Joe left here – and lay the crossword puzzle and the *Bud Lite* coaster inside, along with the grim Polaroid death-mask.

I creep upstairs, undress, wash, and slip under the covers with Annie, wide-awake, staring at her back.

There's no way to tell her what happened. Even if there was, it would take hours. There's no time. Tomorrow there will be *official* questions. I need answers now, or I might find myself 'obstructing justice', complicit, under suspicion, no clue what I'm hiding, or why, or if I *should* be hiding anything. "Annie," I whisper.

If I tell her the whole story, she'll stop me. Of course she will. But I want to trust her. *She's my wife. I love her.* I don't want her involved. Not tonight.

"Annie?"

I just have to get to the Inn, only for a few minutes. I can tell her everything tomorrow, when I know more. She needs to know.

"I left my cell phone in my car..." I whisper.

Annie stays silent.

I know from the sound of her breathing, she's wide awake.

I park the car half a mile from the Twin Lights, under the gnarled jack pines, invisible from the road.

Beyond the neck-high wood roars the rugged coastline, waves breaking on the plutonic cliffs, carbonating the breeze with spray.

I speed-walk along the road, half jogging, in dark-brown chinos and sneakers, watching over my shoulder for motorists... Maybe I'll get myself zonked by some drunken kid with a bat out the window, playing mailbox baseball. I don't turn around completely though. If anyone recognises me, there will be more talk. A homer on the back of the head, I can handle.

The air stinks of road-apples, horse squits, the funky hum beating the air. The first one goes up to my ankle. "Fuck!" I stomp my foot, trying to shake the suede clean. *Jeezus.* The stink is godawful, as I pick my way slowly towards the Twin Lights.

A tired cinderblock wall surrounds the two-story hotel on three sides. Fear clenches round me like a giant fist. *What am I doing here?* It isn't too late to turn around, and go home. Maybe I should just lawyer up, bunker down, and wait for this to pass.

I stop, and stare at the grim, faux manor house – mission brown casements in chipped render, the concrete compartments stacked like shoeboxes behind the main building.

If Diffner *is* here, I have to confront him. I have to know.

I tip-toe through the tunnel in the side of the building, between the reception and a restaurant-bar that reeks – even through the walls – tap beer and mouldy carpet. The central parking lot is still. Frost rims the car hoods. I do my best to look casual. Un-prowler-like. Just a regular Joe Soap, taking a stroll at half-three in the morning.

The rooms are numbered with twenty-inch painted numerals on the doors. Number Sixteen is on the middle of the second floor.

Anxiety grips me more tightly, stopping my breath. I creep up the stairwell, loving the wall, and pause before delivering myself to a final act of violence beyond this door. I can't turn away, for fear of worse to come. Or maybe I'll walk in on a stranger, an anonymous throwback with his leg over a goat. Hesitating before I knock, I test the handle. The door pops open.

Slipping into the room, I'm engulfed by darkness.

The musty odour is poorly masked by cheap apple-scented air freshener. I reach habitually for the light switch, but catch myself. A solitary light in the bleak hotel will scream mischief.

"Clark?" I whisper, immobile in the gloom.

The silence indicates I've arrived too late.

Finally, an anxious voice. "Where's your car?"

"Half a mile away," I complain.

Diffner strikes a trembling pipe match, illuminating his derelict features in a halo of space. He is seated on the far side of the bed in his steaming overcoat. A small travel bag, a wad of tobacco in brown wax paper, and a mean-looking automatic pistol lay on the quilted bedcover. He looks every bit the part of the fearful fugitive, pistol in easy reach, watching the door...

"Did you tell Anne?" He sucks the flame from the match through the nub of his soapstone pipe.

"No—!" I retort, indignant.

The match shakes a final time, and dies leaving the room darker than before, and a bright whorl in my vision. "Did you tell *anybody* you saw me?"

"No. Now what *the fuck* is going on?!"

"Keep your voice down," Diffner spurts faint iridescent pipe smoke.

"How much did Benning tell you?"

"About the crossword?"

"Did they figure it out?"

"I did. It wasn't hard. Where did *you* get it?" I reply.

"Sit down."

I deliberate. Should I fumble my way toward a seat? Stumbling around in the dark is just too ironic. But I'm dog-tired. I have to muster my energy, to shake the walls, to make Diffner talk. I glance at the luminous dial on my watch. "Thanks, I'll stand."

"Suit yourself."

"I want to know... From the beginning. What was that guy doing here...?" *Benning*. I whisper, mindful of people in the adjacent rooms. "Where did you get the crossword puzzle? Benning said you brought it in a week ago. I'm not going anywhere without answers."

Diffner's voice is even softer. "You need to listen to me... very carefully."

"I'm listening."

"You need to go home, pack what you need, and take your wife and your son where nobody will *ever* find you."

A dark chill runs up my spine. "What? *Why?*"

"Join the dots, Bob," he murmurs, quickly, urgently. "Madison gave me the crossword."

"Madison?"

"She found it in Matt's things. She thought it had something to do with why Matt was *murdered*. The *same day* you got an invitation to come to Washington and meet me?"

*Matt was murdered?*

"You never found that unusual?"

*...Yes.* "I thought—"

"We've *both* been set up, Bob. *They* introduced us! They put us in the same hotel, put us on the same plane! And gave us a project to work on together."

"It— wasn't you?"

"They needed to find out *how much* we knew. They gave us the opportunity to talk. I can't believe I didn't see it..."

It's disturbingly cunning. What better way to find out what someone knows, than to provide a sympathetic ear, and listen? "Who did this? Was it Dodd?"

"Higher."

"How is that even possible?"

"*Christ!*" snaps Clark. "I *warned* you this would bring the world down around your ears!"

The fit of rage reminds me of the all-sprinting, all-jumping Jujitsu-lord in the alley, twisting me up like a human bow-tie. "Because of this *crossword puzzle?*" I bicker.

"You tell me? Where did you get the idea about the tablet?"

"I don't know. I guess Matt might have said something once—"

Diffner seizes the edge of the bed. "You have to go. Take Anne and Joe, and disappear. The further, the better! Tonight!"

"Wait! For Christ's sake!" I rub my throat, still sore from the alley. I'm shaking. My whole body feels like it's been put through a wringer. Something still doesn't make sense. "Why are you here—?"

And then, it hits me.

There's another explanation.

A more reasonable one.

*He's doing it. He was actually doing it. The forgery!* "Oh god," I groan. "You're actually trying to pull it off?"

"What?"

"The fake tablet! Why? Is this because of Madison?"

"What?"

"You're actually going *through* with it!" I adjust my stance, still against the door, ready to flee. I recall the first time I took the idea to Diffner, when I was laughed out of the old house - Madison hadn't said much, but she'd agreed with me... Today, Diffner called me back... the double back-flip, going for the idea, then suddenly talking me out of it... I'd been so distracted, I hadn't seen it. "You said - we should leave it *alone!*" I hiss shrilly. "You said, *Matt was a friend. As a favour to him, I want to make sure you let this go!*"

"You're way off." Diffner spits sourly.

"You shot Benning... And—!"

"Did you even *read* the crossword?"

"Yes!"

"What did you think the '*M*' stands for!"

"Look! Whatever you're involved in, I don't want anything—"

"Jeezus!" Diffner thumps the bed dully. "I thought you said you'd *solved it!*"

I seize the door handle, about to run.

"Listen! Forchrissake, listen! The '*M!*' The first letter in the cipher! *That's* the secret!"

The words penetrate the gauze of terror. "What?"

"Here!" Diffner reaches inside his coat and pulls out a damp page of note paper with a spidery diagram drawn on it... "Look!"

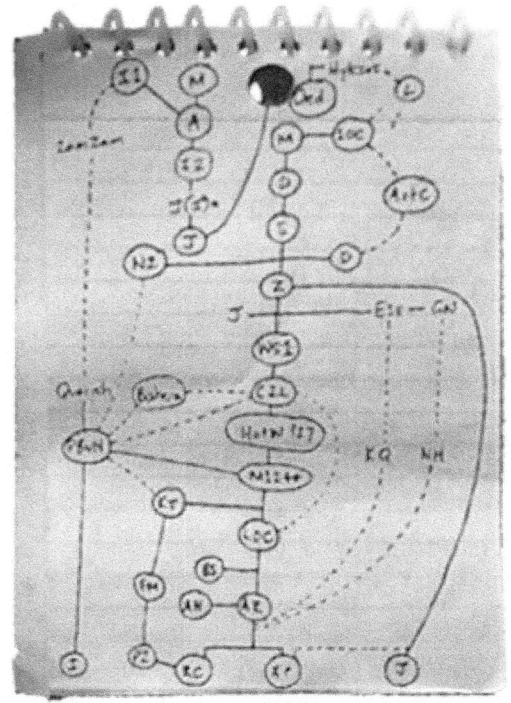

*(Diagram 14 - Diffner's hand-drawn diagram)*

"What's this?"

"The letters in the crossword! See there..." He points to the 'M-A...' in the top left-hand corner of the pad. "'A' is Abraham! 'O-One' and 'I-Two' are for Ishmael and Isaac! It's a history of religion, right back to Abraham, like we discussed! But the *whole* diagram... It's about the '*M*!" There's a tone of hysteria in his voice. "*Before* Abraham! The first king of Jerusalem! The man who converted *Abraham* to god! '*Priest of the most high God.*' It's the first place the word 'priest' – *hiereus* – is *ever* used!" Diffner leans forward. "See! The first priest, the king of Jerusalem, *before* Abraham. His name— starts with an '*M.*'"

I have no idea what he's talking about, if he does. "What?"

"*THAT* is the secret! That is why the tablet stayed hidden! King Melchizedek. '*M*' is for Melchizedek!"

I shake my head, confused. "Madison found this in Matt's things?"

"The first priest, the first church, the first king of Jerusalem. *Before* Abraham... The father of Judaism, Christianity *and* Islam! It's right there: '*And Melchizedek blessed Abraham and said, Blessed be Abraham of the most high God.*' The tablet is written by Melchizedek! It's real!"

"No—"

Diffner growls. "It's in the Bible... 'King of righteousness, King of peace... without mother, without descent, having neither beginning of days, nor end of life; but made like unto the Son of God... Consider how great this man was, unto whom even the patriarch Abraham gave the tenth part of the spoils... And without all contradiction, the less is blessed of the better.'"

"Now *you're* out of your mind," I mutter.

"'I am Melchizedek, the Priest of God Most High... it is I who am truly the image of the true High-Priest of God Most High...' The Father of all churches, before Mohammed, before Jesus, before Abraham... Father of all priests. Jesus is even described as a high priest forever 'after the order of Melchizedek.' Look it up! The son of god, himself! Why doesn't anybody talk about the single most important figure in religious history? Why are there no stories or statues or songs, about the man who started it all?! Why is he kept a secret... Not the tablet! HIM!"

If the notion of a *tablet* from Abraham seemed bold, this was even more intoxicating... that it could be proven...

Diffner eyes me expectantly.

"You're not making this up?"

"Someone is killing everybody who comes close to this! What *else* would make emperors and Pharaohs – Akhenaten, Nebuchadnezzar, Constantine – *all* copy the same god? They *all* ruled empires mad with idol worship. A god for rain, a god for cows, one for tall wheat and short wheat, another one for every different day of the week... Cults vying for control. Factionism. Melchizedek had the solution – one god of *everything*, and – himself, as high priest. He was the first king to do it! A god, so powerful it was forbidden to make statues. *'Give god one tenth of your wealth'*, he said, and they did. And he collected *two* taxes. *'Do as I say, I am god's anointed ruler!'* And they did as he said! He united his people, claimed authority over their lesser gods, and conferred divine authority on himself: god's high priest. The idea thrived. The 'King-Priest'. People traded their lesser faiths. They were obedient. Other kings travelled to *worship* him, to give him gifts, including Abraham! To bow before him, to seek his blessing. All previous systems of belief *and* government were weak prototypes for Melchizedek's state. He started it all!"

Either this is complete madness, or bigger than anything...

"What else could so deeply affect *every future king* who came into contact with this tablet? What could this tablet possibly say that *had* to remain a secret, no matter what the cost? After four thousand years? The biggest secret you can imagine."

I mumble, dazed, repeating myself. "It's real?"

"A secret worth *all* the conspiracy and manipulation. A secret for *all* the Inquisitions, crusades, massacres, suicides, tortures, witch hunts, and holocausts. A secret for which *millions* of people have died..."

The floor feels like it's dissolving beneath my feet, opening over a sea of flame.

"Abraham, Akhenaten, Nebuchadnezzar, King David, Jesus, Constantine..." *M, D, S.* Moses, David, Solomon... "The letters in the crossword puzzle! All of them, were following Melchizedek."

The common link, right down through history... King David built the original temple to store the Ark of the Covenant - 'AOTC'. It's on the code. The temple was sacked by Nebuchadnezzar - 'NZ' - restored by Zerubbabel - 'Z'...

"What are these other letters? *CZL? WS1?*" I ask, pointing at the diagram.

His finger trembles as he leans over the bed, and points at the loci in the middle of the diagram. "'CZL' is the airport code for the city of 'Constantine' in Algeria. 'WS1', is William Shakespeare's first play - the first one *printed*... 'Titus.' The Second Temple in Jerusalem - where the Ark was kept - was sacked by Titus."

The site is still being warred over today... Jews and Muslims... The city of *Melchizedek's* throne... All the centuries of evil. All the wars and corruption... Babylon, Egypt, Rome... All followed this same religion, Emperors installing themselves as high priests. ...Was it possible? A reason to kill so many?

I whisper, my words echoing in the small room, full of sadness. "It's real."

Diffner's brow furrows. "Yes. It's real."

Matt was murdered, for this secret? Madison found the crossword... Gave it to Diffner... Someone set us up to meet, to watch us, and see how much we knew... "Who...? Who wrote the code? Was it Matt?"

"I don't know if it was *from* Matt, or *to* him."

"...What do we do?"

"We *run*."

I'm mute. Physically paralysed. Doomed. "But— there's no proof? We have no proof. Why would anyone want to kill us?" Abraham. Akhenaten. Moses. Nebuchadnezzar. David. Solomon. Mohammed.

Jesus. Titus. Constantine. A line of kings. A diagram of history. Catholicism, Islam, Judaism and Christianity all tied to one man. Hidden, for twenty centuries... It was just an idea...

"What's the connection to the subway attacks?" I ask.

"What connection?" asks Diffner, surprised.

"Benning told me... They found copies of the crossword in the apartments of two of the subway bombers."

Diffner stares into the void between us. "I don't know..."

"I can't run," I mutter. *What about Annie and Joe?*

"Go north, Canada, Alaska. Take cash. Talk to *no one*. If *anyone* finds out you know about this, they'll find you."

"I can't just *take* Annie and Joe and... What do I tell them?"

"Does it *matter–*?"

The room is spinning.

All the world is drenched in blood and I'm sick with fear. Paralysing fear. I just want to go home. And never look back. I want to climb into bed, and wake up, and find it's all been a dream. Nobody would hurt Annie and Joe? Right?

"What are you waiting for? Don't you understand? *Get out of here!*"

I turn toward the door. "What happened?" I plead, with my hand on the latch. "You were going to leave this alone! What the fuck did you do?"

Diffner pales. "I came here to try to warn you!"

"What are you going to do?"

"Look at me! Same as you. I'm going to *run.*"

I don't hear another word. I open the door, and step into the night.

Diffner's final word, hushed through the gap in the door, propels me.

*Run.*

I stumble down the stairs into the courtyard. All I can think about, is getting clear of the hotel. Outside in the dark, I feel eyes on me. Every shadow harbours monstrous agents... A still, small voice in my head, tells me someone is watching. Not god. Not the devil. Worse...

I run from the Inn, gripped by a more acute sense of danger than when I arrived.

'M' is for Melchizedek...

It's almost sunrise. The risk of being seen on the road is too great. The only way back to the car is along the cliffs, through the woods. Witless, fatigued, I bolt in the direction of the ocean, up an uneven trail, scrambling out over the rocky promontory by the sea, through three-hundred yards of brush, thorns, twigs, and hare-holes. Like a logging machine loose in the scrub, I crash through the pre-dawn gloom, panicked... panting.

Falling into the car, I thump the accelerator, and race to the house.

There's a glimmer of sun in the sky over the roof as I brake Anne's car in the driveway.

I leave the car outside, afraid to wake Annie with the garage door. Instead, I sit behind the wheel, frozen, willing myself out onto the front steps, motionless again in the car. Lost in thought.

*There must be somebody I can talk to, to straighten this out...*

I reach for the car's door handle, and– I stop.

What will I tell Annie? There's *no* way to explain where I've even been. Or why. Or what happened. Or what was *still* happening. I have *no* answers. Only more questions.

What the fuck do I do?

If I hadn't seen two men *killed...* if I hadn't nearly been killed myself, if Matt wasn't dead, I wouldn't credit any of it. There's no way of being sure what's real. There's no way I can breathe a word of this, to anyone...What if it *is* real?

I can't stroll back into the bedroom, and ask Annie to pack her bags.

I've never been so exhausted. The fear and adrenaline have drained every last spark from my bones. Panic presses down like a stone.

Movement at the front door catches my attention.

Joe is standing on the stoop, looking out curiously at me.

I force a smile, and climb out onto the driveway. "Hey Joe! What are you doin' up this late?!"

Joe screws up his face. "I'm making breakfast, ding-a-ling."

I force a weak laugh. At sixteen, he reminds me of myself when I was thirty.

*This is fine, right?* Seeing the old man creep in at sunrise?

Smiling graciously, Joe beckons for me to come up the steps. "I'm making eggs. Want some?"

"Thanks. That's nice. But I'm— not feeling too well. I might just go to bed."

Joe shrugs. "Fair 'nuf."

I've barely seen him since Matt died, the day we went fishing. It won't do any harm to go have eggs. Shoot the breeze. I'm fagged and footsore, but it'll take five minutes. It might be the last chance we have, for a moment of peace. Then I'll go upstairs, see Annie, and tell her what happened.

I stuff my frigid hands into the pockets of my chinos, and follow Joe into the kitchen.

Everything is laid out for a cook up. Rashers. Hash browns. I collapse in a chair. "Does Mum know you're using the gas?"

Joe splutters. "Very funny."

"What are you doing today?"

"I'm going fishing," Joe expertly cracks an egg, elbows in the air. "I made a new fly with a bucktail collar. Wanna come try it out?"

He's so free of hang-ups. Not a nervous bone in his body.

"Hang on a minute... I might come with you," I lie. "I just have to go talk to Mum, okay?"

"Awright."

I stand up, and almost walk over to tousle his locks. But he's too big for that now. I amble upstairs and into the bedroom, pausing by the bed.

Annie is asleep.

I'm tempted to sleep a little myself, before I wake her. Maybe I can just lie next to her, for a minute... I take off my burr-filled sweater, and throw it into the robe, then bunch myself up at the top of the blankets. Annie rolls over, bumping my arm, and flinches. My skin is cold. Her eyes come up to meet mine. "Bobby? What's wrong?"

I curl my wrists over my eyes, blocking the dawn at the drapes.

She tugs at my shoulder. "Bob? What is it?"

*What do I say?*

A week ago, everything was perfect. This morning, it's all gone. I'm falling... like an anvil, an anchor, dragged down with the weight of suns... and the ground rushing up to meet me.

"Did you hear from Madison?" I ask.

Annie shakes her head, rubbing her eyes. "Where have you been?"

"I'll tell you in the morning."

"You okay?"

"Yup," I pet her arm.

Annie rolls back on her side.

I lay on my back, unable to close my eyes.

Diffner's revelation, about the encrypted broadcast to the world, had diverted my attention... Who *are* these people? There are too many questions. The clues point to something the size of humanity, buried deep in history... all linked. What are the odds? I'm like the kid herding goats who throws a stone into a hole in Qayla, and uncovers the 'genizah' – the hiding place – Khirbat Qumran, and the Dead Sea scrolls. The scrolls described every treasure in the tunnels and cracks of the Jerusalem temple mount – the sakhra – now the Dome of the Rock mosque, Mount Moriah. Every hollow, every secret chamber. The scrolls described everything, except the most important item... the Ark of the Covenant... *Where did it go? What was inside it?* Somebody must know where it went. Something that important, doesn't just disappear. Not with the handwritten word of god inside. Even before Islam or Catholicism... Why were the contents kept secret? As far back as Moses... If god delivered a tablet, how could it be *lost?*

Diffner's right... This idea needs no proof. It's self-evident. There are a hundred clues, right through history... Once you see it... you can't get around the fact it's there.

Maybe that's why the secret is so dangerous.

Sunlight filters through the drapes. I try closing my eyes for a moment, and see the corpses of Benning and Barne, prone in a mire of blood, eyes cut out.

Is this the day I'll be found dead – eyes plucked from my skull...

# 18. '...LAKE OF FIRE AND BRIMSTONE...'

*Thursday, September 13, 2012*

Annie shakes me awake.

I raise my head, grunting with the exertion, and look at the clock. It's 8:00am. Two hours rest. "I fell asleep?"

"Where are my keys?"

"Keys?" I feel like I've bled to death in my sleep. I groan loudly. "Aaaaargh. *Jeeeeezus!*"

"*Goddammit!* My *car* keys!" Annie *never* swears. She's dressed. On her way out. No kisses. No 'good morning'. She's disappointed she had to wake me. She wanted me to wake up alone.

"Where ya goin'?" I ask, sitting up, dopey.

"Don't tempt me."

'What does *that* mean?'

"I'm going Christmas shopping."

She's riled. Maybe it's about the keys. Or, my disappearing act.

Climbing out of bed, my body aches to the bone. I check the nightstand, and the pockets in my thorny cargo pants.

Annie follows me silently as I plod outside. I notice the mud around the wheel rims of her car, where I parked off the pavement near the Twin Lights.

The car is locked.

I check the ground.

"*Thanks* for this," Anne snaps sourly. She's avoiding eye contact.

"I'm thinking," I try to rub the sleep out of my peepers, but they're raw.

Joe comes out wearing his bright yellow parka, and sits on the first step of the landing.

"Hey Champ, how you doing?"

Joe looks snitty at me too.

"What—?" I turn to Anne, to see if Joe's mood is a surprise. She frowns. Of course; he wanted to go fishing...

I start toward the boy. "Joe—"

"Bob! The *keys?*"

I huff, and stomp back to the front door.

"What's *wrong* with you, Bob?"

"What—?" I turn, and the crunch of tires on the gravel driveway interrupts me.

For a second I'm confused.

It's another silver-grey Lincoln, rolling up the drive. The license plate, EOM – Executive Office – is the same as Agent Benning's.

For a moment, hope fills my heart. Here comes Benning again. But that makes no sense...

As the car draws closer, I see a different man behind the wheel. This one has spidery, speck-like eyes in a blood-shot face. He's bald. He doesn't even seem to have eyebrows. Or they're so faint, they're indistinguishable. He's wearing a cheap suit... the same as Benning.

The Feds are here for me already.

I'm barefoot, in a nightgown, my troubled mind pared back to the rawest nerve.

"Go put some clothes on," suggests Anne.

But I can't move.

The sedan brakes, and the man steps out onto the gravel, squinting.

Annie looks expectantly in my direction, to see if I know who this is.

The stranger walks toward us, and extends his hand to Annie first.

"Hi Missus Travis. My name is Lou Maas." He peers obviously in my direction. "...and— Mister Travis." He's wearing an odd, knowing look in his beady pupils. "I offered to come over and pick you up myself, since your car was impounded. The Sheriff has a lot on his hands this morning!"

I blink, and see a hint of recognition in Maas's face.

...*What does a blink mean...?* I've never felt so scrutinised. Lou's tiny pupils are darting all over me, checking what I'm doing with his hands, how I'm standing...

I remain silent, motionless as a mime.

"You heard about the fire?" queries Maas.

"Fire?"

"The motel, on the way out to Rockport... I think it's called the 'Twin Lights'? Burned to the ground last night."

My eyes dart left. My fingers curl slightly. I gnaw my lip. "The *Twin Lights?*"

Annie looks at me curiously, aware of my reaction.

The three of us are standing apart in the drive. "The Essex County police are still trying to account for everyone," adds Maas. "It seems— somebody set off a car alarm before the fire, waking the guests. But... they're still not sure if anyone was left inside."

Anne has the reaction I should have. "My god, that's terrible."

"Are you alright, Mister Travis?" inquires Maas.

"I'm... fine," I answer.

"You look pale."

"No. Really. I'm fine."

Anne sees my face. "Get dressed, Robert."

I hesitate, wary of leaving Annie alone with this guy, afraid she'll say something she shouldn't. Normally she can be trusted, but she might want to know what I'm not telling her.... Or she might think she's helping... She doesn't know what not to say, because I haven't told her everything.

"That's alright," Maas glances from Anne to me, warily. It's obvious he isn't accustomed to making chit-chat. He's not a regular field agent, not like Benning. I wonder if he's some kind of desk jockey, or a big wheel. But I know from my experience with desks and wheels, Maas is something else altogether...

Inside, upstairs in the robe, I slip on a pair of boat-shoes, polo-shirt and cap, struggling to recall the events of the previous night. Is there any way they can place Diffner in the alley with me? Can I be linked to the Inn? Tyre tracks, footprints, fibres, fingerprints...? How much does this guy already know? I'm not even sure how much *I* know—! Did Diffner start the fire? Is he even *alive?*

Two people, maybe more, were dead in the space of a few hours – in a town where the primary cause of death was fishing accidents. I might as well be strapped into the electric chair, blindfolded, waiting for someone to throw the switch. I hurry downstairs, head aching, and notice as I crossed the entry, how cold the house is.

The driveway is empty but for Maas, leaning unglamorously on the hood of the Lincoln, like a second-hand car ad in a perverted spookazine. "Where's Anni—" I hesitate, uncomfortable using her name.

Maas is impassive. "Your son found her keys."

I avoid eye contact, trying to pretend the observation means nothing. But of course it does. It's obvious I took Annie's car out... after the patrolman dropped me home... Mud on the wheels, tyre prints at the scene... There's enough evidence right there to make an arrest. All Maas has to do is ask: *Where were you last night?*

But he remains emotionless. "Your wife told me I could wait inside, but I didn't think you'd want that."

In Annie's absence, Maas' tone has changed. The nicety is gone.

"I'm sorry about Agent Benning." I try mustering some sympathy and warmth, despite my exhaustion.

"I didn't know him," admits Maas.

"Oh...? You'll have to excuse me if I'm a little distracted," I add. "I didn't sleep very well."

"Me either," replies Maas.

I smile. Great. Now we have something in common. "You must have been travelling all night?"

Maas stares at me for a moment, with his receded eyes. "You had quite a night."

*How so?*

"Running after the shooter? Discharging a firearm..."

I chose the level of my voice carefully. As heavily-laden with innuendo as the conversation has become, I *have* seen two men shot. One of them was a friend. "Did you want to ask me some questions, or should we go to where everything happened, and I'll walk you through it?"

Maas smiles. "I'll ask you *my* questions on the way there, and you can ask me *yours.*"

Something about the situation, feels horribly wrong... But I'm too busy covering my arse to see. I'm mostly just glad Annie is gone. She'd know right away I'm shitting myself blind.

I walk back into the house, switch on the alarm, lock the front door, and follow Maas to his car. Maas sidles into the driver seat, and crosses his arms on the wheel, gazing through the windshield. "It must bother you. The fire at the Inn?"

"Why?" I bluff.

"No?" Maas twists, to look right at me – up close.

"No. What?"

"Isn't that how your father died?"

I start to object, when I realise, Maas isn't talking about Matt... He's talking about my real *father.*

And there it is... Unmentioned, for 19 years. Like lightning out of a clear sky. *Fuck!*

Maas turns the vehicle around, and coasts out onto the road.

*...How your father died...*

I think I'm going to puke.

I barely notice the black van rushing past in the opposite direction, on the usually quiet coast road.

My mind is spinning backwards through time. Even Annie hasn't mentioned my father's death in all these years. I've *always* kept it a secret from Matt and Tessa. In nearly twenty years – it has *never* been discussed...

"You... do some work in Washington," Maas remarks.

"Huh?" I'm still reeling. "A little." I thought Annie was the only person who knew about my father. But of course that isn't true. It was in the newspapers. There would have been clippings... This guy only had to go down to the County library and skim the microfiche. Anyone could find out if they wanted to. Police reports. Neighbours would have recalled the events vividly.

Maas adds, "...it's funny. My office is on Massachusetts Avenue, but this is the first time I've ever been to—" He stops.

I tense, seeing the car parked on the side of the road – over on the verge, near the corner of the property.

Time lags as we draw near.

It's Annie's convertible.

The car rests on an unusual angle, two wheels in the ditch. It's difficult to see inside, the way the sunlight reflects off the plastic rear window of the Merc SL.

I reach for the Lincoln's door handle, even before Maas has begun to brake. "Stop!" I trip out of the moving vehicle, stumble, and run to the driver's side of the abandoned Benz.

The car is empty.

"Annie? Joe?!" I call out, searching up and down the road. There isn't another house for miles. Nothing but woods and paddocks. *Where are they? What happened?*

Maas climbs out of the Lincoln, leaving the engine running.

"Where are they?" I wonder aloud.

I look back into Annie's car, and lean back and check the license plate. It's definitely hers...

I circle around the front fender, looking for a ding or a flat or a radiator leak. But there isn't a scratch anywhere.

Maas points to the picket gate in the stone wall, at the corner of the property, that leads to a path through the woods. "What's down there?"

I dial Annie's number on my cell phone.

Maas walks back to the Lincoln, and climbs in. "Come on. Get in."

I'm distracted, noticing the faint noise coming from Anne's car. I peek through the side window.

Anne's cell phone is beeping, resting in the centre console.

Maas sits in the Lincoln, waiting. "Come on—"

"What?!"

"Don't panic—"

"I'm not panicking!" I yell. What is this?

"She probably had car trouble, and walked back to the house?"

Something about Maas' tone prickles me, but the thought slips. I hesitate, before leaping at the gate in the fence. If Annie ran out of gas – I can't remember now how much I left in the car – she'll be seething by now. She and Joe would have had to walk back to the house, through the horse paddock...

I dial a second number, as I hurry down toward the fence.

"Do you want to *walk* - or *drive*?!" Agent Maas yells, leaning across the passenger seat of the Lincoln. But somehow, he doesn't sound genuinely interested in an answer.

I throw open the gate, and sprint down the narrow path, into the strip of woods.

Maas calls out, behind me. "Hey!"

I stumble down the embankment through the trees, and emerge at the end of the adjacent meadow.

I half-expect to see Anne and Joe in the long grass, and the breeze in the sunlight - hair blowing, swatting at grasshoppers... But the field is empty.

The long granite shelves of the house are visible, six hundred yards away.

It's vaguely possible they could have walked that far. How long were Maas and I talking in the driveway? Standing knee-deep in the millet, I listen as the operator takes my call.

'Mister Travis. Good afternoon. You have eight new messages—'

"Are there any messages from Missus Travis?"

'Let me see... Ah... I'm just looking...'

"Hurry up for Christ's sake."

'Yes. One message.'

"What is it?"

'All it says is... oh.'

"'Oh' what? What?"

'I'm sorry...'

"Just tell me the fucking message!"

'It says 'Call me.' That's the message.'

"What?"

'Would you like your other messa—?'

I disconnect the call. I might have missed seeing them walking back down the road? I turn, and run back into the trees, passing Maas – who's started following me – back through the gate, back to the cars.

"What are you doing?" queries Maas.

Shielding my eyes against the sun, I glance back in the direction of the front gate. The road is empty.

Lou Maas is standing in the ditch, suitably perplexed. "Mister—"

"Did you see that van?" I ask, jiggling the door handle on the Merc. Locked. "The one that drove past?"

"Why don't we go back to the house?"

"If you know *anything* about this, you better tell me," I threaten. "Or I swear, I'll..."

"Or, you'll what?" Maas asks, surprised.

"I'll take your fucking head off! I *swear!*" I turn, and walk back into the horse paddock, frantic... Not hearing Maas's laughter.

"Are you – *threatening* me, Mister Travis?"

"What are you? Stupid? Of course I'm threatening you!" I yell, walking away, looking left and right, trying to decide which direction to go.

And then it begins... *Bwarp! Bwarp! Bwarp!* In the distance, across the field. It's the intruder alarm at the house.

I run.

"Hey!" yells Maas, chuckling oddly. "Where are you going?"

*Fuck you buddy. You hairless imp!* I don't even look back. I run, as fast as I can over the uneven ground, losing my cap, wheezing madly, knees buckling, toward the screaming house. The car. The alarm. The message.

Limbs flagging, wringing my lumbering frame for more speed, I close in on the house. The closer I come, the louder the alarm and all my internal bells are clamouring. I scream their names, "ANNIE! JOE!"

Bouncing over a hundred yards of hare holes and horse mines, I reach the gate in the hedgerow, and fumble the latch. There's a spring on the gate hinge, stiff enough to keep a ten-foot ranch hand from pulling it open with his teeth. I slam through the gate, roaring, and lunge for the door to the pool house, driving it open with a bang.

The moment I gasp air, gas fills my lungs.

*Oh god.*

The heavy atmosphere of the glass-roofed pool house is thick, ribboning with Chlorine... and a more pungent terror. The air is ripe with the familiar odour of sick, and rot, and egg, and bile.

Gas.

My stomach clenches, and I dry-heave, eyes weeping. "ANNIEEEEE!" Swooning, tears squirting down my cheeks – the shrill security siren aches in my back teeth. "ANNIEEEEE?" My voice is lost between the glasshouse and the water, and the blaring klaxon.

I retreat outside – spitting, and gagging – and take a deep breath of fresh air, before rushing back through the doors, down the length of the pool.

The glass doors at the far end of the natatorium are ajar.

The whole *house* must be full of gas...

"AAANNE!" I croak. *Oh god please.* My mind is racing. All it takes now is a spark, and I'm an obituary. A stain in the dirt. This is it. This is the end... *Like Maas said...*

I hurtle into the patterned sunroom, down the hall, smashing a row of pictures on the wall with my shoulder, careening blindly into the kitchen. The stench is everywhere. Eyes swollen shut, retching, I bawl Annie's name in a tight squeak, and I rush for the stove, sending the carving block skidding, twisting the knobs on the burners.

None of them are on. "ANNE!" Red-faced, doubled over, I trip into the living room. The fireplace shimmers with the flow of fumes, and I crash over the bronze coffee table, splitting my shin, and fall blindly onto the regulator.

Rolling, dizzy in the blare of the alarm, half-conscious, I find the dial, and twist it shut. My throat clenches. I'm mute, and blind.

At the back of the house, where I came in, a loud *bang* sends a jolt through my knees, followed by the sound of shattering glass... Loping dizzily, still croaking Annie's name, I run back to the hall and find the busted doors to the pool house swinging ajar... Sweeping through shards of glass.

A soft breeze billows the curtains. Pure gas doesn't ignite easily. It needs just the right mix of air... The gas will rise upstairs...

The alarm stops.

"BOB!"

It's Annie, upstairs.

I bolt into the hall, tripping on the first step.

"BOB- HELP!" It's Annie, but there's something strange in her voice. Worse than fear.

Hauling myself up the banisters, I clamber to the landing, hands squeaking on the timber floor. "ANNIE!" I leap to the bedroom door, and fling it open.

The sight thumps me in the chest like a wrecking ball, knocking me back a step, the air whooshing out of my lungs. Of all the horrors

I have seen since the Boston Southern Mortuary, *this* is my worst nightmare.

Annie is tied to the foot of the bed with heavy black cable ties.

Her eyes are gone.

*Oh god.*

Blood seeps like tears from cruel welts under the macabre slots where her eyes should be.

"Where's Joe?!" she croaks hoarsely, lips quivering, gagging for air.

Tears flood my own eyes. "Hang on Hunny... I'm gonna get you out of here." I fumble with the heavy plastic bonds, pulling at the point where the strap runs through a small plastic buckle, around a rung in the wrought iron bed.

"They took him," she coughs.

The heavy-gauge cable tie bites into her bleeding wrists. It's too heavy to break, and too tightly bound, cutting into her skin. I need a knife. "Hold on!"

"*hurry*," pleads Annie softly. The agony in her voice is heartbreaking.

I turn, scramble into the hall, and trip toward the stairs. *Godfuckingdamn you God!* Stumbling, I run for the sunroom – when the concussion hits me like a wrecking ball.

Heat and gas barks down the hallway, raising me off my feet, cradling me in the air for a moment, shouldering my weight, and firing me through the broken doorframes.

In a protracted upside-down movement, I see the glass ceiling of the pool house shatter, and take to the sky like birds.

Smoke and flame and glass boil sunward.

Then, blackness.

Rocking waves...

The water in the pool smells like Annie. I never swim. Not voluntarily. But the amount of time she spends in the pool, sailing up and down, shoulder blades dancing in her back, I can't imagine what she thinks about all that time. The way she comes up when she's done, wringing her nose, beaming, girlish in her cap and goggles... What makes her so happy in the water? Does it remind her of another time?

I float, rocking to the rhythmic buzzing in my ears. I've skipped ahead. The backs of my arms float beneath me. The skin is red, the layers peeling away like pastry. But my limbs are detached, the puppet-strings cut. I can't feel them... I can't even blink. The water is pink, sparkling, supernaturally cold...

Above the surface, far away, a voice calls my name.

*Bob Travis!*

I feel something touch my back, scraping at me. Scraping. I try to flip myself over, but nothing happens. I can't move. Something pinches at my shredded shirt, towing me through the water, rolling me over.

Lou Maas squints down at me from the tiled pool step, stuffing a gun into his belt, a curtain of ash whipping past his back.

*Thank god! Get Annie!*

Maas presses two fingers to my throat, before releasing my sleeve.

*...What? Hey!*

The strange hairless figure draws out a mean-looking knife, and presses the tip to my eye. I felt the cold steel on the soft skin of my open lid.

*...Hey!*

*It's him.*

My heart spasms. A gout of flame *erupts* from the rear of the house, roiling over Maas's back. The BOOM! shudders in my chest. Maas stumbles, dropping the knife. It bounces off my cheek, into the water.

Maas scrambles away from the heat.

A patch of blue sky opens up, and I'm a boy again.

I can see, *so* clearly? Walking with my father on the sand, the frangipani-print swim trunks tacky on the man's shaggy white pins, his wrinkled back, freckled... Then, I'm sitting on a coarse rug in flannel pyjamas, peeking into a Christmas present... Sitting at the dinner table, wearing a pastel-green seersucker Church shirt, my feet swinging from a purple naugahyde chair, cutlery heavy in my small, freckled fists... Walking to school in my bright yellow raincoat and hat, the smell of new plastic thick in my nose, the buttons impossible – little fingers, sharp loops... And a raging dog as big as a pony pouncing out of an overgrown yard, leaping after me on my rusty bike with its loose chain.... The gut-awful terror of slipping a pedal and being chewed to rag. Nervousness, and surprise, in the schoolroom. The intense privacy of my childhood bedroom, cowering in the closet reading secretly... The profound awareness of my own youthful ignorance, and fear... *Constant* fear of punishment... The rod. The denial, later, I was ever so vulnerable. Growing up... The loneliness... That first unexpected fumbling teenaged kiss... Helen Something... near the library stairs. The redheaded kid who punched me under the swings... College, and sweet, startling Annie. Her irrational, unshakeable love... Matthias in his den... The day Annie and I were married... Tiny, baby Joe, opening his wet, newborn eyes... *Who are you?* The secret realization at that moment, that a man's whole life, he just wants to be as big as his Dad seemed to him when he was ten. It's automatic. The private, terrifying pact. *I am your father. I will care for you.* The unexpected knowledge that *no* man has all the answers, and *all* men seem like giants to their sons. Seeing Joe, gazing up at me to ask me a question... Pretending I know the answer... Dreams, nightmares of my own Father wailing on me, trying to hit back, *really* trying, but the paralysing feeling of moving through toffee... Father flicking my fists away, more riled...

I've never admitted to Annie, about those stark, cold, recurring dreams... Even when my father was grey and brittle, the old man never admitted he was any less than when I was at his knee. He *always* had the answers. He *knew* how things worked...

The darkness comes up slowly, as my head fills with the awful question:

Where are Annie and Joe?

And— Something else. Something that has troubled me all along, that I can't quite place. A connection that goes back, way back, a dotted line – from a half-formed idea, from an event nineteen years ago, out into Reality...

*Thursday, September 13, 2012*

Clark Diffner laid curled in the plastic-lined rear bay of a BMW X5 four-wheel-drive.

The car was fresh off the production line, the smell of new leather mixed with the stench of smoke in Clark's clothes, from the fire at the *Twin Lights*.

The car hit the bottom of a ramp and bounced, the floor cracking Diffner in the chin. The tires hummed on steel, and the light changed from darkness, to orange-tinged flood lamps.

Diffner turned his head, and looked up through a slit in the film-covered window. The car was driving through a giant super-mall-sized car park, stretching three hundred yards long, built entirely out of whitewashed steel.

A row of cars spiralled single-file behind him, up an articulated gangway to the uppermost level, past rows of tightly parked luxury SUVs – Mercedes ML 55s, 350s, 500s and BMW X5s.

A woman in drab red coveralls was driving. Her only acknowledgement of Diffner's presence was a short, furtive glance in the rear-view mirror. She spun the steering wheel, and pulled into the first free parking space in front of a bright red 'NO SMOKING' sign, stencilled on the metal wall.

"Stay down. He'll come get you in a few hours."

A second later, another vehicle pulled in alongside them.

The woman jumped out, yelled something to the other driver, and ducked below the nose of the vehicle, with a rattle of chains, and thump of a latch, then disappeared.

Diffner lay in the back of the BMW for two hours, before the lights went out.

A few minutes later, a young African man banged on the rear window, popped the hatch, and beckoned Diffner out of the car.

Diffner shuffled out over the tailgate, and stretched his legs, glancing around the strange parking lot.

"Don't worry," the young African whispered. "Nobody will find you *here*."

Exactly where 'here' was, was probably the best-kept secret Diffner knew – or at least, it *had* been, until a week ago.

# PART TWO

## 19. '...HE THAT WAS DEAD...'

*Saturday, November 3, 2012*

I thrash awake.

My legs tingle with the pangs of a phantom fall.

I reach for Annie.

Finding the edge of the unusually narrow bed, I raise my head, and the darkened room whirls on a random axis. Sweat burns my eyes, gluing my pyjamas to my skin. I struggle with the linen, trying to kick my feet out of the blankets, and flop hands-first onto the icy floor.

Something yanks on my wrist. A loud *crash* erupts by my head, and pain shoots up my arm. I stumble, draped in a soaked sheet, bashing into a table, a chair... a tree? *Is that a tree? Inside? Where's the damn light switch? It should be right—?*

"ANNIE?" Patting down the walls, I fumble across a handle where no door should be, and fall into a brightly-lit corridor.

Giddiness rolls me over, and I dash full-tilt like a hosed-down Halloweenist into the side of a food trolley. Willying racks of jelly and mucky plates smash against the wall. My skull is pounding with vertigo. "ANNIE? JOE!" I wail. A blurred nurse runs toward me from a night desk. "*Sir!*"

"Where am I?" My tongue feels like a new tennis ball. I barely notice the nurse won't touch me, fearful, hovering nearby, hands raised. "Come back to your room Mister Travis, *Please*," she herds me, with generous arm gestures.

I wonder groggily how she knows my name. "*Where's Annie and Joe?*"

"Let's get you back to bed." Seeing her arm-waving isn't steering me, the nurse reluctantly places a hand on my arm.

Pain jars me. "Where am I?" I seek out her face in the spinning daze. A second nurse comes running. Everything rolls again, and I flick my hands up for balance. The sudden agony jolts me upright. *My skin feels tight, shrunk.*

I allow myself to be towed back into the room, flinching. "What happened?"

The light in the room flickers on, and I see the broken IV stand, the furniture, the Christmas tree tilted over during my mad jaunt. "I'm in hospital?"

A doctor squeaks in on soft shoes. Someone else whispers "He's *awake.*" In a fit, I plead, "Where are *they*–?!"

"Mister Travis." The nurse is adamant. "You shouldn't be on your feet. Get back into bed, please." Another nurse fumbles with a syringe and an ampoule.

"I have to see my wife!" I shrug off the hands. "I *have* to see them!" I try to hold back the waterworks, the blubbering, weepy, gutted, face-aching sobs, but the tears have already begun. I shove the nurses back, sending the bed skidding shrilly on the linoleum, circling in the corral of white-smocked people. "I have to see my *wife!*"

The doctor squares up. "Your wife is... gone."

I sway precariously. "Huh?"

"I'm sorry," the doctor persists. "Please Mister Travis, we—"

"Where's *Joe?*"

The doctor shakes his head slightly. "Sorry, they don't know."

*They?* I search the blurred faces, for doubt. But... they all *know*. They *all* know. My chest seizes up, gripped in an industrial press. I squeak like a bicycle pump, knees buckling. Nurses rush to catch me, and my voice cracks, releasing a wail that rattles the windows. The doctor shouts, but his words are lost in my raw howl.

Sapped, I peer down at my bandaged arms, face dripping three kinds of drool. *Oh, god. Oh, god. No. You fucker. You sick fucker. How could you?*

"Mister Travis, you were in an anoxic coma. You shouldn't even be standing. You need to lie down and get some rest. You've got a lot of work, getting back on your feet."

The nurse seizes my shoulder roughly, jabbing me with a syringe and squeezing the plunger.

They can't be— "What happened?!" I bawl loudly.

The doctor shakes his head.

I weep like I never thought possible, not even as a child. Not wanting to. Wanting to... Not thinking. Not feeling. Like it isn't me crying. It isn't *my* brain, or *my* petty psychological work-up. It isn't *one* thing. It's something fundamental inside, the laws and forces that govern the unnavigated places, deep down in my broken heart. On and on it goes - a supernatural flood of sobs and tears.

Consciousness slips away... sliding away into darkness, like the bottom of the pool...

The second time I wake, a small noise rouses me. I don't open my eyes. I don't want to. I hope I'm dead. I try to find sleep, forever, fumbling for the curtains of unconsciousness.

Their names echo. *Annie... and Joe...*

The void is bigger than all the world. I know now why it's such a powerful idea, Heaven. That they're somewhere else, skipping through clover. They can't just be gone. But— if there's a heaven, there's a god. And if there's a god, he let this happen. There's no way around it. There's no happy ending, no hope of recovery. I can only wait for time to waste me to a bitter, loveless zombie, sitting on the sidewalk in a fold-up chair, flipping the bird at passing traffic.

*This* is where those stormy back-alley hobos came from. The screamers, the railers, weaving incoherently in the street... From gut-wrenching loss. Nineteen years, together... I couldn't keep *anything* together that long. It was her.

The image of her face, blood running down her face like tears, makes me gasp aloud. My lips curl into a sob, lying on my side, curled on the bed like a wounded dog... waiting to die – when an unexpected whisper invades my nightmare.

"Bob?"

It's a woman's voice. More accurately, it's— her.

Startled, I look up, bleary-eyed.

"Bob, are you awake?"

She's sitting across the room, in shadow. *Annie?*

"I wasn't sure if you were awake," she whispers softly. "You've been tossing and turning for an hour."

*...Annie!*

"Sorry I wasn't here when you woke," she apologises, stretching her arms, and purring. "I just went downstairs for a coffee... Figured you wouldn't notice if I stepped out." The misty figure moves softly toward the window. "Do you mind if I open the curtains?"

No. Please... I shake my head...How?

The drapes hiss back. As soon as the sunlight hits her face, I *know* it's her.

But her features are exaggerated. Her hair is longer, blonder. Her cheekbones, more severe. She's dressed in a Chanel suit. I wonder if it's the morphine, or if I've been out of it for so long... Through the window, in spite of the blue sky and sunshine, I can see frozen snow on the ledge. "Where... am I?"

"Saint Ignatius," she answers.

"I thought you were...?" I squint, looking back to her. My eyes won't focus...

"The rescuers reached me – two days after."

*Rescuers?* "I don't understand."

She shakes her head, confused. "Two days after the bomb."

My blood runs backwards.

It's *Madison.*

"Shit. Sorry, for a second I... thought you were..."

"Oh." Madison swishes over to the bed, and sits in the chair next to my pillow. Up close, I can see clearly now.

Her sudden proximity is unsettling.

Madison leans on the edge of the bed, and her swollen breasts threaten to pop out of the flimsy blouse.

Just like every other time I've been alone with her, I want to openly state my dislike for her – maybe now more than ever. Just so it's crystal clear. *I love Annie.* And the fact Madison just *reminded* me of her, just for a sleep-stupored second, curls my toes.

Madison rests her wrists lightly on the arms of the chair. "I came up here as soon as I could get out of New York."

I grumble, unsure what to say.

*She'd made it. Out of the subway? Alive...And Annie never knew...*

Madison sees the nauseated expression on my face. "I like your hair this way," she smiles. "It suits you."

Every conversation I've ever had with her, has turned into a ball-fisted argument. This is surreal, her waiting on my bed like some pal-around old chum. But something about her has changed... She never had the same softness as Annie. There was always something distant about her, hard, and – something else. She always had it. She wasn't like Annie. Not so open. Not so... comfortable. But her eyes have changed. Where they used to be dark, and accusing... They're friendly now, almost pleading now, asking me for something...

I feel the top of my head. It's been shaved. I check my beard. My face is smooth.

"I gave you a shave. You looked like... well..."

"*You* shaved me?" The idea of her touching me up in my sleep is more unsettling than her proximity.

"I looked like – *what?*"

"Like *hell.*"

I grunt. Slack-mouthed and pale, wasted, whiskered, drooling into my duds. And, what? She can't say the word *hell?* "What happened to Joe?"

Madison looks downcast. "They don't know. He's... disappeared."

I consider telling her what Annie said... The words were as clear as if it had all only happened seconds ago. *'They took him!'*

"Here," Madison fetches a compact from her handbag, and hands it to me. "Take a look."

I obey, glad for the distraction. I can't fit my whole head in the tiny lens, but I get the clue. My noggin looks like an old potato.

"You're lucky Bob... You were dead for ten minutes, before the firemen got to you."

"Firemen?" There is no fire station in New Bridlington. Like the ambulance, they'd have had to travel half-an-hour from Gloucester.

"They were on their way back from a fire at a motel."

The Twin Lights Inn. "Well– I wish they hadn't," I confess, staring out the window at the white winter sky.

Madison ignores the comment. "After the first day, they gave you a sixty-percent chance of survival. After the first week, it was fifteen percent. Four weeks ago, they asked me if they could have your organs... Like I said, you're *lucky.*"

I swallow, throat swollen. I'm not sure what else to say. "I guess we're *both* lucky."

"Yeah." Madison sighs.

I reach awkwardly for the pitcher of water on the side table. "Ow..."

She intercepts my hand, taking an upturned glass from a paper doily, and filling it carefully. "Tessa visited as well."

I swill a mouthful of water. It tastes like dish liquid.

"It's the painkillers. They make your taste buds go screwy," explains Madison. "I should go get the doctor. They need to do some tests."

"What kind of tests?"

"I don't know," she lies.

"What?"

"To see if there's any permanent *damage.*"

The type of damage is implied. "My brain?"

"I'll go get them."

"Wait!" I blurt.

And out of nowhere, Madison suddenly beams. "—What?!" It's infectious, that piano-key smile. I can't look at her. It's if she's glad to see me. She leans toward me on the bed.

"Before they come... I need to ask..."

"You're going to be just fine!" She smiles, and for a second I think she's going to take my hand.

I gather up my arms.

She laughs. It's that big Broadway laugh of hers that fills the hall. I smile back. I can't be sure why, I can't help it.

"*There* you are!" she smirks.

I close my eyes. "How long have I been here?"

"Six weeks."

*Six weeks!* Annie would be buried now, cold in the ground.

"For the first week after I got here," continues Madison, "County Sheriffs and State Police were all over the room, waiting to question you." She stows her compact, and walks away from the bed. "You were almost packed in ice, in nine different coolers." Seeing my discomfort, she smiles again. "They're still cleaning up in New York. You've missed a lot. They're saying it will take five years to get trains going again. The stock exchange opened down twenty-percent. Al-

Qaeda and the Taliban are moving on Baghdad. We're sending troops back in—"

"How long have *you* been here?"

Madison shrugged. "A few weeks."

"Every day?"

"I wanted to talk to you, before the police."

"Why?"

Madison looks away, uncomfortably.

"Where are the police now?"

"I'm meant to call this guy as soon as you wake up." Madison produces a Louis Vuitton diary, and plucks out a business card.

"What did you want to talk to me about?" I ask, fearful. "Before the police?" It's all coming back to me. Diffner. Benning. Barne. Maas...

"Not now. Forget it."

"I'm fine. Tell me."

"I... I just want you to know, Tess and I *know* you didn't do it."

"Wh—" I start to query the remark, before it hits me. My voice cracks. "Do what?"

Madison clears her throat. "Sorry, I don't know how to—"

"Christ. What?"

"They think *you* set off the gas at the house."

I struggle for a moment to shut out the dizzying rhetoric in my mashed, numb, bisected brain. I start to sit up, but the tight grip of vertigo yanks my head back onto the pillow. "What...?"

"I just wanted you to know. Tessa never doubted you either." She adjusts her position in the hard, heavy visitor's chair. "You're all the family *we* have left," she blurts suddenly. "When I was in the subway I..." Her voice trails off, seeing my disinterest. She sits back, and clears her throat. "They think you had something to do with the fire at the hotel... They - traced Annie's car there, after the shootings... They say they have your fingerprints on a gun... And— Something about, how your father died. They want to ask you, what you did... with Joe..."

The room starts to spin again.

"...Bob?"

I croak, "how can they think *I* did it?"

"They haven't told me any more than that."

For a horrible moment, I see her again. Terrified, bound to the frame of the bed, her eyes gone. How could they think *I* did it? But there wouldn't have been anything left. Just bones.

Either way, it had been my fault, in a way. I *had* done it to her. I mightn't have lit the match, but – that's what it came down to. Somehow, out of the thing with Diffner, *I* got Annie killed. *I* went to Diffner with the idea... "Where's Clark?" I ask.

Madison suddenly looks downcast, her cheerfulness evaporating. "I hoped you might know."

"Why?"

"They said you were the last person to see him? You saw Clark that morning?"

They haven't figured out Clark was in New Brid, at the Twin Lights Inn. And while we were meeting there, in secret, Madison had still been trapped in New York.

"I better get Lou," Madison stands up.

"Who—?"

"Lou," she repeats flatly. "Lou Maas."

I'm thumped in the neck by a pang of terror. *Lou Maas?!*

"I have to let him know, you're awake..."

I wag my head. "Wait! You met him?"

"He transferred you here from Beth Israel Deaconess Medical Center."

"What?" It hadn't occurred to wonder what I'm doing in Saint Ignatius... a Catholic hospital... "He moved me here?"

"He said— he could make sure, you got better care here."

"Why?"

"You know how I am about *priests*," Madison smiles. "But Lou is different—"

I'm certain, those crucial few minutes in the water must have dudded a chunk of my grey matter. "Maas said he's... a *priest?*"

"It's a bit hard to miss." Madison points at her collar.

The room shrinks... Madison's aspect warps.

"Here," she hands me an embossed business card, bearing the crossed keys of Saint Peter, and the papal miter:

*(Diagram 15 - Lou Maas' business card)*

"He's with the Vatican Chancery in Washington," she explains. "'*Legatus a latere*' means 'from the *Pope's* side.' He's a representative of the Pope."

The card is an exact counterpoint to Clark Diffner's, handed over in that hairy paw outside the Anacostia Institute – just a few miles from the address on Maas' card.

Diffner is – or *was* – the CIA's special envoy to Rome. Maas is *Rome's* special envoy to Washington? This card is *the exact opposite...*

"He offered to perform last rites, when they weren't sure you'd make it."

I'm struck by a simultaneous pain in my eyeballs, and eye-teeth. *Who ever heard of such a thing?* I'm not keeping up. "He's here – *now?*"

"He's been waiting *with* me," she retorts, as if it explains something.

"What does he look like?"

"Pardon?"

"Tiny eyes, red cheeks, no eyebrows?"

Madison screws up her nose. "I guess so..."

I swallow acid. "He's *here* now?"

"He's not back till *five*. Are you - okay?"

"What time is it?"

She checks her watch. "Quarter off."

A sickening dread creeps into my wounded heart.

Now I understand Diffner's desperation in the alley, and at the Motor Inn. The veteran G-man, scared witless. The knowledge something deadly was approaching. Who *is* this man? He showed up at my house, driving the same kind of Executive Office car as Agent Benning. Or maybe it was the *same* car? Now he's a monsignor? CIA Agent, holy father, tomorrow a park ranger, airline pilot... The windows of my mind fog up with the internal conversation. He almost cut my eyes out - my *eyes* - when I was floating in the pool, I'm certain of it. Benning and Barne both had an eye cut out... Matt had cigarette burns... Annie... Now, Maas is waiting daily by my bed? Is he waiting for Madison to give up and leave? It seems impossible... Annie, ambushed on the coast road, and taken back to the house. Maybe she never even *left* the house? I didn't *see* her. Maas drove me just far enough, to give the gas time to spread through the house. Is it possible he set the whole thing up? Madison said Maas moved me to this hospital... It's all so vague, so half-imagined. The way Matt died... Eyes burned out. All the coincidences, pointing in a single direction... And he's *here, now?* Walking into the building this moment?

"I have to get out of here," I plead weakly, not hearing Madison's answer.

She's doomed now, too... Just like Matt. Benning. Barne. Diffner. Annie. Joe.

"I'm sorry Maddie," I bow my head, struggling with the imperative.

"Hey! You know, that's the *first* time you've ever called me 'Maddie'—" she grins.

"You have to get out of here..." The tightness in my throat is like razors. Any show of emotion will make this harder. She has to *want* to leave. "Annie and Joe were *murdered*."

Madison smiles kindly. "It was just an accident, Bob. A terrible accident."

"You have to leave. You have to get *out* of here. And pretend you never spoke to me," and... even as I utter the words, I recalled a similar conversation with Diffner.

Diffner pleaded with me to leave the alley...

Then, again, he told me to run, at the Motor Inn. To accept the exigent reality.

Maddie will be impossible to convince - without knowing the whole story; without *seeing* what I've seen... I can't even afford for her to talk to the police, or fetch the doctor. I wish now, more than ever, I'd never woken up.

I'm still carrying the secret... that everyone is being killed for.

The problem is, I'm not a hundred percent sure what it is.

*...The only reason you're still alive, is because you don't know what's going on...*

Even that wasn't true. The only reason I'm alive, is that Madison stopped the doctors from packing my kidneys in a ziplock.

No matter how I figure it, there's no practical way to force her to leave. There's no reasonable justification. I know her: The more I try, the more she'll argue.

Maddie stands up again, frowning at me, waiting for the delusion to pass.

"You have to go *back* to New York," I whisper. "Something terrible is happening..."

Madison reaches for my hand. "Tell me. I can help."

"No!" I snap, ineffectually.

Clark Diffner had been equipped with facts. I'm still not sure I completely understand everything he even said... An ancient king named Melchizedek? It sounded mad. I'm weak, and disoriented. And... what about Matt? Where do I even *begin* to explain any of this?

"You're in danger," I squeak.

"I better get the doctor..."

I can see the look on her face. They've told her I might be brain-damaged, or incoherent. "Wait!" I grab her by the wrist. "I'm *not* making this up. These people will do *anything* to make sure I don't talk." And even as I'm speaking, I ask myself the question. *Am I losing it? I'm pink, therefore I'm Spam! How much do I really know? How much, of what I think I know... is wrong?*

Maddie leans in close. "Tell me, Robert. I can help."

"You have to *leave*. *N*ow. Or they'll come for you too."

"Talk to me. *Who* is coming for me?"

"Just *leave!*" I snarl severely. "Tell the nurses your dog died, and it's stinking up your apartment. I don't care. Say I never woke up. But—"

"Bob, tell me *who* is coming for us? I know people. You can trust—"

The comment strikes me as strange. *What does that mean?* "No *Madison*! You have to *go!*"

"That's crazy," Madison replies, careful not to insult me directly. "Who would believe me, after all this time, leaving without talking to you? I've been here every day for five weeks, cleaning up after you, decorating your tree, and— you want me to just walk out?"

*Christ...*

She hauls the heavy chair in closer. "I'm not going anywhere until you tell me what's going on."

"*Jesus* Madison! I don't want you here!"

She answers softly, ignoring my anger. "Annie called me, the night before..."

"What?"

She sees she's struck a blow.

"She knew you weren't cheating on her. She was— worried about you... She knew you were involved in something."

"She *said* that?"

"I'm going to talk to the doctor, and see if I can get you something to help you sleep. Then, we'll talk to *Lou*, and we'll jolly well march down there and set things right." She smiles.

I look into Madison's eyes, and know I'm screwed. "*He* killed Annie!"

Madison doesn't even register the accusation. She's already made up her mind, like she knows Maas better than I do, and I've fallen out of my tree. Or maybe, she just realised she's said exactly the right thing to make me talk.

She stands up again. "I'll be back."

"Wait!" I concede. "I was floating in the pool, but I was still conscious. I couldn't move - but I could *see*."

She pauses, frowning.

"He checked my pulse. But he didn't try to help. He put a *knife* to my eye, but then there was an explosion!"

"Bob—"

"Wait. I'm not finished."

"Are you sure?"

"And - he cut Annie's eyes out!"

"That's *ridiculous*," Madison gasps. "You're probably in some kind of shock."

I object weakly. "It was real. It was him!"

Madison glances at the door. "Bob. He's been sitting here praying for you for weeks."

"He probably killed Matt as well!"

"Bob. You're dealing with a horrible loss. It was an accident. It will take time."

My mind is racing... Should I beg, hedge, spit, or seethe? "You think because he's a priest, it confers some special virtue on him? So *what!* He killed *Annie!*"

Madison is aghast.

Saying it, hearing myself say it - *he killed Annie* - my grief is replaced with rage. I try to rise up in the bed, defiant. "If you don't leave now, he'll kill you too."

Madison steps back from the bed. "You want to make this more than an *accident*? Bob? After Matt was mugged, you lost it... You're making up conspiracy theories out of random events! Bob! *You of all people* should know better!"

I begin to argue, to convince her... What about the shooting? It *had* to be Maas. How else did he get from D.C. at three in the morning, to my driveway by seven? How did he know about the fire at the Motor Inn? Maas *had* to be in New Bridlington the whole time? Right?

And then I realise... It doesn't matter *how* I convince her to leave. It doesn't matter if she thinks I'm crazy. Or— if I *am* crazy. It's the only way to get her out of here, before it's too late. "Don't patronise me," I snarl quietly. "How *dare* you criticise how *I* dealt with Matt's death! *You* took one of his friends home from the funeral and *fucked* him!"

Madison frowns. Her impenetrable façade fractures. "It wasn't like that—"

"I didn't ask you to be here. We've never been friends. I don't want you here! Just get out, and let me take care of myself. I don't need your *help*!"

"I'm not leaving."

"I *don't* want you here!"

With a flounce, Madison turns to fetch her jacket and bag from the chair. "Fine." Strutting for the door she whirls, as if she's about to broadside the bed with all her cannons, but... She just sighs, and says: "You were a good man. That's why Annie loved you. Don't let this change you." She glances round the room a final time.

Sitting up as best I can, I wish my face to stone.

Madison pulls on her white-rimmed sunglasses, opens the door, and walks into the corridor.

I listen to the tap-tap-tap of her heels, as she ticks away down the hall.

"*Good morning Miss Travis,*" says a distant voice near the night desk.

I can't hear the reply, if there is one. The footsteps falter. Faintly, the elevator doors rumble open, and Madison taps inside.

There's a confusion of noise.

A door squeals open to the sound of a refilling toilet cistern. *"Madison...?!"* A male voice echoes down the corridor. The lift doors rumble, and thud.

I lay frozen. Listening...

*"Hey there,"* Madison answers loudly.

*"Are you alright?"* asks the disembodied voice. The accent is strange. I strain in the bed to hear it...

*"I have to go home,"* she croaks emotionally. Maybe it's an act, or maybe she's genuinely upset.

*"But, your brother-in-law...?"*

*"I know. Please apologise for me when he wakes. Tell him I stayed as long as I could."*

I'm startled by her complicity. But— she knows I'm listening. She's just as likely to be pointing at my door, and pulling faces... *Bob's totally wigged out. Bob's lost all his buttons. Bob needs help.*

*"Where are you going?"*

There's a long pause.

"I'm sorry," the stranger apologises. "It's none of my business."

*"My— boyfriend called. He's leaving me."*

*"I didn't know you had a boyfriend?"*

*"It's complicated."*

*"Do you love him?"* asks the stranger.

*Who is this person...?! Let her go!*

Madison's reply is loaded, contrived, ambiguous... *"Yes. I love him."*

*"Then I hope it works out."*

"Are you going to sit with Robert now?" asks Maddie.

*"No... No. He needs to sleep."*

*"You have my number. Call me, when he wakes again."*

*"I will."*

*"Good-bye Father Maas."*

And the lift doors close, echoing down the hall.

## 20. '...IN SHEEP'S CLOTHING...'

*Saturday, November 3, 2012*

I lay still, listening to soft footfalls in the corridor.

My mind fires like a shot of salts. What if Maas walks into the room? There's no escape. I don't even know how far I can walk... Where do I run? I have no clothes, no ID, no money. There's nothing to stop *him* slipping into my room, and poking a syringe in my eyeball, right here in the bed. Madison will come back tomorrow, and they'll tell her I died from a mystery complication. And – what if I die? Who will be any worse off?

Eyes closed, I hold still... but my muscles are trembling, cold with dread.

It's over. The cover-up will be flawless. My thoughts bundle together. Can I wrestle my way out? Should Madison have stayed? I could have asked her to call the police... Or would that only add to the list of victims?

There's a faint rustle of cloth.

My anger won't let me go quietly.

*...He killed Annie...*

Joe is missing. *They took him.*

It's better to be pissed off, than pissed on.

But what if I *am* imagining things? I'm not a hundred percent sure... The crossword puzzle... Could it be a coincidence? What if 'Samuel Litthamer' wasn't even Matt? Maybe Matt *was* just mugged... And it was a gas leak at the house... Lou Maas might be a Vatican diplomat, looking for Clark... Maybe I imagined the scene in the pool when I was unconscious? That only left Diffner, whose behaviour had been normal – no mention of a puzzle, or secret tablet, or ancient king – until *after* he thought Madison was dead?

Maybe Diffner and I had *both* gone mad?

I lost Matt. He lost Madison.

I open my eyes an instant before everything turns grey, I see the bald face, the tiny eyes and ruddy cheeks above the white cleric's collar, leaning over me.

*Lou Maas...* I start to speak, but with the cold detachment of a surgeon putting a scalpel into a patient's heart, Maas presses something cool to my face.

It takes a moment to register. It smells like fresh Xeroxes, but stronger. *Much* stronger. Pungent, like the Boston Mortuary. Towelling? I hold my breath, and kick my legs, trying to swing my fists – but my atrophied muscles are like string. Pinned under Maas' weight, I can't breathe...

It's a towel... And the eye-watering odour of poison... *Chloroform?*

Lights blaze in my vision. I swing my arms, looking for a jug, a vase, anything to hammer back at Maas with. I claw at the bed-head with crazed fingers. The water glass falls to the floor, shattering.

My arm strikes the IV-stand beside the bed. I clutch at the drip bag, tearing it off its hook. Fog creeps into my brain, and I snatch at the IV needle taped to my forearm, jabbing it blindly...

The first prick catches Maas in the shoulder and he flinches, lifting his weight.

I gasp for air, see the white collar, aim for it, and the second lunge drives the IV needle into his neck.

He stumbles back from the bed, clutching at his throat, his features stretch in a mask of surprise. I kick my legs out of the bedclothes and fall, landing with my knee on the drip-bag. The fluid from the bag squirts up the tube, into Maas' neck.

The ruddy angular face turns a ghastly shade of grey...

Gagging, Maas' squeaks... and buckles, tearing the blanket off the bed.

For a long moment – I kneel dizzily, teetering, watching Maas clutch at his neck with both hands, then writhing on the floor, eyes rolling upward.

This is real. I know *this* is real.

I crouch down, and swim toward the door on sticky hands. Reaching the corridor, I lean on the jamb, trembling.

The far away nurse's station is empty, blurred...

I look back. Maas is gargling, hand still to his throat, eyes white.

My fists bunch so tight the blood leeches out of them.

Maas shakes his head, eye sockets bulging.

In a mess of limbs I reach for the man who killed my wife, feeble, latching onto his collar – and thump him in the face, teeth clenched.

"Where's my son?"

Maas drawls, groggily. "Goo-do-helll..."

I punch furiously at the bald face, but my blows are weak, as if in a dream. My arms are barely strong enough to lift their own weight... dizzy and drained, I release Maas, letting him slump, a smudge of blood on his lip. "Where is my son?!"

Maas drools, suddenly half-alert, and tries to flick away my hands as I fumble to unbutton his priest's robe. Untying my hospital gown, I peel the Jesuit's garb off his sagging limbs, revealing a tattoo on his forearm... A sword in a shield with three lightning bolts.

Reaching for the door in his underwear, one hand pressed to his neck, Maas leaves a trail of thin red streaks on the linoleum.

I seize him by the jaw. "Tell me! Where's Joe?!"

Maas' eyes roll in their sockets again, spit gargling in his neck.

Squeezing into the priest's habit like a bull seal, I grab Maas by the heels, and tow him back inch-by-inch to the bed, faint with exertion... My muscles turn to acid. I lean against the bed, and prop myself up with one elbow.

Maas grabs at space, eyes on the door – moving in slow motion. He struggles to cry out in a thin rasp. I don't know how long I've got till he straightens out, or someone comes past.

I search for something to club him with. There's a stainless steel bedpan stowed in a wire rack under the bed. It clamours out, and I swing it at the back of his skull.

With a dull noise, Maas flops forward, before swaying upright again. Panting, I grab him by the neck. My stomach is a mess of violence now. The impetus of anger has faded. I'm godawfully sore. If I could just lie down... I raise Maas' head, and hurl it against the floor with all my weight.

*Crack.* He slumps, limp.

The room is still.

Staggering into the adjoining bathroom, I check my appearance in the mirror, and find blood on the collar of the priests' cassock – between the high black lapels. Cupping handfuls of water, I soak my neck, rinse my hands, and lean under the mechanical blower.

Shuffling back into the room in small steps, I take off Maas' shoes, too small for my feet, but squeeze into them, toes mashed. Finally, I stand, waiting for the dizziness to pass, my legs barely holding my weight – buckling, at intervals.

There's nowhere to go now. Maas lays stabbed, and beaten. I have no money... But– *anywhere* is better than here. I just need somewhere to hole up, rest, and figure out what to do.

Decided, I shuffle stiffly out into the corridor, skidding along the wall. I don't have the energy for stairs. I'll chance the lift. It takes every reserve of strength to reach the elevator. Here, out in the open, at the end of the hall near the nurse's station, I stand swaying, black against white, monumentally visible, watching the hallway behind me for movement...

The lift arrives with a *ding!* The doors open.

Inside, I stare at the panel of buttons. L1. G. B1.

The lift doors close.

Shock flutters around in my chest.

When Maas is found, the police will come looking for me. It will be a full-blown manhunt now. Bob Travis. Mentally unstable. Dangerous suspect. Wanted for urgent questioning.

The lift reaches the ground.

The doors roll open on a quiet lobby.

Stepping onto the terrazzo, I circle hesitantly, looking for the door. A receptionist sits behind the front desk. Half a dozen visitors wait on patchwork lounges, reading magazines or staring at the walls as I hobble painfully past, wearing Maas' mincy shoes, and bursting medieval costume, with my shaved potato head.

Seeing the automatic glass doors, I lumber toward them, and they roll open.

Outside in the icy car park, without a coat, I'm *still* sweating like a collier.

Somebody will stop me; I know it, to ask who I am – or where I'm going. I'm lost. I can't hide it. I trundle down the footpath, tripping, driven by fear, turn the first corner, and slip on the frozen snow.

My arms snap out to save my balance, and I catch myself against the wall. Panting, I search the street for somewhere to go... My gaze lands on a public park across the street. A lone mother is supervising a mittened child on a playset. A heavily jacketed girl walks an oversized dog on the snow-shovelled walkway.

I cross, and head for the trees, aiming at a bench half-concealed behind an elm. I stumble onto my ass on the seat, ten metres from the hospital, unable to go any further...

Bent over, panting, my legs are too wasted to stand back up. Perspiration drips off my face in a stream. With a weather-eye on the hospital, I swallow, nauseous. I wish I'd thought of a way to make

Maas talk... If only I was stronger... But there hadn't been time. *This is it... I'm done. Now I'm spent.*

I slump, waiting, as a figure approaches on the gravel path.

"Are you all right, Father?" asks the girl. Her Labrador sniffs around the leg of the bench.

"Pardon me?" My face feels like a billboard. *FAKE PRIEST! ON THE LAM!*

"Are you all right?" The girl's voice trembles. She's nervous.

It takes a moment to get it. She's maybe twenty, a student, but assumes a strange childlike reverence.

"*...Father?*" she asks again, with something like awe.

"Thank you. I'm fine," I slur, searching for an inconspicuous answer. "I'm just not used to this sun," I smile, waving a hand in front of my face.

"Where are you from?"

I wonder if I can just tell her to take off, mind her own goddamn business? I can't even walk away. "Over there," I answer, nodding my head at the hospital.

"Oh."

"I'm fine. Really. Have a nice day," I answer, as evenly as possible.

"Sure... Okay... Bye."

And she leads the big yellow dog away.

I prop myself on my arms, to keep from flopping onto the ground. If I were stronger, I could bum-rush the gates on the 'T' and take the subway... If it's running again. I don't even have money for a cab. What are the odds of getting a Catholic cab driver in Boston? Fifteen years ago it would have been a cert. Not any more. Besides... Where do I go? I just have to get off the street. The cops are going to be looking for me now. If I could lie down for a minute... I need a warm bed, a swig of Scotch, and Annie. *God. I'm effed in the ay. A big black duck in a thunderstorm, in a Monsignor's cassock.*

Outwardly I try to look serene, but inwardly I'm rabid. There isn't anything left to do but turn myself in. Are Annie and Joe watching? What if there's something else, something *after...?* It wouldn't be wrong to check out, now, after all that had happened. Would it? Except, Joe might still be alive. And if that isn't enough, Madison mightn't be safe now either. I've put her in danger too. Maas will suspect we talked. And I'm the only person who *knows* he'll be looking for her now too. In fact, I'm the only one who knows about *any* of it – Benning, Barne, Diffner, Matt, Annie...

I didn't even think to ask Madison what happened to her in New York... What did she say? *...I came up here as soon as I could get out of New York...*

I fumble for a pocket in Maas's robe, and find one concealed at the seams. It's empty, but for a clogged handkerchief.

I've got bank accounts all over the eastern seaboard, but no identification. No cards. I can't think of a single person who'll believe my story... *Gordon?* Gordo would rather call the 'Po' – as Joe would say. And all the days of my life, all those years spent going to work, making Numbers, paying bills, are all suddenly pointless. Out in the cold, I'm confronted with the horrible, godless reality: It weighs heavier, and hurts more profoundly, than anything... This is me; this is how I was, before I met Annie.

I've been wondering a lot lately, what makes a man tie a bomb to his chest, and blow himself to a thousand pieces... Now I know. I *know* why so many people are killing, and being killed for no apparent reason... I know what makes a terrorist. When everything else is taken away, all hope and love, when all you have left is sickness, and bitterness... There's just no reason *not* to destroy.

Rubbing my arms, I hear a faint jingle, and brush against a lump in the cassock near my hip.

It takes a few minutes with numb fingers to find the entrance to the extra pocket, and pull out a set of car keys on a leather ring.

I stare at them for a moment.

*Bingo.*

I stand up, and trudge toward the hospital car park, shoes soaked with sludge. At the corner, I press the 'unlock' button on the key, and hear a dull *thunk* across the lot.

A pair of tail lights flash, in a silver Lincoln.

Madison makes it as far as the exit of the St Ignatius parking lot, before she decides to turn back.

She only intended to make me sweat it out for a few hours... maybe overnight.

She was especially angry that I didn't give a *shit* what she'd been through in New York.

When rescuers reached her on the IRT Flushing Line platform, she'd been huddled in darkness, helpless, on top of the garbage can for almost 24 hours. It felt like a week. It had taken every shred of willpower, without food or water, shuddering in the cold, deep underground, not to let herself just slip into the murky electrified water that flooded the station.

The worst part of all had been the echoes of other people dying in the tunnels.

By the time rescue divers reached her, she was half dead, and – she was fairly certain – three-quarters mad... There had been ghosts in the darkness, too horrible to contemplate. And all she could think about the whole time, was how badly she missed Tessa, Annie, Joe and her fucked up brother-in-law... And Clark. She wished she hadn't been so rough on him.

Still, the decision to come to Boston to stay by her brother-in-law's bed hadn't been easy. Her friends were in New York. They needed her just as badly. Half the city had been gutted, sunk, or burned... It was hard to remember now why she ever bothered to come back. Still, she was in Boston now. And as pissed-off as she was for what had been said, she couldn't just *leave*. We'd *both* lost Annie and Matt, *both* witnessed unbelievable horrors, and narrowly escaped death... Plus, she figured I might still have a clue what happened to Clark – given time. She decided it was okay for me to be fucked up. She knew from experience.

So she circles the hospital, puts her hire car back in the same space it was in minutes ago, and retraces her steps back to fourth floor.

The corridor past my room is empty. The nurses' station is still vacant, and there is no sign of Lou Maas now.

An eerie silence pervades the ward...

The little horror-movie voice inside Madison's head tells her to *turn back*, but it is drowned out by a louder imperative... Creeping past the abandoned nurse's station, a powerful uneasiness climbs up her back. The sensation grows in weight as she approaches the open doorway.

Pausing in the hallway, she hears the sound of movement; rubbing cloth, heavy breathing...

*"Bob...?" she* whispers, *cautioning herself too late.*

The movement stops suddenly.

Stepping forward, she peeks at the empty bed, the strewn linen, and bright red smears on the linoleum. "...Bob?"

"*Help* me..."

The reply comes from the bathroom. "Who's there?"

"It's me... Lou."

Madison rushes into the en-suite, to find the defrocked priest in his undershorts, huddled over the hand basin. She is struck by Maas' sinewed body. His monsignor's garb concealed a lean, muscular frame – and a strange tattoo on his forearm. He's nothing but pale skin stretched over tendons. His astonishing leanness verges on something diseased. The only time Madison has *ever* seen someone with that much muscle definition, is a lifelong heroin addict. And – the scars... All over his shoulder blade, on his ribs, on the side of his neck...

Madison hovers by the door warily. "Father Maas?"

Lou rinses blood out of his mouth.

"Where's Bob?"

"He attacked me!" Maas gasps, dabbing at his bruised forehead. "I couldn't *believe* it..."

"I have to find him." Madison turns to leave.

"Wait!" Lou coughs. He is watching her suspiciously in the mirror. "What—?"

"I know where he went," he offers.

"Where?"

"Pass me that towel." He gestures to the rail.

Madison slips the towel off the rod, and holds it out for him.

As soon as her wrist is within reach, Maas latches onto her.

"Hey!" Madison exclaims. "What the *fuck*?"

"He *talked* to you, didn't he?" Lou growls, his demeanor mutating before her eyes. And instantly, she knows I was telling the truth.

"Huh?"

"He sent you away! What did he *tell* you?"

Madison tries to twist her arm free, and lunges for the door. She's known enough men with bad tempers – or sick ideas of fun – that the move is almost second nature. But Maas' grip only tightens. He lashes out with his other hand, grabbing her by the forelock. The pain, where the hair rips from her scalp, is enough to make her eyes water instantly. But she doesn't scream. She's never screamed in her life. Only a small grunt of exertion escapes her mouth, as she drops to her knees, head twisted back.

Maas drags Madison out into the next room.

As she scrambles for the door, he yanks on her hair again, and pulls her onto her back. "Cry for help," he sneers vilely. "It will do *no* good."

Madison locks him in her gaze, and scoffs. "The worst thing you could do to me is rape me, and you're not man enough!"

Lou stands over her, muscles in his torso rippling with the compression, all the way down his arms to his balled-up fists. "Shut your mouth, whore."

Madison smiles. *Gotcha.* "You can't even hold me down properly."

Lou slaps her across the face. "I said '*shut up!*'"

Catching the look of disorientation in Maas' eyes, Madison laughs again. "Come on. Be a man. What are you afraid of?" With her free hand, she tugs at the waist of her suit pants. It's a familiar game. All men are the same, no matter what they claim to want: If you make them angry, put them off balance, distract them with a little bare skin, their attention goes to the same thing...

She yanks down her pants, far enough for Maas to see her G-string.

She feels his grip loosen for an instant, and wrenches her wrist free, manicured claws hooking into his undershorts, grabbing his balls in her fist.

At first, a look of alarm hits Maas's face, surprised by her strength. Then he tries to pull back – but too late, doubling over in agony. His fist slams into Madison's temple, sending stars across her vision, but she refuses to let go. She *tightens* her grip, digging her nails into the soft flesh around the base of his penis, pivoting her shoulder sharply, twisting her wrist.

Lou howls, and grabs at her arm, driving the tips of his fingers into the muscle. But Madison knows she's already done enough damage. He'll be hurting long after she lets go. The delicate pipes and wires between his balls are all ripped.

As soon as she lets go, both Maas' hands fly to his groin. He crumples to the floor, locked in a knuckle of torture.

Madison raises herself up, tested her bruised arm, and dusting the marks off the knees of her suit. She glowers disdainfully at the curled figure, and coos softly: "Didn't see that coming, did you, tough guy?"

After a moment of consideration, Madison raises a stilettoed heel, and with all of her weight, drives it into the arch of his foot. Maas shrieks in pain. Then Madison inspects her fingernails. Three of them are split. "I just had my nails done, asshole."

She walks out of the room...

Running down the corridor, she slaps the lift button several times, scanning the corridor looking for me... She waits a moment, then heads for the stairs. Swinging off the handrails, she leaps down the stairs two at a time, and bursts into the hospital foyer.

"Excuse me," she asks the receptionist. "Did you see a priest come past here a few minutes ago?"

The nurse hesitates, seeing the cruel welt over on Madison's left eye. But it's a hospital, and she's seen far worse. "Yes, ma'am. He went *outside.*"

Madison leaps for the automatic doors, slapping the glass impatiently, sidling through the gap, and running into the icy street.

Turning the corner, she sees me crossing the parking lot, waving a key-ring.

She rushes toward me, wrapping her arm around my waist, revealing the glowing purple bruise on her wrist.

"What happened?" I ask, spotting the injury.

"We have to get out of here," she answers. "I'll take you to the hotel."

I slump against a parked car, as the ground swoops up.

"Stay here. I'll get the car." And she dashes away.

Propped against a Lincoln, swooning, I wait.

A minute later, Madison brakes her hire car wildly at the kerb, leans across the passenger seat and pops the door. "Get in!"

I push off my perch, and fall inside.

Madison accelerates like a madwoman, before my door is shut.

Her voice is hoarse. "I saw *Lou.*"

My mental fatigue has worsened – as if the car seat, the sudden rescue, Madison's presence, are a magic lullaby. I can barely hold my chin up. "He tried to hurt you?"

"I tried to help him, and the fucker attacked me!" Madison thumps the steering wheel. "Jeezus."

It's strange, seeing her angry. I've never seen her angry. Annie never got angry like this either. Annie used expletives like 'Applesauce' and 'Horsefeathers'. "Are you hurt?" I ask, drifting towards unconsciousness.

"Not as bad as he is."

A smile breaks across my lips, for the first time I can remember.

Madison laughs suddenly. "He'll be pissing sideways for a month." She twists her ankle to check if her shoe is damaged. "Fuck."

And I tell you what, I like her. For the first time ever. "Ha ha!" I laugh. "You're really something," I mumble. I think that's how Clark put it.

Sailing across town toward the Boston Harbor Hotel, Madison diligently adheres to the speed limit. If we're pulled over, neither of us have the energy to make up a story to cover her bruises and my garb. And – seeing the weariness in my eyes – Madison generously postpones asking me any more questions right now.

But I know... the questions will come.

I'll have to tell her everything.

## 21. '...DOWN BY A CORD...'

*Sunday, November 4, 2012*

After twenty minutes hunched on the floor in the shower, hot water pelting my trembling limbs, I hear the bathroom door thump open.

Madison bounces in wearing tight-fitting track-pants, a thin T-shirt, and no bra – carting a bundle of shopping bags.

The steam from the shower obscures the glass just enough to preserve my modesty. Still, I object to the intrusion with an unintelligible growl.

"I bought you some clothes."

I'd probably be dead or in prison by now, without her. It makes it impossible to feel anything but gratitude, despite all our differences. Nevertheless, it's the kind of gratitude you feel for a dentist, after having a tooth yanked.

"I wasn't sure what you felt like eating, so I ordered some eggs," she adds. "You need solid food but I'm not sure you're ready for a rib-eye."

"You don't need to take care of me," I retort. "I'm tired... not *stupid.*"

"Get over it." Madison sashays out into the hotel suite, leaving the bathroom door open. "How are your arms?" she calls from the next room. "The doctor said they were burned."

I inspect the pale, hairless, virgin skin on my forearms. "Fine."

I dry off, and check myself in the mirror. I'm thinner than I used to be, ghostlier, with less hair, less humour, less of everything.

Rummaging through the shopping bags, I find three formats of undergear, jeans, a polo shirt, and a pair of Ferragamo slip-ons. To my surprise, Madison guessed my shoe-size - even if the style is wildly impractical for a man on the run.

I'm half dressed when she walks back into the bathroom, and offers me a highball.

"What's that?"

"'Russian Standard.'"

"I don't—"

"Relax," Maddie scoffs. "You weren't on Bactrim, Flagyl, Tindamax, or morphine - and you're not planning on operating heavy machinery for the next twelve hours?"

I accept the glass.

The food arrives, and I swill some eggs and soft toast, washing it down with milk. Madison sits on the arm of a chair, one leg folded under her tail, searching the internet on the hotel TV for news of the incident at St Ignatius.

"That's strange..." she mutters. "There's nothing..."

"About what?"

"*You.*"

As soon as my fork hits the empty plate, Madison drags her chair over to the corner of the table. "So, from the beginning..."

She listens quietly, sipping her drink, as I describe the events after Matt's death. How - according to Clark - someone set us up.

"*Set you up?*" Madison shakes her head.

"Paired us up in Washington. To find out what we knew."

"But I told Clark to hire you."

"How did *you* meet him?"

"At the funeral."

"It doesn't make sense... What happened to Clark after the motel fire?"

Maddie shakes her head, shrugging slightly.

"He seemed to have it all figured out."

"Have *what* figured out?"

"The crossword by *'Samuel Litthamer'*?"

Madison nodded, sipping her drink. "I found it in Dad's things after he died. The date, and the anagram made me suspicious."

"It contained a code. Like we talked about: Every religion believing in *one* god - Judaism, Islam, Catholicism, Orthodox, Protestants, Mormons. They all have the same stories about an ancient stone tablet, written by God... There are clues... *lots* of clues... Going way back to a king *before* Abraham. I thought we'd made it up, but Clark thought it was *real*. He traced the path of this thing right through history, through Egypt, Babylon, the Roman Empire. They *all* came into contact with this object, and *all* converted to the same God. And... they *all* kept it a secret."

"He found it? The tablet?"

"No. Almost as soon as we even *considered it,* people started getting killed."

"Go back to the beginning..." Madison rubs her temples.

She teases out every excruciating detail, recharging my glass along the way. From my first trip to DC, Agent Benning arriving in New Brid, the explosion at the house... Wherever I miss a name, skim a detail, or something doesn't make sense, she stops me: "How much do you think Dad knew?" I can't answer. "The diagram Clark showed you at the Inn - from the crossword - can you remember it?" *No.* "Does anyone else know about this?" *If they did, they're probably running as well - or dead.* "Did Lou Maas shoot the CIA agent, and Barne Ruberight?" *Probably.* "What's with the eyes - screwing with people's eyes - what's that about?"

"I don't know..." I feel myself getting owled. Ossified. Spifflicated. Obliterous. My liver is out of practice.

"Is he working alone? Maas?"

"One man couldn't do all this," I speculate. He's too well informed, and seems to have unlimited resources. The car. Blending in with the investigators in New Brid... Blowing up the house... Pulling strings at the hospital... Changing his identity...

"Well, at least we know where Clark went."

"Where?"

"You don't know Clark..." she sighs. "He'll chase the fuckers down and wipe them out."

Madison quizzes me at length about a possible connection between the subway bombers... and what Clark said in the hotel room, the night he disappeared.

Finally, she leans back, considers what I've said, and sighs "Clark wouldn't make this up. And he *wouldn't* fall for something without proof."

"You trust him?" I ask carefully. Not because I'm interested in her feelings. Diffner is the weak link... He showed up in *both* our lives just after Matt was killed... Then, after I went to his house and he fought with Madison, he elaborated the Melchizedek story... Then he's in New Brid when Barne and Benning are shot, the hotel burns down, and my house blows up... It's still just as likely Diffner is pulling our strings.

"Yes. I trust him."

"Why did you break up with him?"

"He wanted to fire you after you showed up at his house talking crazy. I asked him not to. He went ahead and made the call to D.C., so I left." She shrugs. "His diagram... The one he showed you at the hotel... Do you think you can remember it?"

"Maybe some of it. Why?"

"Wherever the code points to, that's where we'll find Clark." Madison slides a hotel notepad across the table. "Draw it *for me.*"

"If I had a copy of the crossword..." It's in the desk drawer at the house – inside the puzzle book Joe brought home from Matt's house – along with the *Bud Lite* coaster, and the Polaroid. They're all gone now.

"Draw what you can."

'M' and 'A' through to 'J' I remember, from decoding the cipher on the beer coaster. It's basic Old Testament stuff...

*M-A-I2-J(I)-J-Oed-M-D-S*

Melchizedek ('M') blesses Abraham ('A') who sacrifices one of his two sons... 'I1' and 'I2' are Ishmael, and Isaac. *Which* son was sacrificed, decides whether you're a Jew, or a Muslim... It's the main difference, and the first branch in the diagram... Then Jacob, Isaac's son, was renamed by god to *Israel* ('J(I)'). His son is Joseph ('J') who is enslaved in Egypt. There, it gets tricky. "There was an 'Oed'... short for 'Oedipus', the Greek myth of the King of Thebes in Egypt, who killed his own mother... based on Pharaoh Akhenaten of Amarna..."

Madison nods. "Then Moses leads the Jews back out of Egypt, comes down from Sinai with the tablet, puts it in the Ark... King David brings the Ark to Jerusalem. King Solomon builds the temple..."

Right. "Nebuchadnezzar sacks the temple – Zerubbabel rebuilds the temple... There was a 'WS1' – I'm guessing short for William Shakespeare's first play *printed*... 'Titus'..."

"Titus sacked the temple in Seventy-One A.D."

"...Then I think it was 'CZL'..."

"CZL?" Madison leaps back to the keyboard for the hotel TV internet connection, and types in the acronym. "That's the airport code for the city of 'Constantine' in Algeria. Constantine starts Roman Catholicism."

"Somewhere next was '*HOTW*' with a number. Three... something-something."

"*History of the Wars.*" Madison walks behind me, and leans over my shoulder where I'm scribbling down the letters, breathing on my neck. "By Procopius. The number would be a book reference. Volume three of eight. Followed by a page, or chapter. It doesn't matter. Book 'three' is about Alaric, King of the Visigoths, who sacked Rome in August in four-ten A.D. and took the treasure back to France. What's next?"

"Wow. How do you *know* that?"

"I *read*," she scowls. "How do you *not* know that? Dad would be disappointed in you."

"Then there was an 'M-one-four-two-two'... Or, 'one-two-four-four.'"

"Fourteen-Twenty-Two doesn't fit... Twelve-Forty-Four was the year the Khwarezmians expelled the Crusaders from Jerusalem... That doesn't fit either, if the treasure already left Rome..." Madison drums her fingernails on the table. I notice three of them are cut short. Probably broken in her struggle with Maas today. "It's also the year of the Battle of *La Forbie* near Gaza?"

"You're a freak," I slur.

Madison pours another two fingers of *Russian Standard*, nodding as she gulps. "The Khwarezmians and Egyptians destroyed the Frankish army. That was the Christian Crusader's most severe loss to the Muslims... Not really a fit either—"

"There's *no* way you just know that..."

Madison ignores me. "It *could* be the battle of Montségur. That was Twelve-Forty-Four?"

It's apparent – not *just* for the first time – that Madison is her father's daughter. Moreso than Annie. It's been so long since I've had any kind of conversation with Madison, I'd forgotten. With her Masters in Political Science and International Studies, she's illuminating the riddle with unnerving ease... It also explains what Diffner saw in her – as if he needed *another* reason to sack an oversexed woman twenty years his junior. "What's the battle of '*Montségur*?'"

"It was the end of Pope Innocent Three's crusade against the Cathars."

I draw a line between Constantine, and Alaric. "So what's the link from Alaric to Montségur?"

"The Visigoth treasure, pillaged from Rome, included Titus' loot from the Second Temple. It was hidden in the mountains of the Razès and Sabarthès in Southern France, when the Visigoth Empire fell in the 5th century. The Cathars were a Christian sect, maybe a million strong. The Vatican saw their practices as a threat, and razed the whole civilization during the Inquisitions... They spent *forty years* wiping out every trace of the Cathars... They even murdered *devout* Catholics. Pope Innocent-the-Third instructed his armies to '*Kill them all. God will recognise his own...*' The Cathars had connections between Christianity, Jewish Kabbalist scholars, *and* the Moslem Sufi communities in Spain and the Middle East... All the 'big three' Abrahamic religions..."

"You think the Cathars knew about Melchizedek? Maybe the Vatican was trying to protect its secret?"

"The Cathars are where the word 'bugger' comes from," Madison sips her drink, grinning boldly. "Derived from 'Bulgar' – short for the *'Bulgarian heresy'* – because the Cathars encouraged anal sex as contraception."

"Nice."

"I wonder if there's a connection, with the eyes?"

"'Buggery' and 'Eyes'?"

"No! The leader of the Crusaders gouged out the eyes of a hundred Cathar prisoners, cut off their noses and lips, and sent them back to their homes led by one prisoner with one remaining eye... The contents of the Ark were probably there... During the siege, two Cathars, escaped over the wall of the castle with some kind of sacred object... Some say it was the Holy Grail... It might have been this tablet."

In less than five minutes, Madison has completed nine centuries of the puzzle.

"What's next?" she slaps my shoulder.

"I... can't remember," I mash my temples. "So— This is a well-known story, these Cathars, sneaking out of Montségur?"

"What?! *Yes!* Napoleon ordered the Vatican archives moved to Paris in Eighteen-Ten, and then - *back* to the Vatican, between Eighteen-Fifteen and Eighteen-Seventeen. *He* might have known about it as well. He was a self-confessed atheist, but he also admitted Catholicism was the best way to maintain 'morality and order' in the state... It fits. If Napoleon knew the Egyptians, Babylonians, and Romans *all* did the same thing... You can add Napoleon to the list, along with Akhenaten, Nebuchadnezzar, and Constantine... What's next?"

"Where did the treasure go after that?"

"It could be anywhere... Even if it *was* in Rome. There was a robbery at the Vatican in Eighty-Six."

"Really?"

"Ahuh. During the restoration of the Basilica - three gunmen made it past Vatican security and Swiss Guards with fake I.D.s. The official story was that they fled empty-handed. But, there are twenty-two museums in the Vatican. It's the most valuable art collection in the world. Strange that thieves would leave empty-handed, don't you think? More likely the *Holy See* couldn't say *what* had been stolen."

"You think they stole this *tablet?*"

Madison shrugs again, and pours another drink. "What was next...?"

"I need to think." All my notes, before and after the conversation with Diffner, are nothing but ash.

"Concentrate."

"For chrissake!" I thump the table, sending the dinner plate bouncing to the floor.

Madison looks at the plate strangely, as if it brings back a memory. "This is why we can't have nice things," she grins.

Fucking hell! It's impossible to be angry with her. "It's all *gone!*" I growl. "The notes. The books..."

"I'm sorry," Madison slouches.

"No, it's not you."

"Fine. Then I'm *not* sorry." She bares her teeth in a fake snarl.

I stand up, legs still aching. "I need to get out of this room."

"We're not finished!"

I walk for the balcony door. "I need some air."

Madison leaps up, slipping in front of me before I can get my hand to the latch. "Wait. Talk to me..."

"I need air!" My face is flushed. I'm fried to the hat. There are *two* empty bottles of *Russian Standard* on the counter.

Madison smiles disarmingly, wriggling between me and the glass door, patting me gently on the chest. "Hey, Bobby— I'm sorry. I'm upset as well. This whole thing, Dad... Annie, and Joe. It's horrible."

*Bobby?* I stare at her, astonished. The change in her voice, a few sparks from her fingertips, and I'm placated too easily.

"Let's get some rest..." she whispers sweetly.

I'm being *man*aged. She has had a lifetime of practice at getting what she wants from difficult men. Besides, Matt *was* her father... Annie *was* her sister. Clark *was* her lover. Joe was her nephew, and she *fucking loved* my boy. She's got as much reason as me to want answers.

And she was in the subway attacks... She was there. She lost friends in New York... I haven't given much thought to that side of things. This is her fight as much as it is mine. Swaying on my feet, I wonder out loud, "Why would terrorists have copies of the crossword puzzle?"

Madison shrugs. "They were trained by U.S. security forces in Iraq... What happens every time there's a terrorist attack? People show up to church in droves, and hand the government more power."

"You're not suggesting—"

"The Catholics killed the Cathars to stop them *buggering* around with the Muslims. Maybe there's more to this terrorist attack than a handful of extremists?"

"That's *reedicks*—" I mumble.

"Some people are unbelievably fucked up."

It's terrifying that it's all linked together. "Maybe there's a bunch of Muslim clerics somewhere who want to keep this a secret just as badly as Christians do."

"Let's get some rest," she drags me by the wrist. "In the morning we'll go to Clark's house—"

"You have a key?"

"Yep. He'll have notes..." Madison sees the look on my face, and flicks her hair. "Don't even *think* about going there *now*! You're about to collapse."

"It won't take long for someone to figure out where we are."

"We're fine," she smiles. "I'm not checked in under my name."

I'm about to ask why, but its fair to assume some romantic melodrama. Some ardent ex-boyfriend. Or, a habit formed from too often using married men's credit cards, and avoiding stalkers, and gossip columnists. It's Madison. It's probably *all* the above reasons.

"We need the cipher," I press, gesturing at my partial reproduction. "If we can find out where this tablet is supposed to have ended up—"

"And find Clark," she adds.

"You really *like* him?" I venture, a little too quickly. Like I've been waiting for an opportunity to ask.

"Yeah, I guess so."

The idea of searching Clark's house is seductive. It's one way to find out what he figured out...

"C'mon. This thing has been lying around for four-thousand years. One more day won't hurt." The look on Madison's face is plain. She isn't suggesting sleep for my benefit. She's exhausted too.

The bruise at the sleeve of her T-shirt has turned yellow.

She follows my eyes. "I've had worse," she warns, turning away.

"Okay."

She shoves me onto the sofa, fetches a blanket from the closet, and throws it over me.

I listen while she showers... and drift asleep to the *hissss* of running water.

Rousing at the creak of footsteps, I catch her dimpled tail bouncing past, tip-toeing to the bedroom. Through the open bedroom door, a sliver of moonlight illuminates her spine as she climbs over a pile of pillows.

Sleep eludes me for what feels like hours...

Finally, Madison whispers across the suite. "*Robert?*"

I wonder if I should answer.

"Can I ask you something?"

I could pretend I'm asleep. "...What?"

Madison sits up, clutching the sheet to her chest. "I've known you for... Twenty years?"

"Almost."

"Every Christmas and birthday, I wanted to ask..."

"What?"

"Whenever I brought it up, Annie changed the subject."

"What?"

"The Sheriff said your father died in a fire?"

Something inside me shrivels. I exhale heavily. "...And?"

"We **never** met your family– How come you don't mention them?"

Instantly, it feels like something is springing up that can't be put away again. Something squeezed in so tight, for so long, it had to pop.

"Bob?" asks Madison again, carefully.

"I don't want to talk about it."

"Okay."

But it's already on its way out. The way through it, is to yank it all out in a hurry. "My father ran a church in Akron. When I was seventeen, Family Services came to take me to a foster home. My father thought the *Antichrist* was taking me away, so... He set fire to our house while he and my Mum were locked inside."

Maddie falls silent for a long while, but I can see her still sitting up in bed.

"Shit. That's why you came to Clark's house that morning...? Talking about Waco and Order of the Solar Temple?"

I don't feel like answering. I don't really feel like speaking at all.

"You went back to school, earned a scholarship to MIT, and met Annie..." Madison muses.

The truth is, Annie took my angry, fearful, mangled internal arrangement, and patched me up. I was *shitting* myself the night I first met Matt. My ears were still ringing from ten years of Sunday School... "Annie warned me what Matt thought of religion. I was worried he'd tell her to stop seeing me."

"But he loved you for it," suggests Madison.

I turn over on the couch, so I don't have to look at Madison's silhouette anymore. If I was numb before, there aren't words for how I feel now. The sense of... *drifting.*

I think Madison must have fallen asleep.

Then I hear a creak behind me, and next thing I know, she's wriggling onto the couch. I tense. "Shhh..." She strokes my hair. "Go to sleep."

She slips her arm around me, on the outside of the blanket.

I don't know if she's comforting me, or herself.

My old life – the life that *was* mine, with Annie – is gone, fled over a far horizon.

It's absurd now; the Insurers, the multinational financial institutions, the spreadsheets... handing over Numbers like the pristine milk of the virgin, when it was all bird shit: dead bugs, gravely worm heads, dirty ketchup-soaked fries, green breadcrumbs, and chewing gum... Mix it all together, and it comes out white. Working for the towel-boys of Capitalism. A hundred million Joe-regulars, paying twenty-five-ninety- five a month, so when they get hit by a flying anvil, they get a big ear-ringing payout. All the crashing, colliding, cracking open, spiking into the earth... The annual reports, the prospectii, the EOIs, MOIs, MOUs, and AGMs. The slush funds and earmarked surplus... Trying to keep up with something interminable on a minute-by-minute basis. Keeping it coming in. The hand-shaking, the internal conversations, trying to stay in-good-with-The-Man. Interest in interest. Winding tight the spreads and splits, day-trading, market wrapping, stock-watching, dividends, index points, and P/E ratios. Percentages and points-of-points. Escrows, options, gearing, leveraging, amortisation... None of it matters now.

*None* of it.

All along, it was ass-up ... the idea *any* of it mattered.

Take it all away, and the only things I really miss are Annie and Joe.

I would happily submit to an eternity in Hell – tortured, burned, pulled to pieces – just to see her again... The way she'd say something so funny I couldn't even laugh, my brain was so busy thinking *'that's the funniest thing I ever heard.'* The way she threw in musical words like *'ennui'* and *'ersatz'*. The way she filled my Freudian-type gaps. She was my pal, my poster-girl, my princess bride, all rolled into one. My antithesis. My anima. She disagreed with every second thing I ever said. She wondered why she loved me, but she couldn't help it. I was her one weakness. And – for the first few years – it felt, every day like it was all about to tip over. Any minute, the Devil Himself was gonna come clomping in through the door, and make even. Like there was a bill I forgot to pay. A lit fuse... I could hear it *fizzing* away, while I sat at my desk, singing *'Moneeey... do-n-doo-doo-doo'* and making spreadsheets of spreadsheets in Matt's den, with the double-glazing and the mile-long-drive. But she stayed. She kept loving me.

Now, she's gone.

Whoever said it was better to have loved and lost, forgot to add that it all depends how you lose them.

Gradually, the blinding rage – the muscle memory of that searing moment where I grabbed Maas by the skull and flung it at the linoleum – permeates my limbs.

...Don't let this change you... Madison said. ...You're a good man...

But how can it *not* change me? The fury. The bald-faced, unbridled wrath. And, the question: *Where is Joe...?*

It takes a long time to fall asleep. In spite of my fatigue, my emotions and organs are all spun up together. All the events that led to this strange descent into cryptic purgatory, replay in my head until, finally, my body wins - an image of Annie's last fearful expression - flickers into a feverish, senseless dream.

*Monday, November 5, 2012*

Madison waits till I'm asleep, before she dresses silently, and creeps out of the hotel room.

Driving across town in the predawn glow, she dials my receptionist.

"Hi Ruby, sorry to wake you - what time is it? Oh, it's four A.M... Sorry— You were awake? Oh good. Look, it's Madison, Bob's sister-in-law. We met last year at the Christmas party. Hey, Bob needs a favour..."

Madison parks outside my building, and Ruby meets her fifteen minutes later in the foyer. They ride upstairs in the lift together. "Thank you," Madison smiles gratefully at the dour, septuagenarian crone. "I just need to pick up a few things."

"When is Mister Travis coming back?" asks Ruby.

"You'll be the first to know." Madison touches Ruby's old pruned hand, lightly.

"It's terrible, what happened."

"Thank you. I'll tell him you send your regards."

"Did he like the flowers?"

Madison hadn't seen any flowers. Either they'd been intercepted, or they'd gone to Deaconess after I was moved to St Ignatius. "Yes. They were lovely."

Ruby smiles, before her expression is replaced again with a frown. "We're all praying for his recovery."

"Thank you."

Ruby flicks the light switch, igniting a bank of fluorescent tubes in the office reception.

In the centre of the waiting room stands a polished timber Turing-type Machine in a glass cabinet.

"You don't have to stay," offers Madison. "I know where everything is. You can go home."

Ruby hands Madison a security pass on a lanyard, and returns quietly to the bank of elevators.

Madison crosses the lobby, stepping into the sepulchrally quiet office of Managing Director, Robert Travis. She hurriedly surveys the contents of my desk...

A copy of the *Boston Globe* still sits in my IN tray, folded to the obits. The date reads *Monday, September 3, 2012.*

Madison tosses the newspaper aside, and glances at the row of pink Post-Its decorating the rim of the desk. She collects the tabs on her fingertips, and flips through them...

The first two are in someone else's handwriting... Ruby's.

The second two are mine.

*Detective Cullen, Boston Police Dept.*

*Gordon, SSL*

*Madison, Boston Harbor Hotel?*

*Bill Dodd, Anacostia Institute*

She sits back in my wing-backed chair, and flips through my Rolodex looking for the names on the notes. Only the second name matches a business card...

> *Gordon Daley*
> *Senior Vice-President, Risk*
> *Standard Sapiential and Life*

Madison picks up the phone, tucks it under her hair, and dials the number on the card.

*"Gordon speaking."*

"Gordon. Hi. This is Madison Mueller, Robert Travis' sister-in-law. Sorry to call so early—"

"No, no, no! Madison! I remember you... We met at a picnic with your father. I'm very sorry for your loss—es."

Madison pretends not to notice the clumsy plural. "I remember you too. My father convincing you to hire Bobby in the first place?"

"Boy, was that a mistake," Gordon chuckles awkwardly. "No, just kidding."

"I'm in Bob's office. Bob needs a favour. How far away are you?"

*"I'll be there in ten minutes."*

Madison hangs up, tucked the Post-Its in her purse, and waits, watching the lifts through the open door.

Gordon steps into the lobby with his tie swept over his shoulder. He's short enough that his crop-circle bald patch is plainly visible when Madison stands to shake his hand.

"Miss Mueller, it's such a pleasure to *see* you again! Wow, this place is like a ghost-town. I think I saw a tumbleweed."

"Thanks for coming in so early. I only need a moment."

"Call me Gordo. What can I do for you?" Gordon smiles as he eyed the chair, deliberating whether or not to sit down. "Hey, how's Bob doing?"

Madison doesn't have the energy to answer the questions that will come if she tells him. All she needs is a phone number. "He's going to be fine. He's awake. He asked me to stop by and pick up some work. I wonder if you could help me with a phone number?"

"Sure! Sure. That's great news. What are you after?"

"Bob mentioned something about a job he was working on in Washington? I'm afraid I didn't quite catch all the details. He was after a phone number for—"

"The RUNE Report!" Gordon dips into his pants pocket, taking out his Blackberry. "Boy, I'm glad he's back on the ball. We're hanging on by a thread with those guys..."

"Can you tell me who he was working for?"

"The fella's name is Bill Dodd."

Madison recognises the name from the Post-It. Clark had mentioned him as well. "That's the one. Can you give me his number? Bob wants to talk to him."

"Great!" Gordon reads out the number from his phone, and Madison scribbles it on a fresh Post-It.

"Thank you."

"So... Do you know when Bob will be back on deck?"

"It should be a few weeks. Thanks for your help Gordon. I really appreciate it."

"Great! Great. No problem. Hey, you want to go get a java?"

Oddly, Madison is reminded of a young executive on the IRT Flushing line platform, in grand central station. That had been minutes before... She forces a smile, to cover the spasm that accompanies the recollection. "No thanks. I really have to get back to the hospital."

"Oh, sure. Maybe some other time?"

"Sure." Madison holds the smile.

Gordon dallies halfway between the desk and the door.

"Bye," says Madison, curtly.

"Okay. Bye." Gordon trundles back to the lifts, glancing over his shoulder.

Madison waits for the elevator doors to close, before dialling the number.

*"Anacostia Institute."*

"Hi. Can you put me through to Bill Dodd?"

*"Mister Dodd is abroad at the moment. May I take a message?"*

"Oh. Okay. He didn't mention he was going away. Can you tell me where I can reach him?"

*"I'm afraid he can't be reached. If you give me your details, he will return your call when he is back in the office."*

"When will that be?"

*"In January."*

"Boy, am *I* looking forward to going on a holiday too..."

*"Mister Dodd isn't on holiday."*

"Oh... Of course not. Silly me. Not with the *RUNE Report* still going."

"*Mister Dodd is no longer working on the RUNE report. He's overseas with Advisors from the 'International Center for Terrorism Studies'.*"

Madison smiles pleasantly. "So, he's in Iraq?"

"What did you say your name was?"

"Merry Christmas." Madison hangs up the phone.

She stands up to leave, glancing as she does at the newspaper in the IN tray. And notices there are *two* newspapers there. Retrieving the folded *Boston Globe*, Madison uncovers an older copy of the *New York Times*...

Sunday, September 2, 2012.

She flips through the pages to the crossword.

*Puzzle by Samuel Litthamer.*

"Bingo."

I'm woken by a knock.

Rubbing my eyes, I lean up and peer over the back of the couch.

Madison is dressed, standing at the door. A bell hop wheels a room service trolley into the room. Madison tips the boy, and walks him back out to the hall.

"Rise and shine," she wheels the breakfast trolley over to the sofa. "Look what I found." She tosses the newspaper into my lap.

It's the Litthamer crossword.

And she's solved it, filling in every answer.

"What the hell is a 'Peri-sore-us-cana-densis-capitalis'?" I ask.

"It's a kind of bird," she mutters. "A rocky mountain jay called a 'whisker jack', or a 'camp robber'..."

"Hmmmf."

"I think I figured it out. But I want to check Clark's place first."

I guzzle my eggs, dress, and we take the lift down to the garage.

Madison parks the hire car across the street from Clark Diffner's Beacon Street townhouse.

Crossing the road in the pre-dawn glow, the world looks very different from that sunny morning in September.

I prop myself against the wall as Madison locates the key in her handbag. She twists the lock and swivels inside. "*Get in, get in, get in.*" She drags me by the elbow, imitating the noise of a camera shutter: "*Zzzt zzzt zzzt!*" Her pupils glint in the weak light through the etched glass on either side of the doorway. As soon as the door closes, she twists the bolt, and shoves me toward the double parlour-room with its teetering shambles library.

I allow myself to be towed across the room towards the rear door.

"Hurry!" Madison gestures through the kitchen, to another doorway on the far side of the butchery block. "We have to be *quick.*"

Diffner's study is at the back of the house, overlooking the garden via a tall window.

Madison rushes to the desk, and begins rifling through the drawers. She heaves a ream of paper onto the desk.

I grab a stapled report off the top. The title reads '*Crimes of Genocide, 5th General Assembly of the United Nations.*' I flip it open...

"What if it wasn't a message *FROM* Dad...?" she whispers.

"Huh?"

She's reading a small spiral-bound notepad like the one Diffner showed me at the *Twin Lights Inn.* "'Samuel Litthamer'... What if it was a message *TO* Dad?"

"What have you found?"

Madison's head snaps around, tilting slightly. "*Shh!*"

"Wha—?"

"SHHH!" She clamps a soft hand over my mouth.

There is a scraping noise, from the front of the house.

"GO!" Madison shoves me toward the door at the back of the kitchen, and turns toward the refrigerator.

I trip in the direction of the exit, twisting my neck.

"Quick! Run!"

"Wh–?"

A sudden *crash!* and the *thump-thump-thump* of boots in the parquetry hall drives me to the wall.

"What–?!" I gawk.

A black-faced intruder flies into the kitchen, raising a toy-like machinegun with a foot-long noise suppressor attached to the barrel.

"Fuck!"

Seeing Madison, the figure lets off a whir of automatic fire, buzzing like an insect. *ZZZZZZT!* Kitchen cabinets splinter, stone chips fly off the countertop, hanging saucepans clatter and clang in a thunderous percussion. The light-fitting over Madison's head shatters, showering her with glass.

The sheer *noise* feels like enough to kill a man. The wallpaper bursts to shreds, filling the air with plaster dust... I stare, aghast, at the man in the khaki roll-neck.

Madison ducks and spins on her heel, fleeing the archway.

A second figure leaps into the room in profile, aiming another toy-like gun at Madison. The man moves awkwardly. I catch a glimpse of the grease-painted features in the weak light.

It's Lou Maas.

Madison rushes toward me.

*ZZZZZZZT!* A maelstrom of automatic fire slices open the fridge door like a zip, slashing open the ceiling. Madison shoves me into a panelled alcove in the wall that pops open on a concealed latch.

The last thing I see as I tumble through the hatch, is Lou Maas scrambling forward, sneering vilely, the muzzle of his machinegun aimed at eye-level, spitting fire...

I thump down a set of stairs into a basement, head-first down the well, and hit the tiles painfully, slithering across the cold floor, drooling with fear.

The barrage of fire in the kitchen continues. The house is being fed through a wood chipper. The door overhead slams shut, bolted.

Madison thumps into me, and flicks a switch, illuminating the room. "Fucking hell!"

Parked in the tidy basement garage is the boat-like sapphire chassis of a '60s Monterey Mercury two-door hardtop, surrounded on three sides by timber moving-crates.

Madison flicks a second switch. The automatic garage door hums to life. "Get in," she snaps, sliding behind the wheel, fumbling the keys in fingers slippery with blood.

A loud crack erupts from the top of the stairs...

"Get in!" Madison revs the engine. "Now!"

I look back at the hatch to the kitchen. Another loud *crack* erupts, and splinters spray down the stairs. I run at the car, grabbing at the latch, and fall inside.

Madison drops the sports-car into gear, and reverses into the moonlit Beacon Hill lane. The narrow tree-lined lane is deserted, misty in the predawn haze. Replica gaslights illuminate the brick walls through the fog of the old world.

"Fuck! I think I just pissed my pants!" Madison huffs, checking the mirror. "You okay?"

"Huh?" I squeak hysterically – unravelled, devolved, limbic-brained.

For the briefest instant, everything is still.

An iron gate in the rear wall of the townhouse swings open, and Maas leaps into the lane, bouncing off the side of a parked car, and raises his weapon...

Madison squashes down in the seat, stomping on the accelerator, *screeching* the tyres. A metal spray of bullets peppers the tail of the Mercury, as the car scrapes a sign-post, careening into the side of a white panel-van, and swings around the corner. Madison zigzags down Beacon Hill, the wrong way on the one-way street, veering at the empty approach to the Longfellow Bridge.

I realise I'm trembling, checking myself for holes.

"Could you be any *fucking* slower?!" Madison growls.

"Where are we going?"

"Shut up! Just *shut up for a second!*" The veins are popping in her neck, as she takes her eyes off the road just long enough to cast me a mean stare.

I'm drifting out of my body again, levitating somewhere up near the hardtop's roof.

"Where are we going?" I ask again.

She flicks the small spiral bound notepad into my lap. "Here." Written on the tiny page is an address, and a name from a thousand years ago.

**Vantcha Velajcic.**

"Is that—?" I gasp.

Madison nods. "The lighthouse keeper."

Lou Maas runs from the alley, into the garage of the Beacon Street townhouse, popping the clip out of the Brugger & Thomet MP9 machine pistol. Reaching into his pocket, he takes out a lead sleeve, and slips the magazine inside.

Reaching under his sweater, he unwraps two small round objects, held together by Velcro straps. The small plastic eggs are vibrating busily.

Even with the bullets stored back in their lead sheaths, there is enough ammunition spread around the house now, for the small underarm Geiger-counters to max out on the radiation levels. It's an old-school Russian Cold War tactic to 'tag' subjects with radioactive bullets, aerosol sprays, or impregnated money. Any amateur sleuth can buy an anti-GPS or bug-scanning device from a Radio Shack. But even the Pros *never* think to check for radioisotopes.

The bullets in the lead-sleeved magazine contain slugs made of *105-Ag*, a highly-radioactive isotope of silver. The rate of decay means the signal is spent after about a month, but that's *more* than enough time. The compact MP9 isn't Maas favourite weapon, but it's capable of firing 900 rounds per minute. So it's dead easy to get at least *one* slug in someone - rarely lethal, but enough to follow them from thirty metres away in a crowd.

With a dozen slugs in a car, Maas can track the Mercury by satellite.

## 22. '...WHO GIVES HIM SIGHT...'

*Monday, November 5, 2012*

The atmosphere in the car is blustery, much like that balcony on the lighthouse almost twenty years ago. The pressure of the horror and uncertainty thuds away in my ears. My heart is pumping faster than it's made to.

*...The Lighthouse Keeper...*

I rest my head on the window sill. I've driven this way a thousand times – down Storrow Drive, along the Charles River, between the Longfellow Bridge and Massachusetts Avenue. It might as well have all been imagined, for how strange it feels.

An 8-person racing shell skims the blue waters of the Charles River, parallel to the road. The predawn light projects long shadows of lean bodies across the choppy wavelets.

**Vantcha Velajcic.**

I can barely hear myself think, for the roaring rush of blood in my ears.

Outside the car, the world seems at peace. Beyond the river, in a long tract of land on the far bank, lays the leafy grounds of MIT; the domes and winged halls nudge above a blanket of trees. I look away. That was Matt's former commonwealth, and my own home a hundred thousand years ago, when I first met Annie... Nineteen years ago. The night Matt drove me to the lighthouse keeper's cottage with a first aid kit in my lap, Annie picked me up from the library... just over there.

I notice the knobbled steering white wheel is smeared pink with gore.

"Are you okay?" I ask, pointing.

"Shit!" Madison curses, checks her shirt, and wipes the blood on her sleeve. "Must have been the glass."

She just saved my life, for the second time.

"This is *so* screwed," Madison mumbles.

"Did Clark *ever* mention the lighthouse keeper?" I ask, as much to break the silence – to test my powers of speech – as hoping for an answer.

Madison is silent. Her attention is fixed on the road. "Screwed-Mac-Duck."

The wind whistles in the car windows. I consider getting huffy and trying to take charge. But all I can do is watch the newly unfamiliar landscape roll by. "I met him *twice*," I whisper. I hear my own voice in my ears, flat and distant, like a far-away person. "The lighthouse keeper. It was the night I came to dinner... Matt said Vantcha had an accident..."

"Yeah." Madison glances at me. "I remember."

"Matt said not to say anything." I rest my head back on the headrest, and close my eyes, as we sail past the edifices of Harvard College. "I'd completely forgotten about it."

Madison is distracted, parking the Mercury in a narrow lane. Twitching the steering wheel with slender hands, she pulls the car into a narrow space, clattering past a row of trash bins.

She leads me through the laneway on foot, climbing over a waist-height chain link fence. "This way."

We're in an empty yard, spread with crushed rock. There isn't a blade of grass, not a stick of lawn furniture, not a flower or a shrub – just a flat, bare, austere gravel oblong.

"Something's not right..." she whispers.

"No kidding... We're in someone's *backyard*."

Madison leads the way to the back door, inching open the screen door, and peering inside.

"What are you doing?" I linger, with my rising swell of dread...

"Jeezus!" whispers Madison.

"What?"

She points at the window. "The blinds." Heavy rubber blinds obscure the view inside the house.

Madison slips through the door.

"Hey—"

Peering through the mesh, I see a sunroom, unfurnished but for a single chair, and a small radio on an antique side table. The news plays, of another war in Iraq.

Madison walks brazenly down the darkened hallway. "Hello?" she calls out, disappearing into the shadows.

A light comes on in the kitchen, as Madison disappears through a doorway.

A thickly-accented voice croaks something down the gloomy hall.

Listening at the door, I hear a shuffle of movement, and hushed voices...

"*Robert!*" Madison calls from the lit room.

I step inside. The house is almost empty. No bookcases, no TV, no photo frames. A sudden sickening recollection catches me by the throat. I've being swallowed by unknowns: New people. Strange places. An uncertain future... All the fundamentals have shifted. The *smell* of things is off... The details are askew. Until now. This house I recognise. Or it's contents. The chair. The small lead-light table lamp, that nineteen years ago filled the tiny lighthouse keeper's cabin with an amber glow.

"Robert?" croaks the old man's voice.

I take a deep breath, and step into the kitchen.

At first, Madison blocks my view of the kitchen table.

She moves aside.

The stooped old broom of a man is seated, wrapped in a worn woollen shawl. He looks the same... but for the addition of a wheelchair to his maladies. The crumpled skin hangs in folds around the hollow eyes sockets, and the bony brow.

"It's good to *see* you again, Robert." Vantcha croaks with his strange accent, and holds out his gnarled hand, fingers curled like a clutch of beans.

Decades have passed... I haven't given that night a thought for years. But the details shuffle up now, out the deep recesses of unconscious memory, as Vantcha runs his withered fingers over my knuckles.

Madison watches intently, smiling.

The old man smiles too, toothless now as well as eyeless. I can't look at him, without remembering Annie. And Matt. "I can only offer you biscuits. No cake, I'm afraid." His voice is faint; with barely enough breath in his lungs to form words – hunched in his chair, wrapped shoulder-to-toe in the chequered shawl.

Madison touches him gently on the shoulder. "That's very kind. Thank you."

I remember the bright sweeping lamp of the lighthouse, standing on the balcony. It strikes me like a weight, dropped from the top of that rickety old tower. *...Annie.* "Vantcha," I mutter, breathless, looking at Madison.

Vantcha frowns deeply, the creases around his eyes folding deep into the sockets.

"Can I make you some tea?" Madison moves to the stove, glancing as she does at something on the kitchen table, and casting me a knowing look.

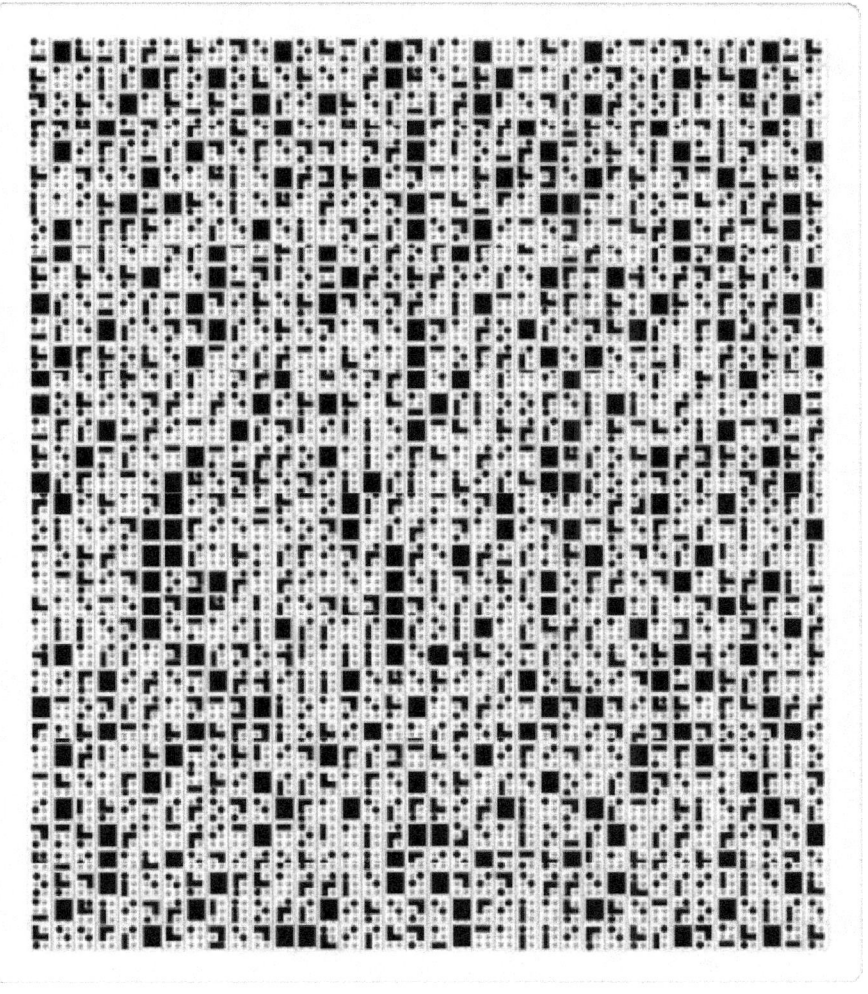

*(Diagram 16 - Completed Braille planche)*

On the table in front of the old man, rests a plastic tablet filled with tiny black pegs. I peer at the intricate array of dots and markers. Beside the tablet, rests a book with a plain white card cover. Surrounded by a pattern of raised dots, is the printed title *'New York Times Large Type Weekly - Sunday, September 2'*

I recognise the pattern on the plastic tablet from the 'punch card.' Six black squares on each row... 36 rows.

"You *knew* Matt did the crossword every Sunday," I whisper.

The old man reaches for the book with his bony claw, touching it lightly.

"You knew he'd see his name..." *Samuel Litthamer.*

Madison pushes two mugs of instant tea toward Vantcha and I. "It's good to see you again, old man."

Vantcha nods his scrunched head. "It has been a long time."

"How have you been?" she asks, softly.

I stare at the contents of the table, darkly. "*You* made the crossword puzzle?"

Madison frowns. "Bob—"

Vantcha raises a gentle hand. "It's alright." He smiles faintly, but the expression twists into bitter remorse. A deep sigh whispers through his parted lips. "I remember you, '*friend*'."

"Vantcha," Madison takes his hand. "Bob's son is missing."

I can't take my eyes off the plastic crossword. This is where it started? With the old lighthouse keeper.

"Sit down," whispers Vantcha. "If you found me, others will not be far behind."

"Did another *friend* come to see you?" asks Madison. "His name is Clark?"

"Yes," Vantcha wraps his hands around his tea.

"You say '*others*' will not be far behind," I sit down. "Who are they?"

"Lujko Maas – that is his *real* name. His father was a guard in the camp at Jasenovic... Not a *Jewish* camp," he adds self-effacingly. "*This* camp was in Yugoslavia, for non-Catholics."

I frown. "I've never heard of such a thing."

"In Jasenovic, I first learned of the tablet. *That* is how Matthias found me, and brought me to New Bridlington to work in the lighthouse... That... is *also* how, Lujko Maas found me—"

Madison interrupts, explaining for my benefit. "There were *several* of these camps, during the war. Catholic extremists formed a terrorist group called the Ustashi, with the aid of the Nazis, funded by Mussolini and the Church of Rome. They overthrew the Serb-Croat-

Slovene government in April Nineteen-Forty-One, to establish a Catholic-Fascist regime... They executed eight-hundred-thousand non-Catholics, at the same time Hitler was exterminating the Jews."

Vantcha places a hand on Madison's trembling arm. "Shhh."

"Let me tell him," Madison offers, calmly. "Ustashi officers within the Yugoslav army, assisted the Nazis in overthrowing the government. The Nazis left the Ustashi in charge. Then the Ustashi began *executing* anyone who wouldn't convert to the *Roman* Church... Many of the Ustashi, the leaders of the concentration camps, were men of authority in the Catholic Church... The President and directors of the Catholic Crusaders. The Ustashi were even based in their monasteries..."

Vantcha remains quiet, listening, head tipped forward.

"The leader of the Ustashi was a man named Ante Paveli ," continues Madison. "The day the German Army entered the Croatian capital – April Eleventh, Nineteen-Forty-One – Radio Zagreb instructed the people to welcome them, and 'seek answers to all questions from the *Catholic parish offices...*' The *Ministry of Justice and Religions* required *conversion* to the Catholic Church by Orthodox persons employed by the Government, or be arrested... In June Nineteen-Forty-One, an *Office of Religious Affairs* was established by Decree One-One-Six-Eight-Nine, in charge of 'the conversion of the Orthodox Church'. Decrees were issued on the 'Law concerning the conversion from one religion to another.' Forcible conversions were legalised... It began quickly. In May, the Ustashi gathered those who would *not* convert, and... executed them. In Karlovac, Sisak, Petrinja, Gudovac, Stari Petrovac, Glina, Stikada, Guduru, Brode, Gudovac, Tuke Brezovac, Klokocevac, Bolac, Jadovno, Lika— Mass executions were carried out. *Nazi troops* were so horrified by the atrocities, that *they* conducted a commission, exhumed the mass graves, took photographs, and compiled reports like *Ustachenwerk bet Bjelovar* or '*The Work of the Ustashi in Bjelovar*.'"

"I don't understand the connection?" I confess. To *us*.

Vantcha speaks. "In the town of Gracac... victims were slain in a butcher's shop. Blood flowed like rain into the gutter. Men were cut to pieces while they were still alive. Whole *districts*, Bosanska Krajina, and Lika, Kordun, Banija, Gorski Kotar, Srem, and regions of Slavonia, were laid to waste... The villages of Vojnic, Slunj, Korenica, Udbina and Vrgin-Most were destroyed. The Ustashi left towns with nobody alive, barrels full of their *blood* in the street as a warning. They used— primitive methods... forks, spades, sledgehammers and saws, to torture their victims. They broke their legs, pulled off their skin and beards, and – they *blinded* us – cutting out our eyes."

Madison stares at me, intently.

"Annie knew this?"

"I have seen... *horrors*," Vantcha whispers, "that you can't imagine... The last thing I saw with my own eyes, was a basket... filled with the eyes from other people in my village..." Vantcha pauses. "*My* eyes were taken to the next village, to convert others. And then I was moved to the concentration camp at Jasenovic."

I feel too numb to be sick. The story is incomprehensible...

"On August third, three-thousand were massacred in Vrgin-Most. *Another* three- thousand, on July twenty-ninth in Pavkovitch... In Baska, Perna and Podgomolje five-hundred-and-forty women and children were locked in their homes, and set on fire. In the village of Crevarevac, six-hundred were burned... At Mlinici Smiljanic, sixty women and children... Five-hundred were slaughtered at Bugojno. At Bihac, in a single day, two- thousand were killed. In July and August, twelve *thousand* more... In Bosanska Krupa district, *fifteen thousand* were killed. All, people who would *not* convert to Catholicism. Forced conversions were planned from Zagreb, legalised by statutory order. In Gorevac, children were impaled... Men had their ears and noses sawn away while they *lived*, or had their hearts cut out. A man and his son were crucified, in Mliniste. Five hundred women and children were hurled into pits and wells in Tusnica and Komasnica. In three months, *one-hundred-and-twenty-thousand people* were murdered. It was the worst massacre. It is the cause of the war in

Sarajevo... And now, years later, they find the Muslims too buried in Srebrenica... It does not *stop.*" There is surprising venom in Vantcha's last word.

"I was a priest, of the Serbian Orthodox church, before I was taken to the camp at Jasenovic. The Ustashi *hanged* Church leaders, to encourage others to convert. Very few of my brothers escaped... They were... imprisoned, hunted down, tortured, and hung. I was lucky... to only lose my eyes..."

Vantcha is speaking now in a disembodied voice. In his blind eyes, the memories replay like a fresh vision. "There were many camps. At Lobor, Jablanac, Mlaka, Brocice, IJstici, Stara Gradiska, Sisak, Jastrebarsko, Ciornja Rijeka... The horrors were... worse than you can comprehend." Vantcha pauses, unable to continue.

Madison touches him lightly on the shoulder. "Testimonies were given at the trials after the war. Jasenovic was— worse than *hell.*"

Vantcha composes himself. "One man who attended the Franciscan College at Siroki Brijeg, a member of the Catholic organization of the Crusaders - on the night of August twenty-ninth, Nineteen-Forty-Two - cut the throats of one-thousand-three-hundred-and-sixty prisoners with a butcher's knife, in Jasenovic. The Camp Commandant was a member of the Order of Saint Francis, Father Filipovic. Addressing a battalion in Drakulic, he killed an Orthodox child with his *bare hands.* As Commandant, aided by other Fathers, he brought about the death of *forty-thousand* men, women and children. The worst horror was the twelve-thousand children... Infants under one year of age were released, but died... because caustic soda had been added to their food in the camp..." Vantcha sighs sadly. "In Nineteen-Forty-Two, the brickworks in Jasenovic were converted into a crematorium. The Ustashi opened an iron door - and pushed the people into the fires... to be burned, *alive.*"

Seeing the pale expression on my face, Madison squeezes Vantcha's wrist. "Robert has... heard enough."

"Is— all this... *true?*" I whisper. "I've... There is - *evidence* for all of this?"

Madison nods. "The Ustashi eventually collapsed, along with the Nazis, after the Vatican changed sides at the end of the war. Ante Paveli , the leader of the Ustashi, found *refuge* at the Vatican... Disguised as a monk, he fled into Argentina, where he formed an Ustashi government, and plotted his return. The Vatican realigned with the Allies... Everyone conveniently 'forgot' the crimes committed by the church. The few who *had* made it through occupied territory to the West, were simply not believed."

"How is that possible?"

"Of course, the Vatican *knew*, just as they knew of the Nazi killing squads – the *Einsatzgruppen* – who executed one-point-four-million Jews. At least four separate letters are *known* to have reached the Pope. And there were more... The Vatican helped many war criminals, and – especially the Ustashi – escape to South America, and laundered millions in stolen gold."

I rest my head in my hands, rubbing my eyes. I'm wary of seeming to dismiss the horror of the story, but I'm at the limit of my confusion. "Why— why are you telling me this...?"

"In Jasenovic, I met an Orthodox scholar who told me the reasons the Nazis were tearing apart the churches, all the Abrahamic faiths, processing Jews, Freemasons, Orthodox Christians, with the aid of the Holy See. He said they were searching for a religious relic, in France... Stories of this relic were recounted by others... Matthias found *me*, sixty years ago, tracing this connection to the camps—"

"I don't understand..." I vaguely recall Diffner mentioning something about Nazi gold in the Vatican, during our first flight from Washington. "I don't see the connection?"

Vantcha gestures at the Braille crossword. "'AH' and 'AR', do you remember?"

I shake my head. "No."

"'Adolph Hitler' and 'Achille Ratti' - Pope Innocent the Eleventh."
"Hitler?"

Vantcha grimaces. "Why— is it so strange? In Nineteen-Twenty-Nine, Mussolini signed a Concordat with the Vatican, guaranteeing the Holy Sees independence as a state, protecting its secret... and Hitler followed with a similar treaty... Why?"

"I don't know. Look, this is all starting to—"

"In Hitler's Proclamation to the 'Catholic German Nation' at Berlin, February first, Nineteen Thirty-Three, two days after being sworn in as the democratically elected Chancellor - after buying the loyalty of the Catholic Party - Hitler said he regarded "*Christianity as the foundation of our national morality.*" He gave the *Wehrmacht* soldiers belt-buckles with the slogan "*God is with us*". His agreement with the Vatican included paying the Church German income taxes collected from Catholics... Hundreds of millions of Marks every year. Hitler called his empire the Third Reich, after the First Reich, the Holy Roman Empire of Constantine. His obsession *led* him to the secret... But he was the Pope's attack dog. *That* is why he occupied France. It was the home of the Vatican for much of the fourteenth century under the Avignon Papacy. It was *there* that the treasure of Rome, the treasure of *Jerusalem*, had been taken by the Visigoths... There, the *parfaits* secretly removed the object during the siege of Montségur. The massacre at Oradour-sur-Glane, the secret Nazi convoys... Parsifal... Hitler's search is well documented. The Vatican were desperate to find the tablet. In Nineteen-Thirty-Five, at the beginning of the war, Hitler established a new arm of the S.S. called *Das Ahnenerbe* — the Ancestral Heritage Society - and its archaeologist Otto Rahn, searched the castle of Montségur in the Pyrenees. Rahn spent months exploring caves there looking for 'the grail stone' - the lost ancient stone, engraved with secret knowledge."

If Madison hadn't pieced together this exact part of the diagram just hours ago, I wouldn't have followed the reference. "M-One-Two-Four-Four." Now she's following the old man's story as intently as I...

"Rahn believed that he'd uncovered the location of Montsalvat, in the Cathar mountain fortress of Montségur. He then died - *mysteriously* - in the Tyrolean Mountains. And just like Akhenaten, Nebuchadnezzar, Constantine, and Napoleon before him, Adolf Hitler made himself head of church *and* state. He was the High Priest of 'National Socialism'. In Nineteen-Thirty-Six, he established the 'National Reich Church.' The origins of the Nazi Party lay in a New Order of the Templars... Nazism was *not* just a political movement. Like the First Reich, Constantine's Roman Catholic church, Hitler was starting a *Church*."

"Hitler *found* the tablet?"

"No."

"I don't understand."

Vantcha reaches into his pocket with a withered hand, draws out a slip of paper, and slides it across the table.

I unfold the page...

It's a more sophisticated version of the diagram Diffner showed me, scrawled on a tiny spiral-bound notepad in the Twin Lights Inn. All the missing pieces are complete.

From Melchizedek, to Abraham, into Egypt... The Visigoths. From the Cathars, back to Rome.

"*This* is the message you hid in the crossword?"

Vantcha tips his head forward again, shadow filling his eyes.

"So— Where *is* the tablet now? Is it in Rome?"

"The tablet is lost. Somewhere, in one of the branches, *somewhere* on its way through history, the tablet was destroyed. It has been searched for everywhere..."

"Then— What's so important, that people are still being *killed for it?*"

"Look at the list..." Vantcha points at me. "This is a map of those who *knew* of the tablet... They're all connected... Back to Melchizedek. *That* is the secret."

"What?" I clear my throat. I remember the evening I first came up with a similar idea, bouncing up like a silver spring, sending me chasing the possibility of a single origin for the idea of god. One god for all. Diffner, the excitement in his eyes when he went to work on the idea... All the pieces in his masterful puzzle... Is it *just* an idea? "But, it existed? The tablet?"

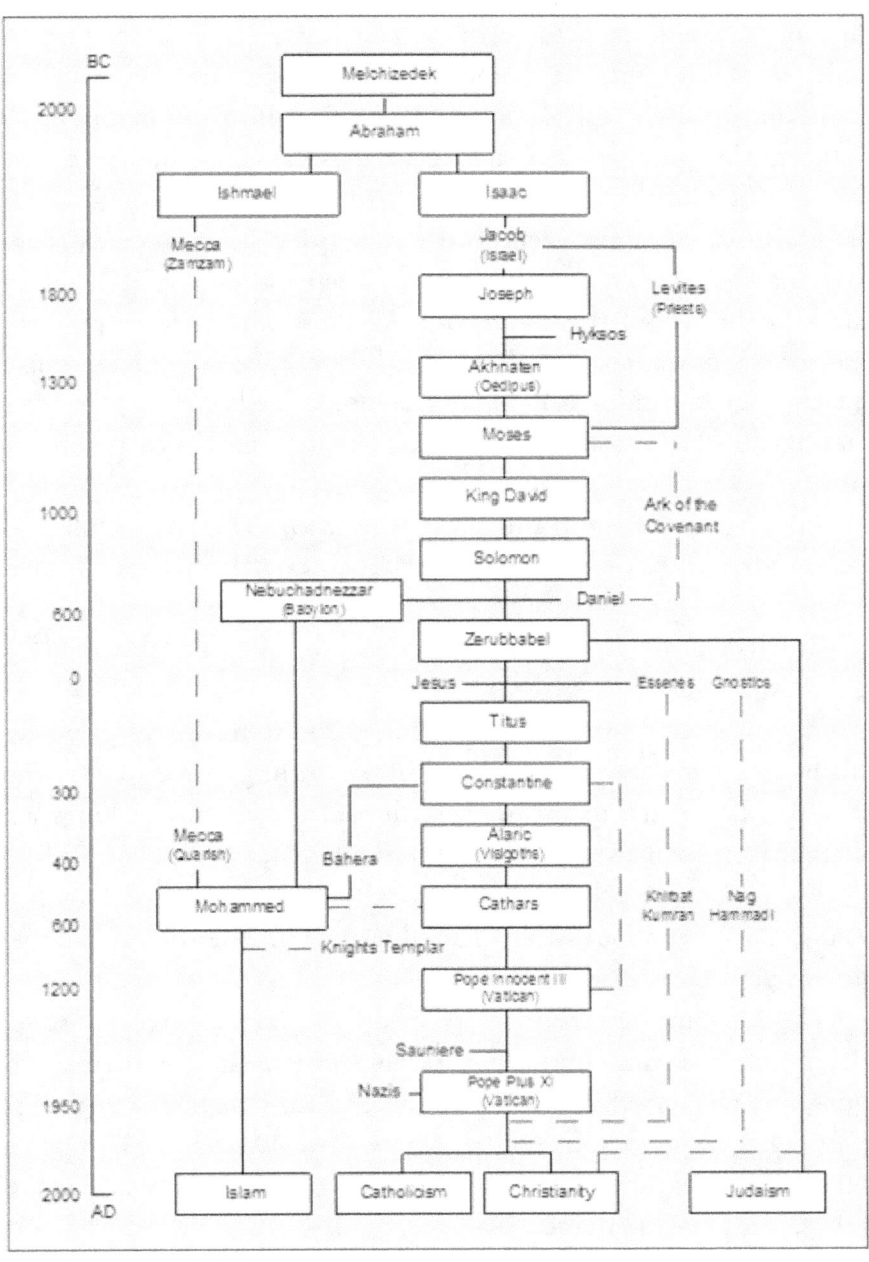

*(Diagram 17 - Completed tree diagram)*

"From Melchizedek, it was passed down to the sons of Abraham, the Pharaohs, Moses, into the Ark of the Covenant... Somewhere the tablet was lost, but the knowledge of its contents continued to Constantine, at the fall of Rome to Alaric... into the hands of the Cathars. The same way *you* appreciate its secret now, but have never seen it. The Christian Knights set out to *seek* the treasure, following the trail back from Jerusalem to the Languedoc. Thousands of people have searched for it, forming secret societies - calling it the Holy Grail, or the Ark of the Covenant... All those who tried to make the *real* secret known were stricken from history, just like Akhenaten in ancient Egypt. And so, it became a deeper secret... People started chasing the shadows. But, the clues all still form a picture... If you *look*."

"I don't understand, if this thing is real, *why* so many people - for *four-thousand* years - how has Melchizedek, and this tablet, all stayed secret?"

Vantcha frowns. "I suppose... that depends, what the tablet said."

I scowl. "It doesn't make sense..."

Why are people still willing to *kill* so indiscriminately to protect this half-obscured mystery, and still others willing to *die* for it? What does this tablet say, to inspire such madness? To convert kings and pharaohs, to invoke such fear... I still don't get it.

"Who *are* these people? Trying to kill us— Lou Maas?" I look to Madison. "What about Muhannad al-Baghdadi? The subway bomber! He had your crossword in his *house!*"

"The Muslim faith *also* has its scholars," Vantcha explains softly. "They seek this same object just as desperately. "It is written in the Qur-an as well, by their prophet Muhammad, that in the end times *'there shall come to you the Ark of the Covenant... and the relic left by the family of Musâ... a sign for you, if you are believers...'* They *all* seek it, not knowing the real reason why."

I sit still, in stunned silence. Staring down at the diagram. I don't get it. I just don't.

Vantcha leans forward, reaches across the table, and taps his old, gnarled finger on the plastic planche. "*Generations* of kings and pharaohs, *all* the leaders of this world – have kept this secret..."

I press my eyeballs with the heels of my palms, and mumble, "what did Clark say when you told him this?"

"He was going to *disappear*. Leave Boston. Leave the country. As soon as possible. If you're lucky, there is still time for you to run."

"Where?" I object. "Where do we go?"

"Did Clark say where he was going?" asks Madison urgently.

"He said he was going to London."

"London?" I blurt.

"Was he going to the British Museum?" asks Madison.

"What? Why?"

Vantcha shakes his head slightly. "I don't think so."

"I noticed something when I did your crossword..."

Madison dives into her handbag, and produces the completed copy of the crossword she showed me at the hotel. Taking out a pen, she begins circling pairs of letters.

"Right through the puzzle, and in all four corners, you hid the letters U-R..." Madison observes, sliding the page over to me...

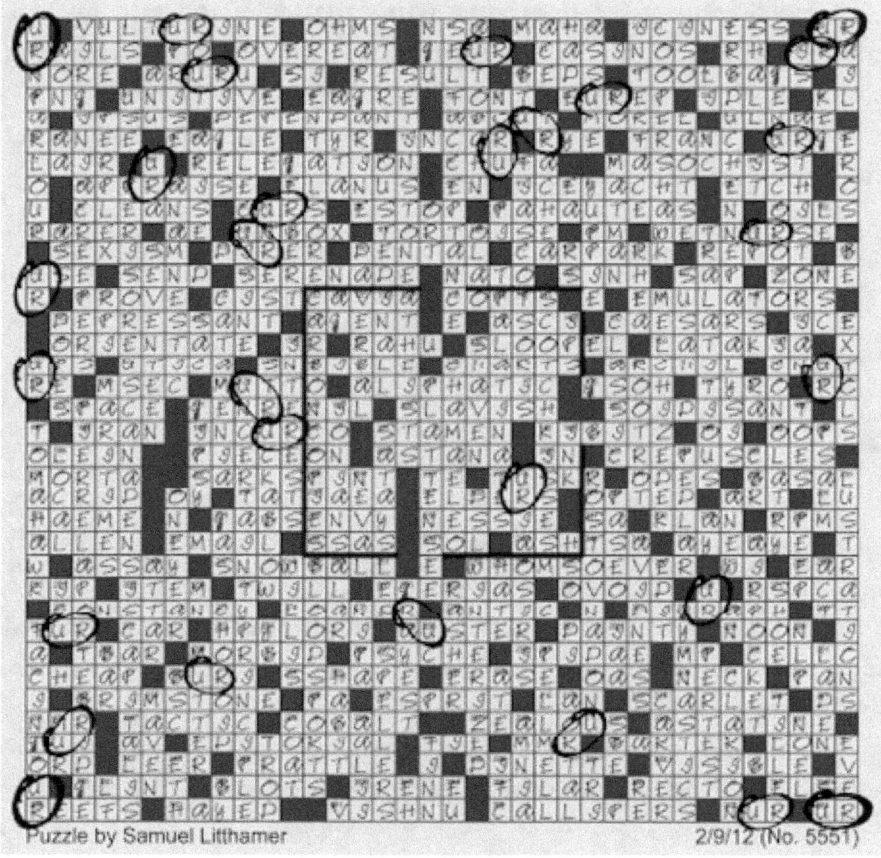

*(Diagram 18 - Madison's crossword, with highlights)*

"Jeezus," I gasp. How did I miss that?

Madison sees my amazement. "It was *pretty* obvious. One down is *'Urnparlour'*? There's no such thing as an *'urnparlour.'*"

Vantcha scowls strangely. "It doesn't mean anything—"

"But... You wrote it?" she accuses.

Vantcha remains silent, his face turned to stone. But he shifts his arms uncomfortably.

"At the British Museum in London," urges Madison. "They have a relic called the 'Standard of Ur'." She looks to me, to see if I recognise the name. "It's a jewelled box from the ruins of the city of Ur, the birthplace of Abraham, dated two-thousand years before Christ. It's part of the Early Mesopotamian Collection. "The box was found in one of the largest graves in the Babylonian Royal Cemetery. In the corner of a chamber, above the right shoulder of an unknown skeleton. When the box was found, the two side-panels had been crushed by the weight of the soil. The bitumen that held the box together had rotted, and the end panels were broken. But... the two sides that *were* intact match the dimensions given in the *Bava Batra* for the size of the tablets in the Ark."

"What are you saying?" My gaze flicks between Madison and Vantcha.

The old man looks frozen.

"The Bava Batra is called the *Babylonian* Talmud," explains Madison. "Because the Jews handed the Talmud down by word of mouth until the captivity in Babylon, under King Nebuchadnezzar, in the Fifth Century Before Christ, when Jewish scholars transcribed it. The Bava Batra describes the tablet – written by god – kept inside the Ark as six *tefachim* by three *tefachim*. A '*tefachim*' is three-point-two inches. The 'Standard of Ur' has the same dimensions."

"The 'Standard of Ur' is the 'Ark of the Covenant'?" I gasp.

Vantcha scowl deepens. "Please—"

Madison doesn't seem to notice Vantcha's objection. "No. It was Babylonian-made. More likely, Nebuchadnezzar took the tablet out of the Hebrew Ark, and put it in a box of his own – a Babylonian. Vantcha, you're *sure* Clark never mentioned any of this?"

Vantcha shakes his head. "Clark didn't want to be followed!"

"We *have* to follow him," I snap, urgently. "I have to find out what happened to my *son*."

"You don't understand..." Vantcha sighs wearily. "There is *no* tablet. It's lost."

I push back my chair with a shriek of metal feet on tiles, startling the old blind man. "I don't care about the *fucking* tablet. I just want to find what happened to my son."

Vantcha hisses. "You *don't* understand!"

"I'm really fucking tired of being told that," I snarl. "So enlighten me."

Vantcha begins to object, but Madison places a hand on the old man's wrist, stopping him. "Bob, if Clark went to London, I can find him."

"As soon as you go anywhere *near* an airport, you'll be caught," observes Vantcha, unhelpfully.

"Clark found a way," Madison retorts.

"We'll figure it out," I growl. "If we have to pay someone with everything I have."

"I'm *only* going to tell you this," admits Vantcha wearily. "Because if I don't... you'll both be killed."

"Tell us what?"

Vantcha slumps. "Clark told me how he planned to escape."

"He *told* you?" I query. "Why? I thought he didn't want to be followed."

"No... But he wanted me to go with him."

## 23. '...THE LIGHT WHICH NO MAN CAN APPROACH...'

*Tuesday, November 6, 2012*

Madison should be back soon.

It's difficult to tell what time it is, through the obscured casements, in the darkened house.

I walk outside onto the empty suburban street.

It's night time again. A light white snow dusts every surface. The tops of the leaves, the posts, and even the moon. Across the street, a cheap Christmas wreath hangs on a wire security-door, as a carol plays cheerfully inside.

*...Here comes Santa Claus... Here comes Santa Claus... Right down Santa Claus Lane...*

On the neighbouring lawn stands an illuminated nativity scene, with a glowing plastic manger emblazoned with the words '*The Reason for the Season!*'

I feel like walking over there and telling them... If they *read* their Bible, John The Baptist's father returned from duty as a temple priest when John was born, in June. Mary was visited by her 'immaculate conception' when John's mother was three months pregnant, putting Jesus' birthday in September or October.

The real *reason for the season*, is the pagan Winter Solstice.

Don't let this change you, Madison said...

There's nothing left, no reason to keep breathing, other than my unholy rage.

I'm alone, except for Madison. It's a gut-awful sense of robbery, like a butcher's cleaver twisting in my gut. I feel like I've been murdered, and I'm still floating over myself in the pool, looking down at a cold, wet husk of someone I don't recognize anymore... I'm not sure how to function. Nothing can alleviate the pain. Annie is gone. And it's impossible in these quiet moments, to plead to god for relief.

But of all the questions still chewing at my prefrontal cortex, the newest is most perplexing: The old blind man is still keeping a secret.

I walk back inside the house, and move into the dim, empty kitchen.

I flick on the light switch.

On the table rests the white plastic tablet – the 'planche' – and an egg-carton palette of black pegged markers. I rummage around the kitchen for a sheet of paper and a pencil – but of course, there isn't one.

I lay the sheet of paper over the planche, and – swiping my finger through the soot on the ring grates over the gas stove – make a rubbing over the raised bumps of the Braille crossword. I take the other page from the table as well – the completed diagram, with the lines and boxes. Folding the two sheets carefully, I walk out to the sunroom, where the old man sits listening to the radio.

"Vantcha."

"Hmmm?"

There's no point asking him anything more. If he wouldn't tell – nineteen years ago – with a gun in his eye and his shoulder pressed to an oven, he won't tell me. "What will you do?"

His face is set as if he's staring, far away.

"Seeya."

I walk out to the street, as the taxi pulls up by the gate.

Madison is dressed plainly for the first time in her life; hair brushed back, no make-up, wearing a chambray work shirt and cap. She looks like Annie.

I climb into the taxi.

"You ready?" she asks.

"Ready."

As we drive away, I remember I'd wanted to ask the old man if the reason he only lost his eyes at the Ustashi camp in Jasenovic, but still kept his life, was that he'd abandoned his god.

The taxi creeps through the Charlestown fog, sneaking out of the green box-girders of the Maurice J. Tobin Memorial Bridge, over Mystic River.

We veer off the expressway, down through the tunnel round the New Rutherford Avenue loop, and double back up Chelsea Street into the old disused dock.

I peer out the foggy window, at the town-scale basement storage room – cluttered with poorly-ordered factories, broken-down equipment, and a litter of old boilers and pipework that may or may not serve some purpose in the life of the city, if anybody knows anymore. Half a dozen giant disused silos flank the expressway, looming over the docks, tops ringed in cloud. To the North, like a dusty old ship in a bottle, lurks the three-masted Washington-era, wooden-hulled frigate – *USS Constitution* – toy-like, in its final berth, midgeted by the bridge, and silos.

Madison directs the taxi driver to a bright yellow security gate, where she nudges me off the seat, hauling a plastic bag half-full of clothes.

She unravels the bag on the pavement, and hands me a Day-Glo vest, with a badge in a plastic sleeve buttoned to the chest. "Put this on."

I doubt it's possible to look any more conspicuous, except if I were still dressed as a priest. "We're *sneaking* in, right?"

"Hardy-ha... Clark told Vantcha—"

"I know I know." I snatch the vest. It feels more like a parachute, and we're about to jump out of a plane. But this is how Clark smuggled himself out of the country, and Madison seems confident she's capable of anything Clark is capable of.

A Hulk Hogan look-alike presses his moustache to the window of the gatehouse, hands cupped to his eyes.

Madison, in her blue-collar gear and work boots, tosses the plastic bag into the weeds. "Come on." She struts up to the gate, and salutes the guard. "Howie!"

Howie nods, points somewhere ahead of us, and goes back to diddling around on his iPhone.

I follow Madison out of the light, unsure what to make of the phenomenal landscape on the far side of the gate.

Beyond the vast expanse of the sixty-five acre concrete apron filled with a thousand parked cars, stands the towering hull of a cargo ship; a seamless steel cliff, ten storeys high, faded orange. The wall of the vessel is emblazoned with a fifty-yard moniker '*Sevresbö Dog*'. The Nordic umlauts on the giant 'ö' are both bigger than the moon.

A strange vertigo wriggles up inside me, as I leer at the stupendous mass: Half the steel in the world, hanging in a wall. The ship is moored in the ice-free, deep draft, weather-protected berth of the Boston Autoport. The ship is a spectacular monument to the human ability to take rocks and hammer them into gargantuan, unnatural shapes.

At the aft of the sprawling vessel, a corner of the hull is set like a wedge. A ramp the width of a freeway hangs suspended from a rack of monolithic hydraulic booms, lying open like a drawbridge onto the apron. At the top of the ramp is a gaping maw, lit like a football stadium. Miniature by comparison, all half-sheathed in plastic, a parade of shiny vehicles weaves across the pavement like caterpillars and rolls up the long ramp into the tail of the giant ship.

I stand for a moment, mesmerised by the scale of the operation.

"The Autoport ships ten thousand cars a year," explains Madison.

Tonight, they're loading luxury SUVs into the dazzling nautical behemoth. There is wonder in it... The spectacle... The complex ballet of the logistics... I wonder where all the drivers disappear to, after they've chauffeured the one-way traffic-jam of SRXs inside the ark.

Then I spot an open-sided minivan loaded with tiny figures in Day-Glo vests, swooping down out of the hold. The van races back to the rear of the long bank of cars, and the workmen hurriedly disembark, running back to the next convoy of cars.

"*Quick*," barks Madison, grabbing me by the sleeve, towing me to the corner of a small shed. The shuttle van disappears back into the ship. "How many were there?" she asks.

"Huh?"

"In the van. I think it was... sixteen..."

"What?" I whisper, fearful. This is madness.

Madison gestures at the long bank of Cadillac Four Wheel Drives. US car-makers build large SUVs in Tuscaloosa, Greer, and Detroit. The domestic market is biggest for these models. Exports from southern factories are trucked to Florida, and loaded onto the ship in Charleston, Jacksonville, and Newark. Then Detroit-made models come to Boston by road. And by ship the whole lot head for Europe, via Trans-Atlantic Roll-On/Roll-Off service to Santander in Spain, across the Mediterranean, and through the Suez Canal. "Give me the vest." Madison flaps a hand at me, keeping an eye on the ship.

I hand it over.

She jams the fluorescent bundle under a rock.

"Okay, that's sixteen. Come on. Quick!" Madison runs toward a lustrous silver Cadillac SUV with a chalk-mark on the tyre. "This one." She pops the tailgate, and climbs into the back, beckoning for me to follow.

Crawling into the plastic-lined rear bay, she pulls down the hatch.

Curled beside me in the cramped compartment, I feel Madison's panting breath on my arm. Our forearms are pressed together at our chests. Her skin is damp with sweat.

The drivers' door of the Cadillac opens, and an African-skinned man takes the wheel, glancing briefly in the rear view mirror. "Stay down," he whispers.

The car jolts as we accelerate toward the ship.

As we race across the pavement, I peer out of the plasticised trunk, looking at the night sky through the tailgate window.

The Cadillac's tyres hit the ramp with a *thwap*, and hum onto the steel bridge.

In a few moments, we're inside the ship.

Through the rear window, I peer up at the bright interior of the *Sevresbö Dog*, lit up like a super-mall car park, and built entirely from whitewashed steel.

The driver spins the steering wheel, and pulls into the first free parking space. "I leave you here two hours. Then I come back."

A second later, another vehicle pulls alongside.

The African jumps out, calling "Hey Buddy!" And disappears beneath the front of the SUV. There is a rattle of chains, and the *thump* of a heavy latch.

I lay in the truck, listening to the sound of other cars, chains, latches, growing more distant.

The last thing I see before the lights wink off, is the excitement in Madison's bright blue eyes.

Clark was here.

Vantcha opens the front door of his tiny house by a crack, his tortured countenance barely illuminated. "Who is it?"

"Vantcha *Velajcic.*"

This time it isn't a question. Maas feels a surprising satisfaction at the old blind man's door. That cold night on the bluff in New Bridlington at the Keeper's cottage, had been the first time he dared confront someone this way. It didn't go exactly the way he'd hoped... He'd given up too soon. He knew that now. To make someone talk, it took more persistence. But he'd had a *lot* of practice since then.

Vantcha falls silent. Even without his eyes, the recognition is visible in his withered expression.

"...I found your name in the Witness Statement in the *Memorandum on Crimes of Genocide* to the President of the 5th UN General Assembly," begins Maas. He'd practiced the line for hours, before that first night. And it's still there, in his most distant memory. "I'm writing a paper on the overthrow of the Serb-Croat-Slovene government. I wondered, if I could ask you some questions about what happened to you during the war?"

Vantcha pales visibly. Now he remembers too.

"My father was also in the concentration camp at Jasenovic," Lujko smiles. Strictly speaking, it wasn't a lie. He'd tricked the old man into thinking his father had been a fellow prisoner. But he'd been one of the *guards.*

Vantcha slumps slightly, and releases his grip on the wheel of his chair. "I won't tell you any more this time—"

"Shhhh." Maas hisses, forcefully. "I want to tell you what I've wished, more than anything... Ask me. What is it, that I've wished?"

Vantcha remains silent.

"I wish it was *me* who took your eyes." Maas leans forward and gently pushes Vantcha's wheelchair backwards, into the darkened house.

The African raps his knuckles on the rear window of the Cadillac SUV, pops the hatch, and beckons us out. "Come out."

There is a confidence in Madison's manner, as if *this too* is nothing. "Come on Bob."

The African leads us to an enclosed stairwell in the corner of the steel parking lot, up a flight of stairs to an iron door. He leans on the hatch with his shoulder, and a heavy squall sucks me out into a thin, harsh rain that stings my skin.

Madison hands me the heavy door, and the gale tears it out of my hand with a *bang!*

Almost swept off my feet by the tempest, I lurch toward the rail as Madison clomps noisily over the steel grill of a catwalk.

The sight that greets us is dizzying.

Boston is spinning away from us, as a pair of tugboats turn the ship at the junction of the Chelsea River. We're a fixed point, and Boston wheels around us in slow motion, myriad pinpoints of twinkling light, appearing and disappearing... It's just like that moment when you recognise the moon is just a reflection: Maybe - right now - the ship is the only fixed point in the universe, and the earth and stars are all spinning.

I'm reminded of Annie again... and that lighthouse balcony in New Bridlington. I don't know why. The metal handrail. The solar system twirling around us, and us - for a moment - at the centre of it.

But it's her sister here, not Annie.

I spot the grand, glowing arch in the wide belly of the Boston Harbor Hotel sweeping into view.

There, in one of the darkened windows, Madison and I shared a sofa the previous night. From that window now, on the deck of the monstrous cargo vessel, we're little more than specks.

*Now* I'm seasick.

The noise of the ship's engines converges in a tantrum of wind, snapping at my jacket.

A pair of painted lines across the flat metal deck, and a flimsy-looking handrail, marks our path toward the ship's conning tower. The maelstrom whistles around us as the African leads us toward another door, in the base of the bridge tower, long hair flicking at his brow.

Madison hands the swarthy stranger a paper bundle from her pocket. With the two of them crowding the narrow walkway between the lower deck and the upper companionway, I grab at an upright, and puke over the side.

The spew atomises in the wind, flurrying out like confetti.

"Ha! *Already*?!" Madison yells, laughing.

Tripping on a steel fin at the base of the external doorway, I fall onto her in the steep companionway, landing on carpet in the dry wood-panelled interior.

The African scowls, and leads us down another white-washed metal stairway, along a hall, past exposed pipes, odd compartments, flimsy red-curtained internal windows, junction boxes, and fire extinguishers – there are extinguishers everywhere – before pointing to a door.

Madison leads me into the cramped cabin.

In the tiny room that follows, the modest decor reminds me of a motor-home, the way everything fits together: The cabinetwork is compressed wood-chip, plastic-coated with a timber lithograph. The bathroom basin folds out of the wall, to make space to sit on the toilet. And the bed – which doubles as a card table – slots between a footlocker, a steam duct, and a wall-mounted septic.

"*Home Sweet Home*," coos Madison.

I test the narrow bed with my tail, before moving to the porthole.

The towers of downtown Boston are still visible from our dizzying vantage point at the top of the ship. Shades of black outline rows of piers, and the oily river boils below. I try to grasp just how many people there must be there, back in that vast arcade of lights. In all directions, as far as I can see, hundreds of cars buzz blissfully. Banks of offices are empty and bright. My stomach knots, as a deep shudder runs through the ship.

The screws have come to life.

The vessel begins to move under her own power.

The collage of light and dark rolls into black nothingness, replaced by the knowledge of deep cold and turmoil.

We're leaving The Whole World behind us.

Madison stands in the doorway of the cramped quarters... She says something, but I miss it.

"Huh?"

"Nobody but Clark's friend knows we're here."

"Okay."

"Stay here, and stay quiet, till we leave Saint John."

"How long is that?"

"Here." Madison hands me a sheet of paper. "We'll be in Southampton in ten days... And lock the door after I leave. I'll rustle us up some food."

"Where's your cabin?" I ask.

Madison sneers. "Ha! Very funny. Lock the door. I'll knock."

I close the door, and lay on the bunk, grinding my back teeth like a junkie. Twenty minutes pass before the rocking begins... At first, it's just a slow swoop. Then a prolonged strain of thumps and lurches rattle under my tail like a saw blade.

The rain drums loudly on the porthole.

There's no turning back now.

The only objective, the only suitable ending, is any kind of ending at all.

Or for time to reverse...

| ALL SCHEDULES ARE SUBJECT TO CHANGE | | |
|---|---|---|
| Ramp Capacity | 150 tons | |
| Max. Height | 5.00 m | |
| PORT | ARRIVE/DEPART | |
| CHARLESTON | 24-OCT/25-OCT | Actual |
| JACKSONVILLE | 27-OCT/28-OCT | Actual |
| BALTIMORE | 1-NOV/2-NOV | Actual |
| NEWARK | 4-NOV/4-NOV | Actual |
| BOSTON | 5-NOV/6-NOV | Actual |
| ST JOHN, NB | 10-NOV/10-NOV | Actual |
| SOUTHAMPTON | 16-NOV/16-NOV | Actual |
| BREMERHAVEN | 17-NOV/17-NOV | Actual |
| ZEEBRUGGE | 17-NOV/19-NOV | Actual |
| SANTANDER | 20-NOV/21-NOV | Actual |
| VIGO | 23-NOV/23-NOV | Actual |
| BARCELONA | 29-NOV/30-NOV | Actual |
| CIVITAVECCHIA | 1-DEC/1-DEC | Actual |
| PIRAEUS | 2-DEC/3-DEC | Actual |
| DERINCE | 4-DEC/5-DEC | Estimate |
| ASHDOD | 7-DEC/8-DEC | Estimate |
| JEDDAH | 12-DEC | Estimate |
| JEBEL ALI | 19-DEC | Estimate |
| ABU DHABI | 20-DEC | Estimate |
| DOHA | 21-DEC | Estimate |
| BAHRAIN | 22-DEC | Estimate |
| AD DAMMAM | 22-DEC | Estimate |
| KUWAIT | 23-DEC | Estimate |

*(Diagram 19 - Sevresbö Dog itinerary)*

Keeping busy for the past few hours has made the time bearable, but lying idly on the paisley bed cover is creeping agony.

I spy a small yellow fleck in the porthole, through the rain. I'm absorbed by the object, where it floats in the cold Atlantic, its bright potential a bristling anomaly in the bitter ocean. Then I realise... It's Boston... nothing more than a single, solitary lamp-light. We're far out to sea now, past the horizon, where the New Bridlington fishermen go. Like the Jew, Jesus. Like the Iraqi, Jonah.

There's a knock on the cabin door, and a whisper. "C'mon. Everyone's asleep."

Stepping into the corridor, I sense Madison's mood is off... like there's a miniature storm cloud over her head. I follow her to the empty mess hall for a lukewarm slab of lasagne, alone at a galley table.

In my feet, through the steel floor, I can feel the engines of the ship fighting with the current.

"We'll be in Saint John in four days," she explains. Her expression is unusually grim. "They'll take on a load of farm machinery. Till then, stay in the cabin. After Saint John, we're in open seas for a week. The only way off this boat then, is in a life raft. We'll be safe. We can go out on deck at night."

I force a smile. It does sound better than hiding in the cabin.

Madison shovels the last of the meal into her unadorned face, scoops up the plates, and walks to the kitchenette. In the dowdy get-up – no make-up, brushed hair – she reminds me even more of Annie. Except for the exaggerated bosom. I'll still bet Diffner's African friend is in his cabin now, spanking off thinking about her.

I listen – with my head in my hands – as Madison places the dishes in the sink, careful not to clink the cutlery. The cautious gesture makes the burst of static that follows, more surprising.

I turn. She's found a small transistor radio on a shelf. With a finger pressed to her lips, she carefully tweaks the dial. The voice on the radio is muffled by static, floating in and out of the room, as the signal tops the waves. *"...Secretary of Defence, Robert Gates today made a presentation to the United Nations on U.S. plans to reinvade Iraq..."*

I glance warily at the door to the mess hall.

"...Gates completed the withdrawal of a hundred-thousand troops from Iraq two years ago, leaving forty-thousand soldiers to provide security, training, and conduct counter-terrorism operations... Today, he ordered the same hundred-thousand troops to go back..."

Madison's full attention is on the broadcast. When the signal drifts back in, the voice has changed. Presumably, it's Secretary Gates: *"...'Iraq is a major source of terrorist activity, and the primary front in the War on Terror...Co-operation between Al-Qaeda and the Taliban was previously limited to a tactical level, fighters alongside one another... This new cooperation has been elevated to a strategic alliance, intent on seizing control of Baghdad...and including the recent subway attacks on US soil... Iraqi immigrant Muhannad al-Baghdadi trained with the Taliban prior to the New York attack... Evidence suggests that the device detonated under the East River matched the bomb-making techniques of Al-Qaeda...'"*

The broadcast erodes to static, and then returns with a news reader:

*"...Al-Qaeda-Taliban forces advance south from Kirkuk toward Baghdad, and Defence Secretary Gate's reinvasion plans gain support from the Security Council... The United Nations announced it would withdraw its civilian staff and a fifth of its peace-keeping troops in Iraq to the Kuwaiti border, amid preparations by U.S. troops for a military strike..."*

"Turn it off," I whisper.

Madison isn't listening. Her cheeks have taken on a green tinge.

"What's the matter?"

Madison huffs, and switches off the radio. "...Come on. I have to get you back to the room."

"Wait, what aren't you telling me?"

"Shhh." Madison leads me back into the corridor to my quarters, where she steps into the cramped space, and pulls the door shut. It's like sharing a payphone.

She stands there for a moment, inspecting her feet.

"What?" I urge.

"I'm not getting off at Southampton."

"What?"

"*Shhhh*...You can still get off. But I'm staying on the ship..."

"What? Where are you *going*?!"

"I spoke to Clark's friend. He says... Clark didn't get off at Southampton, the way he was supposed to..."

The words echo like gunfire. "...Where did he get off?"

"He didn't."

I frown, confused. "Huh?"

"He stayed on the ship... to the last port."

"The *last* port?"

Madison twists toward the door.

"Wait, *why* would he do that?"

"You tell me?" Madison frowns.

I stand immobile, stunned, as Madison steps out of the cramped box.

I'm still standing in the same spot, rocked by the sea, when the floor lurches, tipping me onto the bed. The walls of the cabin squeak like a wheel. I lay there, gazing into the middle distance.

I take out the slip of paper, showing the ships itinerary.

The last stop is Kuwait.

There's only *one* reason Clark would stay on the ship all the way there.

I leap of the bed, and search for a drawer. "C'mon... C'mon..." I rummage through the small medicine cabinet, the tiny cupboard above the fold-down hand basin over the toilet... The object I'm looking for isn't here... I turn, and spot a tiny drawer built into the cabinetry below the Laminex footlocker at the end of the bunk. I rip the compartment open, and there – alone on the bare plywood, just like the room in the Willard hotel in Washington – is a Bible.

I take the worn tome, sit on the edge of the bed, and flick through the thin, filmy pages.

*THIS is what Vantcha was hiding.*

There *is* no mention of the Ark after Zerubbabel.

It's the same as the cave at Khirbat Qumran – where the goatherd threw a stone and uncovered the Dead Sea scrolls: The Copper Scroll contained a list of every treasure in the Temple, where the priests had hidden their holy treasures when the Roman armies approached. But... the Ark wasn't in those lists.

It disappeared *before* the reconstruction of the temple by Zerubbabel.

I flip to Chronicles II, chapter 36, verse 18...

Somebody has already circled the passage, and underlined twelve words.

'...And <u>all the vessels of the house of God</u>, great and small, and the treasures of the house of the LORD, and the treasures of the king, and of his princes; all <u>he brought to Babylon</u>...'

The annotation *has* to be Diffner's. There.

Clark sat in this same 'stowaway' compartment.

He sat in the *same* spot, on the side of the *same* tiny bed, where I'm sitting now... and, marked *this* Bible...

I skim the stories of the Jewish captivity in Egypt. In the book of Ezra, first chapter, verse 7... Looking for more notes.

Cyrus the Great conquers Babylon, and issues a decree that the temple in Jerusalem be rebuilt by Zerubbabel, and the Jews return to their homeland... where the words of the prophet Ezra are circled and underlined:

'...Moreover, King Cyrus brought out the<u> articles belonging to the temple of the Lord, which Nebuchadnezzar had carried away </u>from Jerusalem and had placed in the temple of his god...'

This Bible passage is similar to the Copper Scroll in the Dead Sea scrolls, but it describes a list of items *returned* from Babylon – gold and silver dishes, silver pans, gold and silver bowls...

The Ark is *not* in the list.

The Ark never came back from Babylon.

I thumb through the pages, looking for more markings... It's a Catholic Bible, containing the extra books known as the 'Apocrypha'. Another circled section flips past. I thumb back to it, the book of '2 Esdras', also known as the Fourth Gospel of Ezra... This book was removed from the Bible by Protestants and Jews.

Chapter 10, verse 22...

'...the light of our candlestick is put out, <u>the ark of our covenant is spoiled</u>, our holy things are defiled...'

In the margin of the page, is a handwritten note:

her to eat
m and to
rein I was,

ther, seest
appeneth

full of all
mourning

id are sad,
rieved for

I tell thee,
for the fall

; first, and
d, behold,
on, and a
out.

mourning
multitude;
r one?

fy lament-
I have lost
ight forth

multitude
rse of the

18 And she said unto me, That will I not do:
I will not go into the city, but here will I die.
19 So I proceeded to speak further unto her,
and said,
20 Do not so, but be counselled, by me: for
how many are the adversities of Sion? be
comforted in regard of the sorrow of
Jerusalem.
21 For thou seest that our sanctuary is laid
waste, our altar broken down, our temple
destroyed;
22 Our psaltery is laid on the ground, our
song is put to silence, our rejoicing is at an
end, the light of our candlestick is put out, the
ark of our covenant is spoiled, our holy things
are defiled, and the name that is called upon
us is almost profaned: our children are put to
shame, our priests are burnt, our Levites are
gone into captivity, our virgins are defiled,
and our wives ravished; our righteous men
carried away, our little ones destroyed, our
young men are brought in bondage, and our
strong men are become weak;
23 And, which is the greatest of all, the seal
of Sion hath now lost her honour; for she is
delivered into the hands of them that hate us.
24 And therefore shake off thy great heaviness, and put away the multitude of sorrows, that the Mighty may be merciful unto thee again, and the Highest shall give thee rest and ease from thy labour.

*Spoiled = Hebrew word 'Shacah', to plunder*

*(Diagram 20 - Diffner's note in ship Bible)*

...*There* it is.

I take the rubbing of the Braille planche from my pocket, and Vantcha's printed diagram.

At the place where the Ark went to Babylon, the vertical line is crossed. *'X' marks the spot.*

We'd *all* missed it, in the old man's diagram.

It's not a genealogy.

"It's a treasure map," I whisper.

The original newspaper puzzle contained a 12-by-12 box, in the centre. The box was missing in the planche. The plastic tablet only allowed whole black squares. The only way for Vantcha to place the 'X' in the treasure map in Braille, was to write clues that were out of place... I count out the clues leading up to that point, 12 squares from the top, and 12 from the left. I count every position in the completed planche, where a black box has more than one space to the right, or below.

*132.*

The first clue to the break the normal pattern of a crossword puzzle, is clue number 133.

It's the same position in the planche where the 12-by-12 box begins...

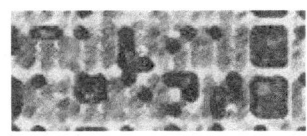

*(Diagram 21 - Planche 'Z' position rubbing)*

And the same place in history, where the Ark was 'plundered'.

I don't need the 6-by-6 cipher on the back of the Bud Lite coaster to decode the two boxes at the end of the two rows.

It's the final letter in the alphabet. The letter 'Z', for 'Zerubbabel' – first king of Israel after the Jews were freed from Babylon.

And the two five-letter words in the 'Z' grid, are 'CAVIA' and 'AGENT'.

'Cavia' is the Latin genus of a large rodent, or a small pig.

*The rat agent has found the treasure.*

As for the tablet's location... it is the clearest clue of all: The one Madison spotted. The word 'Ur' hidden in every corner of the puzzle.

The Ark – and the tablet it contained – disappeared in Early Mesopotamia when Babylon was capital of the largest empire the world had ever seen, now in modern-day Iraq.

After the return of the Jews to Jerusalem, they mourned the loss of the Ark. Their conquerors had customarily carried off images of their gods.

King Nebuchadnezzar had taken the Ark to Babylon, and hadn't returned it.

From there, throughout the rest of the Bible – and the rest of *history* – the temple treasures that were captured by Romans and the Visigoths, contained everything *except* the Ark.

Melchizedek's tablet had first gone to Egypt. Where Akhenaten held it. The Rosetta Stone copied it. Moses *stole* it back to Melchizedek's capital, Jerusalem. Seven-hundred years later it was plundered again, and taken to Babylon by Nebuchadnezzar, and never returned.

For twenty-five centuries, treasure hunters had searched *everywhere* else in the world... except Iraq. Emperor Constantine, the Templars, the Cathars, Napoleon, and Hitler had *all* sought the relic in Israel, Africa, France, and Rome... Maybe they knew its contents. But *all* the Inquisitions, all the wars, and the murders that had continued, in search of this secret...

I close the Bible.

Clark wasn't going to London. Maybe he *never* was. He might have made it up to cover his tracks. Or the old man did.

No. Clark wasn't going to see the 'Standard of Ur.'

He was going to the ruins where it was discovered.

He was on his way to Iraq, to the dust of King Nebuchadnezzar's throne.

He was going to find the tablet.

I move to the cabin's tiny sink.

I slick back my hair, brush my teeth with a foamy finger, sit back on the edge of the bed, take off my shoes, and lay down.

For the first time since Matt died, it makes sense – including that night 19 years ago when Matt took me to Vantcha's cabin.

The old blind man *had* figured out where the tablet was. 'Samuel Litthamer' wasn't an alias. It was the addressee.

*That* was why he sent the message in the crossword. He was warning Matt! Revealing not just the location, but that the *'rat agent'* had also found the tablet.

And in sending the coded message, the lighthouse keeper had set off a deadly chain of events.

The tablet is buried in ancient Babylon.

And all the armies of the Christian world are even now amassing at the border.

Between us and the tablet.

And it occurs to me for the very first time...

The link, to Al-Qaeda and the Taliban...

All the armies of the Muslim world are advancing there as well.

All the folks at home with their microwave snacks, pay-per-view and 5,335 high-def channels have no clue they're witnessing a holy war.

Probably – three thousand years ago – folks didn't know then either.

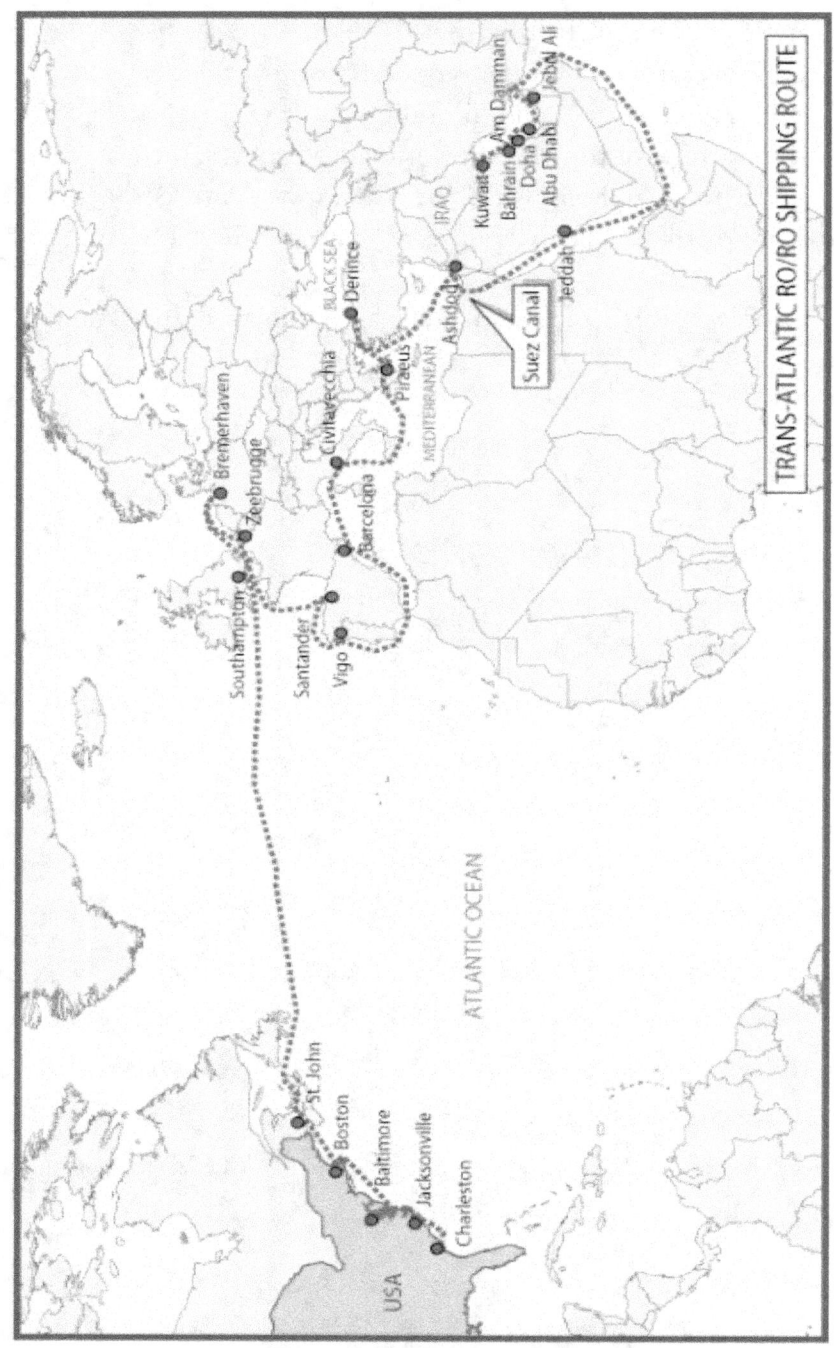

*(Diagram 22 - Sevresbö Dog shipping route, map)*

# 24. '...BROUGHT TO BABYLON...'

*Friday, November 16, 2012*

Seven-hundred-and-forty-*thousand* cars pass through the car-handling facilities at the Port of Southampton every year.

It isn't unusual for a vehicle to be loaded without close inspection; such is the rigmarole of the routine for the dock foremen.

A row of five grey tower-cranes line the edge of the deep draft terminal, standing high over the *Sevresbö Dog*. From the window of the cabin, the only things that are visible are the heavy iron legs of the cranes.

On the apron below, the green farming tractors and harvesters, ochre-orange earthmoving equipment, and white commercial vans are all parked in orderly rows. Faraway across the dock, overlooking the spectacle from the opposite vantage point, are the glass offices of *Ocean Freight UK*.

Lou Maas stands at the boardroom window overlooking the parade of machinery. He nods politely in response to the sales executive, seated at the boardroom table behind him. Maas can see the man's figure reflected in the glass. Behind him, is a mural of the world in Mercator projection – long dotted lines tracing all the available shipping routes.

It is really impressive, seeing it for the first time: the loading of the cargo ship. No passports. No customs... It has never occurred to Maas before. Stowing away on a Roll-On-Roll-Off transporter. He knew the old spook – Diffner – was clever. Lou felt sure however, that the same way Diffner had exploited the low wages of dockworkers and the culture of bribery, he had also been permitted an equally clever rejoinder.

The sales executive was enthusiastically describing at length the procedure for having a luxury sedan transported by 'RORO' shipping to America. Maas caught snippets. He was more interested in the row of white, wedge-nosed Nissan Primastar commercial vans manufactured 94 miles away in Luton. Fourth from the rear, in a row of twenty... He can see from his vantage point, the roof of a van sitting lower than the others. The vehicle is resting heavily on its axles. It is the kind of detail most people missed until it is pointed out... If you *did* notice the van's crouched suspension, you'd be even more surprised to find the key in the ignition doesn't fit the locked rear door.

Maas watches as a tiny figure in a Day-Glo vest climbs behind the wheel of the van.

There is a long pause...

The vehicle rolls forward, and then slows.

Maas imagines the driver tugging at the steering wheel, feeling the van's poor handling. The steering would be sluggish. If the driver took a sharp turn, the chassis would tip with the weight. He might even detect – through that 'new car' smell of moulded plastic – a faint hint of diesel, and something like old socks coming from the cargo space.

Then, the van accelerates off toward the ship.

Maas waits for it to stop... And even as it disappears in through the rear doors of the ship, he still expects it to turn back and reappear on the wide ramp.

Only once the tiny figure of the driver has returned to the apron, does Maas smile.

He turns to the sales executive. "I'm sorry, Mister Carnegie. I've changed my mind. It just doesn't look safe."

The sales executive, with his neat British accent, looked perplexed. "Of course your car would be covered by *insurance.*"

Lou Maas laughs.

Insurance.

*Sunday, December 9, 2012*

The sea outside the Egyptian port of Būr Saʿīd resembles a maritime parking lot.

Ships languish in the hot, hazy light of the Mediterranean. Of a hundred or so vessels crowded around the port, many are larger than the Sevresbö Dog.

The craft are christened in every language – Greek, Nordic, Arabic, Asian...

From my camera-sized window, I recognise insignias from containers I've seen on Massachusetts highways; P&O, Nedlloyd, Mearsk, K-Line, Hapag-Lloyd...The myriad ships and multicoloured containers wait for places in the flotilla, at the wide maw of the Suez Canal.

"Does it always take this long?" I ask.

Madison lounges on the small bed, disinterested.

She's seen the canal before, while sailing from Alexandria to Aqaba on someone-or-other's luxury yacht. She squeezes up to the tiny porthole beside me, and peers out at the strange vista. "There's your reason." She nods at the giant grey rectangle looming on the horizon.

The large shape approaches with startling speed until it fills the sky.

The nuclear supercarrier *USS George H.W. Bush* stretches for 330 metres, and reaches as high as a thirty storey building. It's the largest constant object I've ever laid eyes on. Something strains in his mind as I watch it grow in size, as if my psyche can't quite process the concept. As the carrier slips past us, I can see in the sprawling flank of its hull, the three aircraft elevators connecting the ship's flight deck to hangars below. Dozens of toylike fighter jets and helicopters lurk there in shade, tended to by tiny figurines. As the ship passes breathlessly by, little details tease my mind. At compartments, balconies and walkways along the spectacular hull, miniscule grey-coveralled sailors move purposefully about, tending to the behemoth, like remora on a whale. The control tower – emblazoned with a giant '77' – casts a long shadow across my window. I peer up at the bristling silhouetted array of antennae on the grey spires and crossbars.

"You've never been on a supercarrier?" Madison asks, dismissively.

I refuse to answer the question.

I can imagine why she's been on a supercarrier – so some fly-boy could show her his wings.

"She moves twice as fast as us," adds Madison, with a misplaced twang of pride. "They probably left Norfolk two weeks after we left Boston, and crossed the Atlantic in half the time. They're keeping the canal open for her."

I turn my attention to a handful of similarly sized supertankers lurking out to sea. The distance makes them less imposing.

Queued around the *USS Bush's* flanks are six ships in the Carrier Strike Group: two Guided Missile Cruisers, two Anti-Aircraft Warships, and two Frigates. The fearsome fleet serves as a spectacularly visible reminder of our own destination.

The hulking carrier, and the 6,000 souls aboard her with all their instruments of war, all bound for the Gulf, make me shiver down to my sweetbreads.

Still, there is a small sense of relief at the diversion. The previous weeks have been tedious, waiting in the cabin for days to pass, seeing nothing but ocean, far-off coastlines squiggling at the horizon, and a sequence of identical car-loading ports.

At every destination, Madison and I have hidden, watching from this window as a parade of vehicles board the ship, holding our breath at every footstep outside the door...

With the passing of days, I've grown accustomed to the vibration. It's only when the ship falls quiet that I notice it stop... "We're stopping?"

Madison steps back from the tight space by the window. "We're meeting the pilot boat."

"What for?"

"Ships have to pick up an Egyptian canal pilot and half-a-dozen 'canal line handlers.'"

I twist my neck, trying to see this pilot boat.

"There are no locks on the canal, and no need for lines,' she scoffs. "They're just useless hawkers flogging cheap trinkets and tools they've stolen from other ships, or begging for Coke and cigarettes."

"Can we go ashore?" I ask, hopeful. There's an aching in my feet to walk on dry land.

Madison shakes her head. "The port authority requires papers for cholera and yellow fever inoculations to disembark. We need to stay out of sight till after Tawfik, at the other end of the canal." Madison checks her watch. "That's onety-one more hours..."

I listen to a bustle of activity outside our quarters, glancing at the latch. There's feverish jabbering outside at the new arrivals. The faint echo of the bridge radio crackles with maritime chatter down the hall. I press my nose to the glass, to see the edge of the deck.

An expensive-looking private yacht is manoeuvring ahead of us with its bronze, swim-suited passengers gathered on the fly-bridge to ogle the aircraft carrier.

"What happens next?" I ask.

"Ten vessels in each convoy."

I notice Madison is beginning to abbreviate her sentences, tired of the running commentary.

"Convoys alternate in both directions, passing in the Al-Buhayrah al-Murrah al-Kubrā...the lake. It's half way through."

I stare at the colossal supercarrier, trying again to get hold of the concept of a hundred-thousand tonnes of steel...But the more I contemplate the size of it, the more my dread rises.

The *Sevresbö Dog* hums to life again, and begins creeping past the rectangular prow of the *USS Bush*. The spires of Būr Saʿīd's Great Mosque emerge beyond the sweep of the giant bow; angular minarets towering over the worn, steaming port. Port Saʿīd resembles a mix of old Europe and South America, rattled together: Gaudy, crooked hawkers' stands and sheet-metal rooves sandwiched between elegant Rococo apartments. Seagulls wheel over the marina, spying on the littered harbour.

I move back to the tiny bunk, and sit on the edge. I can feel the gravity of the supercarrier through the wall. "This is insane."

Madison turns, bumping my knees with hers. "What?"

"We're going into a *war* zone."

But we've already discussed it at length. Finding Clark, and Maas, is the only way to find out what happened to Joe. We're all following the same clues. That there's treasure at the end of the road, is just a happy coincidence. *Besides*, Madison says, *Iraq is practically the fifty-third state of America.*

"You can get off the boat, but I'm going," she states flatly.

"I'm going too."

Madison smiles, irrationally.

"How do we find Clark?" I ask. "I don't know about you, but I don't speak Arabic."

"I know a little."

*Shopping in Dubai.* "'I don't think 'do you have this in pink?' is going to help."

Madison frowns. "If I'm there, Clark will find me."

So we'll get a hotel, she'll make some calls, pull some strings at the embassy, and we'll start like that...*Right?* Just as easy as falling off a camel.

It's one of those things: brave and stupid at the same time, depending how it turns out.

There's a long, slow ballet of ships as the *Sevresbö Dog* lines up behind the Carrier Strike Group, and luxury yacht. The convoy powers toward the entrance to the 3,500 year old canal, the original channel dating back to the time of Pharaoh Akhenaten.

As the wall of the Suez creeps toward us, the wide blue of the horizon is replaced with dead flat, arid, infertile, camel-coloured wasteland.

It's Madison's turn on the bunk, sighing as she lies down.

I lean on the edge of the porthole, and watch the desert slip by.

The scenery is broken only by an occasional palm tree, long rows of neatly piled sand, and the odd abandoned shack – speck-like on the flat expanse. Wooden rowboats hug the bank in the shadow of the ships, tiny sails made from tarp, powered by oarsmen in cloth hats.

The shadow of the supercarrier skips ahead of us, visible on the long stretch of placid water and timeless sand.

The overall effect of the parade lulls me into a trance.

Madison begins snoring softly.

I'm startled from my daydream by the crackly transmission of jazzy Arabic pop music outside on the cargo deck. I've lost track of how long I've been standing here. My elbows ache where I lean on the wall. The smell of hotdogs penetrates the tiny cabin. Madison stirs. Together, we listen to the crew and their Egyptian guests, dancing and haggling over sunglasses and tobacco.

Eventually the music stops, and I return to watching at the window.

There's something Biblical about the landscape...It seems fitting that here in this interminable badland, God was born.

The only new diversion along the canal is the surprising sight of a lone military sentry, standing on the shore with a rifle slung on his back. Madison stands, and stretches her arms. "I'll keep watch. Have the bed."

I move to the bunk.

Madison peers out the window. "Hang on..."

"What?"

"It's the Al-Buhayrah al-Murrah al-Kubrā Look..."

I lean over her shoulder.

The shoreline sweeps away from the ship where the lake begins. Nearby a bright, wiry flock of flamingos wade at the water's edge, dipping for fish. A high concrete war monument rises out of the desert, in the shape of a giant AK-47 muzzle and bayonet.

"Hmmf." I side-step back to the bunk.

"We'll be in Qatar tonight," says Madison.

"Can we go out for a walk then?"

"Stop whining."

I stare at the low ceiling. The paint is flaking on the bulkhead. The white enamel is thick with recoats, peeling away in pieces the size of playing cards. In the cracks, I make out a thin layer of two previous colours – yellow and green – and a layer of rust. The regular shapes in the cracks and bubbles look like snow flakes. All impossible. All inevitable...The product of a trillion infinitesimal forces, strands of hair in the brush, stirring of paint in the can, sinews in the wrist, properties and molecules of polymers...As I drift to sleep, I recall vaguely a half-finished thesis. The world again seems impossible...

Strange that the most improbable explanation can even seem *plausible*. That some invisible transcending force is responsible for everything: Sea. Sand. Clouds. Flamingos. Stars. Trees. Rivers. Snowflakes. Faces. AK-47s. That recent events have unfolded the way they have, that each separate moment is its own coincidence – the product of a trillion numerical facts – and every attempt to understand them requires simplification to make them comprehensible, is more terrifying than the size of the aircraft carrier.

Slowly, I fall asleep, drifting through the land of the Bible.

Three-thousand years ago in ancient Iraq, a man turned his back on God and stowed away on a ship …A storm rose while the man slept. The crew of the ship thought the storm was an 'Act of God', punishment for the prophet's rebellion. They took the prophet and threw him into the sea. So the story goes, he was swallowed by a whale for three days.

Sleep takes me again, and I consider that the only thing missing is the storm.

Vaguely, through the fog of sleep, I feel Madison shaking me.

"Huh?"

"You were having a bad dream."

I was. She nudges me over on the narrow bed, and wriggles in beside me – for the thirty-third night in a row.

"Hey, wanna see a trick?"

Jeezus, where is this going? "I guess."

She rolls on top of me, and bunches herself down at my feet so she's peering over my knees. "You have to imagine a higher ceiling… It's much more spectacular."

"Ooookay."

She pushes up into a handstand, facing away from me, putting her feet on the ceiling, knees slightly bent to accommodate the small space.

"That's great."

"Hang on—"

She starts walking backwards upside-down, with her hands and feet, hair tickling its way up my torso. Halfway up, she arches her back, tipping her head so she can see me. "Now, the grand finale." Walking the last few steps along the ceiling, she starts down the wall above my head, until her body is arched, feet at my shoulders. Then she flips upright with a flourish, and lands on her knees above my ears, tail-bone on my chest. "Ta-da."

"Let me guess…You used to date a guy who owned a circus."
She laughs. "That's *one* name for it."

When I wake in the night again, I think I hear Annie crying.
Her shoulders are trembling.
I mean, Madison.

*Sunday, December 22, 2012*

On the lowest deck of the cargo hold stands a row of green farm tractors, harvesters, ochre-orange earthmoving equipment, and white Nissan Primastar commercial vans, all loaded onto the Sevresbö Dog in Southampton. Fourth from the end of a row of twenty identical vehicles, a Primastar van rests lower on its axles than others from the Luton factory.

Inside the van's rectangular cargo space are 24 blue steel barrels on moulded plastic pallets, lashed to deck hooks with orange nylon straps. Surrounding the drums, tamping the cabin wall and side panels, are white plastic 25 kilogram sacks – emblazoned with the yellow HAZMAT diamond, the icons of a flaming orb and the words *'OXIDIZING AGENT'*. On top of the blue barrels is a salad of mining paraphernalia including seven crates of black 18-inch Trenchrite sausages, 80 spools of shock tube, and boxes containing 500 electric blasting caps.

In the centre of the pile, taped to the top of a drum with bright yellow duct tape, is a ruggedised case printed with the label 'Dual ESI Initiator', and beside it – connected by a slender wire – is a radio transmitter.

And at that moment, a faint click…

With a cataclysmic roar, I'm thrown to the floor.

The wild squall cracks and whistles at the window like a whip. Jarred out of the peaceful cloud-cuckoo-land, my ears are split by a cacophony of squealing metal, and the first screams of terror.

It's instantly obvious: The *Sevresbö Dog* and all aboard her are sinking.

Ears ringing like I've been fired out of a cannon, my heart strains fit to squeeze through my ribs. The sudden clamour shoots to my stomach. I lurch unsteadily to my feet. Already, the floor is leaning so dramatically, I'm forced to pedal the length of the small room, propped against the wall.

Where is Madison? "Maddie?!"

I fumble with the latch, and tear open the door – finding others tumbling into the hall, bleary eyed, looking to each other in fear as they scramble for an exit.

*Where is she—?!*

Desperate, I join the throng in the tilting hall in an uphill clamber for the top of the companionway, seeing half-a-dozen others falling ahead of me. I have a sudden, sickening premonition of death in the sea.

Another door *slams* open ahead of me, spilling flailing bodies.

The narrow space fills with crew members tearing at each other's backs.

The panicked, futile press of men compounds as the ship rolls further sideways. The crowd claws and climbs, wailing and bawling obscenities in a cacophony of languages.

I pull back into a doorway, transfixed by the spectacle.

*Is this... a dream?*

My fear is interrupted by the exaggerated hysteria of the others. It's stupendous...

A moment ago we'd all been at rest, eyes darkened, aware of nothing.

Suddenly every man is possessed with the sort of mania that makes men leap from burning buildings, or trample others to death in a sweltering panic to escape the press of a crowd! These men never marvelled that the ship ever floated, the way we marvel that a plane can fly. We did not brace ourselves, as we pulled away from the dock... The reality that we're actually *sinking* is a more acute terror for the surprise. The rolling, shuddering walls, the noise, and the sudden claustrophobia are unexpected...and a more nightmarish twist for having erupted in slumber.

I press my chest to the wall, taking hold of a doorjamb to avoid being dragged backward. Somebody stumbles on the incline, and immediately there's a pile of half-naked limbs kicking around me. The whole ship is raking over with such speed that navigating the hallway is impossible. Detached by my own horror, I spot Madison ahead of me kicking a rakish seaman in the nose with the heel of her boot, propelling herself forward, and the man tumbling backwards, nose bleeding.

The floor is at such an angle, that the tangled knot of bodies begins to break and fall down the companionway, back toward the end of the compartment.

The hue and cry is suddenly lost in a roaring rush of water below.

Braced in the doorway, I peer down, straining to see what happens to those thudding to the bottom of the well. Water is surging in through a doorway, and a great pile of madmen attempts to scale the walls, stamping the less fortunate down into the churning brine.

There is no distinguishing between these men, and animals.

There is no magnificence here. No immortal temperament. Only sickening reality. I marvel at the feverishness of those slipping back to their deaths in the shaft. Their instincts are quickened, to the point where – in a second – they're capable of feats of startling athleticism. A wiry man spies a foothold, and twists his body to collect himself on another man's shirt. Every intention manifests in his wide eyes. And ahead of me, there's Madison, in the midst of the brawl, elbowing her way forward.

I feel no sorrow for *any* of them, except Madison. In this moment, I despise everyone on Earth for their bald lust for survival – and all of them equally – except for this magnificent woman, raging her way through a knot of men…

If I die here, who will know?

I consider returning to my room.

The sea will take all these lives together, and no one will know I was even here. The great secret we were searching to unlock – the tablet, the motive of so many murdered – will sink to the floor of the ocean with us. And—What about Joe?

I fling my arms over the edge of an open door, just as everything comes perpendicular.

With the weight of six or eight others on my back, I hook my elbows into the door frame, and hide my face from the clawing hands and feet. A stray knee clubs me in the ear. I glimpse the open door swinging shut toward me, as it slams across my wrists. I *scream* in pain, but don't let go.

The crew are frantic, finding precarious grips in the inverted landscape. Dangling, spread-eagled across the floor. On light fittings, seams, and bolt heads. Some hold on by the sheer friction between skin and paint.

In the space of a few seconds, the weight that rests on my shoulders multiplies. My grip begins to slip… My bruised arms pull at their sockets. I kick madly to be free, but I'm pinned now, face flushed with *rage*…

A man falls from my waist. Another is dragged away in an avalanche of bodies. I thrust my head about like a brawler, cracking the back of my skull against a brow, and pedal the fallen away. Roaring, vertical, I look up and – to my amazement – see only one figure ahead of me, slipping down the floor above…

*Where's Madison?*

At the end of the corridor, the stairs are empty.

Outside the open door, stands a rectangle of cloud beyond the balcony of the deck, and the sideways rain.

Nothing but a clutch of people on my back stands between me and the sky.

Waves pummel the upturned hull like thunder. If I can just climb a little further! But, I'm held fast. I *long* for the stairs, to be gathered up into a life raft. Then – in a *flash* of white – my hopes are dashed.

The lights flicker and die as the ocean comes crashing through the open hatch.

The tepid waters of the Gulf strike me, uncomfortably lukewarm, like saliva. I press my chin down against the doorjamb, clinging on with it. The sinews in my neck strain as the weight of water presses me down. My arms are ready to snap from my sleeves, and my head about to cave upwards from the jaw, but I can't relinquish my hold. I won't. The water floods over me. Eddies and strange physics of suction tug me in unnatural directions, snapping me like a lure, and still there are those with their arms wrapped around my waist that will not let go... The rush of water *whorls* into every cavity and closet in the ship, colliding in doorways and hallways, pounding against walls, testing my neck and shoulders. A body twists off my back with the force of the sea.

I recognise a bitter taste on my tongue. It's familiar. It was the same, in the crab shacks in New Bridlington... Floating in the swimming pool at the house...Being shot at, in Diffner's house...It's death. My mortality is lurching at me again... But this time it is different. In the noise of my mind, I know that *this* time I will not be missed. Not by Annie or Joe or Matt. This is a secret death, on the far side of the world, in a deep ocean. *Who is left to miss me? Have I even touched the world? ...Have I even left a scratch? ...Who will note my passing?*

There's only Madison...And...if Joe is somehow alive...

Do these two mourners make me any less worthy of survival than those with kinder souls, with wives and children? Those riding on my neck?! Are these other men good fathers? Good people? *Who* deserves to live?

Will my escape cost another man his life...?

And in the storm, just for a part of a second, there is calm in the tepid water around us, as the sea soaks into mattresses and suitcases, bottles, and hollow spaces in drowned men's heads. A quiet stream of bubbles carries their final breath to the surface...

The surging water fills the ship, rising over my head. I push upward on my elbows, still towing a relentless seaman. Others let go in the unexpected calm to make their own way, legs pounding in the dark.

A stray foot catches me in the stomach, punching the precious air from my lungs. I strike my head on an iron edge. Blinding pain belts through my teeth, as I'm shoved aside in the sinking tomb. Animal-madness keeps me kicking upwards towards the light, when I can't think, swimming randomly, thrashing, lethargic...

Grabbing out with blind fingers for the man who kicked me, I find the top of his head with my palm. There is a moment where I decide how to use the advantage, maybe. I can't be sure. I push my way ahead, the physics of free bodies translating my action into sending the other man back. Asphyxiated, disoriented, weak, I reach up...and fumble for a handrail.

One arm wrapped over my skull to nurse the split, afraid of another impact in the maze of rungs and pipes, I hear the yelling and screaming of the drowned, in the busy inner ear of deep-water echoes. And the squeal of twisted metal carries through the water. More softly... Voices...

The best record of the brawl now is the mad pounding of my heart. With curled fingers, I find the first tread of a stair, pull and kick my way upward, glancing off the bulkhead. My lungs are flat, screaming to open. Pressure forces me to pull sea water through my nose and ears. I taste the bitter tang of diesel in the water.

And suddenly I'm breathing air. Gasping!

Bursting through the surface, a red emergency light reveals the space. I'm in an inverted companionway.

A figure shoves past me, climbing to his feet and wading up the incline to the EXIT.

I stand, lop-sided on the submerged wall, and reach for an exposed pipe to pull myself up.

And there she is, resplendent – an unchaste Venus – translucent cotton shirt pasted to her skin. She stands, feet apart, like a romance-novel heroine in a shower of sparks.

I grin, buoyed out of my solitude. 'Madison!''

She beams, rushing forward, seizing my wrist, dragging me upward.

A sudden tide of water blasts back into the corridor, but her grip is fierce.

Bright light flashes through the outline of the sinking doorway. The inverted landscape slips away. Moving upward, quickly – or maybe the shimmering portholes and pillars are descending – I rise through pearl-string bubbles, hauled along by Madison. Her long legs kick rhythmically before my eyes. The sun-like amber of flames above sends yellow beams into the deep. I peer past her swivelling shoulders, and the billowing cotton shirt, to find the foam a few meters overhead, and the source of the amber light refracting around her…

Straining upwards, kicking madly, we hurtle towards the surface, into the blaze of spilled diesel: Unable to stop, buoyed by my lungs, gagging on tainted brine.

A patch of darkness appears in the shimmering ceiling of the waves, my vision blurred with scum and delirium. The instant we burst through the surface, bare and slick, in smoke and flame and death more horrible than those beneath us, I inhale flames.

Acrid fumes of superheated air sear my lungs. Fire licks at my eyes. The underwater stillness and silence give way to *clanging* bells and *screams*. I wail like a gull, surfacing in the trough between two waves where a high shadow hangs above us like a wall.

Madison spins in the water to follow the strange mechanical *whooshing* of some giant unnatural bird, above us. The anvil of the sea presses me down again before I can orient myself, retching, salt water filling my nostrils. A thick film of bunker oil has congealed on my skin. A thousand pinpoints of light skip overhead. But Madison still holds my wrist, pulling me *down* this time, into the frigid sea, away from the flames.

Underwater, skull singing with the pain, arms wasted, unable to govern my movement, too weak to kick, I float tethered to Madison by her tenacious grip. Through the fizz and foam, her bright blue eyes stare at me intently…

My elbow strikes the barnacled hull of the *Sevresbö Dog*. The water around me churns and boils, such that the flames above are briefly held at bay, guttering in the rain. Madison pulls me up again. I look skyward…to see the bright, glowing shape of twenty feet of the yellow prow of the ship standing high out of the ocean above us.

A platform of bow, deck, handrail, and hull loom like the forehead of a giant mechanical man.

In the recessed crown, on either side of the massive rudder, spin the enormous *thumping* screws of the *Sevresbö Dog*, spitting out water in a glistening fan.

Bouncing on the low waves, shielding my face from the heat of the burning diesel, I gaze up at the section of ship suspended above us. The whole vessel dangles beneath this single apex of spinning steel, some phenomenal balance of weight and buoyancy temporarily halting the ships descent. Fused in a dream, I'm caught up in the strange spectacle. The anomaly. And, as I consider the giant propellers, and how they will descend upon me, another man bursts up out of the sea a feet away, towards the keel.

"*HAAAY!*" Madison screams.

The man turns in our direction, and his face shows the blood spurting from a wide-open wound in his skull.

The ship begins to descend… Suction tugs at my waist. The tremendous weight of the improbable force strikes a louder note of fear than all the other terror. It is the pull of gravitation, drawing me into the hammering blades of the giant propellers. I'm pulled back under the water, torn from Madison's grip.

I catch one last breath before being drawn under, as the *Sevresbö Dog* slips ponderously down.

Mustering the last movement in my thighs for each snap of my legs – mimicking Madison's rhythm – I strive for the surface, drained, the weight of the ship and the rush of water relentless. The Arabian Gulf pushes me under, turns me over, dizzying, surrounded by the sweep of churning water.

Numb, I might be drifting into space towards eternity.

*...Maas turns me over in the pool...*

My lungs and stomach and head fill with water, and diesel sings through the cavities.

But my legs kept kicking. Like a winding-down clock.

*Kick, Kick, Kick... Kick... Kick...*

## 25. '...UPON THE DRY LAND...'

*Sunday, December 22, 2012*

The rising sun casts a violet glow on the placid waters of the Persian Gulf.

In the distance, a thin white band divides the matching blue of the sea and the sky.

The surface is broken by flashes of light and debris. Random objects bounce on the rippling surface. A chair, a wet-weather boot, a plastic drum...

A patch of blood crowns the space where I rest my forehead on the fibreglass block.

I lay sprawl, face-down on an orange box, and under my cheek, are stencilled the words LIFE RAFT. I don't know how I got here. *Unless Madison...*

I twist my head. I'm alone.

My limbs dangle in the water. One side of my body glows pink-hot from sunburn. The other is slick with a patina of ash and oil. The only measure of time is the slap-slapping of the water against the floating perch…and the slow track of the sun.

A timber crate thumps against the raft, knocking rhythmically.

Blood trickles down my oesophagus. My skull is ripe with pain. Shaken by a fit of coughing, I wretch an unsavoury coagulate, and roll onto my back, lurching as I almost slip into the sea.

Drawing my feet out of the water, my legs are so sore I'm barely able to hold up my heels. The pontoon tips, almost spilling me into the sea. I lay still, prone, dazed, and daydreaming at the filaments swimming under my backlit lids.

A distant creaking rouses me.

Far away, a fishing vessel whispers over the horizon, its straining mast growing louder, the narrow timber prow coming into focus. It's a '*dhow*' – a traditional Arab sailing vessel – with a triangular lateen sail, and a long beak sweeping up to a narrow point.

A pair of hands hook under my shoulders.

Two bearded men haul me over the low-point in the side of the sweeping hull between the wide rectangular transom, and the upturned bow. The two men wrap a woollen blanket over my shoulders. One of the Bedouins, with a fleece-lined brown shawl across his shoulders, leans over me, blocking the sun, and rasps. "Allaabu Akbar." *Allah is Most Great.*

"Inna lillahi wa inna ilayhi rajiun," whispers the younger man, a teenager. To Allah we belong, and to Him will we return.

At the front of the boat, I spot a third figure dressed in khakis, pressing a pair of binoculars to his face, scanning the horizon, with a cigarette pinched in his lips.

The two Bedouins haul me, arms and ankles, down a narrow ladder into a triangular cabin cluttered with electronics and saucepans, lifting me onto a wedge-shaped bunk. The younger man pours hot water from an old teapot into a mug of powdered stock, and hands me the steaming brew. The man's rough hands remind me of Bert Morney, the fisherman in New Bridlington who dinged Annie's bumper outside the IGA.

The pair of Bedouins whisper, and the older man returns to the ladder, climbing out of the cabin.

"Where am I?" I croak.

The only answer is a stern voice on the boat's radio: "..Unidentified vessel. This is coalition warship Ewe-Ess-Ess- George-Aitch-Double-Ewe-Bush... I am engaged in transit passage in accordance with international law. Request you establish communications, identify yourself, and state your intentions. Over."

At the top of the companionway, the Bedouin barks at the man outside. "Sah, we have to *leave!*"

I hear the American answer. "Not till we find her."

"There's nobody else here, Sah! We looked everywhere!"

A loud thump echoes through the cabin as someone punches the timber wall. "Keep *looking!*"

"Unidentified vessel. You are two miles from coalition warship... I am engaged in transit passage in accordance with international law... You are approaching coalition warship operating in international waters...I maintain no harm. Over."

The man in khakis stomps down the flimsy stairs. His skin is darker than I remember, but there is no mistaking Clark Diffner's mangled expression.

Diffner leans into the bunk, sneering grimly. "Where's Madison?"

"...Clark?"

"Where's Madison! *Hurry!* We don't—"

"I don't know."

I feel Clark's body tense against my side, his knuckles white on the shelf. "Are you sure?"

I recall the vivid image of Madison half-naked in the upturned corridor, dragging me to the surface – pummelled, spitting and screaming, trammelled by the surging sea water.

I nod soberly.

Clark addresses the Bedouin without turning, squeezing his eyes shut. "Five more minutes!"

"In Shah Allah," replies the Bedouin. If God wills it.

The Bedouin leaves the small cabin, and Diffner turns to follow.

"Wait!" I squeak, but Diffner climbs the stairs, and is gone.

I start to wriggle out of the bed, when I hear Diffner bark outside. "Keep him there." A shadow crosses the doorway. Heavy boot-steps thump overhead as Diffner returns to the bow.

I lay still, listening as the boat rocks on the waves, the mast creaking in its footing. There is no more discussion.

The two Bedouins fall silent, hushed by the palpable grief.

# 26. '...CAST OUT OF THY GRAVE...'

*Monday, December 23, 2012*

A small electric lamp lights the cluttered cabin.

I roll over in the bunk, and find the younger of the two Bedouins seated on a stool. The teenager is tinkering with the rusty filaments in the battery compartment of a once-waterproof torch.

The room is smaller than the cabin on the *Sevresbö Dog*. It is another progressively smaller box. "Who are you?" I ask softly, unsure who might be listening at the top of the companionway.

The young man shrugs, the same way Joe used to.

I swing my feet out of the bunk and test my legs. My knees buckle, but snap back before I fall. I steady myself against the bunk. The Bedouin makes no sign of helping me – or stopping me... He just watches curiously as I stumble to the stairs, towing myself on the loose handrail.

Outside on the deck of the creaky vessel, a slender crescent moon reflects on the sea. There is an eerie phosphorescence in the water, that eddies in wide circles around the boat like magic. The air is different here. I feel it on my skin like warm hands.

I search the shadows, and find Clark Diffner silhouetted in the moonlight at the bow, a speck of ember glowing in his lips when he draws smoke.

Laying on her back, one arm slung across her face, white cotton shirt ripped and grey, lays a tall woman with her head on Diffner's thigh.

The lovers reunited. Boy, that moment must have been a sight... Both having thought the other one dead. Of course she made it. Of course Diffner found her: Wonder Woman and Captain God-Knows-What.

Diffner flicks on a penlight, and holds it over the pages of a small book.

I begin picking my way over the piles of rope in the moonlight.

Startled, Clark snaps his head toward me, clapping shut the volume in his hand.

Madison raises her arm. "Bob?"

"Are we still being followed?" I ask, hiding my surprise.

Clark draws a puff from his cigarette.

"How did you find us?" I hang back, unsure whether to sit, half-expecting to be shooed away.

"My man on the ship," Diffner remarks. "I paid the *fucker* five-grand to keep his stinking mouth shut," he growls. "It was the least he could do." He rubs his furrowed brow. "Maddie told me what happened... At the house."

"Do you know where he took Joe?" I ask, brightly.

Diffner shakes his head. "...He traced my car to Vantcha's." *Maas.* "Shit."

There's a hint of blame in Diffner's voice. Madison stays silent.

"*How?*" A shot of guilt rises like bile in my neck, cutting off the question. It's both our faults. If we hadn't gone there, the old man would still be alive.

Diffner stares out to sea. "We're a long way from Boston now..."

"We're a long way from everything," I reply sadly.

"Since you're up, I'm going to use the bed," Madison stands stiffly, takes Diffner's chin in her hand, and kisses him on the lips.

Diffner flicks his spent cigarette into the water. "Maas is clever... He's using the cover of the invasion, to gain access to the site. The bomb on the ship will look like a terrorist attack—"

"It was a *bomb?*" I grab a rope running to the mast, to keep from falling overboard, as Madison slips past me, disappearing below deck.

"With the speed she went down..." Diffner lights another cigarette, "It was a fucking big bomb...Probably a truck. Ripped the whole side right out of the cargo hold."

I feel ill. Maas killed everyone on board just to stop us?

"They'll think it was a terrorist attack...Rammed by an Al-Qaeda fishing boat. It will clinch the DefSec's case for war."

It hadn't occurred to me Maas was behind this as well.

"Al-Qaeda-Taliban forces are halfway to Baghdad," Diffner nods north, over the water. "They're making the big push. Every flip-flop on the Continent is on his way there. And a hundred-thousand Coalition troops now as well."

I scan the horizon. There's a twinkle of light ahead of us, visible only in my peripheral vision. They might be ships, or cities, or planes. "And...are you still planning on going?"

"Hmmm?"

"I found the Bible, in the cabin," I explain, uncomfortably. "Madison found the words in the crossword. Nebuchadnezzar... Melchizedek's tablet is in the ruins of 'Ur.'"

Diffner looks back at the book in his hand. "I'm surprised it took *her* so long to figure it out."

He hands me the Bible and the pen-light. "Isaiah, chapter fourteen, verse eighteen..."

I hook my elbow around the rope, and aim the penlight with my teeth, flipping through the pages.

"'All the kings of the nations, all of them, lie in glory every one in his own house. But thou art cast out of thy grave like an abominable branch..'"

I can see, in the faint light, Diffner is smirking strangely. "The armies of a dozen nations have turned every square *inch* of Babylon, Rome, Jerusalem, Thebes, and the Languedoc...Turned it *all* upside-down, for two-and-a-half-thousand years...Before Jesus was even born, looking for the Ark, and this tablet...Nobody thought to look in *one* place."

"Why?"

"Nebuchadnezzar wasn't buried in Babylon."

Diffner sees the blank expression on my face.

"Nebuchadnezzar was worshipped as a god...He had unbelievable wealth. He conquered the armies of Egypt, took the throne of King Solomon. Eventually, he went mad...and fled the city to live like an animal. He became so unkempt, prowling the wilderness on all-fours, people thought he'd *turned into* an ox to his waist, and the rest of him a lion. '*Like an ox he ate grass, and like a lion he attacked curious crowds...*'"

I whisper the verse from the Book of Ecclesiastes: "'..Concerning the condition of the sons of men, God tests them that they may see that they themselves are like animals..'"

"What's that?"

"King Solomon," I explain wryly. It's the passage I found marked in a Bible in a hotel room in Washington, a seeming lifetime ago: "'*For what happens to the sons of men also happens to animals... as one dies, so dies the other... man has no advantage over animals... All go to one place: all are from the dust, and all return to the dust...*'"

Diffner frowns. "Nebuchadnezzar's son, Amel-Marduk, was made King in his father's place. After seven years, Nebuchadnezzar came back, cleaned himself up, and threw his son in prison..."

"Where was he buried?"

"There are no monumental rock tombs, mastabas, or pyramids in Babylon. The soil decomposes the bodies too quickly... Like the

Chaldean's 'House of Eternity' before them, the underground tombs were made of clay bricks, with corbelled vaults... When he died, Nebuchadnezzar had a grave built into the walls of the palace, like all Kings, where priests could bring him water every day. *That's* where everyone thought he was buried."

"*'...All the kings of the nations, all of them, lie in glory every one in his own house...'*"

"Exactly. That was the tradition since the time of Ninus, founder of the Assyrian empire. But when Nebuchadnezzar's son – Amel-Marduk – was released from prison, people thought his father would return from the dead, and take the throne again ...So...Amel-Marduk had Nebuchadnezzar's body taken out of its grave, an iron chain wrapped around the ankles, and dragged the corpse through the street to prove the old man was gone for good."

"I didn't know that."

"No one knows where he was buried after that, but it wasn't in the same grave...and not in Babylon."

"How do you know?"

Diffner points at the Bible with his cigarette. "The Hebrew word translated there as '*house*' is '*bayith*'. It also means 'city.' '*...All the kings of the nations, all of them, lie in glory every one in his own CITY...*' Except Nebuchadnezzar. He was cast out...The only place no one has looked for the tablet – and the only other Royal Tomb – is Ur. Twenty-five centuries ago, the ancient Sumerian city meant to the Babylonians what Rome – or Babylon – means to us today. It was the birthplace of Abraham...The *very* person Melchizedek first gave the tablet. Before Nebuchadnezzar, Ur was the site of the temple to the Sumerian moon god Nanna, and the later Babylonian equivalent, Sin... that's where the crescent-moon symbol comes from, used by Muslims. The god of the moon. Ur was the birthplace of Nebuchadnezzar's god: the god his son rejected. *That's* where he 'cast out' his father's body."

"Where is it?"

"About two hours drive from the Kuwaiti border."

"I noticed something else," I blurt. "The box in the crossword—"

"Intersects with Nebuchadnezzar."

"—And the cross at the centre of the diagram…'X' marks the spot. Like a treasure map."

Diffner chews his lip.

I glance up at the slender crescent overhead, and remember the moment Annie showed me the light reflecting of the windows of her house… Melchizedek's god became a sun god in the west, and a moon god in the east.

"Ur is where the British archaeologist, Woolley, found the 'Standard of Ur' in the tomb of an unknown King in Nineteen-Thirty…The hollow box is the exact size of the tablet…Aside from that, the place has barely been touched. Saddam was sitting on it for decades. Amel-Marduk sent his father's body and all his trinkets to the ancient capital, where the father of the Hebrews was born… Rejecting his own father's kingship and God, Amel-Marduk cared nothing for a few personal effects. He inherited the wealth of all the known world. The tablet was discarded… somewhere *no* one has searched for thousands of years..."

"When Cyrus took Babylon," I add. "He took the Jewish treasure left in Babylon, and gave it back to the Jews. The Ark was missing."

It's impossible now to draw any other conclusion. It's there in the Bible, when it was first written down…Like an eyewitnesses account, the Bible points squarely to Nebuchadnezzar as the last person to hold the contents of the Ark, and it's being discarded outside Babylon.

The 'mystery hid from the ages.' *The Ten Commandments. The Ark. The Grail. Mohammed's 'well-guarded tablet.'* All one-and-the-same. Buried in a ruin in Iraq.

It's bigger than any secret anyone ever imagined. Jesus isn't even a feature. He's a bit player. All modern Churches are just versions of a faith started four-thousand years ago, at the dawn of civilisation.

I frown. "You're taking a *big* risk, for what still sounds like a hunch."

Diffner takes another long draw on his cigarette. "So are you."

Diffner stares at me. He's more distant than he used to be. And it's not just because I led Maas to Vantcha, or the inconvenience of holding my hand now. I get the feeling he wishes he could throw me back, like an undersize catch.

"You think *he* knows the tablet is there as well?" It's in Vantcha's clue. *CAVIA AGENT. The Rat-Pig Agent.*

"Maas?"

"Yeah."

Diffner nods. "He knew even before he found Vantcha."

"Why?"

Diffner pauses, evaluating whether I'm ready to hear what he has to say. "This thing with cutting out people's *eyes*..."

"What about it?" I answer readily, concealing a twang of pain.

"I thought it had something to do with Vantcha, the way the Ustashi did the same thing...Or the Cathars...But—"

"What?"

"King Nebuchadnezzar – when he conquered the Jews and first found the tablet...He captured the king of Jerusalem, Zedekiah, and... cut out his eyes."

I wince, involuntarily. "You think Maas knew this *all along*?"

"Maybe the 'Z' isn't for Zerubbabel, who rebuilt the temple. Maybe it's for Zedekiah, who *lost* the tablet – and had his eyes plucked out."

Diffner sucks in his breath, sharply. "Or... It's Zechariah! The prophet who described the reconstruction of the temple by Zerubbabel: When the temple was complete, he wrote that God would add the final stone!"

It fits. Vantcha's crossword doesn't just point to the tablet, it points to Maas having located it. All the clues – the whole story, since the very beginning – had been hidden in the crossword all along: The secret of the tablet, its location, and the man who found it. "If he already knew it was here, why was he *fucking around* in Boston?" I snarl.

"Trying to stop anyone *else* from getting here. We're probably not the only ones. Anyone he could find who figured out the puzzle is probably dead... While he waited for this..." Diffner gestures north again.

"Waited for what?"

"The invasion."

"The 'invasion'?"

"He can do what he wants in a war zone...He's C.I.A."

I gasp. "He's *C.I.A.*? How do you know?"

"Let's just say, I recognise the technique."

I feel like I'm going to puke again. I release my grip on the rope and turn to leave, before stopping to face Diffner again. "You think he'll be there ahead of us?"

"Yes."

"I *hope* so," I whisper.

There's only one thing left to do: Find Maas, and make him tell me where Joe is. I don't know how. "We have to make him pay..." I whisper. The kind of scorching retribution that will put god to shame. "For Matt. Vantcha. Barne. Annie. All those on the ship.."

"I hate to say it," Diffner scowls. "After who you've lost... But there are going to be twenty-thousand more bodies by the time this is over."

"We *have* to stop him."

Diffner finishes the cigarette, and flicks it out to sea. "I can't wait to see the look on his face, when the fancy accountant shows up."

"Yeah."

"And Bob?" Diffner whispers.

"Yeah?"

"..Forget it. It's nothing."

## 27. '...UPON THE GREAT RIVER EUPHRATES...'

*Monday, December 23, 2012*

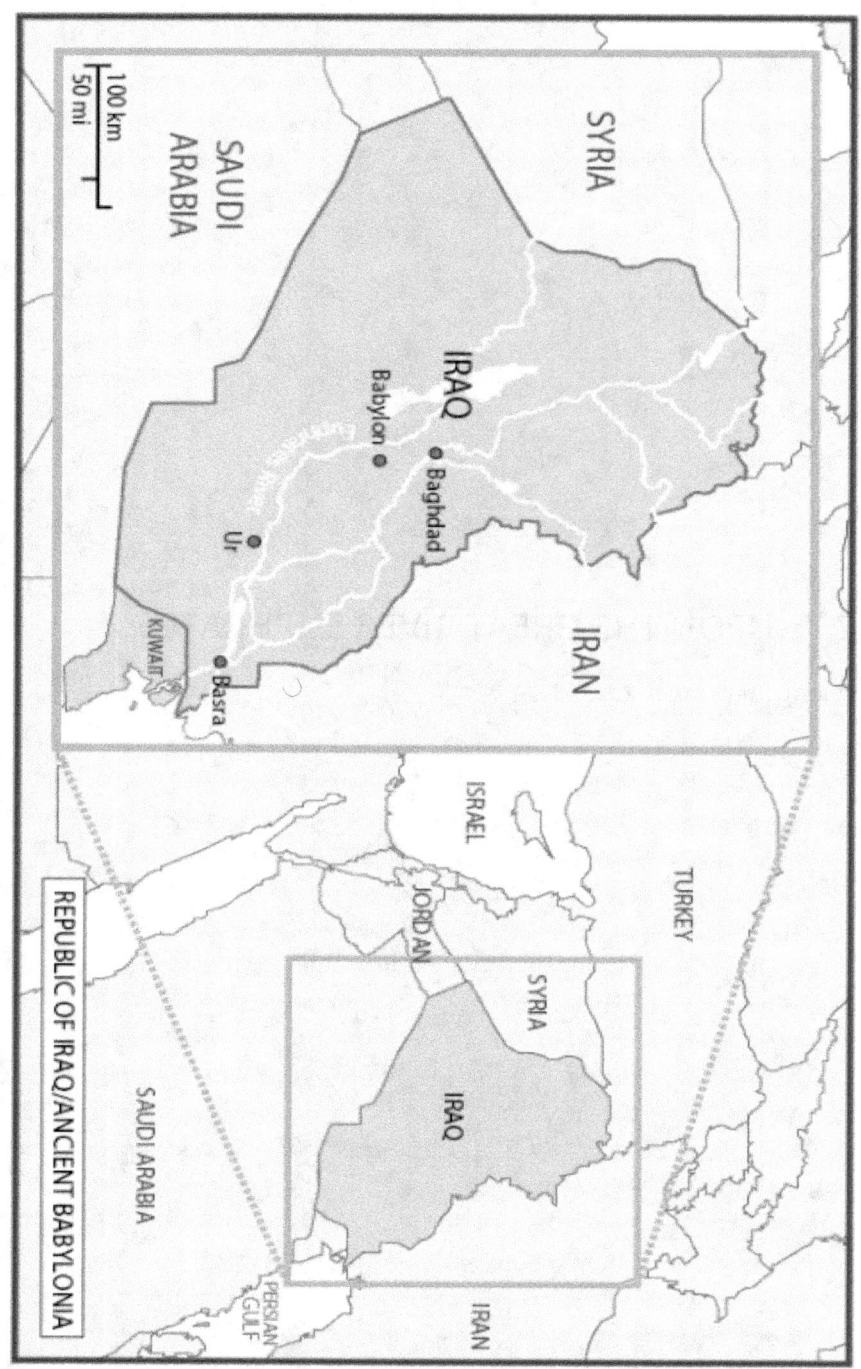

*(Diagram 23 - Iraq and Ancient Babylonia, map)*

The Shatt Al-Arab waterway connects the Persian Gulf to Iraq's only seaport at Al-Baṣrah, at the junction of the great Tigris and Euphrates rivers.

"This is the Garden of Eden," shouts Diffner, above the *thump-thump-thump* of US Navy helicopters in the red sunset sky.

I crouch beside him in the top of the stairway to the cabin, peering out at the river through the crooked slats of the companionway door. Diffner has provided me with a T-shirt and a pair of jeans – the short pant-cuffs revealing my scratched ankles.

Madison is asleep on the bunk, behind us.

The waters of the Shatt Al-Arab are grey and slick with oil. Rusted hulls protrude at off angles from the polluted river. Sickly-looking date palms drop dead fronds along the shore, where they moulder in the water, blackened. The muddy banks are a mire of fallen trees and dead reeds. The smell of rotten fruit fills my nostrils.

*The Garden of Eden...*

"Forty years ago this was the largest date palm forest in the world... a fifth of all the date palms in the world... fires, salinity, pollution, and pests...Ninety-percent of them are dead...That's Iran on the left, and Iraq on the right," Diffner points at the banks. "In Eighty-One they declared war on each other's merchant fleets. This is Iraq's only access to the sea, so they had no choice but to send ships through anyway..."

The creaky *dhow* passes the listing, half-submerged red-and-white hull of a cargo ship painted with the upside-down moniker '*ALSUMOOD*'.

"In Two-Thousand-Six, a tanker with seven-thousand tons of crude oil was sunk here...The river is so polluted; you can almost burn it..."

I shake my head at the hellish riverscape.

"'And the sixth angel poured out his vial upon the great river Euphrates and the water thereof was dried up that the way of the kings of the east might be prepared...'" whispers Diffner. "Revelation sixteen-twelve. The prophecy of the battle of Armageddon."

"Thank *fuck* the river's not dry," I snort.

"The word translated as 'dried up' – *xérainó* – also means 'wasted away.'"

*You're fucking kidding me?* 'So now we're heading into the Battle of Armageddon?'

With a high-pitched roar, a US Navy speedboat rockets past in the opposite direction, throwing a bow wave that threatens to capsize the dhow. An Iraqi flag flutters off the transom beside the Stars and Stripes.

Diffner ducks his head, and I instinctively copy. Madison stirs in the bunk.

"US-Iraqi joint Riverine squadron," comments Diffner, just loud enough to be heard over the thumping helicopters, speedboat motor, surging water, and creaking dhow. "The river is the main entry point for militias smuggling weapons into Iraq...They're patrolling the river for smugglers. Keep your head down."

As the dhow nears the port-city of Al-Baṣrah, the number of small dhows on the widening waterway multiplies. The peaked arches and intricate, carved balconies of Nineteenth Century houses – '*shanasheel*' – appear on the shoreline. The initial impression of grandeur fades as I see more closely: the Arabian homes are crumbling, fences propped with kindling, shutters sagged, holes punched through intricate latticework. The appearance of the structures is accompanied by crumbling piers lined with rusted tugs and freighters, all ringed with old tyres. The water is covered with a rotting carpet of splintered timber, broken Styrofoam, plastic bottles, aluminium cans, and a strange putrid orange spooge. The stench of kerosene and raw sewage overtakes the sickly smell of rotten fruit, making my eyes leak.

On the bank, a row of static black statues on concrete plinths marches by, pointing over the river.

"There are one hundred statues." Diffner points. "In memorial of soldiers killed in the Iran-Iraq war...It runs for a kilometre...Aside from that, Saddam didn't spend a nickel here, nothing – to punish the Shia for the Ninety-Two uprising. No electricity, no sewers, no running water...Then came the drought...Then the war, economic sanctions, militias, and more war...There's nothing left but a raped hell-hole."

A flimsy wooden boat motors past carrying a dozen drunk teenagers in denim jeans dancing on the roof, beating bongos, and gyrating to a scratchy rock song played on a mobile phone. Rusted car bodies line the shore. A tank-turret juts out of a pile of industrial waste in the shadow of a faded political poster... Ramshackle huts lean over in pools of stagnant piss...Hills of piled rubbish, half ablaze, spew dense black fumes into the bloody sky. By the bank of the river a white donkey strains in the harness of a tiny wagon with oversized truck tyres, hooves skidding in the dust.

Iraqi police and Marines in body armour, nursing machineguns, appear on the footbridges and walkways lining the canals that branch off the river. And with an ear-splitting scream, a fighter jet rips through the dusk overhead.

I twitch my head as flies gather round my ears, feeling my gut roll at the stink.

Five-thousand years ago in this ancient city, *writing* was invented...

"Welcome to the birthplace of civilisation," croaks Diffner.

The old Bedouin crouches at the transom of the dhow ahead of us, hunched over the tiller. Hearing the comment, he turns his head. "You came here...For *our* oil."

The Bedouin yanks on the tiller, and the shore approaches.

I turn to see where we're headed, glimpsing a tiled cinderblock pier. At the top of the wharf sits a rusty maroon Tarago minivan with the word '*TAKSI*' hand-brushed in yellow paint down the side. The rear door of the van is propped open with a broom handle.

As the Bedouin sailor hauls down the sail and throws out the anchor, Diffner nudges me up the stairway onto the deck. "Hurry."

"Where?"

"There," Diffner points. "Madison! Come on." He shoves past me, running across the deck crouching, throwing a satchel to the wharf, and leaping after it.

Madison rouses obediently, bounding to the cabin floor.

I follow, barefoot, gagging on the smell, and stumble as the dhow thumps into the ring of tyres around the pier, sending me sprawling into Diffner. Clark seizes me by the collar, and hauls me toward the van. "C'mon! Get in before anyone sees us!"

The van's cargo bay contains a sagging plywood shelf, raised a foot off the corrugated floor by wooden props, supporting a pile of grain sacks. On top, is a scrawny goat with bald spots in its mottled fur. I can smell the animal's sweat and manure from ten paces.

"*Where?*" I repeat.

Diffner points to the tiny compartment under the goat. "In there."

In the improvised cubby-hole – below the sacks and livestock – are a bundle of cases and tent poles, a metal detector, a pick and shovel, and a pair of sleeping bags. The voids on either side of the bundled kit are the size of two coffins. "You're kidding?"

"No." Diffner shoves me toward the nook. Madison runs down the wharf behind us.

"Are you for real?"

"There are no Western civilians where we're going. If we're seen, we'll be shot by Shia militias, or taken for questioning by the Coalition. So it's up to you."

"What about the 'fifty-third' state?" I blurt.

Madison arrives at the tailgate. She's wearing the sandals I saw on the Bedouin boy.

"We can't all fit in there—" I object.

"Get in," Diffner sours. "Or I'll *make* you fit."

I peer at him sceptically, recalling the all-sprinting, all-jumping Jujitsu-lord in the alley, twisting me like a human bow-tie. This is his bread-and-butter. His bash-and-graft. "I hope you know what you're doing."

"Get in," Madison shoves me gently.

"My life, for the past couple months, has consisted of a progressively smaller set of boxes..." I mutter, as I crouch on the far side of the tow-ball. I only worry the *next* box will be six feet long.

I shimmy into the van on my elbows, shoulder blades scraping on the plywood bench, the tip of the pick-axe gouges my thigh, and my jeans snag on a tent pole.

Madison and Clark wriggle together, pressed close, in the similar space on the far side of the kit.

The tailgate slams on my bare heels. "Hey!" Twisting onto my side, I find Madison smirking back at me through the bundles and poles. Diffner is pressed against her back. "This reminds me of a hotel room in Tokyo," Madison sniggers. That's the thing I never got about her – that scares me: the way she skips through life, like the world is her playground. So unlike Annie who stepped so carefully, not making a sound.

I roll over, turning away from the pair, toward the wall of the van – pockmarked with rust. Through a jagged peephole, I see the Bedouin rush past, to the driver's door.

"We'll be there in two hours," whispers Diffner.

It's maddening how close we are to the object that has consumed millions, for three-thousand years. *Two hours...*

With a thin wheeze, the van's engine sputters to life above my head. With a spray of gravel inside the wheel-arch at my hip, we lurch onto the road.

I press my eye to the peephole, forehead bumping against the wall, spying flashing images of the ancient city...The streets are filled with multicoloured drifts of litter – plastic bags, cups, bottles, paper...Clay brick walls dip and swerve. A small boy in a tiny moth-eaten singlet squats over a mud-soaked puppy in the gutter, teasing it with a stick.

The van slows near a shop stall made of plastic crates, piled with bruised tomatoes. Dozens of US army Humvees are parked at intervals down the street. Everywhere, on every corner, I catch glimpses of women shuffling on dusty sidewalks with their bundles, dressed head-to-toe in full-length black burqas. Every woman is dressed the same way – like a Nun's convention – while the boys all stroll around in Eighties thrift-store jeans and disco shirts. And the jaded teenage faces of the occupying forces look on, from under their helmets.

I kick my legs, trying to find a workable configuration for my knees. When I look back through the peephole, the images have changed from camel-coloured city, to belching factories and farmland. A water pipe bounds along the road. Further out, rusting car wrecks flash by, heaped on the roadside.

"What's with all the car wrecks?"

"Some of them are contaminated...from depleted uranium, during the war," explains Diffner. "Or they break down, with no spare parts."

For a few minutes, a boy in faded clothes runs beside the van, screaming at the driver for money.

The crops in the fields look withered, some of them covered with blue tarpaulins to protect them from the radioactive war-dust. Conflict, and drought, and the legacy of economic sanctions have decimated the agriculture here. Screw-worm parasites and a dozen other new crop diseases have hit southern Iraq in the past decade. There's no livestock. Chemical weapons inspectors destroyed vaccine production facilities, allowing an epidemic of hoof-and-mouth to kill a million cattle.

At one point, I think I hear the cry of a rooster, but the only sign of life I see is a pack of wild dogs squabbling on top of a tank barricade made of sand.

I feel the van begin to decelerate. Two hours aren't up yet.

The *rat-a-tat* of automatic weapon fire sounds ahead of us.

"What's that?" shouts Diffner, above the noise of the motor.

I contort at the peephole...

On the side of the road a man stands over a water pipeline, firing a machine gun at a junction in the pipe.

*"...He's trying to steal water,"* answers the old Bedouin from the van's cabin, and accelerates.

As we pass, the farmer glances up from his task, and looks right at the van. I snap my head back, banging it against the edge of a shovel.

The further we go, the factories in the fields become more decrepit, devolving into idle, bombed-out shells. The scenery is increasingly apocalyptic, like all the hellish vials of the Book of Revelations – Pandemics, Climate Change, Resource Depletion, Population Expansion, Energy Security, and Terrorism – have *all* been poured out here, on the Garden of Eden. It's fitting that of all the places on earth, there are more 'Acts of God' here – where god began – than anywhere else on earth.

The car wrecks on the roadside are replaced by a string of burned-out trucks, army tanks, buses, and fuel tankers. The tightly-packed, flipped, twisted, charred wrecks have been bulldozed to the side, forming a mangled steel wall.

"See that?" asks Diffner, sombrely.

"Ahuh.."

"This is the 'Highway of Death.'"

I've seen photos of the infamous thoroughfare on television, but that was ten years ago? The reality is far more horrifying. Or maybe the passing of time has dimmed the images. The scene is made more disturbing, given that the scorched remnants of the massacre remain intact. The wall of rusted trucks forms a grim monument to the dead.

It was the end of 'Desert Storm' – the first of the three invasions of Iraq – when Saddam's troops were in retreat. US fighter planes intercepted the fleeing armour. First they bombed the front and rear of the column, trapping 2,000 vehicles. Then they strafed and fire-bombed the traffic-jam for hours, killing ten thousand people – including fleeing civilians – along sixty miles of highway.

The van's engine grows quiet, as we coast down the shallow grade. There's an eerie silence…

The road is abandoned, but for ghosts.

In the pile of sacks above the cubby-hole, the goat stamps, restless, bleating, creaking the plywood shelf.

"There's a sandstorm coming," shouts the Bedouin.

Another fighter jet thunders by in the distance.

I feel the confines of the tiny compartment press inwards. My breath is short. I'm choking on a cocktail of panic and claustrophobia. Maybe I did die? In the shipwreck…Or the pool? And this is my mythical escort – Madison and Diffner, dead by drowning and fire – leading me from the creaking boat, steered by the old Bedouin, into hell.

The scream of the jet engine is close enough to rattle my teeth.

"Jeezus!" I croak, but Diffner and Madison can't hear.

I roll onto my back, close my eyes, and try to concentrate on staying calm – breathing slowly, through rounded lips.

The Bedouin turns on the radio, listening to a broadcast in Arabic. For the next hour, the roar of trucks on the road becomes more frequent. The aircraft noise grows closer… Louder…

Finally, the combined thump of helicopter blades, screeching jet engines, thundering semi-trailers and tinnitus grows to an ear-splitting *roar*… I clamp my hands to my ears, back teeth buzzing painfully. I twist to the peephole, and spy the drab olive green bodies of trucks flashing by in a convoy. The glimpsed doors of the prime-movers are covered with improvised armour bolted over the side panels.

"Where the *fuck* are we?" I yell, but Diffner and Madison have their hands over their ears as well.

The rusty van veers and nose-dives off the top of the levy, above the barren floodplain.

Gravity and deceleration slam me forward in the tray of the 'TAKSI'. My head *thumps* into the back of the engine bay. I swear, spitting, neck sprained. The van's suspension *squeals* as the wheels hit rough dirt, bouncing me between the sheet-metal floor and plywood ceiling. I grab the wooden shelf and spread my wings against the side panel, punching a bigger hole in the rusted chassis.

The van skids to a halt, filling the compartment with dust. The Bedouin leaps from the cab…leaving the engine running.

I hear the old man panting as he runs to the tailgate, flings open the door, and begins tugging on my feet. "*Yalla! Yalla!*"

I wriggle out of the compartment, grunting, and emerge barefoot in the barren wasteland.

Shielding my eyes from the baking sun, I find *two* visible landmarks in the endless plain: A 3-metre high earthen hill behind us, and behind that, on a wide plateau, rises a stepped clay-brick pyramid the size of a nine-storey building. The aircraft noise echoes from the far side of the hill. In every other direction, the ground is a desolate moonscape: flat, bare, and marked by craters.

Peering at the oddly-evenly-shaped mound, I notice a concrete doorframe at the nearest corner. "Where—*are* we—?"

"Quick! Grab the gear!" Diffner hauls the pick and shovel with him out of the van. The Bedouin slings the metal detector over his shoulder, and stuffs a sleeping bag under his arm. "*HURRY!*"

The Bedouin runs for the door in the low trapezoidal hill, gear rattling around his hips. The goat bleats and stomps in a circle on its tether. I seize the last satchel and sleeping bag, as Clark shoves me toward the concrete doorway...

"Hey—!"

Madison runs ahead of me.

The radio in the 'TAKSI' is still playing, excited voices speaking in Arabic.

Half-dragged to the opening in the level hillside, I see the Bedouin toss the gear, slip off his shoes, throw them inside, and stop...

He turns, blood draining from his face, and looks at the van.

"*Youna?*" shouts Diffner.

The Bedouin turns and looks at Clark. "Baghdad has fallen!"

At first I think he means Coalition troops... But Diffner and Madison are wearing looks of shock.

"They're killing coalition supporters..." murmurs the Arab, darkly.

"Come on!" Diffner hauls me into the concrete cave. I glance back, as the TAKSI accelerates back to the road in a cloud of dust.

"He's *leaving?*" I ask, surprised.

"He'll be back tomorrow with food." Diffner sounds distracted.

"They've taken Baghdad?" Madison marvels. "..*Jeezus.*"

I turn and peer down the long concrete corridor leading into the angular hill. A thin beam of light illuminates a bare room...Diffner leads the way into the chamber, where a tangle of rusted metal concrete reinforcement bars – like hair from an iron giant – drapes through the ceiling, and springs up out of a hole in the floor. Sunlight pours through the perfectly round penetration in the ceiling, where a smart bomb punched through the roof of the bunker, busting the concrete away from the reinforcing steel, blowing a hole clear through to the cement floor. The only objects left in the room are a dusty electric generator that hasn't been touched in a decade, and a chair with a leg missing.

"How is that possible?" asks Madison. "They're fighting with *rocks!*"

"All we had left there was advisors." Diffner kicks at the pieces of broken plastic pipe and the specks of gravel on the floor, throws down his sleeping bag, and slumps against the wall.

"This is a *bunker?*" I marvel, peering up through the neat hole in the ceiling.

Diffner points toward the wall. "The clay tower – outside – is the Great Ziggurat of Ur. The noise...is Ali Air Base." He groans, arching his back. "This was part of the southern 'no-fly zone' between the first two Gulf wars.." Diffner continues, still distracted, talking to Madison – not me. "The Iraqis stopped using the base after Ninety-One. Or, they tried... and it got shot-to-shit during sanction enforcement operations. Then in Oh-Three, the Coalition took it over. It's one of the three bases we didn't pull out of a year ago."

"We're next to an air force base?" I turn and look back at the doorway, muttering to myself. "Is that good or *bad?*"

Diffner sighs, and settles on his sleeping bag. "Get some rest. We'll head out to the ruins after dark."

"Will the Taliban come any further south?" asks Madison.

Diffner shrugs. "It's only 180 miles to Baghdad."

I scan the meagre kit scattered on the floor of the bunker. "You say this guy, from the boat, is bringing back food?"

"...And water."

"How do you know he'll be back?"

Diffner points. "He gave you his shoes."

I pick up the tough, brown leather espadrilles, and stand in the middle of the bunker, shaking my head in disbelief, eyes moving between Diffner, Madison, the door, and the smart-bomb hole in the ceiling.

"We're almost there," Diffner adds.

I start to speak, but words won't form.

"Lay down, Bob. Get some rest," repeats Madison. "You're tired. So, rest."

I can't help but notice she's less argumentative around Diffner than she is with pretty much *everyone* else, ever.

I turn away so the pair can't see the anguished expression on my face. Quietly, I crouch, and busy myself squeezing my feet into the old Bedouin's shoes. It wasn't so long ago, I was curled up on the couch, cradling my laptop, in front of the *faux* fireplace in the living room, flames licking at the immortal ceramic logs... Annie sitting opposite, feet tucked under the cushions, legs knotted into mine as she read Mark Twain. Then the phone rang.

Four months ago.

Now look where I am, with her sister and an old spook, wearing the shoes of a Bedouin. It all started with that phone call in September. *Snick. "Hello?" "Who is this?" "Who is this?" "Bob?" "Who is this?" "It's Madison."* ...Her voice hoarse... *"I'll get Annie." "Bob, wait." "What?" "Dad is dead."*

I throw down the sleeping bag in a corner, and lay on top of it. "*'We're almost there,'*" I mutter.

Diffner remains silent.

I opened my mouth to speak again, but know if I even utter Annie, Matt or Joe's names, I'll crack apart for good.

Madison and Diffner curl together. Diffner stands up every half-hour, moves over, and double-checks the sunlit puncture in the ceiling for signs of O-dark-hundred-hours.

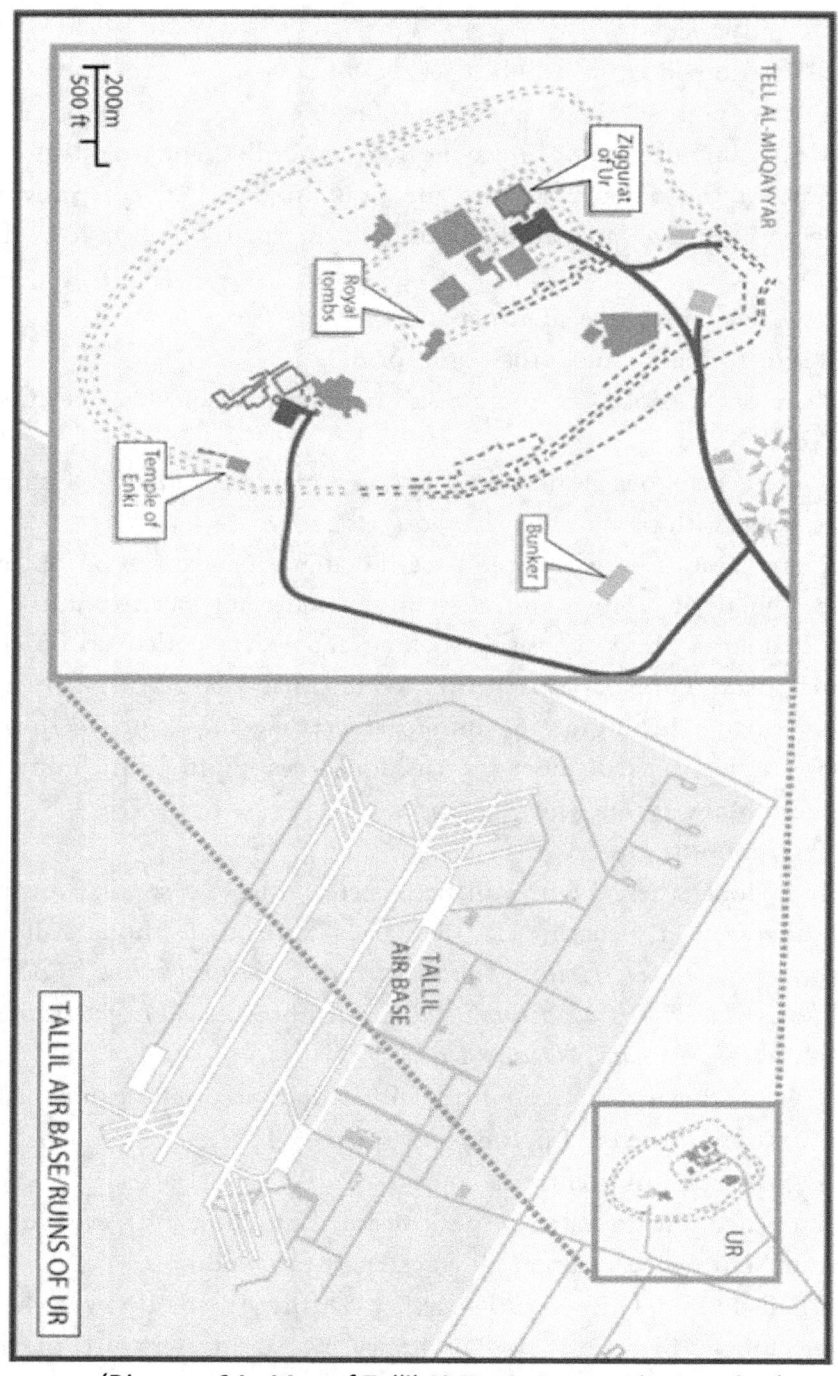

*(Diagram 24 - Map of Tallil Air Force Base and ruins of Ur)*

The roar of aircraft scrambling for sorties is constant: shrill fighter jets, booming cargo planes, the *huffing* percussion of helicopter rotors...

My only relief – the one strand of sanity left to grip on to – is that one way or the other, Diffner is right.

The end is close.

*Monday, December 23, 2012*

Lou Maas stands, hands clasped at his back, feet shoulder-width apart on the tarmac.

He's wearing a faded army uniform: leg cuffs tucked into sand-coloured combat boots, tan t-shirt visible at the Mandarin collar, and a thread-worn patrol cap pulled down hard on his narrow bald skull.

On the peak of the cap is a black, embroidered logo: '*MagCorp*'. As the largest private military company – or 'PMC' – in the Middle East, a MagCorp Officer is as good as being a priest in Boston: everybody looks at you strangely, but nobody asks you any questions.

*(Diagram 25 - MagCorp logo)*

After a week in the Arabian sun, Maas' ruddy features have taken on some colour. The angry red tinge of depilatory cream has faded. There's no need for it here. There are no forensic scientists in southern Iraq...Just sand, and screaming engines.

Across the apron, Black Hawks, Chinooks, A-10s, and transport planes shimmer and shake, in various states of deployment. Ground crews purposefully traverse open spaces under wings, fluttering through jet wash.

The place is a shit-hole, even after nine years of U.S. occupation. From where he stands, Maas can see the rusted skeleton of an Iraqi hangar that has been stripped clean of sheet metal by impoverished farmers. Beyond the airfield, out on the dry wasteland, are sandy Soviet tailfins, and broken fuselages of abandoned Iraqi aircraft. Further on, past a stretch of road, looms the ancient structure of the Great Ziggurat of Ur.

At the sight of it, Maas' excitement is almost impossible to conceal. It has taken twenty years to get here. There have been a *dozen* times when he'd doubted he'd *ever* find it…But – that was all part of the test. God had been testing him, like no man had *ever* been tested.

Beneath his *RayBans*, Maas' spidery, speck-like eyes are fixed on the rear cargo door of the C-17 Globemaster III. The chubby, four-engine transport plane rests low on the sun-drenched concrete apron. The huge girth of the wide fuselage rides on three-tyre-wide wheel racks, protruding from the plane's fat belly.

The sand-coloured vehicle that emerges from the rear of the cargo plane resembles something between a monster-truck and an oversized dune buggy, rolling down the ramp from the payload bay. The strange vehicle has a tiny, heavily-armoured one-man cabin, with a V-shaped undercarriage, and between the two giant sets of soft tyres, hangs a 3-metre wide pair of ground-penetrating radar sensors.

Maas watches as the third of the 'Meerkat' Interim Vehicle Mounted Mine Detectors – or 'IVMMDs' – rolls off the plane before beckoning to a pair of figures in the shadows of the cargo bay. He has to shout to be heard above the noise coming off the airfield. "Bring him here!"

The taller of the two silhouettes shoves the small figure forward.

Tripping off balance, the sixteen year-old boy in a dirty yellow parka emerges in the glare, squinting at Maas.

The taller figure following behind the boy, shouts to Maas above the noise of the air base. "What do we do with *him* now?" It's Bill

Dodd – astronaut-airman, triple Doctorate, and Director of the Anacostia Institute. He looks even more like Buck Rogers now than he did on the podium in Washington. Gone are the Kevlar suit and tie, replaced with a brand-new flight suit. And the chrome teeth and Teflon hair are intact, impervious.

Maas tilts his head down at Joe Travis, peering through his sunglasses.

Joe's posture is one of submission, but his eyes light up when he looks to the spectacle of the air force base.

Maas eyes the boy, with raw contempt. It is true. Robert Travis, Clark Diffner, and Madison Mueller all *probably* dead. In which case there's no need for the boy anymore. But *probably* dead isn't the same as properly dead.

Joe feels the man's eyes on him, through the sunglasses, and tries to return the gaze.

"Take him to the A.B... Just in case."

"In case what?" asks Dodd.

Maas turns, and looks to the hazy man-made mountain of the Ziggurat of Ur on the horizon. "In case that *fucker* still gets there before us."

# 28. '...THAT WHICH WAS LOST...'

*Tuesday, December 24, 2012*

Diffner spreads out a map on the bunker floor.

"This is *Tell al-Muqayyar*," he indicates the round shape on the page. "'*Tell*' is a mound created by an ancient city razed and rebuilt so many times it's a layer-cake of ruins...Like Tel Aviv, *Abīb Hill*... Here's the Ziggurat, and here are the tombs." Diffner points to the centre of the map. "This one, Woolley called the 'great death pit'... There were seventy-three human remains inside...This is where he found the 'Standard of Ur'. It's where we'll find the tablet."

"Let's go," suggests Madison, flashing me a look of anticipation.

Diffner gathers up the shovel, notepads, bottled water, and hands me the pick-axe and the metal detector. "Here." The pair of them creep toward the door of the bunker.

The aircraft noise hasn't subsided in fifteen hours, despite the fact its well after midnight. "They're bombing the *hell* out of Baghdad," Diffner observes softly. "Come on." He pokes his head around the edge of the concrete doorframe. "The faster we move, the less likely we'll be seen."

Then he's gone, disappeared into darkness.

Madison hurries after him.

I trot along behind, lugging my armload of gear. I catch a glimpse of Madison as her moon-shadow disappears at the corner of the bunker.

I follow as fast as I can, leering up at the dark bulk of the Great Ziggurat, backlit by the glow from the air base. The tower, and the ruins all around it, sits on a small hill. The overall effect of the ancient mound, rising in the darkness – the rim of broken clay-brick battlements, and the foreboding stepped pyramid – is fearsome.

I stumble over the flat ground of the ancient river bed, where the Euphrates ran centuries ago. Over these stones, she flowed into a small harbour at the northern end of the ancient capital. There, traders moored vessels of bundled reeds, sailing upriver to Lebanon to buy cedar, and downriver to the Persian Gulf to trade ivory for spices and textiles. Five thousand years ago, during the Early Dynastic Period, in this very place – in this very city, a mile in length – *all* the ideas that shaped the modern world began: Writing. Currency. Construction. Trade. Astronomy. Chemistry. *Religion*. It *all* started here, before the Greeks or the Egyptians refined it.

Here, three Wise Men followed the stars to Jerusalem.

Here, somewhere in these crumbling walls, stands the home of Terah, father of Abraham, first prophet of the faiths of *three billion* Christians, Jews and Muslims in the modern world. Somewhere *else* inside this city was the grave of the Babylonian king Nabû-kudurri-uṣur – Nebuchadnezzar. And there, in that tomb of the last king to hold the world's most sought-after treasure, we hope to find the tablet of Melchizedek...

A fighter jet *screeches* high overhead. I feel the earth tremble under my feet.

I wonder for a moment if the plane has some kind of infrared that might pick out the three figures, running across the open ground. I trip as I run, fixated by the flashing light in the sky. When I lower my gaze, Diffner and Madison are gone.

"...Madison?"

The only clue is the faint rattle of equipment in the badlands ahead.

Then, I notice another noise ...

The sound ebbs through the cacophony of the airbase. It's closer: the rumble of diesel engines, inside the walls of Ur.

Reaching the foot of the *Tell*, I hear a clatter of falling rocks as Diffner and Madison climb the embankment ahead. Stones bounce down the arid slope, pelting my knees. Shifting the metal detector over my shoulder, I scramble up the bank on my hands, arms peppered with rocks, gravel filling the Bedouin's shoes. Near the top of the ascent, large square blocks of clay lay scattered and broken, many bearing arcane symbols stamped in the four-thousand-year-old pottery.

As I approach the uneven ridge, I see Diffner's profile faintly illuminated by the light over the broken wall. The sound of machinery is more pronounced. Clark is crouched behind the eroded stones, peeking over the top, mouth wide in shock.

"What is it?" I puff, as I mount the last few feet of earth.

Diffner ducks into the shadows, beside Madison. "*Shhh!*"

"Wh—" I collapse in the dust, dropping the equipment. "What is it?"

Diffner's eyes sparkle in the moonlit. "See for yourself."

I rise slowly, to peer over the stones.

The scene amongst the partially excavated ruins is like a construction site, lit by portable flood lamps.

Spread out across the plateau, are the broken clay-brick walls of several small buildings – palaces, temples, living quarters, tiny forts. All are smaller than a modern home, most only a few feet high, in various states of erosion. Between the ruins, run temporary electrical leads on posts, floodlights on tripods, a camel-coloured bulldozer and an excavator, and two giant dune buggies, running backward-and-forward over the uneven ground.

On the paved parking lot at the foot of the ziggurat stands a domed, polygonal, taupe tent. Beside the large tent sits a trailer, mounted with a diesel generator, humming loudly. Beside the tent stand a row of palletised containers, and a pair of Humvees.

A dozen men in desert camouflage stand near the entrance to the mobile command post.

"Holy *shit!*"

Madison peers back over the stones.

The resources deployed around the plateau are those of a full-scale military operation. The tent is connected to its trailer by a pair of fat, flexible tubes. "..Army Standard Integrated Command Post System.." points Diffner. The modular trailer-mounted command shelter adjoins a two-wheel HMMWV towable trailer, providing power from an 18kWh generator, and air conditioning for the temporary structure. There are Velcro panels in the sides of the shelter, where multiple TMSSs can be joined together.

"See those?" Diffner points at the pair of strange vehicles further across the plateau – the two tiny, armoured cabins bounce along on monster-truck tyres, traversing sections of ground. At intervals, they roll to a stop, and reverse back over their own tracks. "They're *Meerkat* Interim Vehicle Mounted Mine Detectors.."

"*Mine* detectors?"

"The low tyre-pressure means they can drive over pressure-sensitive mines. If one detonates, the floor of the driver's cabin is armoured, and the structural components are frangible – designed to blow off – and rapidly replaced. Underneath... See? Vehicle-mounted metal detection coils, and ground-penetrating radar."

"There are *land mines* in the ruins?"

"No!" Diffner scowls. "They're looking for the *tablet!*"

Fuck.

The small handheld metal detector slung over my shoulder suddenly feels puny by comparison, despite its weight. "They're using *land mine* detectors?"

"When the radar gets a signal, it pinpoints the object, and activates the marking system in a nozzle on the rear frame that sprays dye on the target."

The group of armed soldiers near the tent are too far away to make out details. All of them have the same shorn scalps, except one...The man at the centre of the group looks like it *might* be Maas. "...Is that *him?*"

In answer, there is a boom and a belch of exhaust from the plateau as the bulldozer roars to life, lowers its blade, and tracks forward. The ground buckles and heaps in front of the machine. Even from where I'm crouched, I can see the ancient paving stones being ripped from the earth, and spilled aside. The earth lies in long piles where it's already been cut, the Meerkat tracking behind the dozer.

"Can they *do* that?"

"Do *what?*"

"To an archaeological site?"

Diffner lets out a snort. "That's *touching...*"

"*Boys...*Let's circle around," suggests Madison. "Over there – get a closer look."

"Where?"

Madison points half-way around the curved wall of the ruin, near the end of the plateau. The earthworks are focused on the centre of the *Tell*, near the royal tombs. To the south is an open expanse broken up by a series of darkened gullies, and excavated walls.

Diffner scrambles ahead of us, feet slipping in the loose embankment as he circumnavigates the *Tell*, crouch-running in the shadows outside the ancient wall.

I follow Madison, traversing the slope awkwardly, dragging the puny metal detector with me. The device clatters on the rocks. I kick loose a small boulder, sending it clapping loudly down the slope...

Diffner and Madison stop, glowering furiously like twins. Even in the dark, I can feel the murderous look in Diffner's eyes.

I hold still, listening for a response on the far side of the wall...

The rumble of machinery continues.

Pausing to empty the rocks from my shoes, I pedal forward, filling the shoe again in the next sideways step. My muscles are weak after the stasis of the past two months – St Ignatius, then the small cabin on the ship. This is the first time I've moved any great distance since the night Barne was shot. Aching, I press on into the darkness, finding the faint figure of Diffner at the southern extremity of the plateau, where he drops his equipment.

At the eastern-most point on the plateau the ruins drop away to nothing – leaving open ground. Diffner bolts out across a paved roadway that leads to the Great Ziggurat.

The air force base buzzes in the distance behind us, made up of a thousand points of light. An unfortunate shadow, the obstruction of a single beam from the base, could alert the men on the *Tell* to our presence. But it's too late to matter. I sprint across the pavement.

Diffner breaks across the open ground at the southern end of the plateau, knees bent, running in a crouch. I watch him in silhouette, as he leaps over the low wall and rolls into a blackened ditch – a hundred yards into the ruins. It's another fifty yards to the cover of the next ruin. After a short pause, Diffner's tiny shadow is up again, emerging from the blackened ditch, running for the wall, and disappearing in darkness.

Madison skips over the wall, following the same tack.

*Fuck.* I set down the metal detector and satchel, collect my nerve, and slide over the wall. Running across the broken ground in the ill-fitting leather shoes, puffing madly, I feel my legs beginning to fail...

Ahead, beyond the ruins, I can see the earthmoving equipment clawing at the ground. Past that, the small group of figures stand by the tent, facing me. Head down, I try to see what the undulating ground is doing under my feet, treading painfully over loose rocks, and broken four-thousand-year-old bricks.

Reaching the point where Diffner took cover midway to the ruins, my knees fold. I land painfully on my hands. Gritting my teeth, I roll onto my back, vision blurred with dust and tears. My lungs are on fire. I struggle to catch my breath. The stars twinkle overhead. The thin crescent moon shines faintly – like a sideways grin. I'm fucked.

Hands tacky with blood, I push myself up again, and try to stand – but this time my legs won't take my weight.

Madison scrambles back to the edge of the hole. "Are you okay?"

I shake my head invisibly.

Madison leaps into the ditch and hooks her elbows under my elbows, hauling me off the dirt. I have the strangest recollection, of moving to pass her at the dinner table, on my way to Matt's den…

"We're *almost there*," she offers.

"Just give me a minute…I'll catch up."

"Come on." Madison ducks her head under my arm, taking my weight.

I flick my legs weakly, as we stumble over the last of the plateau, to the stand of ruins. Diffner is waiting at a corner, through a low archway, near a broken section of wall, where the royal tombs are clearly visible.

Madison lowers me to the ground at the gap in the bricks. "Thanks."

Diffner is ignoring me now.

Fifty yards away, the bulldozer pushes over a wall ahead of the mine detector. The ancient bricks clatter in a heap, spewing dust. We're close enough now to make out faces. Five men stand at the tent, in military camouflage. All of them are unfamiliar, including the men operating the machinery. Nearby, as the bulldozer tears down a section of ruins, the ground opens up into a pit surrounded by razor wire. I can see the top of an old wooden staircase, leading down into a floodlit cavern.

Diffner points. "That's the 'Great Death Pit'…Down that hole…"

I don't fully share his excitement. We're beaten. Maas is here first. Any chance we had of getting our mittens on the tablet is gone.

I swivel on my heel, resting my back against the wall. I glance around the small brick chamber. It's incredible to imagine that someone *lived* in this room, four thousand years ago. *Maybe even Abraham?* He might have sat right here in this spot, thinking *hey, why don't I get half the world onto my idea of god.*

"Fuck!" Madison curses softly, grabbing my sleeve, turning to stare at me.

I follow her gaze, and see the figure rising up the wooden stairs from the pit. "What?"

"A little piece of *home*, right here in sunny *al-Muqayyar...*"

Escorted by two men, Maas emerges from the rotting stairwell that leads down to the underground tombs.

"Maas..." Diffner frowns darkly. "And *Dodd!*"

Maas looks different... *again*. Gone are the cheap suit... and the priest's garb... He's wearing faded army kit: a tan t-shirt, and a brand-new patrol cap embroidered with a black 'M' logo. His skin has a different pallor now. However, the spidery, speck-like eyes are the same. His voice is inaudible above the noise of the machinery, but it's obvious from his gestures, he's locked in a heated argument with *Buck Rogers*.

I feel a surge of anger. If I wasn't so exhausted, I'd run out into the open *now...Smash his bald skull in with the metal detector...*

"He's *'triple canopy'?*" nods Diffner.

"What's that?"

"That tattoo. On his arm... The sword and three lightning bolts... He's Special Forces, Ranger *and* Airborne."

"What does that mean?"

"Someday you'll have to tell me how you got out of that hospital."

"What's the 'M' logo on the cap?" asks Madison.

"*MagCorp*. Military contractors... He either hired them, or he's using them as cover."

"What are they arguing about?" asks Madison.

The bulldozer comes to a stop near Maas. The uniformed operator climbs out of his seat, steps onto the clogged tracks, and leaps down to the dust.

Maas is shouting so loudly now, his words are almost intelligible...

The wind drops, and the phrase echoes over the ruins:

*"It's not here!"*

"It's not here?" repeats Madison.

"What?"

"He said 'it's not here'!"

"It looks like Dodd is taking orders from Maas?" marvels Diffner.

Maas is screaming at the bulldozer operator, his vowels echoing on the breeze over the idling engine. The *smack* carries clearly over the plateau, as Maas punches the man in the jaw, laying him out cold in the dust.

The other men watch silently, waiting to see if the limp figure will get back to his feet. But he's motionless.

"Ouch," whispers Madison.

"They can't find it?" I blurt, surprised. "They've cut out ten feet of earth in every direction..."

"No, it's here." Diffner snorts. "They've just missed it." He smiles, pleased with himself. "We'll wait until they leave, and—"

Maas turns, raises his hand, and makes a series of wild gestures in the air over his head. He's directing the other man behind him to get in the bulldozer. *You. Go there.* Then he waves at the two mine-sweeping-monster-trucks and the excavator, as if pushing them out further from the tombs.

"What's he *doing?*"

I peer sadly at Diffner, and fall back against the wall, defeated. "Same thing as you."

"What?"

"Clutching at straws."

# 29. '...DOWN TO THE STONES OF THE PIT...'

*Tuesday, December 24, 2012*

Diffner flicks on his penlight, casting erratic shadows in the bombed-out bunker.

I follow him into the chamber, dropping the metal detector on the floor. The gesture has the feeling of surrender.

Diffner flings the pick and shovel at the wall, with a disappointing *clang*. "It *has* to be here!" he growls. He uttered the same denial, trudging across the moonlit riverbed. "We *have* to get in and see for ourselves!"

I frown. "You saw all that equipment! If they can't find it...How can we?"

"'The Standard of Ur'...'*cast out as a branch...*'" It *has* to be here!"

"There *is* another possibility," sighs Madison.

"What?"

"...It doesn't exist," she blurts.

Diffner frowns, struggling with the concept – not of the tablet's non-existence, but of Madison's mutiny.

"Maybe there never *was* a tablet?" I add. "Maybe some sandal-wearing loon concocted the whole thing chewing tree-bark in a cave three-thousand years ago… You can just about build a case for *anything* from the mish-mash of—"

"Shut up!" snaps Diffner sternly. "Just shut up. You *don't* make up something like this! You *can't* make it up! There were records, for centuries afterward…For his name to even…"

"Maybe Melchizedek *was* real. Just not the *tablet?*"

"The Bible, the Torah, the Qur'an, *Parzival*…" Diffner shakes his head. "Empires have gone to war over this! The *pattern*! Vantcha's puzzle!" Diffner pointes angrily at his palm, as if he holds the treasure map in his hand. "Babylon, Egypt, Rome, the Cathars…All for a rumour? What about all the *other* tablets… The 'Code of Hammurabi.' The 'Epic of Gilgamesh'. The 'Rosetta Stone'… The box—The 'Standard of Ur'…It *has* to be real!"

Madison shrugs. "Then it's not there."

"It has to be!"

"Where?"

"You said it yourself," I snip. "People have *looked everywhere* else."

"Maybe it didn't go into Nebuchadnezzar's grave?" suggests Madison. "Maybe Nebuchadnezzar's son kept it?"

"Don't start—"

"Think about it…" explains Madison. "Nebuchadnezzar died in Five-Sixty-Two B.C. Amel-Marduk was murdered two years later by his brother-in-law… Then Neriglissar restored the traditions of Nebuchadnezzar. But *he* died three years later—"

I stand, amazed, watching the two of them go through the same routine we have all along: the same routine I've repeated *myself* countless times. The circular logic. Jumping at shadows.

"..After Neriglissar was Labashi-Marduk…" continues Madison. "His throat was cut. Then Nabonidus was elected, but he went mad the same way as Nebuchadnezzar and exiled himself. Twenty-three years after Nebuchadnezzar, Cyrus overthrew Babylon, and what was left of the treasure went back to Jerusalem...*Without* the Ark. So—It could be Neriglissar *or* Labashi-Marduk! They were the *only* Kings to follow Nebuchadnezzar who—"

"Listen to yourself," I snap.

"Or..." muses Clark.

I stand between the two of them. "'*Or*' what?"

"Maybe Nebuchadnezzar wasn't buried in the royal tombs?" Diffner looks down the concrete hallway, into the barren moonlit plain.

"*That's* convenient. An hour ago you—"

"WAIT! The tomb containing the 'Standard of Ur' *could* be Neriglissar..."

"Listen to yourself!"

"Where's the Bible?" Diffner rummages through the satchel. "The reference says Nebuchadnezzar was '*cast out of thy grave like an abominable branch*'...Like a branch off an orchard tree that wasn't bearing fruit...Like *waste*. Scholars took it to mean the way he was dragged through the street...But it *could* mean the way his body was buried?"

"This is ridiculous." I clench my fists. "We should focus on getting Maas."

Madison looks at me, warily.

"What if Nebuchadnezzar's body was tossed in some kind of scrap heap," suggests Diffner. "Along with the objects from his tomb? *OUTSIDE* the city?"

"'What *if*?" I sputter.

"It could be right here, under our feet!" Diffner peruses the pages of the Bible again.

Under a foot of reinforced concrete...?

I stand immobile...Without Diffner, there's no way out of this shit hole. And the old spook is unravelling before my eyes.

"Isaiah chapter fourteen, verse eighteen... '"All the kings of the nations, all of them, lie in glory every one in his own house. But thou art cast out of thy grave like an abominable branch, the raiment of those that are slain, thrust through with a sword, that go down to the stones of the pit; as a carcase trodden under feet.'"

"It's gibberish," I sneer. Worse, it's *madness*. How did *Matt* ever go in for this? That's what made it so impossible to walk away when I should have – *before*. The idea Matt might have believed it.

"The Hebrew word..." presses Diffner, "was translated into '*raiment*' as '*lebuwsh*'. It means '*covered*'. *The raiment of those that are slain*' is saying Nebuchadnezzar is 'covered' with the bodies of the dead. Maybe it was a mass grave?"

"Like the Great Death Pit," rejoins Madison.

Diffner looks to Madison, eyes wide.

I sit down on my bundled sleeping bag.

"'*Buwc*' in the Hebrew is translated 'trodden under feet.'" Diffner tilts the Bible at Madison. "But the word just means 'thrown down' or 'mangled'...He was mangled...In a mass grave... Where waste was thrown..."

"You don't know *where*," I whisper.

"Hang on... '*Yarad*' is the Hebrew for '*go down*' and '*eben*' for '*stones*' is saying he was thrown down, like a stone into a pit. '*Bowr*' for '*pit*' means a cistern, or water well. '*Down to the stones of the pit*' could be mistranslated from 'thrown to the bottom of a well'! The phrase...What it *actually* says is '*You are taken out of your city. Like waste, you're covered in the bodies of the dead, mangled, and thrown to the bottom of a well!*'" Diffner crouches quickly, and draws an oval in the dust. "Here's the ziggurat..." He draws a square near the top of the oval. "This is north...Down here at the south, *near where we were before,* are the ruins of the temple of Enki. Enki – called 'Ea' in Akkadian – was the Sumerian god the creation myths are based on... Before Abraham... *Enki* created man and woman, and placed them in a sacred fruit tree garden called 'Edin'."

"*Ea in Akkadia, ego*," whispers Madison.

"Enki grew angry, and brought a great flood to wipe out mankind, except his favourite prophet Atra-Hasis – Noah, Ut-napištim, Ziusudra – who he gave instructions to build a boat and load '*every living thing into the boat!* That's the original story... '*The Second Book of Enoch*' says Melchizedek, was taken to the Garden of Eden to survive the flood! The reason Enki used a flood to destroy everyone, is that he was the god of *water*. Nebuchadnezzar was thrown in a well! The well has to be near Enki's water temple, on the old river bank?"

I can't contain my frustration. "Can you *hear* yourself?"

A deep boom shakes the earth, like nothing I've ever heard. By bowels slacken. It's like god just stomped his foot in the desert. Motes of dust trickle down from the ceiling. "What *the FUCK*?!"

"Artillery fire," Diffner stiffens. "Insurgents have reached *Nā iñyah..*."

"How close is that?" asks Madison, her bright blue eyes full of fear.

"We have to hurry," Diffner whispers. "We don't have much time."

"How *close*?" asks Madison, stepping past me.

"Two miles." Diffner scoops up the metal detector and shovel.

"What are you doing?" I gawk.

Diffner casts a wild gaze at me. "I'm going to the temple. You stay here...Madison, you can stay or *go* - Up to you."

"I'll go," she whispers, and follows him to the door.

"Wait!" I whirl.

Diffner twists at the doorway, his features lit by the penlight in his hand. "If we're not back by dawn, walk to the air base. You'll be safe there."

"Are you *out of your mind*?" I'm already talking to his back. "Madison!"

Diffner stops. "Robert—You've been a passenger your whole life... Matt carried you. His daughters carried you...*I* carried you...It's time you put your hand to the wheel. *This* is how things get done." And he flicks off the penlight, leaving me in darkness.

Madison lingers, a silhouette. "Come with us," she whispers, touching my hand.

I shake my head. "He's out of his mind."

And before my eyes can adjust to the purple haze in the doorway, she's gone.

I stumble after them to the bunker door, following the faint sound of crunching stones.

The *rat-a-tat* of small-arms fire echoes over the horizon... Bright flashes illuminate the sky, with a delayed clap of cannons.

Entering the flickering plain, I look for their shadows. *"Madison! Wait!"*

But the only answer is the thump of tank battle. The noise of the airbase drowned out by gun-thunder in the desert.

Feeling my way back down the cold concrete wall, I creep to my sleeping bag. Light flickers through the hole in the ceiling.

I stare blankly into the middle distance. A creeping emptiness moves through me. *What if they're all wrong?* What if the old men – Diffner, Matt, Vantcha – *all* lost their minds? What if the few scraps of paper, the crossword, the strange ramblings, the riddles, the seeming clues, are just the fanciful doodles of crazed old men? What if there *is* no such thing as this tablet? What if all these people... the lighthouse keeper, Diffner, Madison, Maas... *all* of them... are just trying to fill the same God-shaped hole?

The black void in my chest twists into panic, flickering with the desert. The sight of Maas and Dodd on the plateau – the roaring machinery and ruptured earth – replay in the cavity behind my aching eyes. The light flashes in the ceiling, and I see the mean shape of the pickaxe amongst the mess of rusted steel on the ruptured floor.

There's nothing left to do.

Skidding my feet through the dust, I reach for the axe handle, and hesitate before closing my fingers on the smooth timber. The act of taking the weapon will seal my fate.

The image of Annie, bound to the foot of the bed, flashes is my memory...Her bloody tears. *'They took him.'*

*Fuck it.*

Screw Diffner. Screw *everyone*. Fuck the tablet.

There *is* only one thing left to do, to set things right…one act, to bring peace.

I'll *kill* Lou Maas myself.

Seizing the implement, I turn and walk to the door of the bunker. With each step, my resolve grows. I jog over the rough stones of the riverbed, pace quickening, no longer tired or sore…

My blood is racing fuel. Eyes fixed on the backlit outline of the ancient city where it rises up from the plain, rage propels me. The mile-long *Tell* looms in the blackness, lit by the storm of gunfire beyond. The closer I come, the more fear and panic grab at my chest. But even as the knot in my ribs grows tighter, so does my certainty. This is all that is left.

*Fuck you buddy. You hairless imp!* I run, as fast as I can over the uneven ground, wheezing madly, knees buckling, toward the screaming house – or hill. The car. The alarm. The message. Limbs flagging, wringing my lumbering frame for more speed, the closer I come, the louder the alarm and all my internal bells are clamouring. I whisper their names, "Annie…Joe…"

Gripping the pickaxe like a sword, I'm a soldier in the armies of Cyrus storming the same walls, two-thousand years ago…Clattering in my armour. Blood-lust burning in my neck. Tripping over the uneven ground, I lope up to the place where the ancient riverbank rises to the crumbled clay-brick parapet. I launch myself up the loose slope, grunting violently. Falling on my hands, I punch the ground with bleeding knuckles. The hickory handle stings in my palm. Gasping, eyes fixed on the top of the rise, a shadow lurches to my right.

I stop.

Peering into the intermittent darkness, I see a black shape…

The shadow stands still.

It's a trick of the flickering light that made it move…

The shadow is a deep rut in the embankment: a vertical channel, where centuries of wind and rain have carved a gully, opening a cleft in the side of the old river.

I resume my climb. My gut is fizzing like an ulcer, like a ripped muscle, *knowing* there's something back there... In that shadow. The primal spine-alert, Middle-Ages sharecropper, and Nuclear man fear-Doppler all stir together... I turn and stare at the black shape, searching for movement. "Madison?"

The shadow gapes back at me.

The rumbling on the far side of the *Tell* grows louder.

I glance to the top of the rise, and then back at the shadow. Releasing my grip on the pickaxe with one bruised hand, I feel around for a stone, and pitch the rock at the shadow.

It disappears with a clatter.

I scuttle a few paces sideways, to see more closely. The nearer I get, the more the hole takes shape... It's a long earthen slot, rimmed at the top with eroded stones.

It *looks* like a deep channel, carved into the hill. Creeping nearer, I kick a larger stone over the worn edge of the crevasse. The boulder disappears and a few short breaths later, the silence is broken by a faint *thump.*

*Well well...*

When the ancients built their cities, they constructed wells near the river banks so water flowed into the deep cisterns through carved channels at the base...Like this. The Euphrates had long ago changed its course, and eons of wind and rain had worn open the hillside, cutting the long, regular cleft into the dried-up embankment. But this is what's left of a well.

Minutes ago I was scoffing at Diffner...But there *had* been clues... It is *possible?*

..You are taken out of his city like waste, covered in the bodies of the dead, mangled, and thrown to the bottom of a well...

All the tiny *pops* and *flashes* that were going off round the world like a disco ball: Bombs ripping through crowds every day, since God-knows when...The abused and brainwashed...The broken families... Sitting at my desk in Matt's den, the red 'R's on the spreadsheet bleeding together, blurred by tears...The abject horror of the subway bombings... The gut-awful sense of robbery... The millennia of madness and division... *What if* there *is* a tablet – here – telling three billion people they share the same God?

*What if* it is at the bottom of *this* well?

Even if there's the remotest chance it was real... it was worth chasing to the ends of the earth. Diffner was right: *This* is how things get done. Someone *does* them.

Sinking my head into the shadow, I strain to see the bottom of the pit...but the moonlight is too faint.

"Clark!" I whisper, turning on my heel, searching the darkness. I struggle to quiet my breathing, listening...But the sound of artillery pounds in my chest. Every other noise in the ancient city – the engines and voices – are lost...

Crawling feet-first into the base of the ancient pit, feeling my way with my heels, I find the floor of the cleft filled with mud and fallen rocks. The hard crust breaks under my heels, and I kick at the loose silt in the floor of the channel with the Bedouin's shoes.

Gripping the pickaxe by the top of the handle, I scratch at the soft ground, breaking up the dirt in clods. Clawing with my hands in the dark, I scoop the spill out of the hole, digging down through three feet of soft earth, before the ground hardens.

Squatting for a moment, clay caking my arms, clutching the pickaxe, I whisper softly. "What am I *doing?*" Kneeling, in a hole in the desert, scrambling in the dirt... It's not probable... But it's *possible.*

I swing the pick up over my head, heaving rocks and lumps of clay over the shoulder of the pit, before pausing again...The artillery has fallen silent. The only sound is the breeze, buffeting the barren slope. Thinking I hear voices, I crouch, listening.

It's as if there is a presence, hovering behind me...

A loud wail of a lone fighter jet, jars me abruptly like a kick in the spine.

The deadly machine rockets through the sky overhead.

Resolutely, I return to my excavation, swiping at the sweat dripping from my nose. Finding a large flat stone, I shovel the earth aside, and resume work with the pick... I've dug down two more feet, when the tip of the pickaxe bites into the ground and sticks, with a hollow *knock*.

Wrenching the tool free, I feel a weight clinging to the end of the tine. Swinging the implement up into the moonlight, a pair of clotted eyes stares back at me, under the dirty orb of a rotted human skull.

# 30. '...HIDDEN THINGS OF DARKNESS...'

*Tuesday, December 24, 2012*

I fall back against the earthen wall. In the dark, sweat trickling down my cheeks, I stare at the broken human remains in horror.

..thou art cast out of thy grave like waste, covered in the dead...

"*Jeeezus* Christ..," I gasp.

I too afraid to contemplate the suffocating magnitude of this discovery... This is how Yigael Yadin felt, in East Jerusalem in 1967, when he uncovered the Temple Scroll in a Bata shoebox wrapped in cellophane and towels, beneath the floorboards of an antiquities dealer's house...Or the goatherd in Qayla, when he discovered a cave filled with clay jars containing the Dead Sea Scrolls...Or Moses, when he uncovered the tablet in a Thebian basement...

Groping at the floor of the hole, something sharp stabs my wrist. "Ow! *Fuck*..." Plucking the point out of the hardened earth, I hold up the curved rib bone. My gut slithers again, and a chill rattles me by the shoulders.

Freeing the head of the pick from the caked dirt, I dig feverishly, kicking at the bones, flinging them over the mouth of the pit. Shovelling the dirt with clogged fingernails, I no longer notice the jabs and scrapes and aching muscles – hauling broken skeletons out of the hole, spilling them down the bank. I fling out dirt flecked with ivory, pulling three more skulls from the ground, before the pick head strikes something hard, *knocking* and recoiling painfully.

Scrambling in the dirt, I feel a flat, slimy surface with an oily smell – like tarmac on a hot day.

Finding the edges of the object, my excitement grows... There's a rectangle the size of a *Monopoly* box, but twice as thick. The surface is strangely soft, and tacky. I prised my fingers under one end, and try to lever it free, surprised by its weight. Tilting the slab onto my knee, I heave it up to my chest, grunting, and shove it up the wall, out onto the loose ground.

In the light of the moon, my hope dies.

The object is wooden, rotted, black with mould.

Pressing the corner of the muddy timber away a bright smudge of fluorescent green appears.

Curious, I scrape with bleeding nails at the bituminous surface, prising at clods of clay and decayed acacia...

The slab *inside* the rotten box is an *iridescent green.*

The object has a mystical, chemical radiance like kryptonite. I recall the moment I first walked into Matt's study and saw the shining Rosetta Stone, suspended on wires in its trophy case. *This* is a hundred times more spectacular! The wonder of it is dizzying. My hands shake uncontrollably, as motes of light craze the surface of the shimmering emerald ingot, haloes of moonlight blooming in the dust... *What is it made of...?*

I notice the mark, where the pickaxe struck the object.

There's a sparkling golden nick in the dimpled green surface.

It takes a moment for the idea to form...

The tablet is made of gold.

*Solid* gold.

Diffner and I had assumed a four-thousand-year-old tablet would be clay or basalt, like other finds from the period... since every other metal would long since have corroded. But neither of us *ever* considered it might be made of the only metal that could survive this long. Even if it were impure...like this...it would turn green! When the tablet was cast in a primitive desert forge, the crude ore must have contained traces of copper, like ancient coins, given the metal object a patina of emerald-green *rust!*

Heaving the tablet sideways, it weighs twice the weight of stone. Its beauty is mind-bending. Taking the pickaxe in my fist, I scrape the muddy iron head down the edge of the tablet and a long, gilt scratch appears, glinting at the edge of the pit.

*It's solid gold.* In early stories of the Holy Grail, the treasure was a stone that fell from Heaven – *lapsit exillis.* Made from the sun. As far back as the Egyptians, gold was believed to come from the sun. The Sumerians, the architects of these very ruins, believed gold was the physical manifestation of god on earth – sunlight in solid form. *Lapsit exillis...* The grail was a 'stone' made of gold...

I'd found it. *The Holy Grail... Moses' tablet...* Leaning close, I see a series of dimples running parallel down the face; columns of tiny wedge-shaped divots, tightly-packed like crocodile scales. The cuneiform cast into the surface is strikingly similar to the Rosetta Stone. *Sumerian?* Maybe Chaldean, or Assyrian? My heart drums loudly in my ears. "I *found* it..." I whisper. "I *found* it..."

Here, in this hole, on a barren slope... The secret behind all the conspiracies and manipulation, centuries of Inquisitions, crusades, massacres, suicides, tortures, witch hunts, holocausts, and bombings... Abraham, Akhenaten, Moses, David, Solomon, Nebuchadnezzar, Jesus, Titus, Constantine, Alaric, Charlemagne, Napoleon, Hitler... The greatest secret in human history – stolen, warred over, whispered, robbed, sunk, and buried, for four-thousand years.

Matt would have given *anything* to be here, to see this.

I want to cry out, but my mouth won't work, it's so full of wonder – and sadness...for all the evil *this* object has wrought.

This changes *everything*.

Tears stream down my muddy cheeks.

"I found it."

Touching the surface gently, I wonder at all those others who beheld it. Every hand that ever held this tablet, Saviour and tyrant, has kept it hidden. All of them – every one – have kept it a secret, buried, returned to darkness, inearthed. Those who even *learned* of its existence, dare not speak of it. Buried for eons, at the bottom of the well, under the *raiment of those that are slain*, a hundred yards from the clay-brick ruin where Abraham was born...

I heave the tablet over, finding more carved dimples on its back.

*Luhot.* Two sides of one tablet. Just like Diffner said.

It's impossible to imagine what the tiny divots might say, to warrant such secrecy. How did a single text do so much damage? *Unless* it actually bore the powers ascribed to it in myth – the Ark, the Grail... Unless – as Moses and Mohammed both said – it *was* carved by God's own hand?

The roar of a diesel engine on the plateau startles me out of my reverie.

I drag the tablet back down into the shadows, and crouch beside it, mindful of my predicament.

What do I *do now*? Carry the tablet to the bunker? It weighs like a fridge. What if Diffner and Madison *don't make it back*? What if we're discovered? I *might have to* rebury it. And come back with Diffner, when it's safe.... *Yes. Rebury it.*

Rolling the ingot into the hole, I shovel dirt back over it. I'm powerfully reluctant to leave it here. But I can't think of another plan. There's *really* nothing else to do. I'll come back.

I'll come back.

The exertion of the past hour sifts over me like sand. Tired, I wriggle out of the pit... Kicking the old, sacred bones back into the well, I skid down the slope on my tail, dragging the pickaxe, and loping wearily into the riverbed.

The *snap-crackle-pop* of small arms echoes over the *Tell*.

It's a mile around the base of the ruin to the place where Diffner indicated the *Temple of Enki...*

Panting, drenched in sweat, arms caked with clay, I peer at the rim of the plateau, searching for movement... Nothing. *Maybe I've gone too far?* I double back, and crawl up the loose bank to the crumbled wall. Ali Air Base spreads out north of me, lit like a stadium. Two miles further, past the ribbon of the modern Euphrates, the city of *Nā iñyah* is in flames. Fires dot the darkened city to the echo of mortar fire. The Taliban are *close.* Thirty minutes walk from here...In under and hour, the battle for the lands of ancient Babylonia will be fought here, at the Tell.

At the top of the moonlit plateau, the bulldozer, monster trucks, and all the other machinery stand idle. The floodlights are extinguished. The only sound there is the faint whir of a small generator at the camel-coloured tent... I can see it...Far away, near the base of the looming ziggurat. A seam of light marks the entrance to the mobile command post. The wind stirs the flap. Lamp-rays strobe across the plateau like a lighthouse.

*Don't look into the light,* whispered the blind keeper...

Annie.

Creeping around the wall, I see figures moving inside the tent.

The outline of the ruin to my right resembles like the broken, rectangular wall of the temple.

Kicking up dust, I plod in a low crouch toward the ruin, slowing as I draw near. I try to silence my weary footfalls on the loose ground. "*Clark?*" I whisper softly, waiting for a reply.

Feeling my way around the wall, searching for the entrance, a sudden movement at my back makes me recoil, ducking into the wall with a loud *woof.*

Before I can turn, a hand clamps over my mouth.

My head is thrown against the stones. I'm lifted like an empty shirt, raised off my feet. Joints screaming, my arm is bent behind my back, wrenched sideways. My elbow *pops.* "Nggh!" I wheeze helplessly, muffled.

The familiar rheumy eyes, and the faded sideburns and eyebrows, the smoky breath and the smile like the underside of a yard tool, leer in the moonlight.

"*Shhh..*" Diffner scowls, as he takes his nicotine-stained fingers from my lips.

"I *found—*" I whisper, urgently.

"SHHH!" Diffner clamps his hand back over my mouth.

I don't understand his reaction... *What?!*

He presses the small binoculars to my face, aiming them toward the ziggurat...

Confused, I follow the old spook's imperative, squinting into the eyepiece.

He is aiming the binoculars at the tent, six hundred yards away, past the Great Death Pit. Magnified through the lenses, I see the Velcro panel at the entrance to the tent. The wind catches the flap, flicking it open.

The yellow parka flashes in my memory – on the stoop, on the final morning in New Brid...

He's sitting on a chair, at a table inside the tent.

Joe...

It's automatic.

I cry out, and lurch out of Diffner's grip, heading for the open ground.

But Diffner's hands are too fast. He seizes me by the collar, hauling me around the wall, inside the temple ruin, where Madison crouches, downcast. She looks up at me sadly, eyes glistening, and whispers my name.

"Shhh!" Diffner hisses.

I search Madison's eyes, then Diffner's. Every thought but Joe is forgotten. "Let me go!"

"Don't be a fool," Diffner seethes. "What are you going to *do?*"

I feel the weight of the pickaxe in my hand. I swing it at his knee.

Diffner wails and stumbles back, clutching his leg.

"Bob!" shrieks Madison.

I break into a sprint, onto the plateau, crying his name: "JOE!"

"*Wait!*" pleads Diffner, too far behind me.

I don't care. The sound of my own shout doesn't even reach my ears. I bawl Joe's name, sprinting over broken bricks, raising the pick-axe.

Diffner limps after me. "WAIT!"

I run, full tilt. My only hope, is that Joe might come to meet me—"JOE!!"

I'm twenty paces from the tent, crossing flat ground, when the floodlights hum to life, sending me reeling. But I keep running forward, tripping diagonally. Something strikes me in the face, and the ground swoops up.

Rough hands grab my arms, and I swing the pick-axe. There is a shriek of pain. I'm not sure if it's me. I swing again and the pick grabs in something, twisting out of my hand. I blink. Two bodies fall backwards – more rush toward me. I'm on my knees now. I hear Joe cry out – desperately: "DAAAD!"

I wail like a dying beast. "*RRRRRGH!*" ..lunging forward. But I'm seized by the wrists, arms wrenched above me, dragged. "JOOOE!"

I'm flung through the entrance to the tent, landing on the panelled floor on my face, splitting my lip like a cherry.

"Stand up!" snaps a familiar voice.

I raise my head.

Joe is bound to the chair. The heavy black cable ties are pulled so tightly at his arms, the sleeves of the puffy yellow parka have split, spilling stuffing. He looks tired. His eyes are red from crying.

I smile broadly, blood smearing my chin. "Howya doin, kiddo? You *awright?*"

Joe stares at me, frozen in fear.

Buck-Rogers steps around the table, smirking. "He's even had a *yut-cut!*" *William Dodd.*

"I don't know why god has kept you alive," marvels Maas. "Stand up!" he snaps again, grabbing me by the hair.

I focus my gaze, staring Maas in his beady speck-like eyes. "Let him go."

"Where's Diffner?" he pries, twisting my head at an angle.

"I don't know," I mutter.

Maas wrenches my neck severely. "He's *here!*"

I manage a small shrug, aware Joe is watching every flinch…every grimace.

Maas turns to the half-a-dozen mercenaries inside the tent, and points at the door. "Search the whole *fucking* mountain!"

"Let Joe *go*," I snarl.

"What?!" Maas sneers.

"Let my son go…Or you'll never see the *tablet*."

I catch a glint of steel, as Maas raises a knife to my cheek. He presses the tip into the soft flesh beneath my eye. "What did you say?"

Blood – or eye-ball spooge – trickles down my cheek. A crippling spasm clenches my teeth. "I *know* where the tablet is…" I spit, determined not to pass out. "Clark *doesn't!*"

Maas grins, pressing the blade at my eyeball. I see a shadow sweep across the ceiling of the tent. I can't tell if it's blindness, pain, my cornea flexing under the knife point, or some optical trick. I suck in a deep breath, and whisper, as evenly as possible: "The only thing I care about is Joe."

"Daaad! *Don't*," pleads Joe. "Leave him *ALONE!*"

Maas smirks, swinging the blade around at Joe. "You bring me the tablet, and I'll let the boy go."

There's a loud *pop-pop* outside, like the sound in Pete Hiptmeyer's bar…the sound of a hammer, driving a nail.

Clark and Madison looked on from the cover of the ruins, as I swung the pick-axe at the first soldier – collecting him roundly in the chest.

"Fuck!" burst Madison, rolling behind the wall.

Diffner watched as another soldier clubbed my skull with a rifle butt, and dragged me to the tent – shouts drifted across the plateau. Minutes later, six men ran from tent, fanning out in pairs.

"They're coming," whispered Diffner.

"What do we do?"

"He *knows* Bob can't be here by himself. He won't give up till he finds me."

"Can we fight them?"

Diffner shook his head. "Go back to the bunker."

"Clark, wait—"

"There isn't time." He seized Madison, and kissed her on the brow. "*Ciao.*" Before bolting laterally out across the *Tell.*

Seeing the leaping shadow in front of the air base, and the burning city, the nearest soldier raised his 16' M-16, and fired.

I hear the scuffle outside as Diffner is dragged into the tent on his knees, leaving a bright red snail-trail. The old spook's right leg is plastered with blood.

Maas steps forward, grabbing Diffner by the chin, grinning. "The *legendary* Clark Diffner!"

Diffner's face is impassive.

Maas grabs Diffner by the jaw, and twists his head, inspecting him like horseflesh. "You should've retired when you could." Maas chuckles.

"Whatever you say." Diffner casts a glance in my direction, then at Joe.

"Robert here tells me he *knows* where the tablet is?"

"*No.* He doesn't."

"I can *take* you to it..." I blurt. "If you let Joe go!"

Maas evaluates me carefully. "We have a deal. Let the boy go."

One of the soldiers draws a large knife, and hacks at the cable ties on Joe's arms.

"Run Joe!" I add quickly. "To the air force base. Don't look back!"

"Dad?"

"Go!"

Joe runs from the tent.

Maas presses a button on his wristwatch. "There... Ten minutes. *Now*, Robert." He squats down in front of me, eyes level. "If I don't have the tablet in my hands in that amount of time, I'll personally go after your son...And we both know what I'm gonna do when I catch him."

# 31. '...FROM HIS EYES AS IT HAD BEEN SCALES...'

*Tuesday, December 24, 2012*

Joe sprints over the plain outside the Tell, in the direction of the sprawling air force base.

He feels his face contorting, tears pushing their way out, and works to keep his eyes open...I had told him not to look back...But—

Nobody ever missed someone so much, was so glad to see them, then lost them again so fast. He's sure of it.

Twisting his neck, he glances over his shoulder.

It's fucking scary back on the hill, that's for sure. It's *hectic.*

Looking ahead again, a shape materialises in the moonlight.

A white horse draped in a chequered saddle blanket, stands grazing at a small crop of grass.

Joe's feet stop.

The memory of Annie comes rushing back in a flood...He can almost still see her...Racing across the horse paddock, forward in the saddle, elbows down in the horse's mane, her own hair flicking in the wind. If only Mum were here too! He'd *never* let her go.

The horse raises its muzzle, and looks back at Joe with dark, pinched eyes under its matted forelock.

Joe stands in the stretch of desert, hypnotised.

There's no point crying. Dad is back *there*... And who was out *here?* Are there scorpions? Maybe jackals? He wishes he'd paid more attention in Geography class... Or whatever subject it is where they cover this stuff. Mum would kick his arse for not knowing. But he *is* glad he *has* paid attention at football practice. He figures he doesn't stand a chance against the army guys on the hill, even if he hulks out on one of them. They're massive, and every one of them has guns *and* knives. Still, he can *outrun* them, he's fairly sure of that. What he *can't* do, is leave his Dad alone up there.

The air force base doesn't seem like such a good idea anyway. He's seen the way the guy called 'Lou' swaggered around there. He was *connected*...

And Dad is in danger...

"'Bye horse," he whispers, picking out the end of the long plateau in the darkness, and running back toward the city wall.

The small cadre of men follow Diffner and I to the rim of the Tell, searching the shadows for the eroded well.

I'm bound at the wrists with cable ties, nudged forward on a machinegun muzzle. Diffner limps painfully beside me, Dodd following behind us.

There's blood trickling down my cheek. But with my hands bound, I can't check where it's coming from. My eye works on ever second blink, and I spy the long vertical shadow in the embankment, walking past...

"I hope you're bluffing," sneers Diffner softly. "He'll kill us anyway..."

Maas' is already restless. "WHERE *IS IT?!*" He looks like he's caught *malaria*. He's feverish, sweating, wild-eyed, swaying on his feet.

I glance at the air base across the plain, wondering if Joe has had enough time now to make it to safety. How many minutes have passed? Nearly ten? "It's here—I think..."

"HURRY UP!" Maas snarls. He points at two soldiers. "You two... Dodd...Go get the boy."

"*Wait!*" I bleat urgently. "...There."

I point to the runnel in the embankment.

Maas shines his Maglite revealing the spill of earth from the well, and he leaps down the slope to the cleft in the rock, disappearing inside. A small sound erupts from the hole. It's surprise, and laughter.

Diffner casts his gaze forlornly at his bloodied shoes. "Fuck."

"It's in a *well*...like you said," I offer.

"You *fool*," whispers Diffner, bitterly.

"I *had* to..."

Grunting with exertion, Maas emerges from the pit, smiling – heaving at the luminescent slab.

He struggles up the bank, heaving the tablet into his arms, and sets it down on top of a large brick, transfixed.

Diffner snatches his breath. "It's *green—?!*"

I feel a twinge of pride...I found it. It hardly matters, that nobody will ever know.

The old spook's eyes bulge. "It's the *Emerald Tablet of Thōth!*" blurts Diffner.

"What?"

Maas and Dodd aren't listening. Maas is busy running his hand over the dimpled surface, his nose inches away from it, studying the impressions...Grinning like a demon. "'*Zechariah's Stone*'" whispers Maas. Another link: Hebrew priests, had a small golden tablet mounted in their head-dress engraved with the name of god...

Diffner shakes his head quickly. "It's all of them! The Grail, Zechariah's Stone, the *Tabula Smaragdina!*"

Maas breaks his gaze from the tablet long enough to look at me, curiously. "Bury them."

"What?" grunts Dodd.

"*Bury* them."

I realise he's talking about Diffner and me.

"Where?" asks one of the goons.

"In the tombs."

I open my mouth to object, but there's no point. It doesn't matter now. Joe is safe. *And* Madison. It's a good deal...

Dodd grabs Diffner, and drags him – still gazing back at the emerald artefact. As Clark stumbles back, his arms fly out, grabbing me by the shirt. I look down at his hands, then his face. There is a crazed, drug-fucked look in his eyes. "What?" I ask, puzzled.

"The *Smaragdine Tablet*!" Clark sputters.

Dodd shoves me forward. *"Di Di Mau. Move!"*

Diffner has lost it. "Wh—?"

*"I said 'Move it!'"* barks Dodd, jabbing his M-16 in my spine, drilling me forward.

"Don't you *see?*" mutters Diffner, clutching my shirt, tripping sideways.

Dodd shoves us to the middle of the *Tell.* "Go!"

Diffner is rambling, not watching his feet, stumbling over the rough ground in a trance. "..I wondered... but *emerald* didn't MATCH!"

I spy the open pit where Maas earlier emerged, via a wooden staircase.

Diffner mutters, madly: "..I found myself across from an old man seated upon a golden throne who was holding in his hand an emerald Tablet on which was written: *'Here is the craft of nature... Here is the secret of creation and the science of the causes of all things. ...I took the Tablet and went out from the crypt. Thereafter... I was able to learn the secrets of creation...'"* Diffner flashes a wild stare at me. "It's Balínús!" he gasps. "'Sirr al-Khalíqa'!"

I'm busy trying to keep my balance ahead of the rough shoves. The floor of the ancient clay-brick 'death pit' is eight feet below the plateau, tilting down through a sagging archway into an underground vault, where the brick ceiling is propped with aged beams. There are dark openings along the wall, some constructed, some broken through old brick.

"Wait!" Diffner cries, spittle flying from his lips, twisting away from his captors. "Don't let him *clean* it!"

"What?"

Dodd pauses, startled.

"It's the Emerald Tablet of Thōth!"

Dodd grabs Diffner, and flings him onto the coil of razor-wire that runs around the top of the staircase.

Diffner stumbles into the metal barbs, unable to catch himself, hands bound, tipping hard into the coiled wire. He shrieks in agony.

"HEY!" I move to help, when a rifle-butt strikes me in the temple. My foot slips on the narrow tread, and I tumble down the stairs into the pit, sprawling, cracking my cheek on the brick floor.

I lay in a cloud of chalk-fine dust, groaning. Heavy boots follow me down the stairs, kicking me toward a crack in the wall. *"Move!"*

Diffner is still wailing, on the ledge above me. His shrill screams are not physical pain… He's still saying something… "Theeeey-thought-it-was-emerald! But-it-was-made-of- gooold! Five-hundred-years in the Ark! Apollonius thought it TRANSMUTATED! He thought it changed from gold! But IT WASN'T ALCHEMY!!"

*The Philosophers' Stone?* Is it possible? All the same myths started with *one* treasure?

"…Melchizedek is THE MAN ON THE GOLDEN THRONE…!"

I'm swallowed by darkness, shoved through the narrow split in the brick into a small, bare rectangular tomb. The air is dry and stale. For millennia, this chamber held the remains of seventy-three dead Babylonians, and trinkets of gold and lapis lazuli now carried away to the far side of the world… There is a squeal at the door to the tomb, as Diffner wriggles through. "BOB!"

*"Hey!"* Snaps a soldier, outside. *"Not in there..."*

*"Separate tombs!"* barks Dodd.

Diffner drops to his knees on the brick floor, at my feet. In the weak light, I see blood trickling from a gash in his brow, rimming his teeth. "The tablet! It turned *green!*"

I struggle to follow what he's saying. But the old man is hysterical...It doesn't make sense, seeing the all-running, all-jumping track-and-field marksman – *Our Man in Rome* – meeting to his own end with such little composure. "Clark—"

"Listen to me! You *have to listen* to me! We can't let Diffner *clean* it! The rust! Or nobody will ever know they're the *same* tablet!"

Dodd argues with a soldier, outside the entrance to the tomb.

"The tablet *corroded!* Before Akhenaten!"

"Clark!" Even in the face of death? He's shot, bleeding...About to be buried alive! And he's still shrieking about the *tablet?* It's like his sanity was snatched away, the moment he laid eyes on it.

"The stories were lost at Alexandria! The tablet laid in the Ark for five-hundred years! It turned *green!* They thought it turned to *emerald!* It's the *Tabula Smaragdina!* The *Emerald Tablet of Hermes Trismegistus!* The Egyptians *said* it contained the *'secret of creation and the science of the causes of all things.'* They thought it turned elements into gold! The beginnings of Alchemy! Because—the tablet TURNED *FROM* GOLD! *It's the 'Philosophers' Stone!'* The Holy Grail! The Emerald Tablet of Solomon! The Ten Commandments! The Ark of the Covenant! They're *all* the SAME THING!"

The sound of the bulldozer roars above our heads. Dust billows down from the ceiling, as the walls tremble.

The light shifts as Dodd wriggles in through the doorway, and seizes Diffner by the neck, dragging him back on his heels.

"Wait!" cries Diffner. "I *have* to talk to Maas!"

The burial chamber shudders.

I watch as Clark is hauled, shouting, back toward the crack in the wall. "Wait! *WAIT!*" he cries, twisting out of Dodd's grip, and leaping back toward me.

"Fuck this," snaps Dodd, reaching around for the M-16 slung on his back.

"No—!" I grab at Diffner.

Clark is looking at me, desperately, as Dodd knocks a banana clip and raises the machinegun at him from behind.

*"They're the SAME TABLET!"*

The burst of gunfire thunders in the chamber. Diffner's shirt pops open, and the bullets skip past me in the dust. I jump back as Diffner jerks forward, hitting the ground with a clap.

"Clark!" I drop to my knees, trying to wrench my hands free of the bonds.

Dodd turns and crawls from the tomb.

Unable to do anything but watch, I see Diffner staring up at me in the faint light, blood sputtering darkly from his lips. "Boobbb..."

A cascade of earth and rocks pours over the doorway, and the last mote of light winks out, swallowed by darkness.

The last thing I see is Diffner bleeding out in front of me. The image hangs suspended in the darkness like a photograph.

I cough on the invisible grit whirling around me... "Clark!" Shifting to my arse, I wriggle to where he fell – toward the sound of choking.

*"Isaac Newton..."* he sputters.

"Shhh..."

He gargles for air. *"Aaargh!"* I can hear his feet kicking in the dirt, clattering amongst the broken bricks. *"Isaac Newton..."*

We're buried. He's shot. I can't dig with my hands bound. There's no way out. "Shhhh...It's *over.*"

*"'It has been thought fit to be concealed by others that have known it...'"* he croaks, gargling blood. *"'... and therefore may possibly be an inlet to something more noble... that is not to be communicated without immense damage to the world...'"*

"What..?"

*"'...There are other things besides the transmutation of metals which none but they understand...' ...Isaac Newton!"*

I feel a crushing sadness…so deep, the darkness *spins*. "Shhh. Hey, at least Maddie is okay," I whisper. *And Joe.*

Diffner gags, lungs rattling like dice. "Even Isaac Newton wrote that the tablet should be kept secret!" he croaks.

I know there's nothing here but darkness. But it feels as if the darkness is shifting. Like there are others here… Or *I'm* dead… floating in space, a distant sun at my back with nothing to cast its light on… Jonah in the belly of the whale… Jesus in his tomb… Mohammed in his cave… *What comes first? Thirst? Hunger? Or madness?* It seems like the worst possible way to die. Mad and parched. And a feeling of being crushed…*Ringing* in my ears…The noise flicks from ringing to *thumping*…then back to ringing again.

At least I saved Joe.

*If there is a God, that's why he let me live…*

Diffner coughs loudly, and I feel his blood soak through my jeans at the knee. "You have to stop him," he croaks.

"Shhh…"

"Turn around."

*What?*

"Turn…around!"

I'm so addled; I think he doesn't want me to watch him die – in the                     dark.                     "Okay." I twist my back to him.

I can feel his breath, damp on my wrists. He coughs again, and blood fills my hands.

Then I feel him tugging at the plastic restraint on my wrists with his teeth.

*Tuesday, December 24, 2012*

At a gap in the ancient wall, Joe sees the bulldozer come to a stop.

He has made it back, just in time to find the dozer rolling back from the edge of the hole. The man named 'Dodd' is standing nearby, watching the action…The dozer driver leaps down out of the cab, and walks in the same direction as Dodd, disappearing behind the giant stone tower.

Joe watches as the floodlights are extinguished, and the last pair of shadows disappear behind the ruins.

*Dad must still be in the tent?*

He waits for stillness to settle over the darkened hill, and counts down from twenty.

*…Four… Three… Two… One… Coming… Ready or not.*

As he creeps out into the open, the sleeves of his parka make a buzzing sound in time with the sweep of his arms. Pressing his elbows to his sides, he places his feet carefully, avoiding the clatter of turning rocks. The only other sound now is the hum of the trailer-mounted HMMWV towable generator.

Impatient, he makes a quick dash across the open ground to the trailer, where he flings himself against the noisy motor. The unit provides little cover. On every other side, he can be seen. He can't stay here…Peering under the wheels, there is enough space to crawl closer to the tent.

Wriggling on his belly, the buzzing noise of friction in his parka, and the clatter of rocks are covered by the hum of the engine.

Joe twists his head beneath the axle of the trailer, and makes out a small triangle of light in the rear of the tent, at the base of a Velcro panel. Creeping forward, he presses his eye to the opening.

Inside the shelter sits a solitary figure.

It's Lou, sitting on a collapsible chair, hunched over, studying something on the table. There is a small black monocle – like an eyepiece from a microscope – pressed to his eye.

Joe watches as the strange-looking *asshole* pauses to flip the pages of a reference book, scribbles something on a notepad, and returns to his monocle... From the low angle, Joe can only guess what Lou is looking at. Maybe it's a copy of *Chicks-With-Dickheads.*

Joe has heard Lou talk about treasure. That's what they're all here for. Lou came back earlier, furious, shouting *'It's not here!'* Then, when Dad was dragged into the tent, he said *'I know where the tablet is...'*

The look on Lou's face now, is curious.

He's staring at the table alternating, between surprise and—horror...

What is he seeing, that makes him react so strangely? What is worth all this *hectic* bullshit?

Joe hears Lou suck in his breath suddenly...

Joe tenses, frozen, eye pressed to the gap in the tent. He's been spotted somehow, sideways through the monocle?

After a long pause, Lou sets down the pen, and slumps in the chair.

Joe's heart is racing...

The monocle falls to Lou's thigh, and bounces onto the floor. The muscles in his maniacal face droop. He's just *sitting there*, staring at the wall, expressionless.

Joe waits...

It looks like Lou has *died*...Maybe he's fallen asleep with his eyes open? There was a kid at school, Malcolm Brogan, who did that... slept with his eyes open. When Malcolm's roommate told Joe about it, he hadn't believed him. So Joe had waited for Malcolm to fall asleep one night, and crept down the hall to the far end of the dorm just to see for himself. Sure enough, there he was, lying on his back, staring *right up at the ceiling*, eyelids half-raised. It was the creepiest thing he'd ever seen...At least, until the day he saw a guy in a black mask chase him down the hall of his house, and wrestle him into a van...*That* had scared shit out of him. But—sleeping with your eyes open, sitting in a chair? He's *never* heard of that.

Lou is just...staring.

Joe makes up his mind that nothing else is going to happen, when he sees Lou's hand move...slowly. Just his hand. Lou reaches into his pocket, and pulls out a pistol.

Joe feels his bladder let loose, ready to piss in his pants.

In a single movement, Lou presses the barrel of the gun under his jaw, against the crease in his neck, adjusts the angle – aiming the barrel at the top of his spine – and squeezes the trigger.

Joe shuts his eyes. *What the fuck?!*

BANG!

There's a *clatter* of something falling to the ground, and a thump.

Panic grips Joe around the throat.

When he opens his eyes, Lou's torso is concealed by the table, where he bounced off the chair, and slumped forward again. A trickle of blood pours off the table onto his knee, puddling near the monocle on the floor.

*...Fuck!*

People are going to come running now, to see what had happened... Maybe lots of them. They'll look around... If they find him, he's in trouble. He's seen something he shouldn't have. *I'm not sposed to see that!* Nobody would believe it, when he told them he hadn't looked.

If he had more time to think about it, Joe guesses he could come up with a dozen smart reasons *not* to go into the tent and see what was on the table...But Lou had just killed himself looking at it...And his father had bargained for his *life* with whatever was up there...

**Right now, Joe just wants to** *see...*

Scrambling under the door flap, he stands up.

Lou's head rests on a shining golden slab; a loose flap of skin open at the back of his bald skull, like a split football. Scattered across the table are jars of green fluid, slimy rags, and an odour of chemicals. There is a notepad filled with scribbled notes.

The bloodied tablet *looks* like it is made of solid gold.

Feet pound in the gravel outside.

Joe turns, and dives back to the rear of the tent, wriggling under the Velcro flap. Even as he pulls his heels under the heavy waterproof fabric, he feels the whole tent-frame shake. Someone shouts: "— *Around the back!*"

Joe scrambles to his feet, and runs.

Seeing the gravel road that leads down off the *Tell*, he sprints as fast as he can.

There are heavy boots in the gravel behind him.

*"Stop—! Or I'll shoot!"*

Torches sweep at Joe's back, casting a frantic shadow on the pavement. His legs make fifty-foot-long shadows ahead of him — pumped up and down...

*"Stop!"*

They're right behind him!

He can hear their breathing.

The road dips. Joe trips forward, barely recovering his balance. A hand grabs the collar of his parka, and he hears the polyester rip.

*"Fuck!"* yells a voice right behind him.

Pulled off balance, Joe stumbles, veering into the dust and darkness. Behind him comes a series of loud *pops!* Screeching tyres, slamming doors... He dares not stop running.

Tripping on a loose stone, he tumbles, sprawling.

Heavy feet pound in the dirt.

He's crying now...Tears stream down his cheeks. *Don't look back!* But he has to. Time's up.

He twists, and a soldier — inches away — reaches out to grab him with a gloved hand...Then there is a confusion of movement, and noise: A long lean figure leaps up out of the shadows.

"Hello sailor."

The soldier turns in the direction of the voice, as a shovel sweeps out of the darkness. The torch drops. Snatching, crouching, spinning... A flash of gunfire. Scrambling back onto his feet, Joe stumbles forward. A pair of arms wrap around his shoulders. "Stop!"

Joe kicks and wails, struggling to free himself, swinging his elbows.

Then he hears his name…
"Joe! Stop! It's me!"
Maddie.

*Wednesday, December 25, 2012*

I crawl through the tiny gap in the wall, kicking the last of the bricks and dirt away, tumbling to the floor of the crypt.

Fingers caked with dirt, I smear dust from my eyes, and peer across the pit.

It's dark.

Nothing but moonlight illuminates the *Tell*.

Creeping up the timber stairs, past the razor wire, to the back of the bulldozer, I see the Great Ziggurat – and the tent.

The ancient plateau is abandoned.

This time I walk slowly – half expecting the floodlights to flash again. But nobody comes to stop me.

Reaching the entrance, the wind snatches the tent flap, and I see two figures: One standing over the other, seated at the table.

The wind stirs again …Dodd has a machinegun slung over his back. He's holding a bunch of notepad pages as he inspects Maas' busted scalp, on top of the golden stele.

It *looks* like Dodd shot Maas in the back of the head.

There is a grim satisfaction, seeing Maas dead.

Did they turn on each other, as they divided the spoils?

Then I notice – on the floor next to Maas's sand-coloured boot – a pistol.

I leap through the Velcro flap, reach for the gun, scooping it up, just like Barne's revolver. I spin, and raise the weapon at Dodd. "Freeze!"

Dodd turns his head slightly to look at me.

His face is pale.

His eyes are glazed, like he doesn't realise what just happened.

He just stares at me...and slowly raises the bundle of paper in his hand.

"Freeze!" I jerk the gun.

Dodd's lips move slightly, like he's trying to form words.

"Drop the gun!" I bark.

Dodd glances down strangely, trying to remember where he is. *What gun?* He looks back at me, an idea dawning on his face. "He translated it..." Dodd whispers.

From the look on Dodd's face, I wonder if maybe he *didn't* kill Maas? He looks devastated. And the pistol had been on the floor.

Dodd murmurs, holding out the blood-stained pages filled with handwriting, looking back down at Maas.

"Drop the *gun, asshole*!" I snap. The pistol is heavy. The grip is clammy in my sweating palm. I can pull the trigger *this* time...No doubt about it. I *want* to.

"Hmmm?" Dodd glances down distracted, unslings the automatic rifle from his shoulder, and lets it slip to the ground.

"Kick it over here!"

Dodd kicks at the gun weakly, sending it spinning.

I look back at Maas, the way the back of his head is popped open, slumped forward...The gun on the floor. Is this *his* gun?

"He shot himself," marvels Dodd, faintly.

*"What?"*

"..When he read it .."

*"What?!"*

Dodd points. "He shot himself... when he read what's on the tablet."

"That's his translation?"

Dodd nods, still mystified.

"Give me that!" I flap my hand at the notes in Dodd's fist, grabbing the pages.

I squint at the dense handwriting, skimming the words as I glance back to check on Dodd:

L. M.                                        ②                                    12/25/12

saying, behold Gamalel has descended and brought me out of the earth and taken me above

the Aeons and the Rulers of the powers and take me away there, with the holy angels and the

Aeons and assured me of my victory at the end of time over all the worldly powers who

oppose me. Behold, I did say, Gamalel hath born witness before the Father of All saying

Melchizedek, celestial High Priest and image of God Most High. And the priests did offer

thanksgiving and I did baptize with water the priests and they were filled with celestial light and

rejoiced and said, Melchizedek, you are Priest of God Most High. And behold, they went

straight ways out into the city and their followers, and overturned the idols and cast out

magicians and sorcerers and returned bearing gifts and singing _____ songs.

And word was taken to the Kenites and the Kadmonites and the Hittites and the Perizzites

and the Rephaims, and the Amorites, and the Jebusites, and the kings of all these lands did

send tithes such that my storehouse overflowed, that they may also be blessed. Now behold, I

am without sons or any worthy follower. And you have risen against the kings of Sodom

and Gomorrah with your servants and smote them and pursued them unto Hobah and are

praised and confederate with Mamre the Amorite, brother of Eshcol, and brother of Aner.

Listen to my instruction, Abraham. Go unto your people and say unto them you are son

of the Most High God. And God has made unto you a covenant and has given you

this land from the river of Egypt to the great river Euphrates. Come tithe unto me and I

*(Diagram 26 - Lou Maas' tablet translation)*

"*Behold Abraham son of Terah, I Melchizedek...*" I murmur... "*Listen to my instruction... Go unto your people and say unto them you are son of the Most High God. And God has made unto you a covenant...And tell your servants that God Most High spake unto you and say I, Melchizedek shall return after I am ascended into Heaven to take the Sons of God out of the earth above the Aeons and the Rulers of the powers with the holy angels...*

"*And behold, this tablet shall remain a testimony to your sons of this covenant that they may also rule, receiving gifts, and their cities have peace and find great increase. And forever it shall remain a mystery that I created god.*"

I look back at Dodd.

"*'..I created god'?*"

Dodd's horror hasn't subsided, with the second reading...

403

I look back at the page, equally astonished.

All the centuries of evil this one mystery has wrought in the world – all the wars, and deception... *This* tablet is what drove Nebuchadnezzar to wander the wilderness as an animal! Isaac Newton wrote that it was '..*not to be communicated without immense damage to the world...' Here* is the reason the tablet has been kept secret... giving life to an aeon of myth and rumour. *This* is why Melchizedek is never spoken of, why Kings and Emperors of every civilisation from Egypt to Rome *all* tore down their old gods... Millions had been killed for knowing the truth... *this* truth... to keep it secret... The answer to the 'mystery hid from the ages.'

The awful, timeless lethality of this tablet — was *not* that this ancient King revealed a common god for all, but that he revealed there was *not*.

The 'secret of creation' and 'science of the causes of all things' is that this man invented god.

And the name of God was not Allah or Yahweh. It was a man. Melchizedek.

Maas, who spent his life seeking proof of his faith, instead uncovered the opposite.

I look back at Dodd. "How's *THIS* for a Remote or Unlikely Negative Event, you sunnuvabitch."

"We have to destroy it," whispers Dodd.

"What?"

"Surely you can *see* that? We *have* to destroy it!"

I shake my head. "No.."

"It will tear the *world apart!*" he shrieks, desperately.

"It's already torn apart!" I snap.

"NO!" Suddenly, Dodd springs at me, teeth bare.

It's like catching a ball.

The recoil snaps my wrist. The powder-fumes jazz in my nostrils like paint, but this time there's no intoxication – no chemical high. Just numbness, as Dodd slumps over Maas, and slips to the floor.

It's finished.

I stick the gun in my pocket, along with the note pages.

Reaching for the tablet, I kick Maas sideways and he flops to the ground on top of Dodd.

Taking a cleaning cloth from the table, I wipe the blood off the ingot, and heave it into my arms. It's even heavier now than it felt on the river bank.

I shuffle out of the tent like a weightlifter, I find the road leading down from the *Tell*.

Skidding my feet, I am halfway down the road to the air base when a ghostly figure appears in the darkness. It's a white horse, draped in a chequered blanket. I see Annie leading a mare down to the creek where the water eddies in pockets, dappled with afternoon light between the shadows of moss-green hardwoods... I see her throwing a rope round the horses' neck, leading it into the water, hair tied-up, long legs wheeling in the gin-clear water, and the horse's shins circling below.

I wish I could go home to her.

*Fuck*, I wish more than anything I could go home and find her there, curled up on the couch reading a book, with her feet stuffed under the cushions.

The white horse looks at me with sparkling eyes.

I'm crying, as a pair of headlights sweeps off the highway ahead, lighting the pavement in front of me – followed by more headlights. Engines rev over the desert wind, racing toward me where I skid along in the road, weeping. A door flies open.

"Daad!"

The light shifts as Joe rushes toward me...

"Daad!" He flings his arms around my neck like springs.

Joe.

"You're alive!" he cheers.

I bury my face in his dusty hair, tears pouring down my face. "I didn't think I'd ever see you again," I croak. Now, with the boy's arms around me, breathing in my ear...it's the happiest moment of my life.

I blink, and see a tall silhouette behind him. She's wearing a black bullet-proof vest, and a combat helmet. "...Maddie—?"

She steps forward, reluctantly. "Where's Clark." But it's not a question. She knows. And she folds, grunting, like she's just been jabbed in the ribs with a broken chair leg.

I'm about to explain, when she looks up at me with those eyes Annie used to make: *Not in front of Joe.*

"Dad!" Joe grins. "Guess what?"

"...What?"

"It's Christmas!"

"Mister Travis," says one of the Air Force Officers with Maddie. "We have to hurry. The insurgents will be here in the hour..."

"Wait...Tell them we found this.."

Joe steps back, revealing the glistening object in my arms.

Madison gasps.

"Tell them we found the relic of Musa from the Qu-ran...Tell them we'll show it to their translators...Don't tell them where it is, just that we've found it.."

"Holy shit," gasps Madison.

There are stories in the Bible of the Ark of the Covenant, and its power to turn the tide of battle, to route whole armies, when carried into war by the Hebrews.

"Mohammed said in the Qur'an that in the end times 'there shall come to you the Ark of the Covenant... and the relic left by the family of Musâ...a sign for you, if you are believers..'. Tell them.." I heft the tablet. "Tell everyone we found it!"

## 32. '...THE KNOWLEDGE OF GOD...'

*Tuesday, January 1, 2013*

In the predawn haze, I find a loose corner on the boarded up door and pry it loose, squeezing into the ashen natatorium.

There's still a smell of chlorine, mixed in with the pungent odour of cinders. But the swimming pool is drained. Soft light dividing the space into rows.

Inside the house, the smell changes to fused plastic, and a memory of gas. The hall is a blackened throat. The drywall has collapsed, leaving a scorched frame that reveals the kitchen, shale island bench like a billiard table, coffee machine like a church organ... All blackened. It's a surrealist snapshot of molten appliances, snapped in a flash of igniting gas. In the living room, the sofa and lamp are oddly intact, but water damaged.

The den is gutted. The books and bookcases are gone. My computer is melted into a knob of silicon and metal and the ceiling sags above it, spilling tatters of yellow insulation.

I take the crispified handle of the top drawer, wrenching it open with a loud *creak.*

Inside are the charred remains of the *Bud Lite* coaster, the grim Polaroid of Matt's death-mask...lifeless jaw, slack beneath the skin. I feel a small sense of relief, that the top half of the image is blackened. And there, the New York Times crossword puzzle that started everything.

Gathering the ashen objects, I slip them in my pocket, and turn to the hallway.

All that remains of the stairs are side rails. Stepping over the blackened ruins, I clamber up the beam, clinging to the charcoal banister, and twist my tail at the top, skidding onto the landing. Pausing at Joe's bedroom door, the sea breeze is cool through the blown-out windows.

I kick through ash, to a fallen shelf and a jumble of objects... A charred catcher's mitt, a fishing hat, a melted GameBoy folded around a swimming trophy, and Matt's *Captain Black* tobacco can full of hand-tied fishing flies. I dust off the boiled can, and slip it into my pocket.

Approaching the door to *our* bedroom, the pain hits me square in the chest...The image of Annie, bound to the rungs of the wrought-iron bed with heavy black cable ties, blood like tears...

From the doorway, my gaze falls on the space at the foot of the burned-out box-spring, where she was bound. A section of the bed has been sawed away by investigators.

I slip to my knees in the damp mess. The feeling of wanting to curl up amongst the ashes overtakes me, wishing for one final embrace... I close my eyes, and wait for the pain to subside, before shimmying back downstairs, trudging through vulcanized debris, and out through the boarded-up door in the pool house.

Madison and Joe stand solemnly by the fence. Madison has her arm around Joe's shoulders. The two of them look at me expectantly.

I take the *Captain Black* can from my pocket, and hand it to Joe. He turns it over in his hands.

"Wait here," I whisper, breathing mist.

"Hurry up!" calls Madison. "I *need* a rib-eye!"

"For *breakfast?*" I turn.

"Yeah!" Joe laughs. "We *both* need rib-eyes!"

I shrug, and whisper through the cold, spun grass. The air is frigid. The tributary is half frozen in the elbow of the creek... where Annie brought horses to swim. I stand on the bank, heels sinking into the slush, and watch the light twinkle in eddies between the ice, in the rising shadows. There is a stillness about this place...and the stream. God once *seemed* like water. We're all made of it...Without it, we died... Immerse yourself in it, and we drown. Maybe that's why he was first imagined by people of the desert. But not anymore.

I know now, every one of us has our threshold where we resort to mysticism to address the unpredictability, the cruel and unfathomable events of Life. We're *all* the same. *God and ghosts.* For some of us, it's as simple as the wonder of the Earth orbiting the sun, seen from atop a lighthouse. Or the good fortune of pulling a fish from a river, and a prayer as the product of our acquisitive nature...For others, its tragic loss... a loved one, a *father* like Matthias, remembered in a musty Bostonian temple... A beautiful, loving wife, taken... Or— it's something about our own precarious place in the Universe, on a fragile, fading planet, witnessed in an academic slide-show at a Washington Think-Tank...

It's the refuge from the stunning brutality of tragedy on an incomprehensible scale, in a subway on a September morning... Or something more personal... abject Loneliness... Helplessness. The unimaginable horror of war, related by a ravaged survivor. The depths of depravity and dehumanisation of a frenzied tangle of would-be survivors, on a sinking ship.

For ancient Kings, it was the need to draw together mad warring cults, in barbaric lands.

In the end, everyone has a point where we *think* we need god.

But what if he's *not* there?

All we'd have is other people.

The stream blurs in my vision. My foot slips into the ice, and I step back quickly, wiping my eyes clear, and climb up the embankment.

In my pocket with the crossword, the beer coaster, and the Polaroid, is a bundle of folded note pages stained with the blood of Annie's killer.

In the past week, the broadcasts of war and terror have been replaced. News of the discovery of the Ark was on CNN within fifteen minutes of arriving at the air base. It would take years to study the tablet properly. The entire history of civilisation would have to be reconstructed: Ancient myths revised, to form a new version of the past. But for now, it was enough that Al-Qaeda-Taliban turned back at *Nāsirīyah.* As news of the tablet and its contents hit the press – how the prized relic had been taken to Washington – Al-Qaeda-Taliban had begun to crumble. It was possible they never intended to push any further south, or disagreed what to do when they got there. *Or* the tablet was all they'd ever been after... Hoping to reach Ur. Intelligence reports suggested there had been a revolt of key leaders in that unholy alliance... And that Syria had withdrawn its support in arms and finances.

Back home, the church had been strangely silent on the subject of the tablet. Except for the Archbishop to say he planned to wait for scientific verification. More likely, they needed time to find a way out of this corner. After all, the 'end times' prophecies of all the major religions based on the tablet – Judaism, Christianity, Islam – all foretold the return of the Ark and it's contents, as a sign of the Messiah's return. It presented an insurmountable quandary for believers that the prophesied relic itself admitted there's no messiah.

'Experts' had leapt keenly into the debate: academics, archaeologists, historians, theologians, Rabbis, Muftis... Many called it a heresy, a fake, a false prophet, demanding its destruction, issuing Fatwahs... The full extent of the madness was made clear.

Most regular people sat back and watched, mystified, wondering what made these people so upset.

The centre shifted, gathering in size, as the edges crumbled.

There have been a few rare voices of reason, agreeing that different faiths have been so busy for so long, staring at one piece of the puzzle – trying to guess the whole picture – now they all tie together...we can see something we never guessed.

The Atheists are happy, calling for the world to put this nonsense about 'god' behind us, and start fixing the mess we've made.

In a few more years, I'll have to redo my projection of relative growth rates of religions. My guess, is that what would have taken 7,000 years before, will now only take *1,000.*

Still, somehow, I hope Annie is watching.

I can't help it. I hope she knows Joe is okay.

I hear footsteps in the grass behind me. Madison stops beside me, at a comfortable distance. "You okay?"

I nod. "Matt would have *loved* to be here for all this."

"Can you imagine?" Madison grins. "Trying to get a word in!"

I've tried telling her what happened to Clark, but she asked me not to. *Not yet.*

"I think Joe's gonna be okay," I suggest.

"Yeah, me too." And she lamps me with those electric blue eyes.

"You know you're his hero now...If you said we're going for tofu salad just now, he'd have gone with it."

"Let's try it out."

"Seriously...Thank you. For everything."

She grins. "Let's wait and see how long *that* lasts."

"..You know, when I was a kid – about Joe's age – I used to pray *every day...*The same prayer..."

"Really?"

"Sometimes for hours. I used to go up this hill behind our house at night, and sit at the top staring at the stars *pleading* with god. *'Tell me what you want from me...'*

"One night I walked up the hill, sat down in my usual place, and started praying. A black cat came out of the trees, walked up next to me, put its paws up on my shoulder…leaned in, and started breathing in my ear."

"Really?"

"I know. It freaked me out. I spent *years* trying to figure out what it meant. Was it a sign? *God?* The *Devil?* Why couldn't he give me something clearer? Is there something wrong with me, not *getting* it.."

"And?"

"Eventually I realised it was just a cat on a hill."

Madison smiles. "Come on." She beckons me back across the field. Joe waits impatiently.

Together, we walk into the sunrise.

### THE END

# AUTHOR'S NOTE

## The Fact behind the Fiction *(Spoiler Alert)*

I recall vividly stumbling across a cursory reference to the Biblical figure of King Melchizedek in an exegetical text, in a seminary library in 1991.

This was the seminary where I was studying to become a Minister. I'd been teaching Sunday School since 16, and dropped out of High School at 17 to attend Bible College. By now, I'd read the Bible cover-to-cover three times, so it came as a surprise to really notice this ancient King for the first time.

Here he was: described as the first 'priest' in the Bible, and first King of the Holy City of Jerusalem – a city that Jews and Muslims still dispute 2000 years later as their respective 'Promised Land.'

How had I missed such a significant figure in theological history?

More importantly, how had *everyone* missed him?

In two thousand years of Biblical scholarship, nobody really mentions the single most important figure in all of Theology.

I began searching for more information about this King.

He blessed *Abraham* – the first prophet of Judaism, Islam *and* Christianity...

Surprisingly, I found that *Jesus* is even described as being 'after the Order of Melchizedek' in the Book of Hebrews – one of the few books of the Bible whose authorship is widely debatable. Melchizedek was named in more than one place as the founder of the priesthood, and originator of tithing a share of wealth to the church.

I'm not sure if it's possible for a non-Christian to imagine my confusion. Other than a cursory mention in a Catholic Mass, King Melchizedek has completely escaped everybody's attention for thousands of years.

A few days later, after several sleepless nights, I requested a meeting with the Dean of the College. I took my findings to his office, sat across from his desk, and asked why nobody talked about this King.

After a brief pause, he answered plainly, "Who?"

My concern deepened, the more I considered it.

Having spent years studying the origins of Biblical texts, the history of the various churches, and – most recently – the original Greek and Hebrew, it was clear that the entire notion of a God was an *inverted pyramid* resting on an infinitely small pivot.

Given Melchizedek's place in history, the way he is described, he is clearly the *only* person on whose shoulders the whole idea of God, and the Church, rests.

That this oversight is an *accident* seemed impossible.

There's just no way I could be the *first* student of scripture to have wandered onto this path? The only reasonable explanation was that the subject was *intentionally* avoided, or worse: purposely hidden.

This led to the *second* of three major discoveries that inspired this book...

I abandoned my plans to become a Minister, and began digging in places I'd previously eschewed as heretical: New Age and Occult bookshops, Apocryphal texts, and the texts of other faiths such as the Qur'an, the Book of Mormon, Dianetics, and so on...

The second thing I noticed, was that *nobody* seemed to have documented the clear pattern of ancient Kings and Emperors from the most powerful civilisations in human history, *all* of whom spontaneously overturned the established polytheistic religions of their times, to replace them with Melchizedek's God.

The stories of Constantine and Nebuchadnezzar are well known, being the orchestrators of traditions that now form the basis of modern Christianity and Islam. The Ptolemys, Charlemagne, Hitler, Napoleon, all attempted variations on the theme.

As I worked on this novel over the past two decades, I've also watched Pharaoh Akhenaten's infamy develop – generating increasing interest in recent years.

Meanwhile, Melchizedek remains largely ignored.

Gradually, with further study, there emerged an intricate web of curious cross-references that linked these rulers together – like the scroll by Akhenaten installed in the first room of the Egyptian Museum at the Vatican, by Pope Gregory XVI. But nothing resoundingly clear.

Ever since Melchizedek, many would-be 'King-Priests' have aspired to the notion of establishing themselves as head of Church *and* State – anointed by God. The idea has intoxicated men of power again and again throughout the ages. They're all well documented, *separately*. The last thing missing was a verifiable connection between these figures and the original King-Priest, Melchizedek – something more than coincidence, or human frailty...

Then I made the *third* and most important discovery:

Stories of sacred ancient relics have always been popular in fiction. Two of the three *Indiana Jones* films have romanticised such myths. Tales have been told of Templar Knights, and the lost treasures of King Solomon, the Ark of the Covenant, and the Holy Grail for centuries. Others have written of Hitler's Nazi *Das Ahnenerbe* (Ancestral Heritage Society) and how the archaeologist Otto Rahn's combed the Pyrenees for the same treasure. Or, the tragic history of the 19th Century priest named Bérenger Saunière, who became inexplicably rich, then died mysteriously. This novel would not have been complete without references to many of these very enjoyable tales. But almost *all* of them revolve around the central character of Jesus Christ, two thousand years *after* Melchizedek – a late player in the scheme of things. And *none* of them note the following facts...

- Parzival, one of the earliest Grail myths, described the sacred relic not as a cup, but as a stone.

- The Qur'an states that the words revealed to Mohammed came from a 'well-guarded tablet'.

- Mormons believe their holy texts were written in ancient times on a gold tablet, sealed up, and 'hid up unto the Lord, to come forth in due time.'

- The Hebrew word 'luhot' translated in the Bible to mean two tablets, as carried down from Mount Sinai by Moses, also refers to two sides of one tablet.

- This one tablet was enclosed in the lost Ark of the Covenant, and Hebrew clerics guarding the box wore an icon of a miniature golden tablet in their headdress.
- One of the treasures of King Solomon – who built the temple that held the Ark – was said to be an emerald tablet inscribed with ancient wisdom.
- A golden tablet left untouched in the Ark for hundreds of years would, by the time it was removed, have turned 'emerald'.
- The 'Philosophers Stone' – to which the power to transmute gold was ascribed – was also said to be made of emerald.
- Sir Isaac Newton wrote to Robert Boyle – father of modern 'scientific method' – that the lost Emerald Tablet of Egyptian infamy should be kept secret, for the damage it could do to the world.
- The possession of this tablet throughout history correlates to a direct line between all the Kings and Emperors mentioned above, who have emulated Melchizedek.

Which of course, informs the plot of the novel: Three riddles, but one.

That all these lost objects – the Holy Grail, the golden tablet of the Qur'an, the Ten Commandments, the Golden Plates of Mormon, Solomon's Tablet, Zechariah's Stone, the Masonic 'Cap Stone', the 'Cornerstone' of the Temple, the Emerald Tablet of Thoth, the Philosophers' Stone, and the 'stone' on which Jesus built his church – are *all* the same tablet, and that it has passed through the hands of every King-Priest in civilisation, is the most elegantly simple explanation for the proliferation of monotheistic religion I've ever heard, and far more credible than the Sunday School version of history.

There's a great deal of factual information in this book – and a lot that has been removed, to make the reading less strenuous. (The original version of this typescript contained extensive footnotes.) All told, it has taken 20 years – since that first day in 1991 in a Bible College library – to compile it into something readable (I hope). The events and locations described have been modified *many* times due to significant events in the modern world, or because books by other authors emerged with similar themes.

For example, Bob's risk analysis on Religious Terrorism – which includes references to prior attacks by Al Qaeda at Khobar Towers, the Kenyan and Tanzanian Embassies, and the USS Cole – was written before the 9/11 attacks on the World Trade Centre, in 2001.

Before 2003, the area around the ruins of Ur was abandoned, until the US occupied the previously abandoned air force base at Tallil – now Ali Air Base – and it then became one of only three bases in Iraq not evacuated.

In 2009, the novel was renamed from 'The Atheists' Bible', when a book of that title was published by another author, and the dates moved forward (a third time) to occur in 2012.

There are a number of hidden ciphers throughout the book. Some will notice them on a first reading. Chapter titles are obvious excerpts from verses in the King James Bible.

The triangular plaza outside the Sacred Heart Church – where Jesus has a pentagram for a halo, and which was a Methodist church before it became a Catholic Parish – opposite the home of the American Revolutionary Paul Revere, was chosen as a location because in Google maps it bears a striking resemblance to the pyramidal symbol of the Illuminati.

Bob and Joe's ages when plotted on the beer coaster matrix spell out the letters for the city of *'Ur'*. The title, *'The Dead See'* alludes not only to the well-known archaeological find at Qayla, and the notion that in death the truth is seen, but also refers to the end of 'The Holy See' – the name given to the jurisdiction of the Vatican. The name of the RORO cargo ship reversed, spells *'God Observes'*.

There are also many intentional parallels between characters in the book, and the Biblical characters of Job, Jonah, Mary Magdalene, Judas Iscariot, and Jesus Christ. But, there are *many* more clues hidden more deeply...

References, dates, place, quotes, names and numbers are mostly real – all except the text of the tablet, which is speculative. All warrant personal investigation. All shed light on facts behind the fiction: *Bahera. Qurayš. Cathars. Warren. Mithra. Enki. Gilgamesh. Procopius. Oradour. Ustashi. Balínús. Newton...*

All are pieces in a jigsaw. But you have to look at *all* of them to see the picture.

I hope you enjoy gathering pieces as much as I have.

*Marcus Gibson*
*January 1st, 2011*

To keep reading visit:

**www.marcusgibson.co**

*To scan this code with your iPhone, Blackberry or other capable device, install a 'QR code' scanning application*

# ABOUT THE AUTHOR

Marcus Gibson's first novel was published in 1995. The gruesome literary thriller sold out in a few weeks. With publication shortly after his 22nd birthday, Gibson broke the standing Guinness World Record for the world's 'youngest novelist writing adult-themed work' by two years.

Prior to the publication of 'D', Gibson won recognition in several short story and poetry competitions. 'D' received favourable reviews in a number of periodicals, and Gibson made media appearances including radio, print, and live appearances on morning and late night television.

Gibson is 37 years old and lives in Melbourne, Australia. His professional career has spanned construction worker, script editor, presenter, corporate spokesperson, producer, software developer, business analyst, knowledge manager, sustainability advisor, and environmental manager in a range of sectors including IT, pharmaceuticals, property and finance, civil engineering, and construction. He continues to write prolifically.

Gibson is a member of the high IQ society Mensa.

# SAMPLE CHAPTER - 'THE PEACE BOMB'

## 1. Kabul, Afghanistan – Night

Chinooks thundered overhead as Flight Lieutenant George Holland parked the stolen Tarago in the darkened Kabul back-alley.

He was dressed in the clothing of the van's owner: the embroidered *kurta* with the woollen, knitted *pakol* – a rough-woven beret with a rolled band – pulled tight over his head. Around his neck he'd slung a striped scarf, to conceal the blood-stained collar.

Lieutenant Holland stepped quickly into the shadows, waiting for the helicopters to pass. Venturing west towards the *Topkapi Hotel,* he circled around the back of the building, past rubbish bins and fly-blown waste where a dog lay in the dust by the kitchen door, watching moths circle in a spotlight.

The sodium vapour lamp lit a concrete apron behind the hotel. Behind chain-link and razor-wire, in the glare of the floodlight, sat a red 1990 Z28 Camaro Convertible. The car was bizarrely out of place in the drab back alleys of Kabul. Nothing else was so clean, so bright, so new, or so well guarded.

A rush of noise shook the screen kitchen door.

Dean Martin was singing *'Powder Your Face with Sunshine'* at full volume, over the chainsaw scene from *'Scarface'.*

George reached for the door, noticing a bearded Pashtun behind a rattly electric fan. The guard was wearing a white knee-length shirt, black waistcoat, and *pagray* turban – and nursing a Kalashnikov, one nicotine-stained finger rested on the trigger-guard, staring across the hall through the open kitchen doorway. In the ceiling above the mercenary's head, a spray of bullet-holes zig-zagged through pink squares between broken mirrored tiles.

The Pashtun was hypnotised by the reflected light of the television...

George took off the *pakol* and bloodied *kurta,* stripping back to his dusty coalition airman's flight-suit. He bundled the clothes, and stuffed them into a bin, then rapped on the door frame. "Hey!"

The Pashtun's head snapped around.

George pulled open the door. "Where's Fonz?"

"Who's there?" shouted a man with a New Jersey accent from beyond the hall doorway.

"George!" Lieutenant Holland turned to the Pashtun. "Tell him 'George.'"

The Pashtun said nothing.

Wahid Fazlija stepped out of the doorway, smiling like Wayne Newton, and walking like John McCain. He wore Wayfarers, a black leather jacket buffed to the sheen of a Porsche headlight, and a Glock pistol in a shoulder-holster over the outside of the jacket. Fazlija – *'Fonz'* – had been raised in New Jersey by Afghani parents, where he'd been a weightlifter and used car dealer. After the fall of the Taliban, he'd travelled to the land of his father to set up business, and do his part to get the country back on its feet – propagating the Capitalist ideal with every intuition. He was a zealous entrepreneur, stifled by the legalities of doing business in America. George liked him for that. He was predictable. Fonz often joked *"if you can't fix something with cash, fix it with more cash."* George guessed the line came from a movie, but he didn't know which. Just as long as the price was right, Fonz would agreed to anything. There was *nothing*, he frequently declared, that he would not do for a buck. That was why George had come here…

"Aaay! Georgie boy! What are you doing here? I thought you were gone?"

"There's been a change of plan."

"There's always a change of plan! Isn't there?" Fonz clapped George on the back, steering him down the hallway, past the Pashtun, using his thick body to block the view into the kitchen. A group of men in a mix of singlets and bullet-proof vests sat around on vinyl chairs, swilling vodka and pomegranate juice, watching an old television on the sink.

Steering George out of the group's view, Fonz yelled "Throw me a coupla *grenaaades*!" Fonz caught the first can of Heineken in his free hand, stuffed it in his jacket, and waved for the second. "Come 'ere Georgie-boy. You gotta see this. I wanna show you somethin'."

"I'm pretty shagged," answered George, resisting. "I just need a room for the night." He carefully nursed a small bundle at his waist, under the flight suit.

"C'mon, you're gonna shit yourself when you see this." Fonz pushed George firmly down the hall, guiding him through a curtain into a well-lit storage room stacked with paper goods and a collapsed ping-pong table.

"I'm not going in there," George braced against the door frame.

"C'mon Pal! I gotta show you something! Take a look at this." Fonz kicked a stack of porn magazines off a salvaged seat from a Russian MIG fighter. "Pretty good hey?"

"Yeah. Nice."

"Take a seat. You oughta be right at home."

"No thanks Fonz. Look, I—"

Fonz muscled George into the room. "Try it out. It's genuine. Have you ever seen anything like it? Go on. We'll have a beer, and you can teach me how to fly, okay? *Har-har!* I wanna get a photo of you in it, with your pilot getup!" Fonz pulled out a cell phone and aimed the camera at the seat. "C'mawn!"

"I just need a room for the night."

"Take a *seat*," Fonz pushed down on George's shoulder.

George dropped into the chair.

"There see? Comfortable! I had to drive down to Kandahar to pick that shit up in the back of the Camaro," grinned Fonz. "I dropped a fifty-gallon Winnebago tank in the trunk so I didn't run out of fuel. Thirteen miles to the gallon—"

"Look," George covered his face, as Fonz aimed the camera-phone at him. "I just want a room!"

"I'll see what I can do." Fonz raised the camera-phone higher, to get around George's hand.

"No photos!"

"I won't tell if *you* won't." Fonz laughed, snapped the picture of George hiding his face, and pulled a can of Heineken out of his jacket. He popped the ring, and chugged it down in three seconds.

"What happened to your flight? You're s'posed to be halfway to Germany, ay?"

"It was cancelled."

"Cancelled?" Fonz frowned. "Bad weather?"

"Something like that."

"But you're still wearing your flight gear?"

"Yeah. I had to get outta there, you know? Needed some space."

"Fair 'nuff. It's busy here tonight, you know. Maybe I get you something else? Girls? Blow? Hey, maybe you like the chair? What a hit! Havin' that in your B-hut, huh? You want it? I'll sell it to you."

"I don't need *anything*. Just a room."

"I'll see what I can do." Fonz turned his head sideways and grinned. His teeth were whiter than toothpaste, leering out of a deep tan. "You ain't in any kind of trouble are you Georgie-boy?"

"No—"

"I mean, like you say, 'no photos'. You're not s'posed to be here, right?"

"Everything's fine." George eyeballed Fonz, hoping his panic wasn't visible.

Everything *wasn't* fine. Everything was *very* badly fucked up.

"Cos...you gotta tell me, if you're in any kind of trouble, George! Could be bad for business. Could be bad for you too! If I don't know what to look out for."

"Look—"

"See, you come in the back door... Let's say someone comes looking for you? You gotta tell me what I should say? Right?"

George considered the possibility, but he planned to be *long* gone before anyone thought to find him here. "I'm just not s'posed to be off-base. It's nothing else."

"You know these guys in the kitchen?"

"No—"

"Private contractors, counter-terrorism experts, security guards, bounty hunters, fortune seekers. You know the type...They're here to collect big RE-wards. They're REAL pissed they missed out on the twenty-five mill for Bin Laden – plus the fame and glory, and movie deals. But most of 'em are after mid-range stuff. You know? A few thousand here and there…while they chip away at a five mill reward for a big fish. 'Rewards for Justice'."

George had heard the story before. In 1984, the US government had passed a law allowing the payment of bounty hunters to catch terrorists. It had been beefed up again under the Patriot Act. The Pentagon had paid out seventy-seven million US dollars to fifty mercenaries so far.

"There's a list of twelve 'wanted men' like al-Libi with rewards up to five *mill* Georgie-boy! That's how half those bastards ended up in Gitmo. Hell, *anyone* who looked like the Americans *might* think they were a terrorist, local warlords captured 'em and handed 'em over for five keys a pop! Too easy. So – you know what happens next?"

"What?"

"Every out-of-work guy with some combat time reads these stories in 'Soldier of Fortune' about 'Spin Ghar' Jack, and they want in!"

'Spin Ghar' Jack was the most infamous freelancer in Afghanistan, even before the Special Forces busted down his door and found eight locals hanging from his living room ceiling in various states of disrepair. Jack had been sent to Pul-e-Charkhi prison, despite fervent claims he was working for the C.I.A. The former Green Beret had earned his nickname after penning a bestselling novel about his role in the hunt for Bin Laden at Spin Ghar. He'd been one of a dozen men to assault the caves in the mountains on the Pakistani border. When the mission went sour, he rented a house in downtown Kabul, and begun kidnapping locals – torturing them in his living room – in his own private hunt for Bin Laden, and the twenty-five million dollar bounty.

"These guys think its gonna be easy money," Fonz slurped his beer. "They get on a plane, come over. Then what happens. Al Qaeda have their own money. They grow three-fifths of the world's heroine, and all that Bin Laden family cash – he's got three hundred flippin' million. The flip-flops decide to work the same angle! Right? They put up a hundred-large themselves for killing a Coalition soldier. So now, there's people running round on *both* sides – with no side of their own – and the worst thing *you* could do Georgie-boy is have *those* guys after you! You know? There ain't no rules of engagement here. If you're wandering around on your own, it's not a big stretch for one of *those* guys to take a mind to grab you. A hundred kees goes a long way in Kabul! Buys a lot of blow! You see? So you gotta tell me, what am I into here? Georgie-boy? You *gotta* tell me."

George returned Fonz's smile, and raised his hands. A few overly entrepreneurial mercs were the least of his problems. After tonight, there'd be more people looking for him than there had been for Bin Laden. The governments of a hundred nations would be throwing *everything they had* at finding him. After this.

"Is this how you get people to buy extras, Fonz?" George smiled. "You just keep talking and talking till they say 'yeah get me some blow'? Cos *really*, I'm just tired. And, I just! Need! A room!"

Fonz gulped the last of his beer, and crushed the can in his fist. "I don't know if I've got a room. It's busy."

"Three hundred bucks," retorted George. A room usually went for sixty. "Let's just pretend I'm getting a *extra*, but I'm not."

"You know I gotta cancel another booking, right?"

"Three hundred."

"Cash?"

"*Three* hundred."

Fonz stepped out into the hall, pulling the curtain closed behind him.

In the next room Dean Martin had moved to *'Money Burns a Hole in My Pocket'* and Tony Montana was back asking *"Min' leavin the door open so's my brother knows everythin sokay?'* The movie had been rewound to the chainsaw scene again.

George sat in the MIG seat, waiting – sweating pouring out of him.

Nobody had ever been this fucked. Ever.

In a flash, he'd gone from being the hero. He should have been the hero! Now he was the bad guy. The baddest guy ever. Badder than Bin Laden.

Because it wasn't an earthquake in Pakistan that had brought the crowds out onto the streets tonight...

No.

It was the biggest fucking bomb the world had ever seen.

## Out Now:

## Coming Christmas 2011...

## And in 2012...